Morningstar

Erin Pizzey is well known for her work in the Seventies with battered wives and their children. She has had a successful career in magazine journalism and is now a full-time novelist. Her previous novels include *First Lady*, *The Consul General's Daughter*, *The Snow Leopard of Shanghai* and *Other Lovers*.

By the same author

ERIN PIZZEY

Morningstar

Fontana
An Imprint of HarperCollins*Publishers*

Fontana
An Imprint of HarperCollins*Publishers*
77–85 Fulham Palace Road,
Hammersmith, London w6 8jb

Special overseas edition 1992
9 8 7 6 5 4 3 2 1

First published in Great Britain by
HarperCollins*Publishers* 1992

ISBN 0 00 647074 2

Set in Linotron Palatino

Printed in Great Britain by
HarperCollinsManufacturing, Glasgow

DEDICATION

This book is dedicated to Jim Krugman who ought to write another book himself; to my beloved Miss Annie and her family; to our students, Shauna, Otelia, Sarah Lee, Lauren, Chad, Judy and Jordie, who have all worked hard and done so well; to Mike and Sue Hundt and the tennis crowd umpired by our dear friend Leon Jackson; to George and Carol Sue Ryan, who provide us all with an example of faith in God; to our cherished gardener, Mr Henry Watson, who so faithfully takes care of us; to Susan Miller at the Cayman Islands Public Library in gratitude for her continuing help; to Richard Curnow, Juliet Clark, Jeff Flook, and Jill Savager at Lloyds Bank; to John McAllister and Ann Aldrich for pasta without parallel; to John and Glenice Ross, who deserve thanks seven times over!

This dedication would be incomplete if it did not include my permanent White Knights: Alan Cohen, David Morris, John Elford, His Honour Kipling Douglas and John Faure. Thank you, as always.

I dedicate this book with special thanks to my agent Christopher Little who remains an infinitely eligible bachelor; to Eddie Sanderson, the best-looking photographer in Los Angeles; to Carol Adams, the best PR in Britain; to my beloved Savoy Hotel and the paradisiacal suite with the breath-taking view of the Thames; to Stella Burrowe at Harrods who dressed me for the marvellous Terry Wogan Show; to John Lampl, the Director of Public

Affairs, and Louise Smith, Special Services Executive at Heathrow, both of whom made our British Airways flight such a pleasure; to Tom Sevik and Charles Glidden at Cayman Airways for their friendship and help; to Sam Bhadha and the St James Court Hotel with its beautiful courtyard and excellent service.

To Graham Harper at Ash Green Travel in London for always looking after us; to our new friends Mauro and Mara Bartolommei at the Al Brunello di Montalcino Hotel in Tuscany; to our lovely Ruth Alboretti who helped us to move to our new life in Italy. May Sonia Potter continue to supply me with amazing hampers from Fortnum & Mason for the rest of my life.

Finally to Kate Parkin, my dear editor for her invaluable guidance, to Eddie Bell for his faith, to Ed Breslin and Karen Solem in New York and to the publishing team on both sides of the pond for all their good work. And above all to Jeff Shapiro, my husband.

To all of us who have been at some time in our lives homeless and penniless, God bless us all.

For now we see through a glass, darkly; but then face to face: now I know in part; but then shall I know even as also I am known.

And now abideth faith, hope, charity, these three; but the greatest of these is charity.

I Corinthians 13: 12–13

Prologue

Michael Morningstar watched the evening cover up the unashamed brightness of the day. Far beneath him, neon lights and streetlights came on and cars flowed in glowing columns of white headlights and red tail lights on the crowded roads. Michael grew happier as the sky darkened.

Michael Morningstar still found it a thrill to look out the window of a building bearing his name. Morningstar Tower rose strong and erect over its neighbours along the Manhattan skyline. The Tower, like the man it was named after, surpassed all potential competitors. In a world of moneyed men and designer buildings, Michael Morningstar and his Tower were the ultimate. They were powerful. They were frightening. They were sexy.

The magnitude of Michael's charisma undoubtedly was related to the fact that, even among the rich, he was richest. Yet there was another ingredient to his appeal, something darker, something deeper within his nature. Michael Morningstar was known to possess an animal-like single-mindedness in the pursuit of getting what he wanted, an untamed lupine hunger that wasted no time on remorse or altruism. His appetite almost resembled cruelty, but it was a hidden cruelty, a residual toughness left over from a childhood that held nothing soft. The name Morningstar echoed an Indian ancestry and an upbringing as hard and as comfortless as the New Mexico desert where Michael, in any way he could, had managed to survive his youth. Now Michael's charming smile and perfect clothes were famous, enticing the world to believe that all along he was born to be a man of position and of culture. Only on occasion did traces of a savage past show through the well-polished cleanliness of his wealthy life, and perhaps it was those very glimpses of savagery that inspired men and women alike to regard Michael Morningstar with fear and envy akin to desire.

Through the window Michael could see the evening had reached a satisfying shade of darkness. Michael felt safer at night. Day was a time when too much could be seen, when predator and prey had to outwit each other in plain sight. The world was better at night. At night, Michael, like the coyotes calling out from the arroyos in the wilderness, could see without being seen. He could hunt, mate, kill, love, all according to his own discretion. Michael stood before the wide window of his office in the sky to watch the comforting night deepen.

He waited for the telephone to chirp on his desk behind him. Impatiently he turned the heavy ring upon his finger. Without looking down he let his fingers play with the ring and its weighty stone. He pushed his fingertips hard against the sharp-edged diamond and liked the way the corners almost hurt. His eyes were lifted to the blackness above the city and he saw the first star.

In the past Michael Morningstar had thought more than once that, had the choice been his, he would have named himself Eveningstar. This sharp guardian of the darkness was far closer to his soul than was its virginal morning counterpart. Michael smiled at the star, the celestial twin of the diamond on his hand. In his head Michael found himself reciting a childish poem. His smile broadening, he spoke the second verse aloud:

> *I wish I may,*
> *I wish I might,*
> *Have the wish*
> *I wish tonight.*

As if prompted by his words, the telephone let out its cricket call. Michael turned to his desk and picked up the receiver. 'Yes?' He did not sit in his chair, but stood at his desk instead. 'Hello. I've been waiting. How's everything in Bangkok?' With his free hand he smoothed down the thick black hair at the nape of his neck. 'Yes, I know it's early in the morning there. You can tell me what tomorrow will be like. What's your news?' His eyes wandered without attention over the surface of his desk while he concentrated on the words spoken down the telephone.

'Good,' he said, nodding. 'Yes, that's very good. So, the supplier in Bangkok is prepared to do business at a reasonable price. I'm pleased.'

He listened some more. Absent-mindedly he used one finger to push a copy of *People* magazine away from the centre of his desktop. The magazine showed a picture of Michael on its cover along with the caption: 'Michael Morningstar: Tycoon With a Heart.' Michael had read the cover story earlier in the afternoon. He especially enjoyed the passages praising him for his philanthropic efforts in various charities worldwide.

'Excellent,' said Michael. 'That ought to give a good little boost to the purchasers in London.' Having got what he wanted from the telephone conversation, he

11

was already starting to grow bored. He tapped a fingernail on the body of the telephone. 'Yes, fine then. Well, great. You can tell the folks at the Bangkok orphanage that they're about due for an infusion. Speak to you again.' Without saying goodbye, he put the telephone down.

Michael felt happy indeed. He took his jacket from the back of his chair and put it on. He tugged the lapels to adjust the garment over his muscled shoulders. He was about to be late for his appearance at a charity dinner at the Plaza Hotel in aid of an organization caring for runaway teenagers, but the phone call had been worth the wait. Michael turned to the window and inspected his reflection while he straightened his tie.

He watched himself and he was made to jump suddenly as something hit the window from the outside with a loud thump. Michael was instantly annoyed, minding that he had been so startled. Michael Morningstar never could bear the thought of anything making him afraid. But in the brief moment after the impact of an object hitting the window, Michael discerned the shape of a falling bird. Pausing to think the event through, he realized that some confused, misguided bird, stupid enough to be flying high after its natural time of day, had probably mistaken the lights of Michael's office for the sun.

Michael chuckled, amused by the irony that the bird, in its idiotic innocence, should bring about its own ungraceful death. Yes, by looking towards Michael's office for safety, the bird had killed itself, and that was somehow very funny. Michael caught sight again of his own reflection in the window and he noticed how good-looking he was when he smiled. His angular jaw and high cheekbones were strong and masculine. He showed his teeth and, struck by the humour of the situation, released an explosive laugh.

Quickly he decided that, were anybody to see him laughing too openly, his public image might be hurt. He changed his expression to something closer to the compassion the fallen bird might deserve. He let his grin soften to what the press, or anyone else watching, would probably have called a sad smile. Michael Morningstar lowered his dark eyes and shook his head from side to side in a gesture that nearly intimated pity.

Chapter 1

'Top of the morning to you, and mind how you go.' Jimmy Donleavy's bright, friendly, familiar voice issued this benediction to Nina Stockton from the radio as she pulled into her drive. Nina switched off the radio, turned off the ignition, walked to her house, and burst into tears.

Nina did not expect to find herself sobbing loudly on her own doorstep. Embarrassed, she stuffed her key into the massive security lock that protected the antique furniture and family silver she had lovingly collected. She pushed open the door, her hand comforted by the brass lion's head, and walked into the large, square, tiled hall. The door swung shut behind her. The thick walls of the double-faced Georgian house secluded her and protected her from the sound of the Monday morning traffic racing down Richmond Hill near London, human beings all of them, on their way to work. This human being was hurting. Nina wryly acknowledged her face in the mirror hanging over the Regency table that stood in the hall, the only piece of furniture except for a pretty Baccarat chandelier.

'Why do I feel so bloody awful?' Nina was pleased when she heard Gemma on the end of the line.

'Because you're a middle class twit suffering from the empty nest syndrome.' Dear old Gemma, succinct as always. 'If you were like my mum, and had to get

15

down on your hands and knees every day to clean a rich woman's house, you wouldn't be so . . .'

'All right, Gemma. All right. I'm not entirely unfamiliar with physical labour myself. I've got a dinner party for eight this evening. Doris'll clean the floors, thank God, but I still have to get the kids from school, do the shopping, feed them, entertain the three other couples who are coming, and do the washing up.'

'Get Simon to do the washing up.'

Nina snorted. 'Simon clean up? Since when . . . ?' She heard Gemma grunt. 'It's all very well for you. You and your girlfriends don't face the problems I have with Simon. Anyway, if I ever do get him to help, he drops everything. Gemma, I haven't seen you for ages. Let's get together.'

Gemma's voice softened. 'I'd like that. Tell me, how did Hamish take to his first day at school?'

'Funny you should ask. I think that's what hurt the most. He shot into school after Susan. He didn't even hold her hand. I know we've been picking Susan up for three years, but I rather thought Hamish would at least acknowledge five years of hard work with a parting grizzle.'

'There's men for you.'

'I suppose so. But then I love Simon, and as for Hamish, he's an angel.' Nina felt tears rise in her voice and threaten to overwhelm her. Some part of her wanted to feel the tears pour over her like a waterfall. The pain was intense, so intense it threw her backwards to the day she stood in front of her own boarding school. 'Don't leave me, Mummy,' she heard herself shrieking. 'Please don't leave me!'

'She'll be all right, Mrs Tolmadge. You just go, and she'll be fine. Come along, Nina. Let's go and have

16

a hot cup of Ovaltine and meet your new friends . . .'

Nina stood in her marble-lined kitchen, staring at the telephone. Hamish had left without a backward glance. Maybe I'm a rotten mother, she thought. And then she realized she had not given Susan a moment's thought all morning. The day Susan first went to school three years ago was a day of rejoicing for Nina and Hamish: another guilty secret. Susan, so like her father, was a hobgoblin of a child . . . That's enough, she stopped her thoughts. Nina looked at her watch. Half past nine in the morning: Doris would be here in a minute.

She opened the fridge door and beheld two defrosted chickens, rear ends up. Parsons' noses, she grinned, remembering the Reverend Simpson in his church in the square behind her house. His nose was thickly larded, punctuated with blackheads, and his nostrils flared.

Nina lifted the casserole onto a butcherblock table in the centre of the kitchen. She took a large German carving knife out of the polished wooden block and began to dissect the two birds. Pity, she thought. I'd like to have been a surgeon, but then Mummy was probably right. 'Marry a surgeon,' her mother had said years ago. 'A *gel* should get married and have her children and take care of her house and family. It's the only thing, Nina.'

In the quiet of her kitchen, Nina held tight to a raw chicken made slippery by its own yellow fat. Look at Gemma, she started to think. She detached the leg from the carcass. I have this beautiful house, she reminded herself.

She looked through the double doors of the kitchen down the green lawn set around with baskets and tubs of flowers. Autumn was colourful in Richmond.

Nina's snapdragons shook their heads at her. Simon was not a surgeon, but Simon was a pleasant-looking man. He was doing very well in the Civil Service. He was a wonderful father to the children and a good husband to her and she knew for a fact he was not the type of person who would ever . . . 'Ow!' Nina sucked her finger. 'Damn!' She put her finger in her mouth and tasted the hot, salty blood. The pain momentarily stunned her. She glanced out of the window for reassurance. The snapdragons, still dancing in the wind, chanted back in unison: 'Dull, dull, dull.'

'Maybe,' Nina replied. She threw the chicken pieces into an orange pot on the gas stove. 'Butter,' she muttered. She chopped six cloves of garlic and three onions. But I wouldn't want to be like Gemma and her over-educated bunch of lesbian friends. The butter bubbled, the garlic turned slightly brown at the edges. The smell of the chicken and the onions pleased her. A couple of months and we'll all be in the Alps for a skiing holiday. Years and years of skiing holidays stretched before her, the children growing steadily larger and larger, Simon rising in the Civil Service, going from strength to strength. And me? Getting older watching them all grow.

She heard Doris at the door and she wiped the tears from her eyes. What an idiot I am, she thought. She put the kettle on for their morning cup of coffee. As she turned to smile at Doris, she saw the long years reach toward the future and for a moment she saw herself twenty years on, tired, dumpy, thick round the middle, her arm around Simon's waist. Well, at least Simon's mother should be dead by then, the awful bitch.

Quickly Nina and Doris fell into their usual

discussion of the various illnesses of Doris's many children. Nina was comforted. The world settled down. The snapdragons were no longer militant. Fresh Nescafé calmed her soul. Today the topic of conversation was Doris's Little Jimmy's tonsils and whether or not they ought to come out.

Doris had been with her since the day Nina returned from her honeymoon to reside with Simon at 232 Angel Walk. Doris was also just married, only Doris was already pregnant. Her Jimmy was now ten. Jane was born two years after Jimmy, and more recently came the twins, Janet and Jenny. Nina had to wait two years before she gave birth to Susan. 'Oh God,' she had prayed upon seeing Susan for the first time. 'She looks just like Simon's mother.' Three years later Hamish was born. Hamish did not look like anybody at all.

She drank her coffee in companionable silence. The casserole rumbled away. Nina poured into the pot a good bottle of Beaune and turned the chickens over. She decided she would use the navy blue tablecloth and her mother's Spode dinner service. 'Doris, could you wash the Waterford wine glasses? I must pop out and find some small beans and a salad for dinner tonight. I'm expecting a side of smoked salmon from Fortnum's, so the van might arrive when I'm out.'

Doris put a cigarette in her mouth. 'I don't know how you do it all. Really I don't. Right then, off you go, and I'll look after everything here.'

Outside in the clean suburban streets the tall plane trees sheltered the Range Rovers, the Minis, the occasional Porsche, and her own dark green Volvo.

Sitting again behind the wheel, she smelled the expensive smell of leather and wood. She looked at her hands that gripped her solid workhorse of a car, the same hands that bathed and washed the children, the hands that wiped bums, picked up puke, and then spent nights making love to Simon. Far too many nights making love, if that was what it could be called, to Simon, who rolled off, turned over, and snored. Her hands had a life of their own. Sometimes, when unsatisfied, she pleased herself and she fantasized about another man in her life. The engine turned and she put her foot down hard on the accelerator. Another guilty secret.

She was off into the traffic. She was a small, thirty year old woman, ash blonde hair cut short around her slim face. A pink mouth. A straight nose and round blue eyes. 'Pretty as a picture,' her father used to say, 'and no trouble to anyone.' Nina edged her way across the aggressive traffic. Today felt like the beginning of a new life. In a few hours she would be racing off to school to collect *both* of her children, and then racing back to feed, wash, clean, cook, and get them both to bed. Susan would whine all through her homework. Hamish would be glued to the television, and Simon would arrive home with two bottles of wine, one under each arm, and a copy of the *Evening Standard*.

There must be more to life than this, she thought at the grocery shop while poring over a pile of small green beans. Shuffling past her, a smelly old man rattled a tin. Automatically Nina dropped in a few silver coins. 'The Lord will bless you, my dear.'

Nina jumped and looked into the blackened sooty face. Her eyes locked with his for a moment and then he continued on. 'Good heavens!' Nina spoke to the owner of the shop. 'Who is that poor old tramp?'

Mrs Porter took the bag of green beans from Nina's

hands. 'That "poor old tramp" used to be a music professor at the Royal Academy. No one knows what happened. He lost his wife. Died, she did. And he went all to pieces. A shame, really. He sleeps in the park, you know.'

Nina drove back to her house feeling shaken. Doris was upstairs, vacuum-cleaning. Eight crystal glasses glittered on the dining room table. Doris had laid the table well.

In the kitchen Nina stuck her nose in the casserole. She added a pinch of butter finger-mixed with flour to thicken the sauce. It did smell good. She topped and tailed the beans and sliced the courgettes. The tramp's bleak brown eyes were still with her when she left the house to pick up the children.

He lost his wife, she heard Mrs Porter's voice. *He lost his wife.* I wonder how I'd feel if I lost Simon. Nina knew the answer, but she did not want to admit to it.

Chapter 2

Nina sat at the end of the long Regency table, her face framed in her hands. Hamish, she knew, was lying upstairs in his bedroom still not asleep. Susan had sulked as usual after school. 'I want to go and have tea with Cassandra.'

'Well, you can't.' Nina was instantly sorry to be so short-tempered, and then she tried to explain. 'I have six people coming for dinner tonight and I must get back. Let's try and make arrangements for you to see

Cassandra at the weekend all right?' It was not all right. Susan moped and Hamish was tearful all the way home. He would not tell her about his day, except to say that some boy had hit him . . .

Nina shook herself and leaned forward to join in the dinner table conversation. She could see Simon talking to his friend Neville, good old rotund Neville, with a face like a porpoise and a waistline to match. His wife Jennifer was a plain, thin woman with a thick red bush of hair. Her face was dominated by hard brown eyes. Jennifer had a double first from Oxford. Now Nina knew she must try and interest Jennifer as best she could. 'I saw the most dreadful sight this morning,' Nina began hopefully.

'Oh really, darling? Do tell.' Jennifer swivelled her head in Nina's direction. For a moment there was a pause in the conversation and fourteen eyes looked askance.

Nina felt herself blush. 'Well, it wasn't *that* dreadful, I suppose. I mean, not in an earth-shattering kind of way. There was this man. He used to be a professor of music at the Royal Academy. And now he's begging at the greengrocer's.'

A definite flake of ice hung in the air.

'Poor fellow.' Neville broke the silence. 'Your wife has such a tender heart, Simon. But it's not quite dinner party conversation, you know.'

Nina shifted in her chair. 'Neville, if you can spend the evening pontificating about the state of the pound, perhaps some of us can devote at least a moment to discussing people who don't and won't see a pound note from one day to the next.' Jennifer, she could tell, was amused by her outburst. Ziggy Lucas and her husband George exchanged glances. *Nina's at it again*, they telegraphed across the table.

Making everyone uncomfortable with her outré ideas.

'If you think the problems of the homeless could be resolved by a shower of pound notes, Nina –' Myles Kinton leaned forward from the other end of the table. He had a sharp nose. A small moustache bristled angrily above his short upper lip, exposing teeth like daggers. '– then I'm sure I could arrange an interview with the Minister for Social Services. She would be delighted to hear your views. And you clearly have so much experience.'

Nina's guests released a few muffled guffaws. She looked around the room. It was time to clear the table for the main course.

Sonia, Myles's American mistress, winked at Nina. 'I'll help you clear up,' she said.

Inside the kitchen, Nina could feel her own face was flushed. Her hands were shaking. 'Why can't I keep my mouth shut?' she demanded, more of herself than of Sonia who was behind her. She rattled the plates into the sink and wrapped up what was left of the smoked salmon.

'Listen, kid,' said Sonia. 'They're a bunch of boring bastards. I'm glad you dropped a bit of doodoo into the works. If Neville and Simon don't stop all the yakkety-yak, I'm afraid I might have no choice but to get drunk and scream.'

Nina smiled. Sonia's ability to get drunk and misbehave was a legend among the senior corridors of power in the Civil Service. Why Myles – neat, tidy, prissy Myles – kept Sonia in his luxurious bachelor pad at all was a matter of not so quiet speculation. 'Sonia, could I leave you to finish the clearing up? I must rush upstairs and check on the children.'

'Take your time. I'll see Simon keeps the glasses full, and with any luck they'll all get blotto.'

23

Nina escaped thankfully. She climbed the stairs up to the first floor. She felt the smooth bannister under her hand and heard the staccato sounds of people talking *at* each other, rather than the quiet cantando of people talking *with* each other. She recalled that in her parents' house, social issues in the Devon village were very much discussed, money was never mentioned, and most of her mother's friends were old China hands so they had years of their lives in common. Maybe that was it: she now lived in a very different world. She must learn not to mix the two worlds. Simon, with his fierce need to transcend his background and to prove to his mother that he would eventually make something of himself and bring glory and fame to the Stockton family name, found conversations at the Tolmadge house boring. Here in his own house at 232 Angel Walk, the cut and thrust marketplace economics, the inside information from the daily happenings in the Ministries, Ziggy Lucas's fruity-voiced references to which Minister did what the night before to another civil servant's wife, such was the elixir of life for Simon. Nina sighed.

She pushed open Susan's door. Even in sleep, Susan's back was turned firmly against the world, her fists tight and belligerent. Nina leaned over her and kissed the child's forehead. Susan's eyelashes fluttered and she mumbled in her sleep. For a moment Nina felt a stab of sorrow for her eldest child, so like Simon. Simon, if crossed, knew how to take his revenge. Over the years Nina had learned slowly – far too slowly – not to cross Simon. When upset, he withdrew emotionally and physically to some remote, dark, inner space where Nina would never find him. Susan had the same tendency. Odd, Nina thought, wandering across the landing to Hamish's bedroom. Passing the children's bathroom, she noticed Hamish's clothes all over the floor. Doris would deal with that tomorrow, thank God.

She heard Gemma's ironic laugh. Nina grimaced. Gemma could snort and disapprove all she liked, but Nina felt herself at this moment trapped by the three-storey house. Upstairs was her wifely life in the huge master bedroom with its luxurious adjoining bath-room. In the bedroom she was Simon's dutiful woman. Sexually available, mostly submissive in the missionary position. Occasionally, if he had quite a lot to drink, more action was required of her.

On the children's floor she was mother. Wake up calls. Baths, bedtimes, and homework to be super-vised. On the ground level she was the children's chauffeur in the hall, and cook in the kitchen. Simon had never lifted a helpful finger in his mother's house and he had no intention of starting a new habit in his own. 'I work hard all day, darling, and I don't think it's unreasonable of me to expect to come home to a clean house and three course meal on the table. That's what wives are for.'

Nina tiptoed into Hamish's room. He was awake. His wide grey eyes, fringed with black lashes, gazed at her sombrely. 'Do I have to go to school tomorrow?'

Nina's face fell. 'But you've been dying to go to school, Hamish. What went wrong?'

'School's okay,' he whispered. 'Except for the big boys. They push us around and they frighten me.' Tears welled up.

Nina put her arms around the small bony shoulders and she smelled the slightly acrid smell of an unhappy child. 'I'll talk to Daddy about it, darling, and we will see what we can do. Don't worry. Mummy will fix it.' She kissed his head. 'You go to sleep now. I'm only

downstairs. I've all these guests to keep happy . . .'
She pulled Hamish's arms from around her neck. 'I'll
be back in a while to see if you're asleep. God bless.
Sleep tight. Mind the bugs don't bite.' She felt Hamish
relax at the nightly prayer.

She stepped quietly down the stairs, pausing for a
moment in the hall, just long enough for the wife and
mother persona to leave and the ever-accommodating
hostess to arrive.

The kitchen was empty. Sonia must have gone
ahead and served the second course. Nina slipped
into her chair, nervously checking the guests' plates.

'Everything all right, Dotty?' Simon looked across
the table at her, reproof hanging over his wide white
brow.

'Just Hamish, Simon. He's being bullied at school.
First day and all that.' She smiled gratefully at Sonia
who grinned back.

'Don't make a sissy of the boy, Simon.'

Trust Neville, thought Nina, to interfere. Nina took
a tentative mouthful of the coq au vin. Not bad, she
decided.

'We sent Christopher to karate classes,' Neville
continued. 'Did him the world of good. After a few
months, he could kick the shit out of any of the boys
in his class, couldn't he, Jennifer?'

Jennifer's face was a portrait of pride. 'He got his
black belt last year.'

Nina chewed the tiny new potatoes. Delicious. First
of the season. Why on earth do Jennifer and Neville
imagine I would ever want Hamish to be a violent oaf
of a son like their Christopher? His neck was as thick
as his head and he had the same shapeless lips and
bottle nose as his father. Nina could see Simon nodding at the other end of the table. Nod, nod, nod, we

26

are all agreed that Hamish Stockton must be a chip off the old block. He shall not go to his father's minor public school; by his loving father's ambition he shall be upgraded to a major public school. Now at five years old, a decision is to be made tonight that this son and heir to the Stockton family seat – Enid's house in Purley – shall be enrolled in a local karate class so that he can be made as violent as any school bully. He can also learn that the world outside 232 Angel Walk is a dangerous brutal place. What is at stake is the survival of the fittest. They all knew that in this dining room on this September night. After all, they had survived. Had they not?

Nina let the rest of the evening slide over her. Must be the wine. She could hear Sonia in the distance. She watched herself serving the tray of coffee in the sitting room. Myles unsteadily put his hand on Sonia's bottom, his fingers inserted in the crack of Sonia's buttocks, drawing Sonia's tight black evening dress up to show the back of her knees. Nina saw a small blue vein in the hollow at the back of the knee. She felt Sonia's embarrassment. She watched George Lucas grin and look at his Ziggy, his wife. Vaguely Nina wondered if Ziggy gave George 'head', which was Sonia's American euphemism for sucking cock. The English were so much more explicit about sex, thought Nina. In speech, but not necessarily in practice. Simon would rather die unsatiated than request that Nina sucked his cock. His way of asking was a general airy wave in the direction of his penis. Hopefully not tonight, she thought.

She watched Simon. He had reached the level of inebriation at which he probably would expect at least a roll on and roll off job.

*

Voices shrilled out into the cool night air. At the door Simon stood with his arm around Nina. Nina inhaled the air and restrained herself from a sudden need to go out to the garden and bury her face beside a sleeping snapdragon. Behind her she felt the wreck of the dinner party. What had all been a miracle of harmony and order was now a broken-toothed ruin of a ground floor. Napkins thrown on to the table, some blotched with food, some with bright traces of red lipstick. The lipstick would be Jennifer's, Nina thought resentfully. It's always Jennifer. The sitting room tables held dirty coffee cups and piles of ashtrays. As for the kitchen . . .

'You go to bed, darling,' Nina said hopefully. 'I'll tidy up a few things.' If she could dawdle for long enough, Simon might fall into a drink-induced sleep.

'Don't be long, Dotty.'

Nina winced. She hated being called Dotty by Simon, but he always insisted that she was scatter-brained and dotty, because his mother truly thought Nina to be a mad woman. Nina knew it was meant affectionately, but it bothered her.

Simon gave her waist a squeeze. 'Pokies?' he said, kissing her on the mouth.

His breath smelled of too much wine. Nina detached herself and walked into the kitchen. She pottered about, pushing leftover food into the garbage bin, and she loaded the dishwasher. She looked at the clock. A quarter past one, she observed. I have to be up in six hours.

The kitchen finished, she yawned and then walked up the stairs. Hamish was asleep. His thin, worried face lay silently on his pillow. Nina felt such a pang

28

of love for her vulnerable little son and then surprised herself as a fierce possessiveness of this child squeezed her heart. She would not let Simon harm him.

She continued up the stairs into the marital bedroom. Good. Simon seemed to be asleep. She removed her clothes and pulled on her nightdress. I'll skip washing my face, she thought, so I don't wake him. She slid as quietly into bed as she could.

She felt Simon's hands between her legs. With a grunt, he rolled over on top of her and urgently tried to push himself inside her. 'Hang on, Simon,' she said, as he eagerly speared her left thigh. She guided him into her body and waited patiently, moving her hips in time with his thrusts.

Simon gave another great grunt and rolled off.

Nina patted his bottom and felt the familiar dribble between her legs. She smiled. Tomorrow she would argue against the karate school and Simon would be so grateful for the sex, she would get her way.

She fell asleep for once feeling that today she had been quite a success as a mother and a wife and a mistress, apart from the dinner table faux pas about the tramp. She would watch what she said more carefully in the future.

Chapter 3

The silence in the house was eerie. Nina put on Verdi's *Requiem* and sang along with the leading soprano. Doris bustled out of the front door at one o'clock, saying, 'Got to take Jenny to the doctor.' All that was left of her daily presence was an ashtray poised precariously on the edge of the sink. Nina loved Doris, but at times Doris's endless stories of kith and kin depressed her. If Jimmy's throat wasn't sore, then her Jane was down with a cold and the two more recent additions – the twins, Jenny and Janet – seemed to snivel endlessly. Doris herself was a walking gynaecological nightmare. Today they spent the morning discussing contraception. The Pill as opposed to an IUD. Or was it UDI? 'IUD,' Doris assured her.

Either way, Nina thought, I have the IUD so Simon can fuck when he wants to. Some day I might have to contemplate declaring UDI and rip the damn thing out. Birth control liberated men, not women, was Doris's final word on the subject. Nina could think of no argument to counter Doris's claim.

Simon, as he bumbled his way out of the front door this morning, had a pleased look on his face. He always did after a leg-over. Nina stopped singing at the memory. Sex, she once hoped, was supposed to be something one did for fun. While growing up, Nina had managed a few fumbles with boys in her Devon village, and a heavy-petting session with Jocelyn, her first boyfriend. But the Major, as her father was called locally, was known for his protectiveness, and even Jocelyn, whose hair was several inches too long, refrained from deflowering the Major's daughter. When she met Simon at a local hunt ball, she was relieved to see that his hair was cut immaculately. As far as the Major was concerned, the sixties were a time of anarchy: 'Whole country gone to pot.' Simon, upon his first introduction, fortunately agreed. 'Are you one of those Civil Service wallahs then?'

Nina smiled. Simon knew just how to win her father over. 'Housing,' he said. 'Important part of the fabric of this country. Contrary to what you hear from the lunatic left, we at the Ministry think we should encourage all council tenants to own their own homes.'

The Major concurred at the time and Nina relaxed, though she doubted very much that her father still held a terribly high opinion of Simon . . .

Fish fingers and baked beans for the children's dinner tonight, she decided, and I'll pick up some lamb chops for Simon when I go to collect the kids from school . . .

The telephone rang. Nina jumped and hurried to answer it. Something's happening to Hamish, she thought. Maybe I should have asked his teacher to keep an eye on him. 'Hello?' She was breathless with alarm.

'Relax, kid. It's only moi.' Sonia's familiar voice made Nina laugh.

'I'm just being an idiot, Sonia. I'm in a panic about Hamish, that's all.'

'And I just rang to say thank you for dinner last night. I enjoyed myself.'

'I'm so glad.' Nina stood in the hall, feeling herself isolated from all the world except for this single voice travelling through wires from Sonia's office.

'Do you want to have lunch tomorrow? We could go to Joe Allen's.'

Nina paused and her brow creased. 'Go out to lunch? I suppose I could. I don't have to collect Hamish from the playgroup at twelve any longer. I can do anything I want between nine in the morning and half past two in the afternoon. Gosh! What shall I do with all this freedom?'

'Get a vibrator or a lover or a three-legged horse.'

'Honestly, Sonia. You have the dirtiest mind.'

'It's working on women's magazines that's done it. How to fuck, when to fuck – All this advice to women. And for those who know how to and when to, the question remains: do they enjoy it in the *right* way? That's what keeps them buying the magazines and writing to me. You should see some of the letters, Nina. Make your hair stand on end.'

'Do you like sex, Sonia?' The question slipped out unexpectedly.

Sonia laughed. 'I'll tell you over lunch, honey. One o'clock?'

'I'll be there.' Nina put down the phone. What on earth will I wear? she thought. What do I have that isn't designed for pregnancy or covered in finger-paint? She danced upstairs and looked forward to having a shower, a long uninterrupted shower. No husband to distract her, no children to whine. I can take the phone off the hook and for once in my life I am by myself. The thought of being alone that yesterday reduced her to tears today filled her with excitement.

She pulled off her jeans and dropped them in the laundry basket. She turned on the shower and waited for the water to become warm. She lifted her T-shirt off and stood twitching her naked toes in the long shag pile carpet.

In the shower, Nina closed her eyes and let the thick, steaming drops run down her face. She reached for the heavy bar of soap, cucumber soap from Crabtree & Evelyn. She slid the bar past her belly, rocking slightly as her fingers found the unsatisfied opening between her legs. To make the moment of pleasure last longer, she ran the soap around her buttocks and along her legs. The urgent hunger of her body made her pant, until she found her fingers caressing her hot, wet vagina. Shuddering, she felt the movement of her body bearing down against her three fingers. Thrusting and arching her back, she moaned and she cried out and the thrusting stopped. There was a silence in the room. Nina stood under the water. She expected to feel guilty. She usually did; today, for some reason, she did not.

At her dressing table, she dropped her towel and looked at her rosy body. Maybe the whole lousy mess between men and women came down to the fact that men pleasured themselves inside women, and women put up with it because it was the price a woman paid for marriage and motherhood, for protection in the marketplace of life. In return, women pretended they liked it and then secretively, furtively, pleased themselves. Or, like Gemma, each other.

Nina smiled at herself in the mirror. Her pink nipples were still taut and her blonde pubic hair was still moist from the shower. Her usually tense shoulders felt relaxed. The bottoms of her feet tingled. Should she try it again, using the rough edge of her towel? No, she thought. I can't be found wanked to death on the floor. Imagine! Mother of two, wife of a successful civil servant, found dead by her own hand . . .

She remembered the one and only time she had tried to persuade Simon to make love in the shower. He refused icily as soon as she made her intentions clear. 'It's bad enough having to get into the shower at all. It's so cramped. You promised to wash my back and that's all. What's the matter with you, Nina? I married a nice, normal girl. You're becoming a pervert. It's that friend of yours. Sonia. She's a bad influence.'

Nina giggled at the recollection. And I'm having lunch with her tomorrow.

She dabbed herself with Shalimar, pulled on a skirt and chose a silk blouse. Silk felt appropriate for the early autumn day.

She arrived at school to be met by a hostile stare from Jennifer. 'You smell like a tart's boudoir, Nina.' Jennifer was red and cross. She was waiting to take her daughter, Hortense, to a violin lesson.

Nina smiled. 'Isn't it wonderful? I feel like a tart. Shalimar always makes me think of sheikhs in the desert, billowing tents, bronze muscular thighs, that sort of thing.'

'I don't have time for that sort of thing. I'm too busy getting the garden ready for the vegetable harvest. You know it's been quite a struggle against pests this year.'

Nina looked hard at Jennifer and tried to imagine her mating with Neville, but could conjure up no image. She couldn't even picture Jennifer having it off by herself in the potting shed. Poor Jennifer, Nina decided. Maybe she writes plaintive letters about not having orgasms to Sonia's Agony Aunt department at the magazine under an assumed name, or maybe she gets turned on by the sight of parsnips and carrots.

Nina spotted Hamish running out of school, his face alight, his hand clutching a sheaf of papers. 'We had drawing lessons, Mum! It was a super day!'

Nina hugged him. His small body smelled of sweat. She could see Susan coming along with her friend Abigail Whitstable. Nina did not like Abigail or, for that matter, Abigail's family. They were pretentious and wealthy. They lived in a big house in East Sheen. Nina often felt that Susan would rather have been born to, or at least adopted by, Abigail's mother than have had the misfortune to be born into Nina's world. 'All right, Susan. *Do* go and have tea with Abigail. What time do you want me to collect you?'

'About six.' Susan waved at her mother with a dismissive hand.

Nina turned and put her arm around Hamish's shoulders. 'Fish fingers and baked beans all right for tonight?' Shit, she thought. I forgot the lamb chops. Simon likes his lamb chops, greens and boiled potatoes. Just like Mummy's cooking, as Simon called it. Nina wished Simon could progress beyond Mummy's cooking, but he could not. At least, not in the ten years they had been married.

Hamish was asleep in the back of the car. His seat belt held him upright. Nina glanced fondly at his sleeping face. Poor child has a randy Mum. Maybe Simon is right. I am mad. A sex fiend living in Richmond.

Chapter 4

'How long have I known you, Sonia?'

'Let me see.' Sonia lifted her head. Her sleek black hair fell in a shining waterfall around her glamorous face.

Seeing the face, Nina felt a flash of envy. Why could she not look like Sonia? Around her, women and men sat at tables in this fashionable, red brick restaurant drinking and eating as if their whole lives were lived permanently in Joe Allen's.

'I think it must be three and a half years at least. I had just moved in with Myles. We met at Myles's place, didn't we?'

'Yes, that's right. I'd heard about you from Ziggy, and I was dying to meet Myles's mistress. I wasn't sure I had ever met someone who was known to be a mistress.'

Sonia laughed. Her luminous green eyes shone. 'You're so old-fashioned, you British. I didn't want to move in with Myles, you know. I was quite happy with my apartment on Kensington High Street. It was Myles who begged me to move in. He keeps asking me to marry him, silly old fool.'

Nina raised a glass of well-chilled Mâcon to her lips. She was conscious of the fact that she was wearing her very best silk camiknickers and a matching brassiere. Over that she had a black lacy petticoat, part of her wedding treasure. And the little black dress she had chosen to wear for this epic luncheon rushed to her knees. She knew she looked good. Now, after two glasses of wine and about to start on her third, she knew she felt good. 'Why won't you marry him?'

The green eyes were wary. 'I'm afraid, Nina. Really scared. I like Myles. I find him amusing, well-read, and intelligent. But he's so very British. *Such* an Englishman. Anyway, that type of Englishman doesn't marry a woman. Men like that are forever married to their public schools and their clubs. What do you expect if you send a boy away to school at seven? Poor little creatures. Most of them become raving little psychos, doomed to a lifetime of emotional and sexual constipation. No, I figure if I do get married, it will be to a good old-fashioned American guy whose idea of a day's hunting and fishing is to take me with him, not leave me with the other womenfolk, sitting over the picnic hampers, competing over who makes the best game pie. I can wait for marriage. I'm in no rush.'

'Simon's not like that at all.' Nina took another swallow of her wine. 'He went away to boarding school, only a minor one of course, but he is kind and thoughtful. A jolly good father for Susan and Hamish.' The words *dreadfully boring* lay silently on the table between them.

'I'd better order some coffee for both of us. I've got to spend the afternoon in the office answering letters from desperate women who can't come.' Sonia wrinkled her nose. 'Sometimes I wish I could call in a load of prostitutes and invite all these letter writers to a symposium. I can't see why not. After all, we're always having symposiums on how to get a job, how to dress, how to do anything you like. Why not one on how to fuck? It's more important to enjoy youself in bed than to learn how to make an entrance into the boardroom.' Sonia raised her hand and a waiter glided up behind her. 'Could you, darling? Could you possibly help us out?'

Nina watched carefully. Could she, Nina Stockton, ever put so much full-frontal sexual innuendo into a simple request for two cups of coffee? Probably not, but then she had never had to ask a waiter for coffee for the last ten years. She let Simon do all that. He just snapped his fingers loudly and was immediately served.

Sonia turned her attention away from the scurrying waiter. 'Nice to make 'em sweat,' she said. 'In your dreams, baby,' she muttered, well behind his departing back. 'In your dreams. Ha! That's all men dream about, you know. Feeding, fighting and fucking. These days you can add fleeing to the list.'

Nina laughed. 'You almost sound as if you don't like men very much.'

'Let's face it, honey. I get miserable letters all day. We Agony Aunts listen to so much agony that sometimes it gets too much for me. I want to write back and say, "Well, dear Mrs Frustrated from Penzance, your problem is that you're looking for a relationship with your husband that you will never have. He sounds a nice enough bloke –" After five years here I can speak English like the English. "– but that's all he is, a bloke. You can't expect him to be Hamlet, Don Juan, and Albert Einstein all rolled into one. No doubt he does like a pint with the lads and he cleans the car on Sunday, and he wants his sex once or twice a week . . ." And frankly, Nina, sometimes I begin to wonder. I'm not all that convinced that Mr Frustrated is the one with the problem at all. I don't think he wants a lecture on foreplay or Mrs Frustrated's sensitivity. I don't even think he wants to discover her G-spot. He just wants to get on with his life without hassle. We *women* are the ones with the complicated needs. I mean . . .'

The waiter returned with two thick white china cups of coffee. Sonia broke off her own thought. 'Bless you, darling.' Her deep growl offered him a benediction and a promise of several nights of abandoned lovemaking. 'There, you see?' she said when he had gone. 'There goes one happy man full of fantasies, but faithful to his little wife all the same.'

'And what do you say to women who write in with questions about "faking it"?' she asked, trying hard to sound casual. She took a deep breath and the wine burned in her cheeks.

Sonia raised her eyebrows. 'That's probably the biggest part of the mailbag, the white lie between the sheets. "Was that okay for you, darling?" "Oh yes." It's the *oh yes* that gives the guilty woman a chance to go to sleep. Once a woman has kids, she suffers sleep deprivation for the next fifteen to twenty years. Sure, most women fake it. Why shouldn't they? Women have a natural cycle built into their biology. Have you read anything about the lunar cycle and women?'

Nina shook her head. 'Honestly, Sonia. I don't read anything any more. I'm lucky if I can get a chance to read the PTA stuff from the school. I know I should, but I honestly don't have time. I don't have a brain any longer, just cream cheese.'

'It's a fact of nature,' Sonia continued, sipping slowly at her coffee in between phrases, 'that women fantasize about men they can't have. But they go off and marry the safe bet, the boring old good provider. It's a purely biological urge to mate with the sure thing to father your children. And that's all very well, but if there's no physical spark between them, after a short while sexual attraction for the woman withers and dies. Except for the time that she ovulates – those days of the month when her body tells her she's ready to conceive. The trouble is, once the matriarchal societies lost their power, the men took everything over, it seems to have been decided that women's bodies, too, were supposed to switch over to male time. Men said what differentiated women from all other female animals was that they were *always* ready for sex . . . Now *there's* a bit of inebriated philosophy for you to think about.'

39

Nina finished her coffee and put the cup down on the saucer. 'But that's not true, is it? I mean that women are always ready for sex? Most of the time, I'm so tired I can barely get up in the morning. By the end of a day with the children, after waiting for Simon to come home, getting his dinner on the table, I'm falling asleep after the nine o'clock news. Which is not to say I don't have some . . . um . . . secret urges of my own . . .'

'That's most women, Nina. You're not alone. Quit the guilt here and now.' She put her hand on Nina's arm. 'Say after me, I am woman.'

'I am woman.' Nina felt fearfully silly. American women are so intense, she thought. She hoped fervently that there was no one watching them.

'Hear me roar.'

'What?'

Sonia's green eyes bored into Nina's face. 'Hear me roar,' she repeated. 'Say it.'

'Hear me roar.'

'Now say the whole thing.'

Nina began in a whisper, bending over the table. 'I am woman . . . God, I can't believe you have me speaking song lyrics! Hear me roar! I feel ridiculous.'

'It's good for you.' Sonia sat back and smiled.

'What? Humiliation builds character?' Nina looked over Sonia's shoulder. Surely no one heard this bit of nonsense.

Someone had, Nina realized, and her face turned red. Sitting at the table behind them were two men. The one facing her had his two hands laced across his slim stomach. On his right hand he wore a large diamond ring. Big enough to be nearly vulgar, Nina appraised. But her eyes crept unwillingly towards his face. He was a big man. What was surprising about

40

his face was his cheekbones. They were wide, causing his eyes to slant upwards. A long, finely shaped nose sat above a firm mouth. The man smiled directly at her. Nina looked down at her cup. 'I'd better go now,' she said. 'I've got to pick up the kids. Good heavens, Sonia! We've been here long enough to make me late, if I don't hurry!'

'The kids will survive a couple more minutes.' Sonia stretched. 'I'll take care of the bill. Lunch is on me, or should I say the magazine? You allow me to give intoxicated voice to my views on the current state of womanhood, and in the eyes of my expense account, that counts as research. Thank you.'

'Any time.' Nina stood up. She fumbled in her bag, aware of the man in the dark grey suit watching her. Nina gave a last sweep of the room. She smiled and waved a hand at the table behind them. 'Who is that man?' she whispered to Sonia. 'Why do I get the feeling I've seen him before?'

'Which one? The blond or the dark one?'

'The dark one. He has the most extraordinary face.'

Sonia studied the face for a moment, then let out a gasp. 'Don't you know who that is? That's Michael Morningstar. No wonder he looks familiar to you!'

Nina was still unsure. 'Michael Morningstar?' she whispered back. 'Oh yes. Of course. The American tycoon. But he looks so different in person. I'm sure I've seen him on television.'

'You'd have to live in a cave not to. I've met him once or twice.' Sonia was visibly thrilled to be seen to divulge the information of one in the know. 'His face has to be one of the most famous faces in the world.'

41

'Hm. But he *does* look different in real life. He's taller than I'd imagined.'

'Not to mention rich.'

'He looks softer though, more human. Don't you think?' Nina noticed that his eyes were still on her as she and Sonia talked sotto voce as they left the restaurant. Michael gave a nod of his head when Nina was nearly out the door and, leaving, she gave him a little smile back.

'To tell you the truth, Nina,' said Sonia, outside in the refreshing air, 'I'm not sure that men that powerful are human at all. I think they're a different breed. A different species.'

'He looks nice to me.'

'*Nice?* I'd be surprised if there were many other people in this world who thought Michael Morningstar was nice. I read an article about him the other day. He's from New York by way of Taos, New Mexico, or the other way round, I mean, or at least so his bio in *Fortune* magazine says. He's part Navajo, part Spanish, and the rest is part mystery.'

'Michael Morningstar,' Nina said thoughtfully. Her hand was on the door of the Volvo.

'Michael Morningstar,' Sonia echoed. 'Now isn't that a name to reckon with?'

Nina laughed. 'And you say you've met him?'

'Well, not met met. I've been in the same room with him before, though. I told you. He's a mystery. I've seen him at publishing parties or at the very rich houses where they all get together to raise money for charity. Who knows? He might even recognize me. I'm not his kind of woman, though.'

'Oh?' Nina opened the car door.

'Uh, uh. He's a heartbreaker. The original. Ladies jump over balconies for him. He likes them young and innocent and then he gets his kicks destroying them. I've seen men like him for years, and I've seen my friends eat their hearts out. Not me.'

Sonia stood on the pavement as Nina's car pulled away. She stood in the busy London street and she thought, But it's women just like you, sweetheart – pretty, bored, rich, middle class housewives – he goes for. Only you don't know you're bored. Michael Morningstar would eat you for breakfast. Sonia resolved that she would keep Nina away from Joe Allen's. Next time they had lunch together, she'd take her some place else, maybe some place in Kew. Michael Morningstar's bat-like wings did not reach as far as Kew.

His domain, on this side of the Atlantic, was based in the heart of London. His home ground was the Morningstar Tower in New York. Michael Morningstar's fortune was made firstly by his marriage to his multi-millionairess, devoted wife Titania, and then he amassed the rest of his dynasty himself. The yacht, the mansion in Georgetown, the summer house in Long Island, the pink palace in Palm Springs, the old-style hideaway in the Caribbean, the villa on the Ionian . . . Oh yes, Sonia knew his listing by heart, as did every woman who made London, New York, and Paris her stalking ground.

But Sonia was content to be settled with Myles, as settled as she ever was. At least sex was fairly straight with Myles. The odd birching, a leftover eroticism from the days when he was beaten with a cane at his public school, was his only perversion. Other than that, he was an easy companion. More or less.

Sonia slipped into her office and groaned. Another huge pile of letters to be answered awaited her. But she was Queen of the Agony Aunts. In the fast-changing world of women's magazines, the editors played musical chairs across London. At least as long as the letters continued to pour in, Sonia's job was safe. She became absorbed in her work and soon forgot Nina and forgot Michael Morningstar.

Michael Morningstar was not so forgetful. He filed a note in the computer which was his brain. The dark-haired woman he could do without, but the blonde . . . She was someone he hoped to see again. He would have to keep his eyes open for her. She shone with an irresistible radiance, a light that touched a dark corner in his soul. It was a long time since he'd seen a woman blush so charmingly. A very long time.

Chapter 5

Riding through London streets usually depressed Nina. Today, however, everything looked different. Everything *is* different, she realized. For the first time in my life I'm alone in my own car, after a fabulous lunch with glasses of wine, and Sonia and I talked about sex . . .

It was a lovely autumn day, the trees down Chiswick High Road yellowed in the afternoon sun. She passed Theodorakis's shop and waved at Nonyos Theodorakis. How nice to have lived in an area so much of your life that you feel yourself truly at home! But then the excitement of lunch with Sonia was that I felt alien, exhilaratingly alien. The man sitting at the next table – Michael Morningstar! – did not know I have two children. He could guess I was married because I wear a wedding ring, but in that room, for an hour or so, I was somebody else. I was not Simon's wife or the mother of his children. Nina smiled and looked at herself in her driving mirror. I was a femme fatale.

She reached the stop light at Kew Bridge. She lowered her shining eyes and then swirled them to the left as a long-bonneted sports car drew up alongside her Volvo. She ogled the tall, fair-haired driver, feeling like Mae West without the tits. As the lights changed, Nina smiled suggestively à la Sonia and then did her Brigitte Bardot pout. The car accelerated away from the Volvo. Oh shit, just my luck, she thought. He's probably gay, or a vicar. Or maybe I just need more practice.

She listened to her favourite radio chat show, Jimmy Donleavy. I'm not nuts, she thought as the phone lines to the show were jammed with callers, almost all of the calls from women. 'I feel close to suicide, Jimmy. My whole life is getting the children up for school, getting breakfast. I kiss my husband goodbye, take the kids to school and then I do the housework. That's not the problem, though, Jimmy. It's so lonely.' Nina found herself nodding to the plight of the woman on the radio.

Jimmy's cheerful Irish voice filled the car. 'Why don't you go down to your local health centre and see if there are any other young women in your area whom you could be friends with?'

'I tried that, Jimmy, but it's hard. I'm shy.'

'What about your local playgroup, Linda? You did say your name was Linda, didn't you?'

'Yes. That's right.'

'Now, Linda, be a sensible girl and promise me you'll pay a visit to your local playgroup.'

45

'All right, Jimmy.' Linda's voice cracked.

Nina knew she was close to tears herself. Nina had cried enough times to share the strange woman's pain. At least I have friends like Sonia. She would want to count Jennifer and Ziggy among her friends, but they were different from her in so many ways, she was not sure her relationship with them could be called friendship.

The next call made Nina wince. 'Jimmy, my old man's at the pub.' The woman was panting with fear.

'What's your name, love?'

'Josie. I can't tell you my last name because of the neighbours. He mustn't find out ever. No, he mustn't . . .' She was babbling.

'Calm down, Josie.' Jimmy Donleavy's voice dropped into a reassuring monotone. 'Just take a deep breath.'

Josie hesitated and then quite suddenly she continued. 'He says when he comes home he is going to kill me. Dead, he says.'

'Have you rung a social worker?'

'Yes. My social worker says he's always saying that. And besides, she has to go to a workshop.'

'Ring the police.'

'I tried the police, Jimmy.' The matter-of-fact voice began to break up again. Nina could hear children crying in the background.

'Are you hurt, Josie?'

'Yeah, I'm hurt bad. He beat me black and blue. And he kicked me before he left. He says he'll kill me.' The pitch of the voice rose higher.

'Go to your local battered wives' refuge, Josie. Where are you?'

'Croydon.'

'Okay, just a sec. I've got it. Croydon Women's

Refuge. Pick up the kids and go now. I'll get one of my producers to ring them and say you're coming. Hurry, Josie. And good luck, love.'

The line clicked off.

Jimmy sounded tired and defeated. 'Thank God for the battered women's refuges,' he said softly. 'To all of you listening to this show who can honestly say, "There but for the grace of God go I," I ask you please to send a donation to your nearest refuge.'

Nina made a mental note to send five pounds to the big shambling refuge in Chiswick. Thank God, she thought, that will never be me. Simon's never hit me in all our years of marriage, and neither of us hits the children.

She switched off the radio and drove the rest of her way in silence. I feel guilty for thinking about sex without Simon. It's sort of unfaithful. Maybe I shouldn't have sexy luncheons with Sonia. Perhaps properly happily married women only stay properly and happily married if they remain in their shells like snails. I will try to make it up to Simon . . .

Poor woman. Nina thought again about Josie whom she had heard on the radio. She tried to imagine what a battered woman would look like. I suppose worse than when I broke my nose skiing in Italy.

That was before the children came. Lovely days on the slopes and nights with Simon's friends singing songs and drinking grappa. Then bed. Big roaring fires . . . We ought to get away together, just by ourselves for a week.

She could see the school walls. She parked and walked up the street. A few leaves tumbled from the tall trees, spinning and twirling to the ground. Maybe something inside me has changed. She kicked at the golden leaves. Maybe I'll never be the same again. The years of children at home all day have gone by so fast, now that they're over. No more having to run to keep up with myself. Now that Hamish is in school, too, I have hours to myself.

She joined Ziggy and the other women waiting to collect their children. 'I've just had lunch with Sonia, Ziggy.'

'Did you have a good time?' She sounded envious.

'Hm. Very good, as a matter of fact. You know, I could get quite addicted to long luxurious lunches.' She could see Ziggy was not really interested. Nina grew silent.

The school door opened and various women remade alliances as they picked up their children, made arrangements for tea, and departed, shooting bolts of information at each other. 'Fiona got a first at the gymkhana!' 'Robyn and Bruce swam two hundred lengths last night!'

'Poor little buggers, the lot of them,' Nina mumbled. 'Bye, Ziggy.'

On the way home, Susan and Hamish bickered in the car. 'Well, you stay away from me in the playground, Hamish. You're much too young to tag around with my friends.'

'But I'm frightened of Teddy. He says he'll beat me up.'

Nina turned and looked at Susan over her shoulder. 'Susan, he is your brother. You should look after him.'

'I knew you'd say that.' Susan kicked the back of the driving seat.

'Don't do that, Susan.' Nina felt her throat constrict.

Nina and Simon each had been raised as only children. They deliberately had had two children of their own to address what they felt was a gap in their lives. Now Susan was refusing to make good their promise to each other. That's not fair, Nina reminded herself. Simon and I made the promise, that our children would love and care for each other. Susan never agreed to anything. And anyway, Hamish *could* be demanding. 'Tell you what, kids. I need to drop into the shop and get Daddy his favourite lamb chops. So why don't we all have an ice cream?'

She saw Hamish's face light up. Susan scowled. But then, Susan always scowled.

Chapter 6

Upon arriving home, Nina felt her newfound excitement drain from her body. Once in the kitchen, the familiar rituals kept her hands and her feet busy, but her brain, she imagined, ceased to send frantic signals to the outside world. It concerned itself instead with instructions on the length of time to grill the fish fingers and when to open the tin of baked beans. Her body still smelled of Shalimar and her silk petticoat swished around her knees. 'Susan! Hamish! Come and have your supper!' The afternoon was drawing to a close.

Hamish wandered into the kitchen, followed by Susan who complained, 'I can't even begin to understand these sums.'

'Wait till your father comes home, darling. He'll help you. I'm no good at maths.' She saw the look in her daughter's eyes. Enid's eyes – her mother-in-law. How strange to have a daughter who is such a replica of someone as alien as Enid Stockton!

Susan smiled and sat down. 'Will Daddy be late tonight?'

'I don't think so. We were all late last night, so I think we'll have an early night tonight.' Deftly picking up a tray, she laid two places at the table in the centre of the kitchen. Both children sat down. 'For what we are about to receive, may the Lord make us truly thankful.'

'Amen,' concurred all three voices.

'Cassandra gets to have supper whenever she wants. She just goes to the fridge and helps herself.'

'Well, that's nice for Cassandra, Susan, but we don't live like that.'

'Cassandra's mum says you're old-fashioned.'

'Maybe I am.' Damn Ziggy, thought Nina, with her ridiculous name and her precocious daughter. Of all the girls to befriend at St Miriam's, why did Susan have to pick Cassandra Lucas? 'Baked bananas for pudding,' Nina said brightly. She looked at the two faces. My children, she thought. The reason I've lived like this for the last eight years. She cleaned the first plates into the sink and then put the pudding bowls down. She reached for the brown sugar. 'Susan, will you stick the bowls in the dishwasher please when you're both done? I need to go upstairs to have a shower and change.'

Susan frowned. 'Why can't Hamish do the dishes?'

'He can, in a year or two. For now he helps Daddy in the garden.'

'And that's hardly ever.' Susan's face cleared suddenly. 'You look quite pretty today, Mummy. Where have you been? You're wearing make-up.'

'I'm beginning to get used to my new life with both of you at school during the day. I have time on my hands.'

'Ziggy Lucas is having an affair.'

Nina felt her jaw drop. 'Really, Susan. How can you say such a thing? Who on earth told you that?'

Susan's light blue eyes glinted. 'Cassandra says she caught her mother in a clinch with Neville. He had his tongue down her throat and everything.'

'You watch too many American films on television. Cassandra's probably just making it up. I must rush, Susan. Your father will be home soon and he'll expect to have his dinner ready.' Nina ran up the stairs.

Ziggy and Neville? she thought as she turned on the shower. She removed her clothes and dropped them into the laundry basket. Did George know? she wondered. Of course, she told herself, people had affairs, but it was strange to think of it so close to home. Years ago, when Nina had time to read, Barbara Pym's characters were always talking themselves in and out of love affairs. But not your own friend, Nina thought, climbing into the shower. We've known each other for years, Simon in the Ministry of Housing, Neville in Social Services, Myles in Transport, and George – poor old cuckolded George! – in the Ministry of Agriculture, all four men having met at Oxford, now with their four disparate wives. I'm the most disparate of them all.

Nina stepped out of the bathtub. She dried herself and pulled on a pair of jeans from her closet. Simon had his own dressing room, but she chose to have a big walk-in American closet built in the bathroom. She sighed. Where was the woman who felt like an escaped butterfly? Nowhere. She had returned to her daily life with a bump. Those few hours were a hiccough in time, and her life with Simon would go on. Now to tackle the last part of the evening – dinner with Simon.

Everything was ready by the time Simon reached his front door. He pushed the key into the lock. 'I'm home,' he called out.

Susan was first to greet him. 'DaddyDaddyDaddy!' she shouted as Simon gathered her in his arms and gave her a hug.

'Miss me, Posie?' he said, swinging her off her feet.

'I need you to help me with my maths. Mummy can't do it.'

Nina watched the look that passed between Simon and Susan. The look seemed to say, *We two know each other. The rest of the world can keep out, because sealed between us is a relationship that no one else can share.* That look between them had been there from the time Susan was first able to focus on her father's face.

Simon put Susan back on her feet, kissed Nina on her forehead, and patted Hamish who stood silently by his mother. 'Good day at school, son?'

Hamish nodded.

'I think we'll have a look into karate classes for you. Teach you to fight, eh?'

Hamish looked at his shoes and said nothing.

'What's for dinner, mother?'

'I'm not your mother, Simon. I'm your wife.' Nina decided to keep the irritation out of her voice. 'It's your favourite. I've made a curried soup with celery, and then chops, new potatoes and peas, followed by a brie.'

'Sounds lovely.' Simon carried his briefcase into the drawing room. 'Angela sent you a present. She says husbands should give wives presents regularly to

52

show them that they are appreciated.' He pulled out a bottle of sherry. 'Good choice, wouldn't you say?' He held the bottle up to the light. 'Nice colour. Nina, let's have a glass before dinner.'

'Can I, Daddy?' Susan was standing close to her father. Too close.

Nina felt excluded. 'Why don't you get on with your homework, Susan?' Nina knew she sounded sharp. What with Simon's secretary Angela's condescending attempt at befriending her, and her daughter's efforts to annex her father's attention, Nina was feeling beleaguered.

'I'll be along in a minute, Posie. Let me just have a glass with your mother.' Simon patted Susan's bottom as she turned to flounce out of the room. For yet another moment, their eyes locked. Again came Nina's excluded feeling. Hamish felt it, too. He had always been locked out of his father's affections. It caused a bleakness about his face. Nina put her hand on his shoulder. 'Hamish, why don't you go over to the china cabinet and bring me two sherry glasses?'

'Okay, Mummy.'

Nina watched him as he walked towards the large display cabinet. The drawing room was a big square. The windows still retained the old indoor wooden shutters, now patinaed with age and polish. It was a graceful room, and one of Nina's favourite moments was now. She snapped on the table lamps.

Simon sat in his stuffed armchair, his glasses glinting in the light, reading the *Evening Standard*. Hamish returned with the two Waterford sherry glasses. 'Can I have a sip of yours, Mum?'

'Of course you can. Why don't you go into the kitchen and watch the television there while Daddy and I have a little chat? We haven't seen each other all day. Run along.'

Hamish nodded and was gone.

'Shall I pour, Simon, or you?'

Simon folded the newspaper carefully. 'I'll pour, dear.'

Nina watched Simon walk over to the drinks trolley. The trolley or, rather, some madman's artistic folly, made her laugh. Sonia loved the thing and was always pestering Nina to sell it to her. Nina noticed that the brass screws that held the trolley together needed cleaning. I'll worry about that tomorrow, she thought. She ran her eyes along the rim of ostrich skin that stretched around the glass oval of the trolley's upper shelf. Pure 1920s kitsch, she thought . . .

'Dreaming again, Dotty?' Simon sounded impatient.

'Sorry, darling. I was just thinking about the drinks trolley.'

Simon opened the bottle, filled his glass, lifted the sherry to the light, and then sniffed. 'Good choice.' He sipped from his glass. 'What a very good choice. I'll tell Angela in the morning.'

'Could you pour me a glass, darling? After all, Angela said it was for me.'

Simon laughed. 'Well, it's sort of from both of us. You know how it is. Angela asked if I'd done anything nice for you recently. "Other than the other?" I said. She caught what I meant. Old Angela's no fool.' Simon tried to look roguish. 'Anyway, "Not that kind of present," Angela said. "Have you bought her something nice?"'

'"Tell you what. I'll give you the money, Angela, and you go and choose Nina something she'd like."'

'How did you know I said that?' Simon's eyebrows took off in surprise.

'You always say that, every time you bring a present home.'

'Do I really?' Simon sighed. 'I must be getting old, I suppose. Still, I'd better give Susan a hand with the old maths. Call me when supper's ready.'

Nina left the room which glowed in lamplight. She walked into the kitchen and made a note on the magnetic pad on the front of the fridge. BRASSO, she wrote.

Hamish stood up from the beanbag chair on the floor of the kitchen. 'Can I have a sip now?'

Nina handed him her glass. Hamish took a sip and made a face. 'Anyway, darling, it's time for pyjamas and bed. Is it a bath night or a wash night?'

'Bath night,' Hamish laughed. 'I've got all my underwater divers ready.'

'Okay. Can you manage by yourself?'

'I'm five now. I'm not a baby.'

'Off you go then. I'll be up to tuck you in after dinner.' She heard Hamish run across the hall and she imagined him running up the stairs. She used to have to carry him up those stairs in the early years, before he reached the age when he learned to manoeuvre himself step by step on his bottom. At last the wonderful day had come when he shouted, 'Look, Mummy!' and she had run out to see him grimly hanging on to the handrail, walking down towards her. At the bottom he flung himself into her arms and they hugged. How silly, she thought then, to feel so proud. How silly, she thought now as she stirred a spoonful of cream into the soup on the stove, to mind so much when Hamish says, 'I'm not a baby any more.' At some level, Hamish will always be my baby. Nina lit the grill for the chops and checked the dining room.

The table was laid for the two of them. She lit the candles in the silver candelabra, a present from her aged Aunt Persephone. Nina loved to eat by candle-light. After a child-filled day, detergent-smelling hands, and hair limp from exhaustion, there was nothing like fresh clothes and a quiet drink before dinner and the candles to keep the magic in their marriage. 'You're too romantic,' her friend Jennifer protested once. 'Christopher, Hortense, Neville and I just pig it out in the kitchen. We don't have time for all that nonsense.'

Well, maybe Neville does after all, Nina grinned as she saw Simon crossing the corridor to enter the dining room. 'I'll be along in a minute,' she said, returning to the kitchen. She poured the soup into her Chinese rice bowls. The smell of curry caught her nose. How I would love to go to India some day! She carried the soup into the dining room. 'Wouldn't it be lovely, Simon, if we could visit India?'

Simon broke the Melba toast between his long, pre-cise fingers. 'Never been there and wouldn't want to. After what the old man told me about the place, I'd sooner die. Mother's house is *still* full of Indian bric-a-brac.'

'Some of India must be nice though.'

'I don't know. I suppose so. By the way, mother says she'd like to see us for Sunday lunch.'

'Oh dear. I'd hoped to have Gemma around on Sunday, Simon. I haven't seen her for ages.'

'With or without her lover?'

'*With*. Marietta is awfully nice. I don't know her very well, but I've spoken to her on the telephone.'

'Nina, before you go inviting those sort of people

into our house, mightn't you consider what the effect will be on the children?'

'I don't think there'll be any effect, as you put it, on the children.'

'Now Dotty is getting defensive. Aren't you, Dotty?'

Nina felt herself growing very cross. 'But I suppose you think it's quite all right to invite adulterers into the house, as long as they're not dabbling within their own gender.'

'What on earth do you mean?' Simon held his spoon at mouth level.

'Neville is having an affair with Ziggy.'

'How do you know that?'

'Your own daughter told me this afternoon. She saw them French kissing in Ziggy's drawing room. She saw for herself when she was with Cassandra.'

'Good heavens!' Simon put his spoon down. 'Good heavens! How awful for George. If anything like that happened to me, I'd . . . Well, I can't imagine what I'd do.'

Nina looked up at him. Simon appeared startled. Immediately Nina felt solicitous. 'Simon, I'd never be unfaithful to you. I'm not the unfaithful type. Honestly. Here. I'll clear the soup. Would you like a glass of red wine?' She picked up a wine decanter from a side table and poured. She pushed his wine glass towards him. 'Drink up, Simon.' She left the room.

'Wonder if poor George suspects,' she heard Simon mutter.

Poor George indeed. Nina bent over the spluttering lamb chops. I'm not the unfaithful type, she told herself fiercely. Mentally she caught sight of Michael Morningstar in the restaurant, the man with the thick

dark hair and high American-Indian cheekbones –
they must be Indian. She thought of *The Song of
Hiawatha*. The heavy metres of the great epic poem
began to thrum in her mind. *'By the shores of Gitche
Gumee . . .'* She put a pat of butter on the peas. *'By
the shining Big-Sea-Water . . .'* She added a splash of
cooking wine to the gravy in the grill pan. *'Stood the
wigwam of Nokomis . . .'* She pushed a fork through
the boiled potatoes. *'Daughter of the moon, Nokomis.'*
She took out a big Victorian serving platter complete
with indentations for peas and potatoes. The two
chops looked bewildered by the size of the plate, but
it didn't matter. It was better than three trips backwards and forwards.

Nina arrived in the dining room with the main
course and a plan.

'How about I telephone Gemma tonight, and if
she's free, I'll go over there one evening?'

Simon's head jerked up. 'You mean I'll be here
alone with the children?'

'Yes. You'll be here with the children. They'll have
a wonderful evening with you alone, and I can go out
by myself for the first time since they were born.
Please, Simon. It's such a good idea.'

Simon was trapped. He ate his lamb chop in
silence. Bother the woman. Why does she have such
silly ideas? A woman's place is in the home, whatever
nonsense those ugly harridans bellow about on the
television screen. All the fault of those lefties in the
BBC.

Nina cut into the brie. 'I love that brie smell,' she said,
smiling at Simon. 'Gemma says fine for tomorrow
evening.' She put a wedge of the cheese on her plate
and then cut a sliver. 'Perfect. It smells like sex. Here,

58

have some, Simon.' She pushed the cheese plate towards him.

'Brie does not smell like sex, Nina. It smells like brie.'

'Do you really think so?' Nina was dreaming.

'You've got sex on the brain, Nina.'

'Have I? It's your turn to load the dishwasher, Simon.'

'I don't have a turn to load the dishwasher.'

'Well now you do.'

'I say, Nina. You *are* in a mood tonight.' He wiped his cheese knife on the rest of his water biscuit.

Nina cleared the table and loaded the dishwasher. She went up the stairs thinking what a rollercoaster of a day it had been. She kissed sleeping Hamish on his brow. She pushed open Susan's door. There on the desk stood Simon's sherry glass. Susan was also asleep, a smile on her face. She can be so nice when she wants to, Nina thought. Maybe things will get better when she's older. Eight is such a difficult age. I wish we lived in the country. Then Susan could have a horse. But then Simon wouldn't hear of living in the country.

Nina was reading when she heard Simon coming upstairs. Maybe we can really make love, she thought, the way we used to.

Simon emerged from his dressing room in his striped flannel pyjamas, pulled the bedclothes open, and Nina held out her arms. 'Not tonight, darling,' Simon said, falling into bed. 'I'm getting a headache. Too much on the brain, what with you going out tomorrow night and leaving me with the children. I'd better get some sleep.'

I thought it was wives who had headaches. Nina

snuggled into her pillow. Oh well. There's always imagination. Her hand found its way between her legs. She smiled into the darkness and Michael Morningstar, with his high cheekbones, smiled back. What wickedly perfect teeth he had, she remembered.

Chapter 7

This being Saturday morning, Simon stayed upstairs and read the newspapers in bed while Nina gave the children a cooked breakfast in the kitchen. When the coffee was ready she took him up a mugful – two sugars, no milk – along with a plate of toast. Nina was full of excitement at the thought of a night out with Gemma ahead of her.

She put the coffee on the bedside table and kissed the top of Simon's head. He gave a small grunt of acknowledgement, but was too absorbed in the newspaper to produce an articulate greeting. Nina stepped back and observed Simon sitting up in bed, his newspaper held out before him, and she wondered whether or not he knew she was in the room. Simon gave his newspaper a brisk snap to rid it of wrinkles. Nina's eyes were caught by a photograph on the side of the newspaper facing away from Simon, the side facing her. And, as if looking into her own face, the large photographic portrait of Michael Morningstar appeared from the flat surface of the newsprint.

Nina sat down on the bed by Simon's feet to better see the picture and the story. From the glimpsed lines of the text, she could tell that the article was a personal profile of the world famous multi-millionaire. Slightly too far away from the page to read the story clearly, she was more interested in the picture anyway. What struck her was that, having seen the man in real life, having watched his actions and his gestures, and having returned the smiles and nods he had given to her, she now thought that this photograph looked different from any of the ones she had seen in the past. Suddenly the face in black and white had depth and shape for her, for she knew what the jaw looked like from the side, when the head was turned. She knew how the mouth moved when not frozen in the elegant but distant smile it held in photographs.

'Shopping today, Dotty?'

The eyes of the pictured face were not the impersonal eyes of a celebrity. They were human eyes capable of real expression and unspoken communication. Those same eyes had looked into her own in the restaurant, and now, as she studied the printed image, they appeared once again to find her out in particular. Yes, the eyes, the mouth, the whole face did now hold a different demeanour than in the past. The person was real, and Michael Morningstar was looking at her. Maybe she had been in his thoughts when he sat for the photo. Perhaps he had even imagined her in front of him when he looked directly at the camera, trying to convey through the newspaper a message that he was thinking of her, too. After all, he had nodded especially at her. Not at Sonia, only at her. And she had waved back.

When was the photo taken? It couldn't have been since her lunch with Sonia. There couldn't have been time – not much, anyway – for a photographer to take the picture, develop it, send it to the newspaper, have the newspaper print it . . .

What was she thinking? Nina asked herself. *Of course* Michael Morningstar wasn't thinking about her when he posed for his portrait. How could she let herself dream something so absurd? Fantasizing is becoming a bit of a habit lately, Nina said to herself . . .

'I said are you shopping today, Dotty?'

'Hm?' Nina raised her attention from Michael Morningstar's sharp, dark eyes to the blank, questioning eyes of Simon who watched her with growing impatience over the upper edge of the newspaper.

'Yes. It's Saturday. I was just reading a story on this page . . . I always shop on Saturday.'

'Indeed you do,' said Simon, laying the newspaper down on the bed. 'So it's time for us to make our shopping list, isn't it?'

'If you say so.' Nina's gaze remained on the newspaper which lay with Michael's face down.

'Children going with you?'

'Hamish is. Susan doesn't want to.'

Simon reached for a notepad and a pen on the bedside table. SHOPPING, he wrote across the top of the page, and Nina heard the pen scratch the paper.

As if without caring, she turned over the newspaper and read the piece about Michael Morningstar while Simon got on with his list. The article said nothing new, nothing she hadn't read before in many other newspapers and magazines. But the picture, with its insistent, intelligent eyes . . . Those were eyes that understood you when they beheld you. You could keep nothing from those eyes, expect none of your secrets to remain secret for long. Nina felt furtive as she looked at Michael Morningstar with Simon so close by. She felt guilty of a betrayal, though surely it was madness to imagine that Simon would see her doing anything other than reading a perfectly ordinary article in a perfectly ordinary newspaper . . .

'You know how important it is to make a list, Nina, or we end up running out of things. You always forget to buy *something*.'

The words *running out of things* struck her ears, when spoken by Simon, as if the last trump had been sounded. She looked up from the newspaper. 'Oh, don't be silly, Simon. I can always pop next door if we run out of loo roll. Or there's always *The Times*.'

'Don't be vulgar, Nina. Why should I even consider using *The Times* for such a purpose when all it takes is a little bit of organizing? If you would only shop at a proper, modern supermarket, like Jennifer does, instead of patronizing those grotty little foreign shops, our lives would be much more efficiently run, to say nothing of cheaper.'

'I hate supermarkets, Simon. You know that. Why don't you come with me? George always goes with Ziggy.' Ziggy's name fell between them.

'Yes. Well. I may not be the best of husbands, and I may not escort you to help you shop, but I do provide lavishly for you, and you do have full-time help. So we'll write out this list together, and you promise me you will go to a decent supermarket, won't you?'

His languid hand held the pen poised to write the list. Nina looked at the gold ring on his little finger. Who's vulgar? she thought defensively. Men with mothers called Enid and a house in Purley don't have real family crests. And to try to carry off wearing a crest ring as if it were truly ancient and venerable must surely be the absolute zenith of pretentious vulgarity . . .

Nina put her brain on hold. Simon began to list the shopping, item by item, according to the order in which the items appeared on the shelves at the supermarket. Starting at the door, she must enter and work her way around until she got to the exit. How useful it must be for him to have a photographic memory of the inside of a supermarket, and how safe he must have been to be raised by a mother who kept a life's supply of loo paper in her store room so that her family need never risk the perils of running out! Of course, should the ultimate evil – constipation – visit Enid's only son, there were rows of suppositories at the ready in Enid's bathroom cupboard. If those didn't work, there was a malignant-looking contraption lurking in the back of the same cupboard.

Breastfeeding and constipation were Enid's two main subjects of conversation. No wonder poor Simon has a morbid dread of running out of lavatory paper, thought Nina. Looking down, she saw that the face of Michael Morningstar seemed to be laughing at her from the newspaper on her marital bed.

Simon sat hunched over his list. There was a slight hiatus when he reached the question of whether to guide Nina to the right or to the left when she arrived at the final aisle. Photographic memory triumphed and Simon sat up with a smile. 'There you are, darling. All the hard work done. Now all you have to do is decide which vegetables you want to buy.'

Nina ran her eye down the list. 'Must we have kidneys?' she said. 'And you know Hamish hates liver.'

'Offal is awfully good for you.' Simon guffawed at his own pun.

Nina tried to manage a smile.

'Tell you what. I'll cook tonight when you go off with your girlfriends.'

'That's good of you, Simon.' Nina stood and kissed him again on the forehead. The sight of his coffee mug, sitting on his plate of toast, irritated her, because she knew that she would be expected to make a second trip upstairs to carry the crockery down to the kitchen once Simon, leaning on his pillows, had emptied them. 'You can take your plate and mug down yourself,' she said.

He opened his eyes wide. 'My, we are in a bad mood today, aren't we?' She took the list and left the room.

Hamish was waiting for her in the hall. She could see Susan slumped on one of the beanbags at the end of the kitchen, talking into the telephone.

'Come on, Hamish.' Nina opened the door to a mild autumn day. 'Let's have an adventure. Let's play truant from the supermarket and see what Porch's fish shop has today. Then we can sneak off to Nonyos and Stathis Theodorakis's grocery shop and get some *real* food.'

Hamish grinned.

Chapter 8

The last time Nina had visited Gemma's West Kensington flat – ages ago – Gemma had been living alone. Now Nina would have to share Gemma with her friend. So far Gemma had not used the word *lover* to describe Marietta, Nina reflected as she drove along. I know I'm supposed to be liberal and all that these days, but I can't imagine Gemma in bed with another woman. But then, Nina reminded herself, she couldn't imagine dry, intense, politically active Gemma in bed with anybody. Gemma's bed was usually awash with books, ashtrays, and political tracts. It was the political earnestness that tended to push them apart.

Nina was nervous as she turned the car into the dismal, long road where Gemma and her friends plotted the overthrow and destruction of the English establishment. The road was suitably shabby. The shops supported tattered awnings and not much else. The occasional restaurant appeared along the road, as did a lone fish and chip shop. Nina found the block of uninspiring 1930s flats and parked her car. No long lines of Porsches here. Instead there were Ford Escort vans and old rust-encrusted Consuls, some settled forever, their tyres removed, permanent residents of the gutter beside discarded coiled bed springs and three-legged prams. The dim, gap-toothed overhead lighting gave the landscape a surreal look. Nina felt too well-dressed for the surroundings. She grew aware that her car was not only foreign but was also a luxury. She felt the curtains flicker behind windows in the flats. The sounds of loud music and multi-volumed television sets overrode the intermittent piercing cries of a child. Why did Gemma have to live in such a dreadful area?

Nina hurried to the bottom of the stairs. As she turned the corner she smelled the stale, musty smell of urine. JOE FUCKS MARY screamed the graffiti up the smeared walls. HURRAY THE IRA said one piece of plaster. DEATH TO THE CAPITALISTS promised another.

Nina ran up the stairs and knocked on Gemma's blue front door. Gemma opened the door on a chain. 'Who is it?' she said.

'Me, you twit. You asked me to dinner, remember?'

'Oh.' Gemma sounded relieved. 'Of course it's you.' She shut the door again and Nina could hear her fumbling with the chain. 'I'm just being stupid.'

Nina felt the hair rise on the back of her neck as a sharp scream rang out from the treeless playground across the road behind her. Gemma opened the door. 'I really don't know how you can live here, Gemma. It's a ghastly place. Dante's *Inferno* pales by comparison.'

'Welcome to the real world, Nina. This is how most people live.' Nina could hear the familiar impatience of political dogmatism in Gemma's voice.

'Then thank God I'm not most people.'

Gemma grinned and her voice turned warm. 'When the revolution takes place, darling, you *will* be like most people. Each according to her need. No one will be poor or hungry. Anyway, come and meet Marietta.'

They walked down the corridor to Gemma's sitting room. The flat always reminded Nina of a ship. The rooms were uncompromisingly white and square. The windows were placed so as to give an unimpeded view of an outdoor blank wall. Standing in the doorway was a tall woman. She held her hand outstretched. 'I'm Marietta Luscova.'

Nina was surprised. 'You're not at all what I expected.' She felt the blood rising in her face. 'I mean, that sounds awful, I . . . I just didn't know what to expect.'

Marietta laughed. She had very fine hazel eyes, a wide sensuous mouth, and her shining, sleek, black hair was tied back in a bun. From each ear dangled a lovely lapis lazuli earring set in heavy gold. Nina realized that Marietta was extremely beautiful. She had a large curved nose which, rather than detracting from the beauty of the face, made it different from all other faces. Marietta's features spoke of far off lands, thick plush carpets, walls hung with tapestries, silken fleet-footed dogs. What was she doing in dingy St Stephen Street? Marietta saw the question in Nina's eyes. 'I met Gemma at a women's conference in Holland last year. It was love for both of us.'

Nina looked at Gemma. She smiled back. 'We've been together for a whole year now,' said Gemma shyly. 'Let me get you a drink.'

'Damn,' Nina said. 'I meant to bring a bottle of plonk, but by the time I got all the washing done, I guess I forgot. I'm sorry, Gemma.'

'Don't be.' Gemma moved into the sitting room. 'Come and see how Marietta has improved my life.'

Nina laughed. 'I say, Marietta, you have made a difference!'

Gone was the dentist's waiting room look, the uninspired old sofa and back breaking stuffed chairs. Instead Marietta must have scoured the neighbourhood for good solid Victorian furniture. There were two massive spoonback chairs. 'We re-upholstered those ourselves.' Gemma's eyes were shining. Nearby sat two smaller nursing chairs and a walnut drop leaf table. The ugly windows were obscured by thick green curtains with matching pelmets. The room, for the first time in Nina's experience, had a warm and cozy feel to it and Nina found the tension in her neck and arms flowing away. 'Here,' offered Gemma. 'Have a glass of wine.'

Nina accepted with a smile and said, 'You really

have changed.' Wine in Gemma's home used to be served in a thick drinking glass. 'What a pretty wine glass!'

'To be a revolutionary, you don't *have* to suffer,' Marietta laughed. 'Though English people like hair shirt.'

'Come on, Nina. I'll show you the bedroom and the kitchen.'

Nina followed Gemma's straight back up the corridor again.

'Here you are.' Gemma opened the door.

'Good heavens! Now that really is a miracle!' No longer was there the tiny camp bed with its thin unwashed pillow. Instead, the floor of the room had been covered with thick brown carpet. A big double mattress lay on the floor. Stacked up against the wall were huge square European pillows in brightly patterned silk pillowcases. The bed was dressed in Irish linen sheets and a fluffy midnight blue blanket. Large pots of green plants stood around the room and suspended from the ceiling over the bed was a multicoloured Tiffany lamp.

'Our bed,' said Gemma proudly.

Nina stood in the doorway nonplussed. She was bursting to ask *What do you do in it?* but she was also deeply embarrassed. 'What a beautiful room!' she stammered and she blushed. She could feel Marietta's eyes on her. Marietta's eyes were undisturbed pools of watchfulness.

She said, 'Come along, Nina. I'll show you the kitchen. This is my special place. I love to cook. Gemma is out working all day, so I cook. She comes home to a nice place and a beautiful meal every night.'

'Lucky Gemma,' Nina found herself laughing. 'I

69

cook, chauffeur, and bottle-wash all day, and then I cook a three course meal for Simon.'

'That's called enslavement to a man.'

'But I love Simon and my two children.'

Marietta's eyebrows rose. 'I once said those words about my family when I lived in Hungary. That's where I'm from. I was a wife and mother.' She shrugged. 'What a life! No life. All was for the children and the man, and then . . . Poy! His mother! She spoiled him into a monster! He still has my children . . .' Her expression grew distant and pained.

Nina was afraid to touch that pain. 'Well, it smells as if you've cooked something magnificent tonight.'

'It's just a goulash. We start with mint and cucumber salad and then we proceed.'

'It all sounds – and smells – wonderful.'

Marietta stretched her long body and smiled. 'Let's eat.'

Over dinner Gemma asked Nina to tell her everything happening in her life.

'Actually,' said Nina, 'there's nothing much to catch you up on. Except to say that Hamish has started school, and Susan wants to join the Girl Guides. We have to go and see Simon's mother, Enid, in Purley tomorrow.'

'Ah! The great bourgeoisie, nowhere so alive as in England!' observed Gemma, evidently unable to stay away from politics for long.

'I guess you're right.' Nina took a spoonful of goulash. 'That's absolutely marvellous, Marietta.' Nina took another mouthful, swallowed, and said, 'You must give me a little to take home for Simon.' She kicked herself. Why must she keep on bringing up

Simon? Perhaps because the three of them sitting comfortably at the walnut table made her feel complicit and nearly illicit. She had to admit to herself how quickly at home she felt in a world where there were no demanding children, no intrusive male presences. She ate her goulash.

After a cup of gloriously harsh coffee, Nina stood at the front door. Marietta hugged her goodbye. 'Come again soon, Nina. We will be friends. I can tell.'

Nina returned the hug. Gemma walked her down to the car. 'What do you think of her, Nina?'

Nina breathed deeply. 'I think she's fantastic. I really do.' She opened the car door and looked at Gemma. 'Does your mother know?'

Gemma's voice was a whisper. 'She's met Marietta several times, if that's what you mean.'

'That's not what I mean.'

'Well, no, Nina. And she will never know. My mother wouldn't understand in a million years.'

Nina kissed Gemma on the cheek. There was a dreadful misery in Gemma's eyes. 'As long as she makes you happy, Gemma, I'm happy.'

'Thank you, darling. I needed to hear that.'

Nina drove away, her foot hard down on the accelerator. Suddenly she badly wanted to get back to the safe world of Richmond and her husband and the children.

Chapter 9

Driving back to Richmond, Nina felt exhilarated. Now I've got lots to think about, she said to herself. I can tell Simon about my evening out. I won't be boring for a change.

Leaving the shabby roads behind her, she enjoyed passing the familiar landmarks. Hammersmith roundabout, people milling about, some on their way back from the Palais, some just standing and talking. Nina noticed their faces as she flashed past. These people looked so very different from the people who stood in the pubs in Kew and Richmond or the people in the small restaurants along the River Thames. These people looked alive, as though they shared an electricity of their own.

The car moved down the Kew Road and the traffic was thin. Mostly expensive cars. Nina saw a few disapproving wives gazing at her alone in her car. Irritation in the women's eyes because she, Nina, was a dangerous figure alone in the night, the blonde that might one day take the man away who so patiently drove his platinum-plated wife back to their expensive nest in Richmond and the bourgeois wastelands beyond . . . Hearing her own thoughts, Nina laughed at herself. I can tell I've spent an evening with Gemma, to think of things in terms of the bourgeoisie . . . Enid, she groaned. Oh well, at least I don't have to go to church and listen to the Reverend Simpson carry on about his personal relationship with Him up there. Visiting the widow is a good Biblical excuse. It would be nice if we could get our hands on a bit of the widow's mite . . .

She turned the car into Angel Walk. Such a lovely road. She saw her usual parking space. The house loomed a welcome in the starlit night. The dug-up bed of the last flowers of autumn breathed a sleepy greeting. The white latch gate clicked and Nina put her key in the lock. She paused before she pushed open the door and checked her watch. Half past eleven, the numerals flashed green. How often had Simon come home at this time after late meetings or dinner with fellow civil servants from his Ministry? Half past eleven meant that Nina waited for him on her own in the sitting room. She loved the half past eleven return. Simon would push the door open and call hello into the dark, children-sleeping night. *I'm here, darling.* And Nina would come through the hall to kiss him. Then they would pour a last drink – whisky for him, brandy and soda for her. The quiet uxorial hour after Simon returned from the fray to his home and his hearth and his wife . . .

Nina smiled. Now, for the first time, she would call and he would answer. She stood in the hall and she called, 'Simon? I'm home.' But her voice trailed away in the silence. He's fallen asleep, she told herself. She walked through to the drawing room. No, the sofa was strewn with cushions. Several lay on the floor. A tin of Coke and a screwed-up packet of crisps remained on the coffee table. Susan, she thought. Why can't she pick up after herself? She bent down and replaced the pillows on the sofa. She took the empty tin and the crisp packet into the kitchen. The dustbin was filled with the Chinese takeaway containers. Some of the cashew chicken had slid onto the

73

floor. The sink held a stack of plates and knives and forks, all unwashed. I'll deal with it tomorrow, Nina decided, a great tiredness stealing over her. Simon must be upstairs reading.

She climbed the stairs, carrying her handbag. Both children were asleep. Hamish was sleeping in his vest and underpants. He'll have to have a shower before going down to Purley.

She pushed open the door to the bedroom. The room was drowned in silence. Simon lay on the bed. He had not thought to leave a light on for her. He was soundly and solidly asleep on his back. Nina could hear the slight snore. She inched her way by instinct to her side of the bed. She removed her clothes and slipped her hand under her pillow to find her nightdress. She pulled it over her head and let the silk settle.

Once in bed, she lay back, longing for a moment to be sitting in Gemma's bedroom with Marietta, the three of them talking. Instead she was here with Simon, her night out unshared and unappreciated, the chaos in the kitchen an unwelcome return home, a reminder that her role in Simon's life was that of mother of his children. If she defected, then there was a price to pay. Though the price was no more annoying than a piece of grit in a tennis shoe, it was also no less annoying.

Nina picked up her alarm clock. She set the alarm for a quarter to eight, a little early for a Sunday morning, but she would have to get Hamish up early to take his shower. She tried to fall asleep, but thoughts and images kept chasing through her head. She did not dare wake Simon. Slowly sleep crept over her, but her dreams were disturbed. Several times she jumped awake.

In no time the alarm shrieked and she had to get up. Groggy, she sat on the edge of the bed and remembered the state of the kitchen. She poked Simon. 'I've got to get Hamish into the shower, Simon. You get the coffee this morning.'

Simon rose out of his sleep, blinking his eyes. 'That's all very well, Nina. I babysat for you while you raced about with your dyke friends. *You* get the coffee. I'm tired. Hamish was difficult.'

'I can see that.' Nina controlled herself. 'We have to get off to visit your mother and I must get Hamish out of his vest and knickers. Why didn't you see he had a bath?'

'I did. I sent him upstairs.'

'Simon, Hamish is only five years old. He needs to be supervised. Otherwise he starts playing and he forgets.'

'I could bathe myself at five. He's a little git, because you spoil him.'

'First of all, Simon, you did not bathe yourself at five years old. You had a nanny. Remember?'

Simon grunted. It was the usual Simon grunt when he knew he had been found out but wouldn't admit it.

'Secondly, Simon, Hamish is not a spoiled git. You just ignore him too much. Anyway, get up and let's get moving. It's going to be a long day.'

Simon sat up and swung his feet to the ground. He knew he had pushed Nina too far. 'Did you have a nice time?' he offered.

'Yes, I did have a nice time. And you'll have to get used to the idea that in future I will have other nice times and you will have to babysit.' Nina left the room. Even Doris gets time off to go to bingo with her girlfriends, so why shouldn't I?

*

75

She bent over Hamish and she smiled. Hamish was asleep, his long eyelashes resting on his cheek, his hands full of his favourite soldiers. 'Hamish,' she called quietly. 'Wake up.'

Hamish's eyes rolled open. 'I missed you tucking me up,' he mumbled.

'Just as well, young man. You didn't have your bath, did you?'

Hamish giggled and stretched. 'No. But I missed you, Mum. You won't go out again by yourself, will you?'

'We'll see, Hamish. We'll see.' A sense of hopelessness descended upon Nina like a brown pall. Why shouldn't I go out for a night if I want to? She remembered her mother's two nights a week. Those were nights she cooked supper for her father and they both ate supper off trays on their knees in the library, if it was winter, or in the garden if it was a warm summer. Lovely memories.

There was no sign of Simon, and Nina needed a cup of coffee. Her mouth was dry from an unaccustomed amount of red wine. She grimaced as she walked down the stairs. She heard the hiss of the shower on the children's landing. Susan was already moving about in her room.

Nina turned the corner into the kitchen and then remembered it was Sunday. No Doris. She must clean up the mess by herself. But first she would give herself a cup of coffee. She put the kettle on and sat on a chair by the kitchen table. Sod it, she looked at the bullying dustbin and the mess of plates. But it was not worth irritating Simon. The whole day would be a day of tiptoeing around Simon and his mother anyway. Whatever resentments they held about each other usually settled like crows on Nina's shoulders.

For years now, Nina accepted it as a fact of their married life together.

The kettle whistled. Nina filled her mug with boiling water. The brown crystals in the bottom of the mug dissolved, letting out the healing smell of instant coffee. Five more minutes, she promised, and I'll clear up.

Chapter 10

'Susan, do stop pinching your brother.' Nina turned around in the car and marvelled again at the resemblance between Susan and her grandmother, Enid. Nina said, 'Hamish, move over. Don't crowd your sister.'

'I'm bored,' Hamish whined. 'It's too long to drive to Grandma's. Anyway, there's nothing to do when we get there.'

'You can water the garden for her, darling. Your grandmother would like that.' Nina wished she could whine like Hamish. Really, the situation was impossible.

She sat back in her seat and shut her eyes. The night had been too short. She was tired. Not just tired, she realized, but fed up as well. She would much rather be tucked up in bed reading the Sunday papers than doing this miserable drive down to Purley, passing row upon row of horrible houses, Sunday people on their way to church or the pubs or both.

Simon beside her had a self-satisfied smile on his

face. Good husband driving wife and produce of his loins to visit mother on a Sunday. Nina resisted an urge to poke him in the ribs. 'What are you thinking about, Simon? You look as if you've swallowed the canary.'

'I'm thinking about mother's roast beef.' His grin widened. 'Nobody cooks roast beef like mother.'

'Nobody cooks like your mother, full stop,' Nina snapped. Mentally she added *Thank God*.

'She did offer to teach you, darling. You were the one who didn't take her up.'

'Thanks, but I don't need a lesson on how to cook three different kinds of mushy potatoes or how to drown Brussels sprouts. If there were a National Society for the Prevention of Cruelty to Vegetables, I'd be the first to join.'

'You're only jealous, Nina. Come on. Admit it. My mother was a wonderful wife, a wonderful mother, and an excellent housekeeper. We can't say that about you, can we, Bonkers?'

'Why does Daddy keeping calling you Dotty and Bonkers, Mummy?' Hamish was looming between the front seats. His breath smelled of chocolate.

'It's just Daddy's silly sense of humour . . . Oh, Hamish! You've dribbled chocolate down the front of your blazer.' Nina hunted through her handbag in vain. 'Simon, let me have your handkerchief, will you?'

Simon felt she should have brought a handkerchief of her own, and he told her so, but he handed over his anyway.

They entered the darkest Purley suburbs. Small, mean houses fronted the road. The car ran down a long hill and then took a wide corner. Enid's widow home sat back behind Purley Station. Not long now. Nina squared her shoulders. I mustn't make a fuss. It's only three hours every few weeks. I'll be nice to the old bitch. Dear Lord, it is Sunday, and I will try, but I need help. Lots of it.

The car turned into the immaculate drive and came to a standstill outside the large mock Tudor house. 'Come on. Everybody out.' Simon looked rather like a bloodhound scenting his prey, his thin nostrils flared.

He's glad to be back home with his mother, Nina smiled grimly. Simon, when she married him, was a thirty year old bachelor living with his mother. He was now forty. Nina wondered if he longed to return to this house.

The door opened and Enid stood blinking in the sunlight. 'Simon, darling!' she shrilled.

She's got wattles like a turkey, Nina observed. Today the wattles were flushed with pleasure.

Enid put her arms around her son and planted a smacking kiss on Simon's mouth. Hamish was already wiping his cheek and looking nervously at his mother. Nina reached out and pulled Hamish to her side. 'Hello, Enid.' Nina put her hand out to repel the advance. She deftly tucked Hamish behind her back and marched swiftly through the front door.

Susan dutifully allowed Enid to clutch her to her thin bony chest. 'Susan, dear! I have such a lovely outfit for you. After lunch, we shall go upstairs and try it on.'

Susan and her grandmother exchanged looks. Nina, watching from the hall, knew what that exchange meant: time for treason. Nina and Simon would do the washing up, and Susan would spend the time upstairs in her grandmother's bedroom telling Enid her version of all the minutely-observed family events.

Nina turned on her heel and followed the sounds of Hamish touring the ground floor. Hamish was always a nightmare in his grandmother's house. All, over the place there were tables at waist-level covered in bits of china.

Enid was inordinately proud of her acquisitions. Most of her life was spent scouring the local antique shops for bits and pieces. She could no longer collect furniture, as the house already bulged with over-stuffed Edwardian chairs. Grandfather clocks ticked loudly in every room. Small carriage clocks tocked amiably to themselves on mantelpieces. Antimacassars clasped the backs of the sofas and grasped the arms of the chairs. When Enid did sit down, she crocheted these hideous things. Nina had several sets buried underneath a pile of sheets in her linen cupboard. Enid's inevitable Christmas presents: antimacassars from hell, thought Nina, as she looked at the familiar evil sight. 'Hamish?' she called. 'Let's go into the kitchen and wash the chocolate off your blazer.'

'Really, Nina. Sweets before luncheon?' Enid asked.

Why can't she just say *lunch* like everybody else? thought Nina, scrubbing at Hamish's blazer. Why did Hamish have to let her down? Still, so far he hadn't dropped anything or banged into one of the many Brasso-smelling Indian tables that lurked like large bronze tarantulas in dark corners. There were many dark corners in the gloomy big house. Simon's bedroom was still as he left it – his Oxford pennant plastered on the wall, various trophies for rowing and for golf on his side-table. At some point during the day, Simon would slip away to sit in his bachelor's room, no doubt brooding over the days when he was free and unencumbered. 'There, Hamish. The chocolate's off. Now go quietly into the drawing room and sit down. I'll be along in a minute.'

Nina washed down the sink. Enid was a fastidious cook. Even now, with the roast hissing and popping in the oven, saucepans full of vegetables and before long, perfect Yorkshire pudding sitting stiffly in the cake tin, there was no smudge or mess anywhere to indicate that a real person had been doing real cooking. Oh well, she thought. These beastly blow-outs just make me feel fat and awful. Still, Simon and the children love every moment of it. At least Susan does.

She wandered back to the drawing room and sat down.

'Now, darlings!' Enid came bustling in. 'I'll just have a glass of sherry with you, and then I must get on with the cooking. Simon,' she smiled at him as he walked into the drawing room, 'darling, do the usual for us.'

How can a grown woman simper like that? Nina marvelled.

Simon gazed back at his mother. 'Righto,' he said.

This house is full of signals between people, she thought. The look between Simon and his mother completely excluded Nina.

Simon poured a thin stream of sherry into a sherry glass. 'There you are, darling,' he said, handing the glass to his mother. Enid's wattles flushed a brighter purple. Her face blotched. 'Oh, thank you, Simon.' She paused. 'You don't know what it means to have you here. I've been so lonely since your father died.'

Here we go. Nina waited for Simon to put his arms

around his mother. They both stood glued together. The inevitable embrace always followed the also inevitable demand for affection. In her first married years, Nina tried to be sympathetic. After all, Stockton had quietly yellowed away with cancer eating at his throat and had even more quietly died. Nina did miss his presence. But now, several years later, she found herself less sympathetic and was quite surprised at her feelings of disgust at the whole of Enid's repeated performance.

Simon detached himself from his mother and Enid walked off with her sherry in her hand, no doubt to snivel over the potatoes. There was a silence in the room. Susan seemed engrossed in her shoes and Simon handed Nina her glass of sherry. Nina wrinkled her nose. Too sweet. She gave half a glass to Hamish. Might send him off to sleep after lunch.

'How can anyone eat turnips? Ugh!'

Nina looked at Hamish. In front of his hanging head lay a plate filled with his most hated vegetable. 'Hamish doesn't eat turnips, Enid, and neither do I.'

Enid sat at the head of the table. Simon had just finished carving the roast beef. He sat in what had been his father's chair. 'Nina,' said Enid, 'I do expect a young growing boy to eat all his vegetables. Otherwise, he'll be "you know what".'

'Constipated!' Hamish said loudly.

Susan giggled.

'Not at table, Hamish,' Enid blushed.

'I'm never constipated, Grandma. Am I, Mum?'

'No, dear. But if you can't eat the turnip, how about trying the parsnips? They're lovely.'

Hamish looked down at the pallid lengths of parsnip. 'I like it better the way you do these, Mum. All brown and crispy.' He poked the plate with his fork.

'Tact is not Hamish's strong point.' Nina tried to cover.

'He takes after his mother, doesn't he?' Simon was grinning. 'I can always trust Nina to put her foot in it. Come on, Hamish old boy. Eat up. It's not often you get a piece of roast beef like this. Still buying your beef at Gower's place?'

'Yes indeed, dear, and both Mr and Mrs Gower ask after you every time. I told them you'd be coming down for the day with the children and they gave me this roast at a reduced price. They both send their regards. Oh, and I saw old Mrs Bridges at the post office. She really is quite crippled with arthritis now. She might have to retire next year, but she says she's looking forward to her retirement.'

Nina sat back. Both children for the moment were occupied with eating. The dining room furnishings were as busy as those in all the other rooms. The dining table was a ponderous oak creation. The wood was dull and heavily stained and the legs bulged under the chisel of some demented Edwardian designer. The matching chairs were hard and uncomfortable. As usual, the table was filled with different plates and serving dishes. The final effect was to make the table look more like a jumble sale than a meal taken by five people. 'Nina, Mother is offering you a glass of wine,' Simon interrupted her reverie.

'No, thank you, Enid. I think I'll just stick to water.'

'Nina has a hangover, haven't you, dear? She left me all alone to babysit while she went out with her two peculiar friends on the razzle.'

'They are not peculiar, Simon, either of them. Your mother knows Gemma.'

Enid's mouth turned down in disapproval. 'Isn't

Gemma the girl who's involved with all sorts of nasty politics? Believes in, well, you know . . .'

'Constipation!' Hamish shot in helpfully.

Nina laughed. 'No, not constipation, Hamish. Other things you'll understand when you're older. Yes, Gemma is politically minded. Most of the rhetoric I'm afraid I don't understand myself, and never will, but I do agree with her about the issue of homelessness. Everyone has a right to a roof over their head. And Simon of all people should support that statement.'

'Hang on a minute, Nina.' He put one of his hands in the air. Nina looked at his flat, lineless palm with distaste. 'Just because I'm in the Ministry of Housing doesn't mean I support your loony leftist friends. There are plenty of people out there who could perfectly well go out and get themselves a job and put a roof over their own heads, if they wanted to.'

'You're out of touch with real life, Simon. There are no jobs and there are no places to rent.'

The awful squalor of last night's streets seemed all the worse sitting here in a cluttered house set in acres of suburban land.

'I mean it, Simon.'

'Good heavens! A night out with her friends and my wife is a raving pinko! We'll have to put a stop to that, won't we, mother?'

Enid looked pained. 'I really don't know what has happened to the young these days. I never went out without your father. Ever.'

'Well, my mother does.' Nina felt belligerent. 'My mother helps run the village. And now that Hamish is at school, I will have to find some volunteer work for myself. I can't sit at home all day and do nothing. I saw a man up around Chiswick the other day. He was homeless, Enid . . . He had been a music professor, but he lost his wife and the will to live. Yet no one seems to care . . .'

'Oh dear, Nina.' Enid wiped her lips with her paper napkin. 'Come along, children. Let's take out the plates, and I'll get the sweet.'

Susan stood up and picked up her plate. 'What's for pudding, Grandma?' she asked.

Enid flushed. 'Ah, well. Um. It's Daddy's favourite. Meringues. Come along, Hamish. Carry your plate carefully into the kitchen.'

Nina groaned. Hamish obediently carried his plate across the room. Around his empty place setting there were sizeable amounts of potatoes and escaped vegetables. Nina stood up and brushed as much she could into the palm of her hand.

'Don't let's discuss politics with Mother, Nina. It always upsets her.'

'Fine then,' Nina agreed. 'What shall we talk about, Simon?'

'I don't know. How about the garden?'

'You talk about the garden. I'll try and see that Hamish doesn't make too awful a mess of the meringue. At least he hasn't dropped his plate.'

Susan returned and slipped into her seat, followed by Enid who was carrying a large mound of meringue. Where on earth, wondered Nina, does she find the recipes for such disgusting puddings?

'Mummy?' Susan's voice was bright and cheerful.

Nina felt her spine stiffen in anticipation. 'Yes, darling?' Nina knew that voice of Susan's. In the tone was the warning rattle of a snake about to strike.

'Why do you call pudding *pudding* and Grandmother calls it *sweet*?'

There was a moment's silence.

'It's called sweet . . .' Simon began.

'. . . lots of different ways of saying . . .' Nina heard herself charge forward.

'. . . used to be sweet, darling, and then the savoury . . .' Enid contributed, her dewlaps quivering.

'I see,' Susan concluded. 'Like Mummy says *napkin* and Grandma says *serviette*.' Susan's eyes raked the grown-up faces. 'You know, when Daddy is at Mummy's house, he talks like Mummy. And when he's here at your house, Grandma, he talks like you. Don't you, Daddy?'

'I don't know, pumpkin. All I know is I want my favourite meringue pie. I don't care what you call it.' He put up his plate and smiled at his mother. Why, Nina thought in disgust, does he become a child again in his mother's presence? Maybe all men do. She looked at Hamish. Hopefully Hamish won't when he grows up.

'Ah! This is lovely!' Simon shovelled a large spoon-ful of the pie into his mouth.

Nina gingerly pushed her portion around with her spoon. The meringue was dry and brittle as it should be, but the custard underneath was a grey-green mess. *It looks like snot but it's not.* She silently recited the old school joke to herself and wished very much she could share the joke with Hamish.

When all had finished their pudding, Enid said, 'Children, let's go and see if Grandma has a surprise for you.'

Susan held Enid's hand. 'Oh goody, Grandma! I love presents.'

The child will win an Oscar at the rate she's going, thought Nina as she watched them accompany Enid out of the room. She started to clear the table.

She heard squeals of excitement, and Hamish came to the door of the dining room brandishing a tank. 'Wonderful, darling,' Nina said without conviction, brushing past him with her third load of dirty dishes. From the drawing room she could hear Simon's loud confident voice. 'The Director of Housing says I have an excellent chance . . .' She lost his voice once she was in the kitchen.

Why doesn't he ever talk like that to me? she wondered. Back came a cold little voice that whispered, *Because he knows you're not interested*.

Nina piled the last of the plates into the sink. I'll need a cup of coffee before I tackle this. She dried her hands and walked into the drawing room. 'What a wonderful display of flowers, Enid. They can't be from the garden, can they?'

Enid smiled. 'Simon sent them for my wedding anniversary. That dear secretary of his never forgets a thing. Do thank Angela for me, Simon.'

Nina felt furious, but she knew she must wait.

'Come along, Susan. Let's go upstairs and you can try on a few things and we can have a chat.' Enid stood up.

Susan had a pile of new clothes on the floor. 'I'll pick these up for you, Susan. You go along with your grandmother.' Might as well get the Judas hour over with, she thought. She bent towards the pile of clothes. 'You spoil them, you know,' she called to Enid's retreating back.

'That's what grannies are for, isn't it?' And Enid was out of the room.

'Why didn't your bloody secretary remind *me* that it was Enid's wedding anniversary? I should have sent the flowers.'

87

'Because, Nina darling, she's my secretary, not yours, and you never remember anything. Why should you take the credit?'

Nina bit her tongue. Only a few more hours and she would be away from this awful house.

'I think you should be careful.' Enid's voice was shaking.

Susan, standing beside her grandmother in the drawing room, gazed innocently at her mother.

'Careful?' said Nina. 'How do you mean?' She noticed that Enid had redone Susan's hair so that the child now had a scraped-back ponytail and she was wearing the pink jersey that Enid had bought for her. Why is it, thought Nina, that an hour alone with the old witch and she comes downstairs as if she belongs to Enid rather than to me?

'Run along into the kitchen, Susan, and put on the kettle,' Enid instructed.

Hamish was still asleep on the sofa. Too much sherry. Nina pushed his legs over and sat down. 'Careful of what, Enid?'

'Careful of that friend of yours. That Gemma.'

Nina sighed. 'What on earth has Susan said to make you so upset? Gemma's been an old friend for years.'

'Yes, but you didn't say anything about *her* new friend.'

'There is nothing to say, Enid. Simon was teasing me, and Susan probably overheard and got it all wrong. Anyway, what does she know? She's eight years old. I don't encourage her to snoop, Enid, and neither should you. I . . .' Nina could hear Simon coming down the stairs after his post-prandial pilgrimage to his bedroom. The discussion between the two women was truncated, and Nina sensed, half with relief, that it would remain that way.

Simon ambled into the room and smiled vaguely. 'You two having a tête-à-tête?'

'Just girl talk,' chirped Enid. 'Could you get the coffee from the kitchen?'

Simon left and returned, wheeling in the trolley, Susan behind him. Hamish stretched and yawned. Nina wondered why she felt outnumbered. She had only Hamish on her side.

Chapter 11

I hate Mondays. Nina put her pillow over her head and contemplated Simon's back. He lay with his knees drawn up and his right hand in between, clutching his penis. I wonder if all men sleep like that? Maybe he thinks it will fall off in the night. More likely he's afraid Enid might creep up and cut it off and have it bronzed, along with his first pair of baby shoes.

It always took Nina a few days to forgive Simon after a visit to Enid's. She knew it was unfair and they never discussed her feelings. Simon didn't ask for sex during these few days, but then Nina often wondered if such visits did not satisfy Simon at some deep level she could not reach.

Simon was always in an excellent mood after making the trip to Purley. Still – Nina reached out and shut off the alarm clock – he'll have a good day today, even if it is a Monday. She stretched and slid out of bed. She stood under the shower and prepared her Monday list of events. Fresh vegetables and a chat with Mrs Porter at the greengrocer's after dropping the children off. Back home for coffee with Doris. Then what?

The day reached out unbearably long ahead of her.

Telephone Sonia for a word . . .

She turned off the shower and walked back to the bedroom. Simon was waking up. 'Coffee?'

'In a few minutes, Simon. I'm just getting dressed.'

Simon opened his eyes and then rolled over again. 'Toast?' he said hopefully.

No point in arguing. Nina pulled on a pair of warm tights, readjusted her panties, and wondered how many husbands looked at their naked wives and were reminded of toast and coffee? It was an ongoing battle between them. She didn't mind giving him a plate of buttered toast at the weekend, but she balked at the idea of breakfast in bed for him too often. I am not Enid, she reminded herself grimly. She put on an old comfortable dress. 'Okay, Simon,' she said loudly. 'Toast. But only today.'

Simon snuggled into his pillow. He was smiling in his half-sleep. He looks younger than Hamish sometimes, thought Nina.

She marched downstairs. She smelled the coffee in the automatic percolator. Sausages and bacon sizzled in the pre-set oven.

She put on the record of Tchaikovsky's *Romeo and Juliet Overture*. She turned it up too loud, making the music fill the house. She grinned. Simon didn't like classical music. He said he liked jazz. Simon had a wooden ear. Nina knew she was being mean, but then it was a Monday. 'Hamish! Sausage and bacon! Susan, breakfast!' Nina clattered up the stairs. She was wearing her Dr Scholl clogs. She liked the clogs. They reminded her of Holland and tulips and small boys with their fingers in dykes. What a silly word to call a woman! Gemma's just Gemma. 'Susan?'

Susan was ready. Hamish was not.

'Go ahead, Susan. Breakfast is laid. Could you put some toast in the toaster for Daddy?'

'Sure. I'll take it up for him with his coffee.'

'Thanks, Susan. You're a love. I'll have to get Hamish going.'

Hamish was staring at his mother through a hole in his knickers, which he had on his head. 'Hamish, this is not a vest. Those are your knickers.'

'Oh.' Hamish's voice was owlish and he blinked.

'Come here, idiot.' Nina pulled the offending article of clothing off his hand. 'Let's get moving.'

'What's for breakfast?'

'Sausage and bacon. And then I'll make Savoy Toast and you can have some of Granny's Devon marmalade. Quick. Teeth and hands and face washed. Let's go.' She passed Susan on the stairs. 'Thanks, darling. I'll go and serve breakfast. We have lift-off with Hamish.'

Susan flitted up the stairs.

So far Monday was turning out to be a good day.

Savoy Toast was a family favourite. Funny how such a simple recipe could give so much pleasure. Clarified butter, that was all it was. She brushed a pile of toast with the drawn butter and carried it into the dining room. A blue china plate lay on the table heaped with sausages and bacon. 'Hortense and Cassandra are on a diet,' Susan said, reaching for a sausage.

'Hang on, Susan. We haven't said grace.'

'Oh, Mummy. You can't believe in all that.'

Nina bent her head. 'Thank you, Lord, for our food and for this day.'

'You don't say grace when Daddy is at the table.'

'I know, but Daddy and I compromise. It doesn't upset him if I say grace when he's not up for breakfast, and it makes me happy to thank God for our food. There are so many people who have no food.'

Nina passed a plate to Hamish. Susan helped herself. Nina smiled at her children. This was a part of her day she liked best. She exulted at the bite of the Colman's mustard on her sausage, then a snap of bacon and a munch of toast.

'You never diet, do you, Mum?' Susan's voice cut across the chewing silence.

'No, I don't.'

'Everyone else's mother does.'

'Do they?'

Susan nodded. It was a complacent nod. There was no malice in it. It was just a reminder to Nina that she was habitually different to the other mothers at St Miriam's.

Nina acknowledged her failure with a sigh. 'Well, actually, I don't need to diet. I'm lucky, really.'

'Neither does Ziggy have to, but she says at your age you get cellulite on your bottom.'

Hamish snorted. 'You said a rude word,' he chanted.

'Shut up, Hamish. Bottom is not a rude word.'

'What's cellulite?' Hamish spluttered his toast.

'Don't talk with your mouth full,' said Nina.

'Cellulite,' Susan explained, 'looks like pin cushions.'

'How do you know?' Nina asked.

'Ziggy showed us her bottom last time I was there.'

'Say that again?' Nina shook her head.

'Ziggy showed Hortense and Cassandra and me her bottom.'

'You mean she had no knickers on when she showed you?'

'None of us had any clothes on.' Susan was getting impatient. 'We were in their swimming pool.'

'But I packed you a swimming costume,' Nina said faintly.

'I know.' Susan stood up. 'I'll take my things to the sink.'

'Thank you, darling,' Nina said for the third time that morning. 'That's very kind of you.' She heard Simon in the hallway.

'Goodbye, family!' he bellowed as he rushed past.

Nina raced out of the door after him. 'Simon, wait a minute!'

'What's the matter? You look as if you've seen a ghost. Has something happened?'

'I don't know. Susan just told me she's been swimming in the nude with the Lucases. I mean, none of them had any clothes on at all.'

'You silly goose, Nina. That's perfectly normal. Not everybody is as prudish as you are. It's the seventies, not the fifties any more.' He patted Nina on the bottom and set off for his car.

Nina stood in the driveway, the wind chasing leaves at her feet. She felt entirely confused. If one of us is the prude, she thought, then surely it must be Simon. Since when has he been so uninhibited?

She went back into the house. The children were in the hall. Nina knew Susan had heard her father's laughter. Susan's eyes were alight with amusement. Oh, why does it have to be a war between us? Nina wondered as she drove them to school. Will it always be a war?

A second cup of coffee with Doris, after putting away the shopping, and mentally Nina worked out what tonight's dinner menu would be. Inevitably conversation got round to the health of Doris's many offspring.

'The hospital says Little Jimmy's got to have his tonsils out, no two ways about it.'

'Maybe that will make a big difference and he'll be healthier overall once he gets it done.' Nina tried to be cheerful.

'There's a two year waiting list at the hospital.'

'Oh, is there? Still, get him on the list, Doris.' Thank God for our private medical insurance policy. Nina picked up her mug of coffee. 'Actually, Doris, I'll go upstairs and collect the dirty clothes.' She left the kitchen feeling guilty. Poor Doris. Why must life be so hard for her? She had a useless husband, that was why. Unlike Simon, who worked hard for his family.

The telephone rang. It was Jennifer. 'Thursday?' said Nina. 'For coffee? Okay. Sounds fun. Fine. Half past eleven. I'll be there.' Hanging up, she realized she had just made arrangements for her first morning coffee in someone else's home without Hamish to accompany her.

For a moment Nina felt childless. She decided to ring Sonia for comfort. Sonia was always good on occasions of momentary despair.

'Go and buy yourself a really expensive dress,' was Sonia's offering. 'That's my professional Agony Aunt advice. Besides, it's what I do when I'm feeling depressed.'

'Simon would be furious.'

'Just tell him you bought it for him, and then give him a bit of nookie. It always works. Don't show him the bill until after you've had sex. Go on, Nina. You're not his slave, and I'll bet he has a cupboard full of clothes.'

'But he has to, Sonia. It's for the office.'

'Get off your ass and go shopping. When the going gets tough, the tough go shopping.'

Nina smiled. 'It sounds positively sinful to go out shopping for myself with a cheque book.'

'A bit of sin would do you the world of good.'

The two women agreed that, since they so enjoyed their last lunch together, they should meet for lunch on Friday. Sonia suggested the Gay Hussar instead of Joe Allen's. Nina had half-hoped that, were they to lunch at Joe Allen's again, she might even see Michael Morningstar. And he would see her in the new dress she planned to buy. Would his wide cheekbones shine, and his smile scrunch up his eyes, and his mouth curl with admiration? Now she would never know . . . But Sonia seemed insistent about going to a different restaurant this time. Nina gave in.

As she put down the telephone, Nina decided with finality that Sonia was right: a shopping spree was exactly what she needed.

She opened her appointment book. *Thursday. Coffee, 11.30 Friday, Lunch.* Good heavens! I'm a lady of leisure with appointments! She put her appointment book in her handbag and got off the bed. I *will* buy myself a dress, she thought, opening up her cupboard. Before her hung a row of clothes. All pregnancy stuff. I'll get rid of this. She began to pull out an assortment of dresses and trousers. Soon the cupboard was pruned of her pregnancies. She folded the

95

clothes carefully and carried them downstairs and gave them to Doris who no doubt would have occasion to use them herself soon enough, or she could sell them for a bit of extra cash. Nina was happy either way, as long as the clothes were no longer in her own cupboard. That part of her life was behind her.

She left the house, started her car, and headed for London's West End, the chequebook in her handbag at the ready.

Chapter 12

Nina felt ridiculously wicked. She stood on the escalator at the back of Harrods, after finding a convenient parking place. God must be watching over me, she smiled as she gazed at the droves of shoppers. She had to push her way to the dress department. Once there, she found her heart beating fast. Her excursions to Harrods so far had always been with the children. Children made her anonymous. With them, one in each hand, she was a wife and mother. Anyway, with the children she had never dared enter the women's department. They went to the children's department, a visit to the pet shop, and then a quick cup of tea. Her own clothes Nina usually bought in Shepherd's Bush Market or in Kingston.

The carpets muffled her footsteps. The air was clouded with perfumes. So many different types, they clogged Nina's nose. 'Can I help you?' A tall kindly woman stared down at Nina. Nina noticed the woman was immaculately dressed in a black shirt-waist dress, black crocodile shoes, and a large string of pearls.

Nina wished she had made more of an effort in dressing herself. 'Yes, please,' she said nervously. 'I would like to buy a dress.'

'What kind of dress, madam?'

'Well, sort of a good one for going out to lunch. A bit formal.'

The woman smiled. 'Let's go and have a look, shall we?'

Nina trailed behind the tall figure. Around her were other women, some with children, some with friends. She wished desperately that she had Hamish with her, or even Susan, who was always such a pest to take shopping. Without the children, she felt naked and vulnerable.

The sales lady paused in front of a row of dresses. 'Madam is quite small.'

'I know.' Nina felt wretched and apologetic.

'Let's have a look at a few of these.' The sales lady pulled several dresses off the rack and expertly fanned them. 'A nice cut on the bias there. Notice the detail on the back pleat.'

Nina stood transfixed. They were all lovely dresses. All of them. She wanted to buy the whole rack. She found herself breathing hard. 'I'd like to try the blue one and that one and, oh, I must try the grey. That looks lovely.'

Inside the changing room, Nina looked at her flushed face in the mirror. She pulled the grey dress on first. It had a round neck, a pleated box top, and a bell-shaped skirt. A thin belt with a gold buckle finished the outfit. Nina loved the cut. The blue dress caught the colour of her eyes. She imagined walking into Joe Allen's wearing the blue dress and Michael Morningstar's face smiling at her. Ah, my swan! he might think . . . Stop it! she said to herself. He probably wouldn't even notice me. And we're not having lunch there anyway. Why do I have Michael Morningstar on the brain?

The third dress was for late evening. It was cut low and Nina could see the top of her still brown, summery breasts. Oh yes, she thought as she slowly twirled around. I must have this one. 'I'll take all three,' Nina said, uncomfortable in her old, scratchy day clothes.

'Does madam need any underwear?'

Nina paused. In for a penny in for a pound, she thought. 'Yes, I will need a strapless bra for the evening dress.'

'Certainly. This way.'

Nina pored over the wisps of underwear. My goodness, she thought. It's been such a long time since I wore anything other than cotton knickers and sensible bras. She fingered the bras.

'And these are the matching camiknickers, and the petticoat, madam. Such a lovely colour, that eau de nil, don't you think?'

'Oh, I do think so, I really do.'

The sales lady sighed. Such a dowdy little thing, she thought, but such lovely blue eyes and an angelic face. She so often saw women like this one, married young to men who couldn't love them. Obedient, faithful, good wives, good mothers, but no sparkle in the eyes. Still, this one looks as if she was at least attempting to break out.

'Um, how much is the set? I mean the petticoat and the bra and the . . .'

'Fifty-five pounds, madam.'

Nina blanched. Fifty-five pounds for three pieces of silk she could contain in the palm of her hands . . . But then she had a private moment of wondering what it would be like to slip off her low-cut dress and stand exposed in her sensible white Marks and Spencers knickers . . . 'I'll take it,' she said.

'You'll not regret it, madam. I can promise you that.'

Walking out of Harrods clutching the huge green bag, Nina reminded herself that she had just spent four hundred and fifty pounds of Simon's money on clothes for herself. Simon will kill me.

Later, in the quiet of her own house, she hung the dresses carefully in her cupboard. She ran her hands over the fabric. The grey dress spoke to her of tea at the Savoy Hotel, Michael Morningstar – now a permanent fixture in her fantasy world – lying back in his chair, intense hooded eyes gazing at her, long pale hands toying with a cup of tea, fingering a smoked salmon sandwich, nibbling on a green sliver of moist cucumber . . . The blue dress whispered back a walk in St James's Park, bread to feed the pelicans, the tall commanding figure striding ahead of her, the elegant head set on the wide shoulders . . . And then there was the evening dress. The bell of the silken skirt pressing against his legs. Her waist in his hands . . .

She closed her cupboard door. 'You stay there until I confess how much I spent to Simon,' she told the dresses. I'll wear the knickers and the bra tonight, and then I'll tell him in the morning about the rest.

She walked downstairs and began to cook a special dinner for later that night.

*

Nina felt like a traitor. There had been occasions in the past when she had overspent her housekeeping allowance, but today? Though she shared a joint account with Simon, only rarely did she write a cheque. Simon usually spent the last few days of the month with his head in his hands bemoaning the bills. They were always in danger of being 'in the red'. Simon regularly waved the bank statement in front of her face, saying, 'We must cut down, darling, or we'll be in the red.' Nina did not quite know what to make of those conversations. In her background, money was never discussed. Either you can afford it or you can't, was her mother's sensible attitude. Yes, Nina remembered wearing a cousin's coat and several of that same cousin's dresses. Secondhand clothes seemed quite natural. It never crossed her mind to object, but this orgy of accounting for each penny spent, the shaking hand and the loud cries over the bills mystified her.

Now, however, she would have to explain the expenditure of four hundred and fifty pounds. She picked up the children and listened while they bickered all the way home. She wondered why they had to fight so much. 'Righto, children,' she said as the car pulled up at home. 'Out you get. Susan, do your homework. I'll get supper organized. And then it's television time.' Thank God for television! she thought. The answer to a busy housewife's prayers.

Two tins of spaghetti hoops, ice cream and chocolate sauce . . . I won't even to try get anything healthy down either of them tonight. Her hands were trembling as she prepared the veal for Simon. The aubergine pâté was creamy and full of garlic. After the veal, she would serve bananas baked in demerara sugar and brandy. 'Susan, Hamish!' She heard their feet on the stairs. 'You can eat in the kitchen tonight.'

'Why?' Susan asked, arriving at the kitchen doorway. 'Why aren't we eating in the dining room?'

'Because I'm cooking your father a special dinner this evening.'

'Why? Is it your anniversary or something?'

'You know it isn't. No, it's just that he's been working so hard recently, I decided to give him a treat.'

She resented the look in Susan's eyes. Can an eight year old girl be jealous of her own mother? Susan's eyes said yes. Very. 'You behave tonight, Susan. I want you both in bed and lights out on time.'

Nina filled their plates with spaghetti hoops. The television kept up a loud commentary at the end of the kitchen. Nina cleared away after they had finished eating and she laid the dining room table. By the time she heard Simon's key in the lock, she had bathed and changed and now stood in the kitchen wearing the silk underclothing that had cost fifty-five pounds.

'I say, you look nice this evening, Nina. Where's Pudding?'

'Susan and Hamish are upstairs, darling. I thought we'd have a quiet night, just the two of us. You've been working so hard. And anyway now I have both children at school I have more time to cook.'

Simon put his briefcase down on the table in the hall. He pulled Nina to him. She could smell the familiar smell of his office on his clothes: stained coffee cups, other people's cigarettes, and a faintly perplexing smell of perfume. Simon kissed Nina inexpertly, missing her mouth. 'Lovely idea,' he said. 'I'll go up and say good night.' He took off his winter coat and handed it to Nina.

'Are you doing any work tonight?'

'Not tonight, Josephine.' Simon wiggled his eyebrows suggestively. 'If we're to have a quiet night alone, my briefcase can wait.'

'In that case,' Nina tried to smile seductively, 'I'll put it in your dressing room, Napoleon.'

'Mummy, Hamish is singing. I can't go to sleep.'

Nina had just served the veal. The aubergine had been a huge success. The veal lay in a marsala sauce beside tiny peas and new potatoes. 'That child, Simon! I asked him to leave us alone.'

'Be quiet, Hamish!' Simon bellowed from his seat in the dining room. He put a forkful of veal into his mouth. 'Tastes really good, Nina. A little more effort, and you could give my mother a run for her money.'

Nina winced at the mention of money.

'Hamish is in the lavatory, Mummy. I need to go. Can I use yours?'

'All right, Susan, but no more interrupting!'

'Thank you!'

And she heard Susan run up the stairs.

'Here's to us, darling.' Simon poured her another glass of wine.

Nina felt the cool of her petticoat and the sigh of the silk between her thighs. Silk and wine go well together, she thought as the liquid slid down her throat. 'You sit, Simon. I'll get the baked bananas.' She was bending over the oven when she thought she saw Susan creep into the dining room behind her. 'What are you doing, Susan?' she asked as she walked back into the room carrying a serving plate with the bananas. Her oven gloves protected her hands from the heat.

'Nothing. I just saw this Harrods bag in your dustbin. It was all folded up, and I wanted to ask you if

I could use it for a satchel. I left mine at school and I need to take my PE gear.'

Simon took the neatly folded bag from Susan's hand. 'Have you been shopping, Dotty?' His enquiring, tidy fingers plucked at the bag. 'We have been shopping, haven't we?' He pulled out the bill. 'Nina!' His face drained of colour. 'How on earth did you manage to spend four hundred and fifty pounds?'

Susan looked at her mother's face. Nina moved aside to let Susan run from the room. 'It's like this, Simon. I needed some decent clothes. I'm the one that has always had to do without whilst you and the children come first. I know it's a lot of money, but I just had to have something decent to wear.'

'To deposit and collect children from school? That's all you do. Why do you have to be so well-dressed for that?'

'That *is* all I do, Simon. But in the future I want to do more. I have to.'

'We're ruined, Nina. Absolutely ruined! In one day you've put our main account into the red. I'll have to make an appointment with Mr Jones at the bank and apologize. I can't have a cheque with my name on it bounce at the bank.'

'Can't we just take some money out of the savings account?'

'You're joking! Touch capital? Nina, my father'd roll over in his grave. Never touch capital. It's all you've got. I'm truly shaken, Nina. I can't tell you what you've done to my confidence in you.' He waved his hand in front of his face. 'No, don't give me any pudding. I'm too upset. I'll get my briefcase and work in the drawing room.' He stood up.

Nina sat at the table. 'I'm sorry, Simon. I didn't

mean to upset you. But I'm not sorry I bought the clothes.'

'Mother is right.'

'Your mother is always right, Simon. I'm a bad lot. Go on, say it.'

But Simon walked out of the room. Nina sat by herself and ate the baked bananas.

Anyway, she thought as she washed up the plates, at least I didn't have to sleep with him. She grinned. That wasn't too bad. And I still have the clothes.

Chapter 13

There was no way around it. Simon was intent on doing his famous impersonation of an Egyptian mummy in a sulk. Actually, when he sulked, his nose got pointier and his mouth pursed like a cat's arsehole. Nina was reminded of a furtive rhyme from her childhood: *Cats on the rooftops, cats on the tiles, cats with their arseholes wreathed in smiles*. But no smiles from Simon.

Nina was scrubbing her teeth. She grinned at her face in the mirror. I'll wear jeans to school and then, with old po-face out of the house, I'll change into my new blue dress and wow Jennifer and Ziggy. What on earth will we talk about without children? Tupperware? Not with Jennifer. Tupperware isn't biodegradable. I'd better get Simon a cup of coffee and some toast.

Nina ran down the stairs. 'Breakfast!' she yelled out. 'Come on, Susan, Hamish, let's get going!' For once, both children were up and ready. No doubt Susan had explained Mummy's huge crime to Hamish and they were waiting to see if there was to be any fall-out. Susan will be disappointed, thought Nina.

She poured a cup of coffee and jammed two pieces of toast into the toaster. She took a sip. Nice, she thought. Strong Blue Mountain from Fortnum's. She looked out of the French windows. Although autumn, the sun was warming the mellow bricks at the back of the house. Nina felt the warmth enter her bones. She was excited and restless. She did not know why. Usually the idea of Simon sulking was deeply upsetting and distressing, but today it was just a fact. Four hundred and fifty pounds equals two days of Simon moping about the house and dropping hints at the ruination facing them all. Children forced into comprehensive schools, holidays abroad cancelled . . . The list was boring.

Ting. The toast jumped up, properly browned and awaiting butter. Five minutes and Nina was back in the bedroom. 'There you are, darling. Toast and special coffee. Jamaican Blue Mountain.'

'What's wrong with Nescafé?'

'Nothing. Nothing's wrong with Nescafé, Simon.'

He lay on his back, his hands folded on his stomach, his nose in the air. He looks like his bloody mother, thought Nina, bending over the bed to kiss him. 'I'm off early today. I've got to deliver the kids and then have coffee with Jennifer. What time will you be back for supper?'

'I don't know, Nina. I'll be late, so don't wait for me. I'll get a bite to eat on my way home.'

Usually Nina found herself frantically begging, *I'll put your plate in the oven. I can wait for you* . . . But today she felt no such compunction. 'Okay. I'm off now. See you later.'

'Drive carefully.'

Nina snorted. 'I always drive carefully, Simon. After all, I'm not the one who's had three accidents.' She slammed the door of the bedroom shut. Three days and he'll be randy and then the sulk will be over. All so predictable and all so boring.

Nina bounced into the dining room. What I need is a holiday. Maybe Simon and I can drop the kids in Devon and have a long weekend together. We're getting far too jaded with each other.

Having dropped the children at school, come home and changed into her new blue dress, Nina drove herself to Jennifer's house, listening to her favourite radio programme, the Jimmy Donleavy Show.

'He doesn't beat me, Jimmy. It's not that. He would never hit me.'

Nina's hand tightened on the car wheel. 'What does he do?' Jimmy Donleavy's voice was calm and reassuring.

'He just shuts me out. If he gets cross, he pulls away. He won't speak to me. He pretends I don't exist.'

Nina sighed. Was there this endless, baleful cry of women everywhere in the world? Did the radio programme tap into some mystical universal source of female misery?

'I'd be better off if he'd hit me, Jimmy. At least I'd have a bruise to show. This way, there's nothing.'

'Can't you sit him down and explain to him how much it hurts?' Jimmy tried to sound optimistic.

'No, Jimmy, I can't. The night my mother died he

went out. He said he couldn't stand the emotion. He thinks emotions are dirty, ugly things.'

'Have you tried marriage guidance?'

'He won't go nowhere. Not him.'

Nina turned the dial. The woman's voice was too close to her heart. Would a black eye be less painful than three days' worth of Simon sulking? Yes, she thought as she turned the corner over Kew Bridge. A while ago a black eye would be preferable, but now I finally don't care. I'm a different person. There is a new me. One not festooned with children nor beholden – that's the word – I'm not beholden to Simon or to his mother.

Truly, lunch at Joe Allen's had been an eye-opener. Her first lunch in eight years without children attached to her skirts. Now for Nina it was as if her life were to begin properly.

She had been a much-loved only child, a schoolgirl, and then a secretary. She drove up to Jennifer's house and remembered the first time she saw Simon. No, she reminded herself. It wasn't the first time. She saw him first at the hunt ball in the country. But it was in London that they came to know each other and first singled each other out as special to each other out of all the people in the world.

She had signed on at a temporary agency. It was her first week in London and her mother and father settled her into a flat which she was to share with two friends of hers. The flat was in Dolphin Square. Both parents felt she would be safe and secure inside Dolphin Square's massive bulwarks. She watched her father's old black Rover creep out of the underground car park and slowly join the Sunday evening traffic down on the Embankment. Along the River Thames, the buildings were lit up with lovely, wonderful, fairy-tale windows. The lights winking along the river and the bridges proclaimed a perpetual blessing on the city.

She got a two week placement at the Ministry of Housing. A bossy woman with white pointed glasses scrutinized Nina at the interview. 'Shorthand?'

'One hundred and twenty,' Nina offered.

'All right. How about typing?'

'Forty words a minute.'

'Can you use a dictaphone?'

Nina nodded. It was difficult to understand the sharp, angular London accent. Nina was used to the slow pace of Devon. Here she felt swept off her feet but exhilarated by it all. The Ministry of Housing, off St James's Park, turned out to be a rabbit warren of small rooms. The First Secretary was a charming white-haired man who preferred discussing Wordsworth and Keats to dictating memos. Then she saw Simon standing by the First Secretary's desk. The sunlight fell on his bent, fair hair. He looked so grave. He was explaining a point of procedure to the First Secretary. 'All right, Stockton. All right!' The First Secretary was fretful. 'It's Friday and I need to get off to play a round of golf. You see to it, will you, old fellow? By the way, this is Nina Tolmadge. She's with us for two weeks helping out. Could you stay and give Mr Stockton a hand, Nina? I'd be very grateful.' Nina nodded. Most certainly she would give Mr Stockton any hand he wanted. Nina was in love . . .

She parked the car and walked into Jennifer's house, still aglow with fond memories. 'You look dressed up like a dog's dinner, Nina. It's only coffee, you know.'

Jennifer stood in the long, narrow Victorian hallway. Along the walls above the stairs to the first floor were children's paintings and macramé hangings. Bowls and dishes were piled up in dusty corners. Jennifer was wearing two long handmade earrings. 'Come on in. Ziggy'll be over in a minute. And she's bringing her friend Cal. Let's go into the kitchen and put our feet up. It's ages since we've had time to girl-talk.'

Nina followed Jennifer into the kitchen. Unlike Nina's white, cheerfully modern kitchen, Jennifer's kitchen was dark and humid – dark because no attempt had been made to scrape away a hundred years of depressing brown varnish and humid because the family washing drooped from chairs and piled onto the floor.

Trying to sound more helpful than rude, Nina said, 'Really, Jennifer. I don't know what I'd do without my washing machine. Do you think Neville might buy you one?' She eyed Neville's bulky underpants. How on earth could Jennifer make love to a man who wore such awful knickers? But then she doubted if Jennifer made love to anything from the way she bitched about Neville.

'You take your coffee with milk and sugar?'

'Thanks.' Nina lifted the offending undergarment from a chair and sat down.

'I don't want to own a washing machine, Nina. I don't want to pollute the earth with detergent.'

'You haven't changed.' Nina grinned. Jennifer poured the water into two of her handmade tumblers. 'These are nice.' Nina held her large, brown earthenware cup in her hands.

'I'm making some for my stall in Portobello. What do you think? Of course Neville thinks I'm absolutely mad. With our income, anything I make just goes on tax, but I felt I just had to have some creative outlet for myself. There must be more to life than cleaning a house.'

Or not cleaning it, thought Nina. 'I do know what you mean. Now Hamish is at school and I have time on my hands, I'll have to find something to do.'

The front doorbell rang. 'That'll be Ziggy and Cal. You sit tight. I'll let them in.'

Nina sat in her chair and stared at the room. Jennifer lived in a big, generous house but resolutely refused to do any housework. Consequently, the place always depressed Nina. She had stopped asking why Jennifer didn't get some help, because she already knew the answer: Jennifer insisted that housework was men's oppression of women and she was taking her stand against oppression. But Neville works all day in the office, Nina had tried in vain to point out on past occasions. Wouldn't it be reasonable for Jennifer to do her share at home?

A pity, Nina thought. Could be such a nice house.

Jennifer ushered Ziggy into the room along with the woman called Cal. 'Hi. I'm Cal, short for California.' Cal shook Nina's hand. Her grip was too strong. 'Nice to meet you, sister.'

Nina tried not to look surprised. 'Yes,' she said. 'How very nice. Did your mother call you California? I mean, it's an unusual name, I must admit.'

'No, I took the name when I came out.'

'Came out?'

Jennifer looked at Ziggy who was standing beside Cal.

'Came out,' Ziggy explained. 'You know? Told people she was a lesbian.'

'Oh. Of course.' Nina felt as if she had been caught off-guard. 'Sort of like being a deb, but instead of

110

bowing to a cake at the Queen Charlotte's Ball, you, er, come out.'

Cal smiled. 'Dig it? Hey, Jennifer, you got any beer?'

'Knowing you were coming, I put some in the fridge for you. Ziggy told me you'd die for cold beer.'

'You're a sweetheart.' Cal sat down.

Nina tried not to stare. Cal was built like an oil derrick.

'How did you meet Ziggy, Cal?' Nina felt her obligation to keep the conversation from dying on its feet.

'Usual way two people meet. I saw her walking along the road and liked what I saw, so I whistled at her and she waved back. We got to talking. I'm almost part of the family now, aren't I?'

Ziggy blushed slightly. 'Well, George practically faints with excitement when he knows Cal's coming to dinner.'

Nina's eyes widened.

'If you ask me, your George is probably something of a closet queen himself. I mean that in a nice way.' Cal held the beer in the palm of her massive hand. She had yellow eyes. Ziggy pulled up a chair and then Jennifer joined her. 'Yep. Looking at him, I bet he'd be right up for the feel of a whip across his ass. It's English men and all their Tom Brown's schooldays stuff. Or am I way off target, Ziggy?'

Ziggy nodded. 'George likes to wear my underwear sometimes, if that's what you mean.'

'Are you *serious*?' Nina wanted to leave. After all these years, she was hearing things about friends she did not want to hear.

'Neville bought me a vibrator the other day,' Jennifer put in. 'He says I can use it if he's too tired to get

111

it up. These days he's usually too tired, and I don't see why I should sacrifice my right to my sexuality. After all, we women don't have to hang about servicing men, do we?'

Not for the next three days, I don't. Nina sipped the last of her coffee.

'Cal has deepened my understanding of our position to men in relation to our capitalist society. Isn't that right, Cal?' Ziggy looked unsure.

'Perfect, Zig. Women are oppressed by men. And that's the truth, the whole world over.'

'I don't think it's as simple as that,' said Nina, feeling it was probably a mistake even to bother to talk. 'I mean, I think of people like Simon's parents, when Simon's father was alive, and I honestly can't believe *he* was the one doing the oppressing. No, I think it depends much more on the relationship . . .'

'I told you she'd be a hopeless case, Cal.'

Jennifer was smiling.

'I'm not hopeless, Ziggy.' She found herself growing angry. 'I'm an old-fashioned Devon farm girl. You make me feel like Rip Van Winkle. I see you and Jennifer at dinner parties with your husbands. We discuss our children and where we're going for holidays. Your new plans for building onto your house. Our husbands sit in the drawing room while we run in and out of each other's kitchens getting coffee and after dinner mints. But the fact remains, whether we like it or not, we can sit here drinking coffee precisely *because* we have three husbands working in their offices to pay our mortgages.'

There was an uncomfortable silence. Three pairs of eyes disapproved of Nina. Oh hell, she thought. I promised myself I'd keep my mouth shut. Last time I upset my own dinner party, talking about the music professor, and now . . . She finished her coffee. 'I think I'll go now, Jennifer,' she said quietly.

Jennifer said, 'I think you had better go, Nina. The problem is that you live an uncommitted life. You aren't involved in the changes that must come if we are to live in a more equal society, a less selfish place.'

Nina made a face. 'Listen, Jennifer, what you mean is that we all have to keep our lives in compartments. Get up in the morning and you and Ziggy go into the wife and mother mode. Get children and husband off to work and school. Now, at eleven in the morning along with the Nescafé – decaffeinated, of course, because you've decided that caffeine is evil – you go into your urban revolutionary mode. But at three o'clock you drop the revolution and kick into the competitive mother mode. Back to school, pick up the kids, off to swimming and gymnastics, and music lessons, karate, and ballet . . . The whatever-the-children-can-do-you'd-better-market-it mindset. Then it's back to the house and wait for the old man to come home. Well, jolly good for you, but I don't live like that. I love Simon and my children, and I think you could begin your revolution by cleaning your house. I'm sure your family would be grateful.' Nina knew she was standing on a very sore corn. Everything was coming out with far more anger than she would have intended. But she could hardly bear the irony that she knew from Susan all about the indiscretions of Ziggy with Jennifer's husband, Neville. And here was Jennifer holding forth from a stance of unknowing self-righteousness . . .

'I'll clean my house when you get on better with your daughter. Clean or not clean, Susan would prefer to live here, and you know it.'

'Here or anywhere she could do as she pleases.

113

She's a very spoiled child, Jennifer, and that's what I'm up against there. Simon has no idea how to relate to children, especially a girl. He treats Susan as a cross between a pretty doll and his mistress.'

Ziggy said, 'That's very true. Actually, sometimes I get the feeling there's no place for me between George and Cassandra. I'm beginning to think the sooner I send her off to boarding school the better. Then maybe George and I can get something of our old lives back.'

Nina stood up, finding accusations of Ziggy's adultery nearly spilling unbidden from her lips. 'I'm thinking of asking my mother to have the children for a long weekend and then Simon and I can go away, just to spend some time together and see what we can recapture.'

Cal shook her great leonine head. 'You English broads. I'll never understand you. American women are light years ahead of all of you. American women have fought for their freedom and their right to have a career, their right to explore their own sexuality.'

'So, Cal.' Nina felt the hairs on the back of her neck stiffen. 'What have you achieved with all this freedom? Your right to look at home on a construction site? Be the pet hero of your revolution in the dining rooms of Kew and Richmond? Give your hosts a thrill with inside stories of the forbidden lesbian life?'

Ziggy's hands were shaking. 'Really, Nina! I don't think you should be talking like this to Cal.'

'Bourgeois revisionist,' Jennifer said, sniffing loudly.

'Oh, do shut up, Jennifer! Since when did you swallow a dictionary? Go and throw some pots. I'm leaving. See you later, at our spoiled children's over-priced exclusive private school. What is it this afternoon, Jennifer? Guitar lessons for Hortense? Judo for Christopher?'

Jennifer sat at the table, her face white. 'Christopher needs to learn to control his male violence.'

'And I suppose Hortense needs to play the guitar so she can sing protest songs?' Nina smiled. 'No hard feelings, Cal. I just don't agree with any of this trendy nonsense. Goodbye.' Nina walked out of the house.

This was the first time she had left Jennifer's house after a full-blown argument. Usually Jennifer's condescension irritated her and she just swallowed her anger. But in the last few days of freedom, Nina felt a bubbling sense of confidence. And her confidence, like her freedom, needed preservation. Protection from Jennifer, from Ziggy, and even from Simon, her own husband. He will sulk, she thought as she got into the car, but so what? He'll get over it.

She felt homesick for a moment. Homesick for her mother and her father. Old-fashioned, Simon called them. Nina never remembered a quarrel between them. Her father deferred always to her mother in the house and he took control of the outside world. 'Poppycock' was her mother's often used word. 'Balderdash' her father's. But Nina knew that her parents loved each other very much, without there being a need for too many overt shows of affection between them. Her father would never sulk the way Simon did.

That evening Nina had a surprisingly pleasant time cooking homemade pizza with the kids. Even Susan seemed to enjoy getting covered in flour during her efforts at twirling the dough in the air, and Hamish was clearly delighted to count out the pepperoni slivers as he laid them carefully out, making sure that each slice of pizza would contain the same amount. Nina and the children shared a happy dinner in front of the television set until it was time for them to go to bed.

With both children upstairs and asleep, Nina sat by herself and wondered how late home the unforgiving Simon would be.

Around eleven she heard his feet crunch up the path. Then came his cough and the sound of his key in the lock. She rose to her feet, filled her glass and walked out to greet him. 'Had a good day?' she asked hopefully. She scanned his face in the light of the hall. He looked glum. She stretched out her hand to take his coat.

'Not too bad. I spoke to mother and she says she'll cover your cheque at the bank until the end of the month. She's really very angry with you, Nina. She says you've been irresponsible.'

Nina felt her heart beat faster. 'Why did you ring your mother, Simon? You could have taken the money from the savings account. You know you could have.'

'And lose a whole month's interest on four hundred and fifty pounds? Don't be such an idiot. This way mother will cover us until the end of the month, no interest lost, and next month I can take the money out of the housekeeping. We can manage without wine for dinner, and you can stay away from Theodorakis's grocery and Mrs Porter's expensive vegetable shop. Strict rations, darling. Strict rations. Besides, mother says the amount we spend on food is quite ridiculous.'

Simon was feeling vindicated. There was nothing Nina could do. She stood in the hall holding his coat. She hung the coat on a peg in the wall. Phew!

Someone in the office certainly overdoses on that horrid scent, whatever the hell it is.

Later, after a hectic bout of lovemaking, Nina lay back on her pillow. Tears slid down the sides of her face. Why does sex with Simon have to feel more like a wrestling match than my idea of making love? Simon always seemed to be somewhere she could not follow. Lovemaking was never a matter of lips tenderly touching lips, or tongues sliding and gliding in between soft crevices. Lovemaking with Simon was like mountaineering, Nina trying to accommodate his increasingly hard thrusts until finally he reached his summit and, gasping and groaning, rolled down the slope into oblivion. Sometimes Nina wondered if Simon liked making love to her at all.

Tonight, for a moment, their eyes locked. Hers questioned and his refused to answer. The meeting of the eyes caused a momentary pause in the thrusting, and then he came down on her mouth brutally and the thrusting continued. This must be what it's like to be raped, she thought as she struggled to contain his driving penis, but he's not a rapist. He's my husband.

She fell asleep crying.

Chapter 14

It was not lunch on Friday with Sonia but what happened *after* lunch that left a deep and permanent impression on Nina's thoughts. Lunch at the Gay

Hussar was a treat. Nina was glad she had made the effort to dress nicely – she wore her expensive silk underwear and her new grey dress – for she felt very much in keeping with the atmosphere of the elegant yet comfortable Hungarian restaurant. Sonia was fun, as always, and listened with interest to Nina's recounting of yesterday's coffee-time clash with Ziggy and Jennifer who, for all their efforts to be revolutionary, still seemed more suburban than Nina could ever be. Sonia laughed at the way Nina told the story, and Nina, too, found herself laughing at how awkward it had been to say nothing about Ziggy's affair with Jennifer's husband Neville when she was sitting right there in Jennifer's own house. And as for Cal . . .

But what mattered most came after lunch, when they were leaving the restaurant. Nina was in full savour, treasuring her sense of independence and rebelliousness at having another woman-to-woman lunch with Sonia, discussing why so few couples seemed really happy, speculating whether or not there would ever be anything like a truce in the war between men and women. She and Sonia had their coats on when Nina, one step ahead, reached to open the door on their way out. Just then the door opened. Nina pulled back her hand.

The doorway was suddenly filled by the tall shape of a large man, the form made to look even bigger by the wide shoulders of the man's generous camelhair coat. Where the coat opened at the chest Nina could see the lapels of a smooth wool suit and the beautiful fabric of a Liberty silk tie. The tie was folded over by a clean, crisp collar which itself held the golden curve of a strong neck. Slowly raising her eyes, Nina spied the smooth skin at the jaw and her heartbeat quickened. The lips of the smiling mouth parted to reveal perfect teeth. Above the high cheekbones, onyx eyes looked into her own. 'Ah,' he said, sounding pleased but not surprised. 'It's you.'

Nina was speechless for a moment until she found the presence to smile back and say, 'It's *you*.'

From behind her, Sonia held out a hand and introduced herself. The man was polite but he did not look at Sonia, even while she shook his hand. His eyes remained on Nina. 'I've met you once or twice before at various dos,' Sonia said, trying to sound calm, though she was evidently excited to be grasping such a well-known hand. Clearly she had forgotten for the moment her instinctive fear of Michael Morningstar, the same fear that had prompted her to suggest lunch at the Gay Hussar instead of Joe Allen's in the first place. 'And this,' she said, almost reluctantly, 'is my friend Nina Stockton. Nina, this is . . .'

'Michael Morningstar,' said Michael Morningstar. 'I was hoping I would see you again.'

Nina could hardly believe that her fantasies had in fact been justified. He *had* been thinking about her since they first saw each other at Joe Allen's. Yes, she *did* hold a place in his heart, as he had captured a special place in her world of dreams.

'Funny, how we all seem to like the same restaurants,' she said, thinking her words had sounded idiotic and inadequate.

'Remarkable coincidence, wouldn't you say?'

'Mind-boggling!' said Sonia, though neither Nina nor Michael noticed.

'It's only our timing that's unfortunate,' Michael said, looking over her shoulder. She followed his eyes and saw a wealthy-looking elderly man rising from a table across the room at the sight of Michael, his lunch companion. Michael bowed his head in a gesture that said *I'll be over in just a moment*. Nina recognized the older man's face from the newspapers. Yes, she was certain he was prominent in the House of Lords. 'I'm due for lunch with . . .'

'We were just going,' Nina demurred, afraid of what might happen if he invited her and Sonia to join him at his table. She might stay all afternoon. She might never want to leave. And she had the children to collect soon . . .

'But we will see each other again,' he said. 'I'd like that.'

'If coincidence holds out,' said Nina as, dropping Sonia's hand, he held hers.

'I'm sure it will.' His voice showed a strange certainty. He looked to Sonia. 'Goodbye.'

He released Nina's hand, walked past her, and joined the man he had kept waiting. Nina did not want to leave the sphere of his attention, though the whole encounter, she realized, could not have taken more than thirty seconds.

'Huh!' said Sonia on the pavement outside when the door had shut behind them. 'I'm not used to being the wallflower. I tell you, Nina. He has eyes for you.'

'Oh, don't be silly!' Nina could feel the colour rise in her cheeks.

'I'm dead serious. I'm an expert when it comes to reading the signs. But listen to me, he's someone to steer clear of. Though he is *gorgeous*,' she emphasized. 'I'll give you that.'

Nina shook her head, pleased to have been the recipient of his special recognition. 'I really don't think he recognized me from Joe Allen's,' she said aloud, happily flustered. *But he did*, a voice within

her whispered. *And he said he wants to see you again.*
I'm sure we won't ever see each other again, she said
to herself. How often can a person count on running
into someone like Michael Morningstar? But, despite
herself, she let out a sudden little laugh of joy.

You're being stupid, she told herself as she drove
alone in her car back towards Richmond. Exchanging
hellos with Michael Morningstar, touching his hand,
looking into his eyes, being told he wants to see you
again . . . It's all stuff that's good for fantasy and not
much else.

But what fantasies! He had given her fuel for many
fantasies to come, she knew. And, if nothing else,
she was grateful for that.

Chapter 15

'Do let's go to the cinema, Simon.' Nina saw the
Lyme Regis cinema as the car rolled down the steep
hill towards the sea. 'We haven't been to a local fleapit
since we had the children.' Nina felt exuberant after
sitting in Simon's car, mentally pushing aside a vague
sense of guilt at leaving the children with her mother.
Not too much guilt over Hamish, who waved goodbye from behind his grandfather's cricket stumps.

Major Tolmadge had aged as finely as the bottles
of port first laid down by his father when he was
born. Hamish too had his own bottles of port awaiting his twenty-first. 'It's not fair,' Susan had argued
once when the subject of port had been raised at a

family gathering. 'Girls should have port laid down for them, too.'

'Girls don't drink port, Susan,' her grandfather replied at the time, and Nina felt guilt's moist fingers take her by the throat now at the memory.

The older Susan got, the less Major Tolmadge seemed to understand her. Today, as they left Susan sulking by the gate, Nina saw the puzzlement cloud the Major's eyes. 'It's kids today, Pa,' she said as she tiptoed to kiss his greying cheeks.

'Girls don't play cricket,' Susan whined as Nina hugged her goodbye.

'Of course they do, darling. I used to play when I was your age. It's a fabulous game. Or, if you want, you could go and help grandma. She's pickling cabbage for Christmas.'

'I hate the smell of pickles. I hate cabbage. I want to ring Hortense. Grandma won't let me. Why are you leaving me here, Daddy? I want to go with you.'

Simon cleared his throat. 'Your mother and I need a little time on our own.'

Nina winced at the stricken look in her daughter's eyes and then she saw rage roll in like a tidal wave. The little figure squared its shoulders. The thin hands clutched the gate. 'Like Ziggy and Neville, you mean?' The child's features contorted.

'No. Not like Ziggy and Neville, Susan. Daddy and I are married to each other. There's no adultery involved with us.'

Now sitting in the car, Nina very much wanted to discuss this event with Simon, but she promised herself that this would be their happy weekend together, their attempt to rediscover the magic of those days before the children came along, the days when they were free to go where they pleased.

Nina squeezed Simon's hand. 'We'll get to the hotel in a few minutes, and then we can catch the afternoon show at the cinema. You can buy me a box of Black Magic chocolates. Remember those? I haven't had a box for ages.'

'We must go away more often,' he smiled, glancing at her flushed face.

They parked the car on the Cobb and Simon carried the two blue matching suitcases into the quaint hotel. The owner of the hotel introduced himself as Mr Bob. 'We've been fishing folk here all our lives.'

Nina smiled at his round weather-beaten face. He preceded them up the long rickety staircase, through the corridor, to a double bedroom on the top floor. Mr Bob put the suitcases down, pulled out a bunch of thick brass keys and opened the door. 'What a wonderful view!' said Nina, walking towards the windows.

'Yes. Really first class.' Simon followed Nina to the window.

'I'll leave you now.' Mr Bob nodded his head. 'The bell is over there. Just ring the front desk if you need anything. We serve dinner from seven until nine o'clock. We go to bed early round here.' Mr Bob left quietly.

Nina stood and looked out across the sea. The waves were choppy, like restless white-maned foals careering across windy fields of steel grey. 'I do so love the sea,' she said.

Simon put his arms about her. 'I do so love you, darling. Time for a quick one before we go to the cinema?'

Nina elbowed him away, surprised to find herself feeling suddenly irked. 'I'm not about to sit with my diaphragm leaking spermicide in a cinema, thank you. You'll have to wait.'

'You didn't say that when we first started making love. You couldn't get enough of it back then.'

Nina looked at her husband. 'That was a long time ago. I've changed in the last ten years. Having children changes women. You still have the same job you had before I married you. The same friends. Only now you have a wife to come home to. In a funny way, I feel you've really always been a bachelor. But things do have to change from now on. I feel there's too wide a gulf between us, Simon, and it's getting wider. No, I don't want to make love right now. Maybe later, after dinner, when we're more relaxed. I just want to go back to the days when we used to joke and laugh and you bought me a box of Black Magic chocolates. We can just sit together in the darkness and hold hands.'

'If that's how you want it.' His voice was surly.

Nina felt the awful pressure. I wish sex with Simon didn't feel like this. She so much wanted to lose herself in passion, but invariably she ended up feeling like a car being filled at a petrol station. Sonia puts up with it. Jennifer puts up with it. Ziggy screws both Neville and George, so she must be getting something out of it . . . All I get is boredom. I wonder, once you stop fancying a man, does it ever come back again?

She lifted her suitcase onto the bed and unpacked her night clothes that were folded neatly on top. 'Look, darling.' She softened her voice in an effort not to be too harsh. 'My negligée from our wedding night. Let's make this weekend fun.'

'All right, Dotty. We'll do our best. Let's go down for lunch.'

*

Nina and Simon sat at a table in the dining room. 'It's quite an ugly room,' Nina whispered. 'I hope the food's good.'

'Not a bad wine list.' Simon's nose was quivering. 'What about a light claret with a rack of lamb? We haven't had lamb for quite some time.'

Nina held out her hand. 'Let me have a look, Simon. I think I'd rather eat fish, if they have something local on the menu. I'll have half a bottle of Pouilly Fumé, if you don't mind.'

'You've been taking more and more of an interest in wine lately. I thought you left that sort of thing to me.' Simon's eyebrows were up. 'I usually choose the wine. In a restaurant. Male prerogative and all that.'

'Not these days it isn't.' Nina smiled. 'I had a lovely bottle of Pouilly Fumé with Sonia at lunch.' She felt dangerous, simply mentioning to Simon the lunch after which she had met Michael. 'It has a beautiful, woody, smokey taste, like a summer bark smell and autumn leaves. Anyway, I don't see what the fuss is all about. I chose a good bottle the other night at home to go with the veal, didn't I?'

'Sonia again. Really, Nina. She's a person of loose morals.'

'Then so are Ziggy and Neville.'

'I suppose so, but it's different.'

'Really? I don't see why.'

'Well, we aren't about to quarrel over it, are we?'

'No, we definitely will not quarrel. But why is Sonia different from Ziggy and Neville?'

'To begin with, she's so very American. You know how aggressive American women can be.'

'In one way,' said Nina, 'but they're also successful,

125

and maybe self-assertiveness is a small price to pay for success.'

'Self-assertiveness? There's an American phrase, if ever I heard one.'

'Ah, look!' She pointed to the menu. 'They do have locally caught salmon. I'll have that.'

'If you insist, Dotty. I'll have the salmon, too.'

'No, you said you wanted the lamb. Have it if you want to. We're not Tweedledum and Tweedledee.'

The waitress appeared at the table. She was young and pretty. Her two perfectly-shaped breasts wobbled under her black silk dress. 'Do you want a starter, darling?' offered Simon.

'No thank you, dear. Just the fish.'

'Two salmon steaks,' Simon ordered, 'with Béarnaise sauce. And a bottle of the Pouilly Fumé, please.'

'Peas and new potatoes?' The girl's mouth was a pink lipsticked pout.

How the hell does she keep her lipstick on? Nina wondered. Mine's gone a minute after I've put it on.

'Yes, please,' said Simon, handing back the menus and giving the waitress the benefit of his warmest-looking grin.

The girl turned and her bottom seemed to be an independent part of her anatomy. Nina watched Simon eye the girl. He doesn't look at me that way any more, she mourned.

They sat in the bay window, both looking out to sea. Nina felt as if she were sitting with Simon in a perpetual scene on a postcard. All that had to happen was that a hand would come out of the clouds and pick up the card and tilt it on its side, and plop it into one of the postcard stands next to the fat lady in the red bathing suit. Then time would stop, both of them captured forever. The ultimate snapshot. A pretty blonde wife with her handsome husband on a week-end of seaside marital bliss.

'What on earth are you doing, Simon? Put it away.' Nina's raised voice coincided with a hushed moment in the cinema when the film's villain was hunting for the heroine in a quarry with the intention of killing her.

'Shush, Nina.' She could see Simon shoot from his slumped state to sitting bolt upright.

'Shut up, you silly bitch,' said an anonymous voice in the darkness.

They could hear giggles running around the cinema.

'I was only adjusting myself.'

Nina was horrified. 'But where would you get an idea like that, Simon? Off Neville, I suppose?' she hissed, glad that the place was in darkness. 'Were you trying to jerk off? Most men would sooner die than be caught wanking in a cinema,' she said, thinking that Michael Morningstar, for one, would never do such a thing.

Simon placed his mouth close to her ear. 'Some women like doing it in the cinema. *They* find it exciting.'

'Well I'm not one of them. I think it's disgusting.'

'Am I very much mistaken, or weren't you the one who thought we might try it in the shower?'

'A private shower's one thing,' she said seriously, 'but a public cinema is quite another.'

The killer was closing in on his victim. 'Shh! I want to watch the film.'

Nina studied Simon's profile in the light flickering from the screen. She wasn't so much shocked by Simon's behaviour, but more by the sound of her own voice. I sounded as if I was talking to Hamish, telling him to put it away. I'm beginning to treat Simon like a child.

Later that night she lay beside her husband. She smelled of Shalimar and bath oil. She nuzzled his ear. 'That was a lovely rack of lamb we had for dinner,' she said, feeling the peppery red wine still on her tongue. The wine had created a tingling between her legs. She wanted everything to be good, to be as it used to be. She let herself be moved by the wine and the food. 'Let's make mad, passionate love.'

Simon rolled over onto his stomach. 'I can't,' he said, his face in the pillow.

'Why not? Are you too tired?'

'No. Well actually, yes. I'm exhausted. Let's just go to sleep.'

Nina hugged him briefly and kissed the nape of his neck. She lay back on her pillow. He must have come in the cinema, she thought, and can't get it up again. Well, women can have wet dreams, too. She sat up for a moment and then looked out at a patch of night through the curtains. Must I always lust in my heart for Simon to be more, if not for Simon to be someone else? I mean, dear Lord, I'm already an adulteress in thoughts. She remembered the face that smiled into her own at the door of the Gay Hussar . . . Oh well. I'll dream about him, but I'll never be unfaithful in the flesh. A vow is a vow, she reminded herself, and she was connected to Simon by unbreakable vows.

Chapter 16

Simon awoke on Sunday morning with a huge erection. Nina, stirring beside him, felt the urgency of his fumbling fingers between her thighs. Still flushed with last night's wine, she spread her legs and let him enter her. They moved together in a well-remembered saraband. This was not just lust; this was the recreation of their ten-year communion, a communion which had produced their beloved children. This felt as much a time of consolation as of passion. Nina ascended the peaks and descended the valleys of sensation, and she imagined them both in the sea outside the window, the waves surging through her, mounting higher and higher. She could hear Simon's voice shouting in the distance. 'Sshh,' she said, putting her hand across the gasping mouth. Then she lost herself in their explosion. They both fell back panting.

Nina removed her sweaty hair from her face. She rolled into a hollow beside Simon's spent body. 'That was wonderful,' she said, her voice singing with genuine relief that they had not forever lost their desire for each other. 'That was absolutely marvellous. It was like all our vows put together. Oh, Simon.' She let out a light, contented laugh. 'All my bones feel loose, like jelly.'

Simon sat up slowly. He looked down.

Nina rolled up in a ball beside him. 'What's the matter, Simon?' She sat up. She put her hand on his cheek and turned his head. 'Simon? Are you crying?'

He hung his head. 'I have something to tell you, Nina.'

'Oh, come on, Simon. It can't be that bad. Is it your job?'

'No.' He seemed to suck all the air out of the room. 'I want to marry Angela.'

'Angela? Angela?' Nina stopped breathing. There was no air to breathe anyway. All the oxygen had been swept into the black hole created by his secretary's name. Nina finally exhaled. 'How long has this been going on?' she said hoarsely, picking her way through the shards of her marriage.

'For two years.' He took both her hands in his. 'I've been meaning to tell you. Lots of times. I didn't start off intending . . . I mean, I thought it would only be an affair. You and I were rowing and we weren't making love much. And Angela was so understanding. I couldn't help myself. Anyway, she's pregnant, Nina. If I didn't tell you, she would have herself. She's already tried to.'

Nina smiled grimly. 'She doused your coat with her scent, the bitch!' Nina surprised herself. She felt like a dentist poking at a sore tooth. Does it hurt here? No, not really. Then how about there? Yes, a bit . . . Funny, she thought. I should be devastated, but I'm not. A prod. Oh yes! It hurts there! 'You fucking bastard, Simon! How could you lie to me for two whole years?'

'I don't know. It wasn't easy. But for your sake, I didn't want to hurt you.'

'Didn't want to hurt me? How long would this have gone on if she hadn't hit you with an ultimatum?'

'Probably a lot longer, if she hadn't got pregnant.'

'Do you love her?'

'I love you both, Nina. I should have married Angela and kept you as my mistress. Angela is for marriage . . .'

'What *do* you mean?'

'I mean she is the sort of woman my mother would approve of. She knows how to take care of a man.'

'Yes, most secretaries do. It's part of the job. Remember, I was a secretary when I met you, but I didn't go around pinching other women's husbands.'

Simon sighed. 'You're a brick, Nina. Really, you're taking this awfully well. I rather thought you'd be devastated.'

Nina looked at her newly-painted toenails. 'No, Simon. *Noblesse oblige*, dear. In times like this, we were taught at school to think of the Queen of England and ask ourselves how she would handle it. If this is what you want, Simon, then this is what you can have. I think I'll take a shower and go for a walk. I've lost my appetite, but I will be back for lunch.'

If Her Majesty were upset, Nina said to herself, she would probably have a walk around her garden at Balmoral. I'll have to make do with a windswept beach. At least it was empty. The wind was raw and tore at Nina's face. She stuffed her hands into her coat pockets. Head down, she trudged across the beach towards the Cobb. In her mind she saw Simon's face when Susan was born, the way he awkwardly held his first child, pictures of holidays in Portugal, both children playing on the beach there, Nina in her blue bikini, Simon holding Hamish's little fat hands as he tried to walk . . . Yes, she did feel a terrible sense of anguish. Of failure. Of looking backwards at the four of them, the sun still shining . . . But also – to her guilty surprise – she felt a tremendous sensation of lightness, of a cloud being lifted, an elation of sorts. She began to run quickly towards the Cobb. Faster and faster she ran until she felt her feet leave the ground and she was flying.

Winded, she walked out to the end of the Cobb, the arm of stone that curved protectively around the little bobbing boats. She gazed into the water and saw the bladderwrack seaweed pregnant with evil. Let them all go to hell, she thought, picking up a discarded strand. All of them. POP! The sac exploded. That's for Simon and Angela. The sac expelled a faint smell of death. POP! Ziggy and George. POP! Jennifer and POP! That Californian woman, Cal. She threw the bladderwrack into the sea. 'Today,' she said loudly to a passing gull, 'I begin a new life.'

'Caw,' replied the gull. Splat.

Nina looked down at the white blob on her shoe. 'That's for luck!' she yelled as the gull rolled over in the wind. It called in agreement and Nina laughed, her voice following the bird as it floated high over her head.

Chapter 17

'I think . . .' Nina sat down for lunch. 'I really feel it would be better if you went back to London, got yourself packed, and left the house.'

Simon appeared surprised. 'Are you sure you want to do this? I mean, it's all so fast. Shouldn't we go together and tell your parents and the children?'

Nina took a spoonful of hot soup. 'Simon, you've asked me for a divorce in order to marry Angela.' She felt ice trickling down her throat, despite the hot soup. 'You have lied to me for two years. I want to get it over with. I'll tell the children and my parents myself. Besides, my father would probably horse-whip you if he saw you face to face.'

'Would he? That's awfully old-fashioned, Nina. After all, people have affairs all over the place nowadays.'

'Not in my family. We are old-fashioned. We have traditional standards and I intend to live by them.'

Simon finished his soup. 'I did rather expect you'd ask me to stay.'

'Did you? Well, you got that wrong. Very badly wrong. After we finish lunch, I shall drop you off at Axminster and you can make your own way home. You're to be gone when I get back to London.'

'Are you sure you don't want me to come with you, darling?'

'Don't call me darling. I'm not your darling any more. You're Angela's darling, and good luck to her.'

At the train station in Axminster, Simon got out of the car looking bemused. Nina tried not to laugh. This is not how true confessions take place in novels, she thought. Simon's lost his script. I'm supposed to beg and plead and he's supposed to have orgasmic dramas running back and forth between Angela and me. No. Never.

'Goodbye, Simon. I'll be back on Monday with the children. I expect you to be packed and gone. By the way, leave a cheque on the hall table for the housekeeping. I'll telephone you when I get back and we can discuss finances.'

Simon patted Nina's hand nervously. 'Well, good-bye. I'll speak to you soon.' He lowered his head to look more closely at her. 'Are you sure you're all right?'

'Perfectly sure. Run along.' My God, she thought as she drove off, there it is again – my talking-to-a-child voice.

She drove the car efficiently and well. She felt tears fall again, but she was crying not for Simon the man but for Simon the confused, over-protected, mother-damaged boy. I thought I could change all that, she explained to the trees lining the road. An earnest black and white cow raised a mournful eye. He could have changed. We would have been happy, but the boy in Simon was dead. Nina knew, driving towards her parents' house, that she would have been pulling a corpse along with her for the rest of her life. Simon, at the end of the day, was a selfish narcissist, locked away in a world of his own. Even now as she wept, the sense of relief came back.

She drew up in front of the house and prepared herself to break the news, first to her parents and then to the children. Hamish was a bit young to understand the full implications, but Susan would be very vulnerable.

The door opened and Susan came running to the car. She played with the cow gate which protected the flower garden from marauding farm animals. 'You're divorcing Daddy.' She swung on the gate. 'You've kicked my daddy out of the house.'

For a moment Nina was thrown. Was the child a mindreader? But then she gathered her composure.

Simon must have telephoned from the station, the bastard. Already he engineered things to put her in the wrong.

'No, Susan.' She climbed out of the car. 'It's not like that. Really it's not. Here. Let's go into the house and talk about it.'

'I don't want to talk about it. Daddy was crying. I hate you, Mum! I really hate you! You made Daddy cry.' Susan's eyes were filling with tears. 'He has to go and live with Angela. You made him!' Her voice rose hysterically. The screams brought both grandparents to the door.

'Whatever is the matter, Susan?' Mrs Tolmadge ran down the path to the gate. Major Tolmadge stood in the doorway, his hand on Hamish's shoulder.

Susan pushed away her grandmother's arms. 'I hate you all! I want to live with Daddy.'

'What's happened? She talked to her father on the phone, and then she ran outside.'

'Let's go in, Mummy,' said Nina. 'I need to talk to you.'

Mrs Tolmadge looked at her daughter's strained face and puffy eyes. 'Trouble, Nina?' she asked softly.

'Yes.' Nina hugged her mother. 'But nothing we can't handle.'

She sat with her parents in the familiar, comfortable library. Hamish, still innocent of the drama, watched television in the kitchen with the cleaning lady. Somewhere outside Susan was suffering, but for the moment there was little Nina could do.

'That's all there is to tell you.'

Major Tolmadge's face was full of colour. 'What a cad that man is!' He put down his teacup. 'Never did like those dubious neckties of his!'

'Daddy, you can't judge a man by his ties.'

'The hell you can't! He'll never darken my door again, I can tell you that.'

'I don't think he'd even try, Daddy. He was never very comfortable here anyway.' Nina looked at her mother. 'You know, Hamish will be hurt, but I'm most worried about Susan. Simon had no right to tell her the way he did. He certainly wasn't crying when I left him at the railway station.'

'Maybe he hadn't really thought the whole thing through, Nina. And he certainly didn't expect you to take such quick action. Perhaps when you dropped him off, he finally realized the total consequence of what he'd done.'

'To be honest, Mummy, I'm shocked by my own reaction. I'm sad, and I'm sorry, but part of me is not surprised.'

Major Tolmadge rose to his feet. 'I'll leave you two to talk. I'll go and find Susan and take her into town. There's little to do on a Sunday. Maybe we can feed the ducks on the mill pond and I'll buy her an ice cream. An ice cream is always a good idea if one is upset.' He walked stiffly over to Nina, bent over and kissed her forehead. 'Don't worry too much, my dear. You're better off without him. You'll see that in time, though things'll be rough for a bit, I expect.'

Nina dreaded looking at him. She could hear the frog in his throat. She knew her father would never allow himself to think *I told you so*. She knew ten years ago that he was unhappy with Simon. But he held his peace and now he was grieving for her and for the children. Nina felt an awful ache. She had hurt her mother and her father, but at least her mother would understand, and afterwards her mother would translate all those feelings and emotions to her father.

'You see, I think I believed that eventually Simon and I would have a relationship rather like you do with Daddy,' she said when she was alone with her mother. 'I knew at the beginning it would be difficult. Right from the start Enid said I was the wrong woman for Simon. I didn't tell you at the time, but she actually told me that she hated me and that the marriage would be a disaster. I suppose that's why I worked so hard at it to begin with. You know, I was out to prove her wrong somehow. But oddly enough, I feel that in little ways I must have known something was going on over the last year or two. I mean,' Nina wrinkled her brow, 'I began to notice other men.' She bit her lip. 'Is that an awful thing to admit?'

Christine Tolmadge shook her head. 'No, I don't think it's an awful thing to admit. If a marriage goes sour for long enough, the eye will start to wander. After all, you are human, you know.'

'Hm. But the worst confession is that the marriage was sour from the start. Jennifer, Ziggy and I married our husbands because we wanted to get married. That was all. You know, Ziggy and Neville are having an affair, right behind Jennifer's back. Susan told me so.'

Mrs Tolmadge's mouth registered shock. 'Isn't she a little young to know things like that?'

'Not these days. Not London children. What they don't see on television, they see in the streets and in their friends' homes. Things have suddenly gone haywire in kids' lives. I sometimes think I'm the only one left stranded in this little rowboat which has signs attached to it saying, "Do not be rude to your parents", "Table manners are important", "I'm your mother, not your best friend."

'Jennifer and her daughter talk about sex with each

137

other. I don't mean just the facts of life; I mean adult sexual knowledge that I wouldn't dream of discussing with Susan. Anyway, there's not much I can do with her. Hortense and Emma and Cassandra and Susan behave as if they're eighteen already, not eight. Still, I won't let Susan wear nail varnish or make-up. She thinks I'm a witch, and I know she puts it on when she's with her friends. All I can say is that in my own little boat I'm trying to reach a shore called sanity. And now, with Simon wanting a divorce, I have no paddles.'

'You have the two of us.'

'That means the world to me, Mummy. And maybe I can get a part-time job and . . . And, I don't know. Begin a life.'

Christine Tolmadge got up and walked over to her writing desk. She pulled down the flap and took out a long envelope. She walked back to her chair and sat down. 'I know Daddy will agree with me.' She pulled out a piece of thick paper. 'This is our will. The bulk of the estate goes to you, as our only child, when we're gone. But I'd imagine you might need money now. When you've had time to talk to Simon, after the shock wears off, we can work out the details. There's no point in you being short of money with the children now just because you're due to inherit a sizeable amount after we die.'

'Oh, don't say *die*, Mummy!' Nina put her chin in her hands. 'I don't ever want to think about that. I expect Simon will let me stay in the house. After all, we bought it very cheaply ten years ago without much of a mortgage. You gave us such a huge cheque as the deposit, we're almost clear. So if I get a part-time job and he pays towards the children's bills and school fees, we'll manage.'

Mrs Tolmadge tried to hide her concern. She knew they would not manage. Nina, in all her innocence, did not understand a man like Simon. Mrs Tolmadge had seen many such men come and go in the lives of her friends. Some had left bruises and broken bones, but those had mended over the years. Some – more typical of Simon and his ilk – left no bodily damage, but broken hearts instead. She had watched her beloved daughter slowly fade, gradually lose her sense of humour. Now she would at least see to it that Simon's final treachery would not be financial, too. 'I think you ought to go and talk to Hamish, darling, before Susan gets to him first.' She put her arms around Nina and they stood quietly in the calm room.

Nina breathed in deeply the smell of the books and the leather, the warm milk and flower smell of her mother, so familiar, so much loved. 'All right. I'll talk to him.'

Christine saw her leave the room and then she dropped her head in her hands and she cried for her daughter.

Chapter 18

Nina dreaded the journey back to Angel Walk, Richmond. She spent the last night in the bedroom of her childhood lying in bed, staring out of the window that had seemed so huge when she was five – Hamish's age. She stretched out, alone in bed after ten years of sleeping beside another body. She cried yet again at the thought of the sadness in Hamish's eyes. 'You mean,' he said, looking at his mother, a small frown on his brow, 'that Daddy won't live in our house any more? Where will Daddy live?'

'He will live with his secretary Angela. You know Angela, that nice lady?' For fuck's sake! Nina thought while telling him. This is difficult. 'The one that looks after him at the office?'

'Why does he want to live with her?'

'That's a good question, Hamish. Why indeed? Sometimes these things happen. But you can still go and stay with him whenever you want to.'

'Susan says he's going to have a baby. Is that true?'

'Yes. It's true.'

'It won't be a boy, will it, Mummy? I don't want Daddy to have another boy. Only me.' It was then that Nina finally broke down. She left Hamish after a hug and she retired to her bedroom.

I didn't know it would hurt like this, Lord, she prayed. I really didn't know. The look of desolation in the children's eyes haunted her.

How odd, Nina thought. A day ago I was a married woman, and tonight I am on the eve of a divorce.

Walking into the house in Richmond was not as daunting as Nina had feared. When she actually managed to get the children into bed their first night home, she sat with her glass of red wine by the fire in the drawing room.

Simon's cupboard upstairs was empty. He had also taken her classical record albums and several of her carefully collected antiques. But then Simon by himself had collected nothing. Very little of the house reflected his taste. Most of the furniture, the paintings, and the carpets came from Devon, Nina's Aunt

Persephone being the main benefactor. Nina smiled, as always, at the thought of Aunt Persephone. She was a tall, gaunt woman, a strong image from Nina's childhood. 'If a thing's worth doing,' she heard her Aunt's voice, 'it's worth doing well, child. Do it again!' If I survive all this, Nina promised the flames licking the coal, it'll be because of women like Aunt Persephone. She's never relied on a man. Still, it would be nice if one day I could find someone who could love me the way I am . . . Goodness! She wiped her eyes. I never realized one did so much crying.

She poured herself another drink and dialled Gemma's number on the telephone. There was a silence on the other end after Nina said what she had to say. 'Are you there, Gemma?'

'Yes, I'm here. I'm just a bit stunned. It's all rather sudden, isn't it?'

'Not really. He says it's been going on for two years.'

'And the bitch is pregnant?'

'Hm. The worst part of it is, although I feel awful for the kids and furious that Simon could lie to me like this, there's a part of me that's . . . I don't know. Almost *pleased*. Pleased to be rid of him. I did love Simon at first . . .'

Gemma said, 'I did try to warn you. But you always were stubborn.'

'Yes, but I really did believe that he was as brilliant as he said he was. After all, he had a first from Oxford. He had Myles and George and Neville for friends, all such worldly men. There I was with four O levels. To begin with, he seemed like a dream come true. I was the little country mouse from Devon. My parents used to make him laugh. And can you believe it? I used to think his mother was so glamorous and fashionable! Then everything changed. I had Susan and Hamish, and I guess I grew up. Hang on, Gemma. I'm going to pour myself another glass of wine.' She spilled it. 'Damn!'

'Do you want me to come over, Nina?'

'No. I'm feeling a little woozy, but I'll put myself to bed and I'll be all right. I just needed to hear your voice. I wanted to say I love you. I'm sorry for those Simon-years when I lost touch with you.' Nina felt the wine fumes in her nostrils. She sneezed. 'Anyway, Gemma . . . Are you there, Gemma?'

'Still here. Good night, Nina. I love you, too.'

'That's all right then, Gemma. I'm glad someone loves me.'

Nina put the phone down and lay back on the sofa and sobbed. What an idiot I am! She sobbed loudly. Why am I crying?

Jimmy Donleavy's voice on Tuesday morning was a steadying influence. Both children sat in the back of the car while Nina drove. Susan's voice was exceptionally cheerful. 'I suppose I'll have to tell Hortense and Emma that Daddy has asked you for a divorce.'

'I suppose you will.' They had already had this conversation at breakfast.

Hamish's face was white in the rearview mirror. 'When can we see Daddy?' he said. 'I haven't seen him for two whole days.'

'I'll telephone him at the office and I'll arrange a time for you both to see him.'

Nina was almost surprised. She had assumed it would be Susan who would have been distraught, for she was far closer to her father. But Hamish was the one to look more bereft.

'Whatever your problems, it's hard to be too

142

unhappy on a fine sunny day like today.' Jimmy's voice caused Nina to look out of the window at the trees lining the road. It was a lovely late autumn day. Most of the leaves were gone. They lay in matted piles along the roadside.

At the school, Nina walked behind Susan holding Hamish's hand.

The headmistress already knew that Nina and Simon had parted. Nina telephoned her yesterday to tell her why the children missed a day of school on Monday and would start their week on Tuesday. 'Any chance of a reconciliation?' The voice was distant and signalled distaste for the whole subject.

'No. I'm afraid not. There's another woman involved and she's pregnant.'

'Oh dear. I am sorry, Mrs Stockton. Aren't men incontinent? Really, you would think at his age, and in his position! But then women really are their own worst enemies. In my day, we stuck together and made men behave themselves. Men can be such animals, and it's up to us women to civilize them. My late husband, Mr Burns, always agreed with me. Oh well, I'd better get on. Thank you for telling me.'

Today, approaching the school, Nina saw Hortense and Emma waiting for Susan at the gate. They must know. Nina felt herself blushing. This is ridiculous. Of course everyone knew. The schoolyard telegraph would have been raging all day yesterday, and Emma and Hortense were probably the chief operators.

Hortense and Emma rolled their eyes at Susan who rolled her eyes back. They communicated news through schoolgirl telepathy. Exciting news! Something happening in the usual boring grown-up world in the super-boring universe.

Susan darted off without saying goodbye. A little

143

crowd of girls followed her and Ziggy joined Nina at the gate.

'You've heard?' Nina forestalled Ziggy's question.

'Yes. I heard from Jennifer. Angela, huh?'

'Yes. Angela.'

Ziggy took Nina's arm. 'How do you feel about it?'

Nina looked squarely at Ziggy. 'I don't think the Angelas of this world should pinch each other's husbands.' She saw Ziggy's face crumble. 'Nor should you. Of course I'm upset, not just for me, but for the children. Kids need two parents. They need to know that they have a mother and a father who won't betray the family.'

'You always were old-fashioned, Nina. It may be like that in storybooks, but that's a far cry from real life.'

'You don't love Neville, do you, Ziggy?'

'So you know about that?' Ziggy sighed. 'It's not a question of love. I'm at a stage of my life when I find I'm terrified of my mirror. I wake up and look at it every day, and there's one more line to count. Neville is a way of feeling young again. Whispering down telephones. Making secret lunch appointments. Trysts in anonymous hotels. It keeps my blood racing. It makes for a change from boring old George.'

'But what about Jennifer? How can you double-cross her? She's supposed to be your friend.'

Ziggy shrugged. 'Jennifer half-suspects, I think. But even if she did know, she'd prefer it was me than somebody else. She knows I don't really want Neville on any sort of permanent basis. And this way Jennifer isn't about to lose her husband or her style of living. No, I rather suit Jennifer. We play a sort of dangerous-seeming game, but really it's perfectly safe. Neville thinks he's fooling both of us, but then

144

we sort of share him. It's quite sexy, you know. She tells me all the intimate details that happen between them, and naturally I'm discreet enough not to counter with any anecdotes of my own, but I still think she can feel it in the air. Puts some unspoken friendly competition into the whole thing, if you see what I mean.'

'I don't see, Ziggy. I don't see any of it. Frankly the whole idea makes me as uncomfortable as hell.' She could see Jennifer in the distance. She wanted to hide. She bent down to kiss Hamish. 'Darling, there's your friend Ben waiting for you. Run along.' She pushed the thin little shoulders and then she fled.

I can't bear any more discussions like that, she thought. I'll go home and telephone Simon. I must get this first phone call over with, and then somehow we'll manage a severed relationship. Most of all, we have to be civilized. She made a face. Why do we have to be civilized? she asked herself. Why, when Simon has betrayed me for so long, has lied to me and impregnated another woman, and finally left me in favour of her, why do I have to be civilized? For the children's sake, the trees waved their branches. For the sake of the children, they reminded her. And a huge old oak glared at her. You know perfectly well you don't want Simon back, so there's no need to be uncivilized. Nina knew that was the truth.

Chapter 19

'You see,' Nina leaned anxiously over the desk of the Star Employment Agency, 'I'd like a part-time job. Nine-thirty to two-thirty or three in the afternoon.'

The woman behind the desk was on her third crimson nail. The smell of nail polish mingled with the smell of too many typewriters chattering away behind the woman's back. 'D'you do audio?'

'Yes, Mrs Dullman.' She read the woman's name from a badge attached to the aggressive breast.

'Shorthand?'

Nina smiled nervously. 'I'm a little out of practice, but I can brush it up. I passed the exam at college.' She held out her certificate.

Mrs Dullman stretched a taloned, supercilious hand.

Nina looked around the room. I feel old, was the first thought that came into her head. Dreadfully old. Don't be silly, she reasoned with herself, you're only thirty. The big three-oh. All I have to show is a certificate that says I can do shorthand and I can type forty words per minute, and that should be that. She gazed at the bent heads of the audio typists. Sod, she thought. I really don't want to do this.

Mrs Dullman handed back the certificate. 'You *were* well-trained, my dear.'

Nina winced. 'But things are different now?'

'Most men want . . . Well, you know. They want

dolly birds. But you already have children. Men don't want secretaries with children.'

Nina felt her shoulders sag. 'They're at school all day. They won't be in the way.'

The woman paused. 'I tell you what, Mrs Stockton. I'll keep your name on the books. I'll give you a tinkle when a job comes up. But don't count on it, will you?'

'I won't count on anything.'

'Daddy?' Susan's voice trembled. 'Can I stay the weekend with you?'

Susan was hunched over the phone, white-faced and apprehensive. Nina, standing in the kitchen, heard Susan's end of the conversation in the hall.

'I miss you, Daddy. Can't you come by to say goodnight?'

Nina sighed. She knew Susan wasn't sleeping at night. She stood at the child's door listening to her rolling over, readjusting her pillow, and wrestling with her bedclothes.

'Please can I stay? I'll help Angela and I'll wash up. Hamish wants to stay, too.'

So, thought Nina. Children already make plans without the grown-ups. This must be what a divorce is all about. Funny, you use the word *divorce* about your friends, and you read about divorce among famous people, and then it's just a word. But you have no idea what it really means until you encounter it yourself. My daughter has a plan which she made with Hamish to go away for the weekend with their father and his mistress. They didn't think to discuss it with me . . . She realized that the mere notion of the whole thing hurt her. They ought to be furious with him on my behalf, she said to herself. After all, he betrayed me . . .

'Mum? Daddy wants to talk to you!' Susan held out the telephone. 'I really want to stay with him. Tell him, Mum. Tell him.'

'Hello?' Nina said into the mouthpiece.

'It isn't convenient, Nina,' came Simon's immediate voice. 'Angela and I have to go and see mother.'

'I think Susan's welfare comes first, Simon. Daily telephone calls hardly make up for an absent father. I'll have them both ready for you on Friday. You can pick them up after school.'

'But . . .'

'No buts, Simon. It's your turn.'

'By the way,' he said.

Nina's heart sank. She knew that voice well. Simon was thwarted and angry.

'I've seen my solicitor,' he continued, 'and she says you'll have to move out of the house. We can sell it and then split the profit.'

'Oh no, Simon. I can't sell this house.'

'Why not? I can't afford to support two families. It's unreasonable for you to expect me to. Pay two mortgages and school fees as well? Impossible.'

'Maybe you should have thought of that before you impregnated your mistress.'

Nina heard her own voice shouting. She knew Hamish and Susan could hear every word she said, but for the moment she did not care. Why hide the truth? 'You be here on Friday afternoon and collect the children, and you are not selling this house. Do you understand that, Simon? I've put ten years of my life into this house, and the children were born here. You've put us through quite enough without us losing the roof over our heads.'

She could hear a cold silence on the other end of the telephone. Simon, she knew, had made up his mind. She was aware of the futility of her own words.

'I don't see why you should live in the lap of luxury while I have to pig it in East Sheen.'

'The reason you are pigging it in East Sheen is that you fucked your secretary. If she was good enough for fucking in East Sheen while you were married to me, then that ought to be good enough for you now. *You* committed adultery, Simon. Remember? Anyway, I've got people coming for dinner tonight, so I'll say goodbye. Do you want to say goodnight to Hamish?'

'All right, but I do think you're being very unreasonable, Nina. Selling the house is the obvious solution.'

'Solution for whom? Certainly not for me. I don't have a problem that needs solving. Hamish!' Nina yelled. 'Come and say goodnight to your father.'

She put the telephone down on the table and walked into the kitchen.

I can't lose you, she whispered as she looked around the room. Simon can go, but not the house. Whatever they lacked in their marriage was expressed in the house. All the passionate love and sensuous feelings that had been dormant in Nina during her life with Simon were reflected on the walls of the house, in the furniture, and in her garden. The house was now her own domain. The few weeks that had gone by since he left felt like a happy dream. Not always happy . . . There were moments when, like Chicken Licken, she felt the sky might fall on her head. That's not because of Simon, she reminded herself. That's because I'm used to being part of a couple. It's true.

She opened the fridge. I'll cook spaghetti Bolognese. That way I'll feed the children first and then Gemma and Marietta later.

Hamish came into the kitchen, his face drawn and tearful. 'I don't want you to get a divorce, Mummy.'

Nina hugged him. 'I know, darling. It's awfully hard on children.' She heard Susan running down the stairs.

'Can we stay the weekend, Mum?' she asked.

'Yes, darling. He's looking forward to having you.'

'Oh goody!' Susan danced around the kitchen. 'I wonder if he'll take us out to a restaurant. That's what Melanie's dad does. He takes her out to the Hilton Hotel for a proper grown-up dinner. Just the two of them. Of course, we'll have Hamish.'

Hamish looked at his mother. 'I can stay with you, Mum, if you're lonely.'

'Oh no, Hamish. You have a fabulous weekend. Don't worry about me. I've got lots to do. I'm sorry for all of us. Getting divorced is always a beastly business.'

'Daddy wants you to sell the house.' Susan's eyes were watchful. 'If you sold the house, we could live near Jennifer.'

'No, we couldn't, Susan. We bought this house ten years ago when it was relatively cheap. Anyway, I'm not selling the house and that's final. You'll see, Hamish. In time you'll find out that Daddy and I are much happier apart.'

Hamish hung his head. 'But kids want a mum and a dad living together in the same house. You were happy with Daddy some of the time, weren't you?'

'Of course I was. There were lots of good times.'

Susan smiled serenely. 'I want to live with Dad.'

Nina froze. 'Really?'

'Yes.' The girl nodded her head vigorously. 'Really.'

'Well. We'll have to see. Have you asked him yet? And, you know, Angela would have to agree, too.'

'Oh, she'll agree.' Susan grinned. 'She is going to be my step-mother. I've always wanted one of those.' Susan scampered back up the stairs.

Hamish took Nina's hand. 'I don't want to lose my bedroom.'

'I promise, Hamish. Whatever happens, I'm not selling the house.' Nina kissed his nose. 'Now run along and I'll call you when supper is ready.'

Chapter 20

'He says he's talked to his solicitor and he wants to sell the house.'

Nina felt her voice tremble. Her fingers tightened around her glass of wine.

Marietta leaned across the table. 'He said, he said! Why do you listen to him? He can't put you out of your house until Hamish is sixteen, and then if Hamish goes on to university you're safe until the children are off your hands.'

'He says he can't afford to pay the mortgage and the school fees at the same time as maintaining Angela and the child.'

'Too bloody bad!' Gemma refilled her glass. She stretched out her legs and looked quizzically at Nina. 'You look awful. The bastard's really upset you, hasn't he?'

Nina stared into her wine. 'I can face losing Simon. He was my husband for ten years, Gemma – that's a long time – but . . . I don't know. What was missing was the fact that we were never friends with one another. For Simon everything was a competition. Poor little Susan is completely confused. One day she is the adored daughter, and then the next he's gone. I know she thinks it's all my fault . . . But actually it *does* make much better sense for him to be with Angela, and for me to get on with my life. Though it's not going to be as easy as I thought to get a part-time job. Do you want some more spaghetti either of you?'

Gemma declined and said, 'At least we can come and visit you when we feel like it. Simon's disapproval kept us away.'

'Oh, it's not just the fact that the two of you live together. It was also that Simon resented *any* friends that I might have who could embarrass him. I'll get coffee.'

'No, you sit down, Nina. I'll get the coffee. You sit and talk to Marietta. She has a law degree.'

Gemma left the room and Marietta smiled. 'Don't think you're the only one going through all this. I lost the house, and my ex-husband got custody of the children because he told the judge that I was a lesbian.' Her face drained of colour.

'Do you still see your children?'

Marietta was silent for a moment. 'I'm not allowed to see them. My husband keeps them with him in Hungary. I'm not allowed to go near them or visit them or . . . I'm trying all I can, everything I can. Maybe, if everything goes well . . . Some day.' She lowered her face and wiped her eyes with a long, elegant finger. 'It's bad luck to say too much.' She smiled. 'I want to see them very much. Who knows? I'm trying in all sorts of ways.'

'I'm sorry.' Nina could feel Marietta's pain. 'It must be terrible for you.'

'They know I love them. My only hope is that when they grow up and get to know me, really get to know me, they'll realize I *am* their mother. Sexual preference should be a private matter. And their father has no moral right to keep them from me, whatever the judges say.' She was silent for a moment again, then made an effort to pull her thoughts back to the room. 'Listen, you're facing a difficult time right now. We have to think about how you are going to handle Simon. Tell me, given how well you know him, is he capable of really going through with taking steps to get you out of your house?'

'I don't know. I am rather shocked, especially for Hamish. He's such an insecure little boy . . . And anyway, I don't see Angela going for the whole idea of Susan moving in.'

'How would you feel if Susan did go and live with them?'

'Sad, I guess, but not all that surprised. Enid had such a hold over Susan as a child, and for so many years Simon and his mother shaped her. They treated her like *their* child, as if I was nothing in her life. I was too young to argue with them, and also too insecure but when Enid had had enough and Susan was no longer just a pretty little doll with ringlets and ribbons, Enid lost interest and dumped her back on me. Naturally the poor child was resentful. Fortunately Enid was not at all interested in Hamish. He's too much like my side of the family for her to want to have too much to do with him.

'So you see, it's all a mess, and has been for years.

But until something like this hits you, like Simon moving out, you don't see the mess yourself. You live day by day, coping as best you can. I'm luckier than most. I have Doris to help in the house, but still, I'm dead by the end of the day.'

Gemma carried the tray of coffee into the drawing room. 'Come on,' she said. 'Let's put our feet up. We can do the dishes later.'

'I suppose,' Nina heard her own voice pleading her case as if to a jury, 'I wasn't all that good a wife. I hate housework, and I could never remember to put the knives in the knife slot and the spoons in their slot and then the forks . . . I used to enrage Simon because I left the dishes in the dish rack, but I just couldn't see the point of putting them away in a cupboard only to get them out a few hours later for the next meal. However much I think about it, I feel a failure.'

Marietta put her arm around Nina. 'Don't think you're a failure. Women are conditioned to feel guilty for everything from the moment they're born.'

Nina pulled a cushion onto her lap. 'The biggest surprise to me is that Simon is still Simon. He betrayed us and he got this woman pregnant, and somehow *I* end up as the single parent with two children. Jennifer and Ziggy treat me with pity as though I'm no longer in the club. The club, I realize, is all those women married safely but not particularly happily. Maybe Sonia has it right. She has her job *and* she chooses to live with Myles. Maybe she's wise to stay out of marriage.'

While Nina spoke, Gemma held up the wine bottle to ask if she wanted another glass.

'No. Thanks, but I'd better not drink any more. I can feel myself taking to the bottle these days a little

154

too much. It's just that I can't sleep at night, I feel so restless. I . . . I've never been alone, I realize. I got married so soon after I moved to London from home, and I expected to be married to the same person all my life.'

Gemma looked at her watch. 'Let's get the dishes done, and we'll have to get back. I have a big meeting to prepare for. If the children go to Simon's place for the weekend, why don't you join Marietta and me on Saturday? There's a meeting for people interested in the issues of homelessness in our area. I think you'll like most of the people involved. They're not ranters and ravers. They're people who genuinely care. How about it?'

Nina smiled. 'Sounds marvellous. It'd be good for me to go out and do something and get my mind off my own problems.'

The three women cleared the table, talking as they moved in and out of the room. How peaceful this all is! Nina thought, women working together. How unlike an evening with Simon. I'm not anxious at all. This is just a pleasant night with two friends.

'Goodbye, Nina, and thanks for the dinner. It was excellent.' Marietta hugged her on the doorstep.

Then Nina hugged Gemma. Gemma's was a thin body that always seemed to hold a nervous and intense posture. But the embrace was warm. Nina's cheek rested against Gemma's red hair. 'Thank you for coming. It's wonderful to have you back.'

Gemma laughed. 'I waited, Nina. I'm not altogether surprised this has happened. I know you're hurt, but it will pass. And one day you'll look back and realize it was the best thing that ever happened to you.'

Nina tucked her head in Gemma's shoulder.

'Gemma, I bless the day I first met you. I'll look forward to Saturday.'

'Great,' said Marietta. 'You'll pick us up at the flat about nine o'clock, yes?'

'I'll be there,' Nina promised.

She watched Gemma and Marietta walk together, their hands linked, down the road to the nearby tube station. And she realized how natural it looked for these two women to be walking together as a couple. Why, she asked herself, do they seem to belong together? Maybe it's because Marietta and Gemma really take care of each other. Marietta has lost so much. Thank goodness I still have my children. And for now, the house.

She climbed the stairs and got into her own bed. The notion of Simon demanding sex or entering her body ever again, she realized, revolted her. I think I'll take a vow of chastity. Sex just complicates things. Any sort of sex. Why does sex have such power in relationships? If Gemma and Marietta were to share a flat without sex between them, nobody would mind. But because they do have sex together, many people do mind terribly . . . I mustn't start thinking too much, or I'll never fall asleep.

But it was too late. Her brain already turned round and round. Gemma, Marietta, Cal, Ziggy . . . Will Angela's baby look like Simon? How will Susan and Hamish cope with a new half-brother or sister? Will Simon try and force me to sell the house? He can't *force* me . . . At last Nina dropped off to sleep.

Chapter 21

'So you see, Reverend Simpson, I have to agree to the divorce.'

There was a silence in the vestry at St Peter's church. The Very Reverend Simpson made a steeple out of his hands. He poked at his bibulous nose. 'Have you been to see a marriage counsellor?'

Nina shook her head. 'In a funny way, we've really not talked at all. Simon confessed to his affair, and then I asked him to leave.'

'You asked your husband to leave? Just like that? After ten years of marriage?'

'Well, he wants to marry Angela. And she's pregnant with his child. I thought it would be a bit odd if he stayed with the woman he didn't want when obviously Angela wanted him very much.'

'Mrs Stockton . . .'

Oh, shit. She could feel a sermon arising from the Reverend Simpson's belly.

'What God has joined together let no man cast asunder. You took your vows in this very church ten years ago. Your mother-in-law was wonderful. She still comes to see me when she's in London. Of course, you encountered difficulties in your duties as wife and mother. Simon is a very senior civil servant. And I think you tried in your role as helpmate. As much as dear Enid could, she sought to influence you, but ultimately failed because you were somewhat reluctant, perhaps, to accommodate yourself to the yoke of . . .'

'Simon was the one who failed, Reverend Simpson. He committed adultery, and for two whole years he lied to me. Doesn't adultery have the shock value it used to? I don't know why, but I had expected you'd be somewhat outraged by his actions.'

'Even a man in my position cannot be blind to practical wisdom as well. The truth is, men who stray tend to be the ones who aren't properly loved and – ahem – taken care of. I mean in the full sense of the vows. With my body I thee worship . . . Did you *worship* Simon?'

'Did I *worship* him?' Nina felt her face taking on the colour of anger. Reverend Simpson skewered her with his rolling turkey eyes. Why don't you say *gobble gobble* while you're at it, she thought, and let me get the hell out of here.

'Women used to know their place,' said Reverend Simpson, not waiting for an answer. 'All this rocketing around will only lead to tears. Do you want me to speak to Simon?'

'No, thank you, Reverend Simpson. I just felt that you should know, rather than hear about the divorce through gossip.'

The Reverend Simpson put his hand on Nina's shoulder and shepherded her out onto the front porch. 'I do hope we shall be seeing something of you on Sundays.'

Nina marched determinedly to her car. No, you won't, you sanctimonious bastard, she thought. Why should you make it *my* fault when all that time Simon was off worshipping Angela's body?

*

Later that night, with the children firmly tucked in bed, Nina poured herself another glass of wine. She watched the late news and filled her glass again with the last of the wine. At the sight of the empty bottle she said, 'Oh shit.' She spoke out loud then caught herself, experiencing the fear that talking to herself might become a habit.

The house was too quiet. October was leaving the garden and now November beckoned. Tomorrow I'll clear the leaves, she promised herself.

Tomorrow would be Friday. Already Susan had her suitcase full of clothes. Hamish settled for his backpack: a minimum of clothes, but a maximum of soldiers and guns. The sight of the packed luggage hurt Nina. She decided to ring Sonia, thinking Sonia might come round for dinner tomorrow night.

'I didn't wake you, did I?'

'No, honey. I'm just finishing my nightcap, then I'm off to bed.'

'Where's Myles?'

'At his club, I suspect. How are things going?'

'Oh, sort of okay. Are you free tomorrow night, Sonia?'

'Tomorrow night?' There was a pause.

'Hm.'

'Tomorrow night's no good. Um, Angela's invited everyone to dinner. Jennifer, Ziggy . . .'

'You're kidding.'

'No, really.'

'The bitch! I can't believe she's wasted so little time nicking my friends!'

'Don't worry about me, kiddo. I'm one friend who won't be won over. But I thought I'd go and be your fly on the wall.'

'I can't *believe* she'd actually invited everyone I know!' Nina was furious.

'Promise you it's true. Myles and I got our invitation. "Eight o'clock, dress informal . . ."'

'I bet the invitation was embossed.'

Sonia laughed. 'How did you guess?'

'Angela always was tacky.'

'Listen, I'm sorry I can't be with you, but I'll sure as hell report on the event.'

Nina decided it was a good idea to have a scout in the enemy camp after all. 'Thanks, Sonia. Oh, listen, can you do me a favour? Can you keep an eye on the children while you're there? This is their first weekend away from me. Actually, Susan has spent loads of weekends with her grandmother, but Hamish is usually too frightened to be away. And this is different, somehow.'

'Sure thing, Nina. But don't worry yourself too much. They'll be all right.'

'Simon wants to sell the house.'

'What?'

'I said Simon wants to sell the house.'

'The hell he does! Listen, sweetie, don't let him bully you.'

'If only he did bully me, or hit me, I might feel better. But he's always so fucking reasonable when really he's being cruel as hell.' She knew she was drunk, but she relished the anaesthetized feeling. 'It drives me mad. He has all these buzz words and in the end I always come out feeling he's right and I'm the one who's unreasonable. If he gave me a black eye, I would at least have something to show people so they could see what he's really done. Instead, he just refuses to discuss anything. If I try to talk about the children, he clams up. All he's ever comfortable talking about is money. I suppose he's feeling strapped for cash.'

'Isn't Angela working?'

'No. I hear she's given up work, the clever bitch. And she has no intention of throwing her "at home" parties in a flat in East Sheen for long. Not while the ex over here is sitting in a Georgian house in Richmond. She wants a new house and a hot-line to Harrods. It's bad enough being divorced, but it's awful to feel threatened with homelessness.'

'Stick to your guns, Nina, and I'll phone you after the dinner party. Consider me your secret agent.'

'Okay, Sonia. Thanks.'

'Sleep well.'

Nina put the phone down and stumbled slightly on her way upstairs. She vowed she would have to cut down on her drinking. But not yet.

Nina did not allow Simon to enter the house. As soon as he put his key in the lock, she opened the door with the suitcase and the backpack at her feet. 'The children are ready, Simon. Here are their things.'

Simon stood awkwardly on his own front doorstep. 'Aren't you going to invite me in?'

'No. This is my house now, and you're not welcome.'

'We'll see about that.' Simon's eyes clouded. 'Angela wants to talk to you. We both want to talk to you.'

'I'll bet you do. And the answer to everything is no.'

Susan ran into her father's arms. 'Let's go, Daddy, before you start arguing with Mum.'

'I'm not arguing with your mother, sweetness. I'm just trying to make her see sense.'

Susan turned in her father's arms. She gazed at her

mother. 'I don't want you to fight with Daddy any more, Mum. If he wants to sell this house, why can't he? After all, I want to live with Angela and Daddy. Hamish says he'll stay with you.'

'Oh does he? Hamish!' she called. 'Turn off the television and get your coat. Your father's here. I am not selling the house, Susan. Not under any circumstances. Get that straight. You want to live with Angela and your father? Talk to them about it.'

'I say, Nina. I mean it's far too early to think about things like that.'

Susan detached herself from Simon's arms. 'Hortense said she'd choose her father over her mother any day.'

A moment later the car was gone and Nina stood alone. Rake the leaves she commanded herself. Keep busy.

At eight o'clock Nina sat in the drawing room with a butler's tray beside her. On it was a Greek salad. Olives, feta cheese, and rings of fresh purple onions. Beside the salad she had a plate of garden peas and new potatoes, and a grilled fillet steak with an anchovy and butter sauce. She poured herself a glass of white wine. Despite the effort she made to feed herself well, she could not enjoy her food. Her thoughts were of the dinner party Angela was throwing. They'll all be sitting down about now, she thought. Susan and Hamish are probably in bed. I wonder if they have a room each . . .

She could see Angela's humourless efficient face, with its rabbit-like teeth which seemed forever smeared by traces of lipstick. Two little lines permanently creased above her eyebrows, carefully permed hair, and those dreadful teeth . . . Angela – once a secretary, now a senior civil servant's intended bride. All thanks to a carefully planned pregnancy. Clever cow.

Restlessly Nina switched on the television. It was a documentary on homelessness. Usually Nina tended to turn off such gritty stories of misery and suffering, but her curiosity in the subject was piqued by the old tramp she had met who had once been a music professor and by the conference she was to attend with Gemma and Marietta. She decided to watch.

She quickly recognized the presenter's voice. It was the voice of Jimmy Donleavy. He stood by a bonfire surrounded by huddled people. Bundled up in rags they circled round him as if he were the answer to their prayers. 'Merely talking about these people will not house them.' Jimmy held the microphone out to a young-looking woman. 'Why are you here?'

'I took to the streets after me husband beat me. The social services said I'd have to go back to him or else they'd take the children into care, so I went back and 'e gave me ever such a good hiding. He kicked me and said he'd kill me if I come back again. They took the kids anyway. Put them into care. You see, he's got another woman. That's why he don't want me back.'

Tell me about it, thought Nina. Her eyes filled with tears.

Jimmy touched the woman's shoulder. 'You'll do better without him in the end, love. You don't need a man like that.'

Nina watched Jimmy's face. It was a very Irish face, broad and thoughtful. The image on the television screen was too dark to see the colour of his eyes. His body was square and compact.

'Here comes the van!'

There were a few scuffles as the waiting people swarmed around the mobile soup kitchen. Nina watched Jimmy walk gingerly around some cardboard boxes. The final shot of the documentary was a close-up of Jimmy Donleavy. 'We cannot ignore the plight of the homeless in this day and age. There is no excuse for a wealthy developed country not to see that the poor and the homeless are cared for. So far, the Government has done very little to change this appalling situation. Tomorrow there is a community meeting for all people interested in taking real action to confront the problem of homelessness.' He gave the address where the meeting would be held. 'Personally, I've given my support to the excellent work that's started up at Latchmere House in Shepherd's Bush. Those of you that can, please come to the meeting. Homelessness can only be stopped if we all pitch in. This is Jimmy Donleavy, saying good evening to you, and mind how you go.'

The close-up revealed that Jimmy's eyes were deep blue. She smiled at him. 'See you tomorrow,' she said with delight.

She finished her steak and sipped her white wine. No Simon to tell her off any more. I'll drink white wine with red meat if I want to. Of course, she was not as homeless as those poor wretches in the documentary, but Nina sat in the house feeling homeless anyway. The house she loved was in peril.

Nina sat and contemplated tomorrow's meeting. For the first time since Simon had disrupted her world, she felt she had something to look forward to.

Chapter 22

Nina had a hangover. Acknowledging that these days hangovers were a rather common event, she groped her way to the bathroom. She managed a dry retch and grimaced at the strain on her stomach muscles. She picked up her toothbrush, but the thought of putting it in her mouth made her feel worse. A cold, cold shower, she decided. Standing under the icy water, she felt better. Not only better, but also penitent.

She wandered into the bedroom with a towel around her waist. She looked about the bedroom and smiled slowly. Over the past few traumatic weeks, her personal touch had changed the room from the anxious arena of sexual ambivalence to a peaceful, cheerful haven. Two large potted plants she bought last week gave the room a softer glow. A brilliant scarlet scarf lay on the back of the chair. She had a mess of books and papers on 'her' side of the bed. She let the towel drop to the floor. That's not my side of the bed any more; now the whole bed is mine.

Downstairs, still undressed, she found the Saturday newspapers waiting on the floor beneath the letterbox in the front door, along with a letter from her father. She read the letter first while she waited for the kettle to boil. '. . . We do worry about you, darling, and we would like to know more about your plans . . .' the letter said.

The kettle whistled and she turned it off. She

watched the coffee granules melt into the hot water. She savoured the suddenly chilly moment when she opened the fridge door to take out the milk. Her naked nipples retracted, sharply forming tight, almost painful, buttons. She put the milk back. Time to get moving, she warned herself. I've got an hour left before I pick up Gemma and Marietta.

She hurried back up the stairs into the bedroom. What on earth should I wear to a conference on homelessness? She was going to a place with two friends and the only other face she could expect to recognize would be Jimmy Donleavy's. She decided on the tweed skirt outfit.

Impulsively she picked up the scarlet scarf and wound it around her neck. She smiled at her reflection in the mirror. I'm becoming a person again. I look in the mirror and I see me.

She pressed the top of the atomizer. Shalimar, she gloated. Lovely, lovely, Shalimar.

Nina was glad that she had perfumed herself with Shalimar. Not all of the bodies packed into the Town Hall seemed to have been recently washed. 'Who are these people?' she hissed at Gemma, sitting beside her.

Gemma wore a pair of jeans with a thick turtleneck sweater. Marietta was in black overalls with a white blouse. Her smooth black hair was pulled back. 'These people,' Gemma smiled, 'are all here mostly because they're homeless. But there are also people like us who want to help.'

'Why didn't you warn me to wear jeans? I feel silly.' Nina tried to hide her crocodile handbag underneath her seat.

In front of her sat a row of black men wearing black

166

berets, black shirts, and the darkest of dark glasses. Nina pointed a nervous finger at the stiff back in front of her. '*Who's that?*' she mouthed.

'A Black Panther,' said Gemma.

'I thought this was about homelessness.'

'Hm. But lots of sympathetic causes turn up to air their views, too.'

Pretend you're the Queen Mum, Nina told herself as she always told herself in times of uncertainty. She tried a kindly smile and sat back and contemplated the crowd around her.

A small woman came onto the stage after a few minutes of restless jostling among the crowd. She spoke in an Irish accent that was impossible to follow. Whatever it was that made her so cross, she spat invective at the audience who cringed like whipped dogs. When the woman ceased to rant, she walked to the front of the stage and said quite distinctly, 'All of youse are part of the solution, or you're part of the fokken problem.'

Several individuals got up carrying tin pails. There came the satisfying rattle of coins dropping into the buckets.

Nina found all of this extraordinary. 'What problem are we supposed to be part of, Gemma?'

Marietta, sitting on her other side, put a hand on her arm. 'All socially-minded people must act in concert. Housing and homelessness is only one issue on the full social agenda.'

One of the men in front broke ranks and ran onto the stage. 'Cry freedom for my brothers!' He raised his fist in the air. 'Cry freedom for my sisters!'

Marietta and Gemma seemed singularly unembarrassed at this public display. Both thrust their right fists in the air. Nina raised her hand. 'You look as if you want to go to the loo, twit,' Gemma corrected her. 'Make a fist.'

'What for?'

'It shows solidarity.'

'Solidarity? Gemma, this is silly. Women like me don't have solidarity unless we give it to our husband because he's constipated. Simon suffered severely from solidarity.' Nina tried to remember a time when she felt more out of place.

Gemma began to open her mouth, but Marietta silenced her. 'Leave her alone, Gemma. This is all new to her. We can help her understand later.'

Later went on for a good long time. Children tottered around the room. The smell of hot bodies and full nappies punctuated the gusts of sweet-smelling cigarette smoke. A large dog ambled on and off the stage.

Nina grew bored and restive. Too many long words, too many yells and whistles. But then came a silence. Jimmy Donleavy stood on the podium of the stage. He said, simply and quietly, 'Good day, friends.'

For once there were no catcalls, no insults and no jeers.

'I am here today to say that whatever your political persuasion, we must all be united in the fight against homelessness.'

Everyone clapped. Nina felt as if the world gone mad was now sane again.

'We can judge a country by the care it takes of its poor and its elderly. Just as every child has the right to a mother and a father, so every child has the right to a roof over his or her head.

'We *like* to tell ourselves that surely everyone is provided for in a nation as enlightened as our own, that our safety net is securely in place, that for all who cannot fly, the net is ready to break their fall. Friends, I tell you what you already know: there are tears in the net. Wide, gaping rips. Too many people, ordinary people like ourselves, are falling through and hitting rocky ground beneath.'

There was a concentrated silence in the audience as Jimmy Donleavy spoke. Evident in his words was the fact that he was a clear-thinking man, a man who tempered his passions with reason but who nonetheless was fully capable of harbouring passionate beliefs. He said that ending homelessness was the responsibility not only of the government but of each individual conscience. His gentle, fluent, effective words spread his sincerity throughout the room.

'What is homelessness? Homelessness is the hard ground that most of us complacently ignore. But in our ignorance, we turn our backs on too many people falling and hitting hard. It's high time that we turn away no more, but hold on to each other, to give each other strength and comfort. If we all support each other, then no family need be alone and on the streets. No one need fall.'

He was interrupted by rousing applause.

'Some of you may have seen the documentary last night on television. I'm here to say that before I made that film, I was just an ordinary bloke who did a good enough job as a radio DJ. I heard other people's problems down the phone-in line, but I did not see them. Oh, Jesus!' His voice cracked. 'When we made the film, I saw the suffering face to face. Did I see suffering! And I tell you, friends, life looks very different on the streets than when viewed from the inside of a radio studio.'

He's going to cry, Nina thought. She glanced at Marietta and Gemma. Both women were staring at Jimmy. It was as if he were being judged.

'All I could do was pray, and it's been a long time since I said my prayers with such conviction.

'In researching the documentary, I met a man with his wife and two children under Blackfriars railway bridge. His family's meal consisted of a few dinner rolls he found in a dustbin. He explained to me that not long ago he had been perfectly healthy and they had a nice little council house in Fulham. He and his wife loved each other and the kids. Then he got rheumatoid arthritis and the doctors told him he couldn't work. The council came after him for the rent. The Social Services said they had no accommodation, but they could take the children into care. I – big shot that I thought I was – said to him, "Don't worry, mate. I'll telephone the people that can help you." I went back to my office and made a call to a charitable organization which purports to be an action group for the homeless. Do you know what this expensive charity replied? They said, "We don't take individual cases."

'"You don't care if these parents lose their children?" I protested.

'"I'm sorry, Mr Donleavy," they said again. "We don't handle personal cases."'

Nina was genuinely horrified. She knew battered children were taken away from dangerous parents, but surely state care wasn't supposed to take children away from good but impoverished parents.

'Anyway, I got in touch with another group, the good volunteers over at Latchmere House, and *they* fought hard for this family. I'm pleased to tell you the family are now back with their children,

170

rehoused in a liveable home. That was when I agreed to become a public spokesman for Latchmere House. And the volunteers there are owed our thanks for their work.'

His congratulations were greeted by more applause and he held up his hands to stop the ovation. 'I come from a broken home. I myself was homeless when I was seventeen. Homeless, my mother dead, and my father a violent and alcoholic lout. I wanted a different sort of life for myself but I've come to realize that I can't stay away. The homeless are my own people.' He paused and cleared his throat.

'All I want to do this evening is to ask that you, too, not look at the need and walk away. I ask for your help. Real help. A sign-up sheet is being circulated for those of you willing to volunteer at any number of good programmes, such as Latchmere House, who daily fight against the growing evil of homelessness within our own community. I ask for your time. Give of your time. Give of yourself. I don't care what your politics are. The problem is bigger than any political theory or bias. Our only hope is people helping people, and God help us all.'

He was clapped and cheered as he stepped down from the stage.

Nina signed the sheet when it came to her. What useful skills did she have? the sheet asked. 'Well, I can type,' she said aloud.

'Put that down,' said Gemma. 'And what hours are you free?'

'About ten in the morning, by the time I get the kids to school, until two in the afternoon.'

'We could do some evenings at Latchmere House,' said Marietta. 'What do you think?'

Gemma said she thought they should.

Marietta wrote their names down. 'I'm tired of sitting in on endless, fruitless hours of coffee shop discussion with well-meaning, middle class students. Let's go and find the man. I was really very impressed.'

Nina stood up, clutching her embarrassingly expensive handbag. She walked awkwardly behind Gemma and Marietta. They belonged here, with their casual clothes and their various badges.

Automatically she took the leaflets handed to her. Gemma and Marietta located Jimmy and were making arrangements and getting addresses. 'Latchmere house is in Hammersmith,' he said. 'Right on Shepherd's Bush Road. Very accessible.' He smiled at Nina over Gemma's shoulder.

'I'm one of your devoted listeners, Mr Donleavy. I'm so pleased to meet you.'

Nina knew her words sounded lame. What was worse, she felt her own accent to be conspicuously middle class, which made her feel inappropriate in this room full of people. Was she the only woman in the room to have enough money to sit in her Volvo while her house was cleaned for her? 'And I agreed with everything you said today. It's a terrible feeling to have the roof over your head threatened or taken away. I mean, that's not my situation, not exactly. But you never know. And you can love your house one minute, and all of a sudden someone tries to take it away . . .'

She realized that her words were words of fury. She also heard that everything was coming out badly. 'What I'm trying to say, really, is that it's still scary to have someone like my ex-husband, or soon-to-be-ex, trying to move you out of your own home. So I think

I can at least imagine a little bit of what the poor people you were talking about must feel like. Not that it's the same thing at all, but I just . . .'

She began to hate herself for being such an idiot until Jimmy looked at her with true reassurance in his eyes. 'It's never easy to face losing a home you love. And when things go wrong in middle class homes, middle class women can find themselves very lonely indeed because they have no one to tell their troubles to.'

Nina was relieved. 'I knew you'd understand,' she said. 'And most women are too ashamed to even admit they're being booted out. They leave bravely, say they've always wanted to live in the country. "So good for the children, horses and dogs and Wellington boots . . ."' Nina stopped talking. 'I'm so sorry,' she said. 'I don't know what got into me. I don't usually make speeches.'

'That's all right.' Jimmy took her hand. 'You obviously know my name. And you are . . . ?'

'Nina. I'm Nina . . . Tolmadge.'

Gemma grinned. 'First steps first, Nina. At least you got rid of his name.'

'Stockton, really,' Nina corrected herself. 'I'm afraid I can't pretend that quickly to be unmarried.'

Jimmy smiled. 'You've written down that you'd like to volunteer and do some work at Latchmere House. That's wonderful, Nina. We can use all the help we can get. What can you do?'

'Well, according to the employment agency, not much. I can type and make coffee, but that doesn't seem to matter any more.'

'That's my girl. It's a start. And I promise, once you get your feet wet, you'll see how habit-forming volunteer work can be. But come in and type what

173

needs to be typed. We'll see where things go from there. There's no end of work to be done. There's as much to do as you're willing to do. Coffee and typing it is. I drop by the Latchmere House office whenever I get a chance. I'll see you there.' He waved and was gone.

'Smug bastard, once you get a close look at him.' Gemma grunted.

'Oh, do you think so? He didn't seem that way at all to me.' Nina looked at her neat, polished shoes. That's my girl, he had said. *I wish I were his girl*, was the unbidden thought. I guess I'll have to shop at Oxfam from now on, she thought as she followed Marietta and Gemma out of the hall.

Chapter 23

Nina was pushing her way through a crowd of people and trying to follow Gemma and Marietta. The only other time she had been so near to panic in a crowd was at Harrods' yearly sale after Christmas. This, however, was not a Harrods crowd. 'Where are we going?' She grabbed Gemma's arm.

'To the pub.'

They found the car and Nina drove down long, narrow, treeless streets. 'How can people live here?' She did not mean to ask that question out loud.

'Nina, you're very spoiled. Most people have to live like this.'

Nina knew Gemma was right. They had been good friends since the time Nina arrived in London.

Gemma happened to meet Nina one day in a Russell Square spaghetti house. Although Gemma, a student at the LSE, had little in common on the surface with her, a secretary, Gemma took a liking to the shy country Nina. She introduced her to long walks along the River Thames and she tried to educate Nina about her own concerns.

It was a hopeless task. While Nina could weep over a story of a battered child, she could not focus on Gemma's esoteric lectures on the ills of society at large. For Nina only individual people were real; grand conceptual plans had little meaning. Even today, Nina had responded to the personal message given by Jimmy Donleavy yet was adrift in the political reasonings as to the roots of the problem at hand. Yes, homelessness had something immediate to do with Nina's life, Gemma knew. Nina had spent many nights twisting in her sleep dreaming about removal vans . . .

'Take a right turn,' Marietta directed, 'and then a sharp left.'

They were in the heart of a rough-looking neighborhood in Earl's Court. 'Don't you ever get afraid down here?' said Nina.

Gemma, sitting in the front passenger seat, shook her head. 'We are perfectly safe. We have nothing worth robbing. And anyway, people round here know us. It's our patch. There's a sort of bush telegraph if anyone new comes into the territory. We'll get asked questions about you, probably.' She grinned. 'Down here *you're* out of place, but where you live *we'd* be out of place. Funny, isn't it? Here people who have nothing also have nothing to hide from each other. Nobody needs to keep up appearances. We're all in the soup together. But once you start moving up in the world, then the need to conform and not to let the neighbours see your flaws gets bigger and bigger. There's the pub over there. Pull in at the car park.'

Marietta and Gemma pushed their way into the Saturday drinking crowd. 'Hi, Stanley,' said Gemma.

Stanley raised an eyebrow. For a huge man, he had a surprisingly childish voice. 'I've lost Kit, the little bugger. He was here only a minute ago.'

Nina saw that Stanley's eyes were full of worried tears.

'He'll be back in a minute, Stan.' Marietta put her arm around his waist. 'Come on. Have a drink with us, and don't get yourself into a state. Here, Nina, meet Stanley. You sit over there with him while we get the drinks. Stanley drinks beer. What will you have, Nina?'

'A gin and tonic, please. Can I pay for the first round?'

But Marietta was lost in the crowd and Nina found herself sitting next to Stanley. She had never found herself with a man beside her who also wore lipstick and eye shadow. Stanley peered at her, his thick fingers stole across the table to feel her brown jersey. 'That's a beautiful jumper,' he said. 'Lovely quality cashmere. Where did you get it?'

'At the Scotch House. I get all my cashmere there.'

'You must be rich then?'

'No, not really. Well, sort of middling. Actually, I'm about to be divorced, so I won't be buying much more cashmere.' How could she possibly be baring her soul to a man whom Simon would describe as a freak or a poofter?

'You must be so sad. I should get rid of Kit, but

we've been together for seven years now.' He sighed. 'He just cannot stay faithful. He's up some back alley right now, I expect, even as we speak, shagging some sailor and probably catching God knows what! I think he does it to make me jealous.' His eyes again filled with tears.

'Don't cry, Stanley.' Nina cupped his chin in her hands. 'You'd be better off on your own if your relationship makes you this unhappy. That's what I'm in the middle of discovering. I kicked my husband, Simon, out. He's gone off to live with his mistress, and for the first time in my life I'm living on my own.'

'No kids?'

'Yes, two. But this weekend they're with their father.' Nina smiled. 'Today has really been sort of an adventure.'

'To see how the other half lives?' There was no malice in the voice, no impatient snap as there often was in Gemma's. Just a quiet intensity, a gentle intuition.

'Maybe so.'

'You're friends with Gemma and Marietta?'

Nina nodded. 'I've known Gemma for years, but once I got engaged to Simon, we sort of drifted apart. Gemma sees Simon as the Number One Enemy of the People. I always thought she was being ridiculous, but now I'm not so sure. Maybe she was right all along.'

'They're a wonderful couple, those two. I envy them.'

Marietta elbowed through the crowd, Gemma following her. Nina took a sip. The gin was strong and the tonic sharp. Good heavens! she heard a voice in her head whisper. I'm sitting between a homosexual

177

and two lesbians. For a moment she felt a sense of unease, but then she smiled at Gemma and Marietta. 'Here's to you both,' she said and she raised her glass. 'And here's to the re-emergence of the phantom Kit.'

Three gin and tonics later, Kit did appear. He was a tall, fair-haired boy. What a waste, Nina thought, looking at him. He's quite beautiful. Kit stood behind Stanley, his graceful hand on Stanley's shoulder. 'Miss me, lover boy?'

Nina studied Stanley. She would be amazed if he were any older than thirty-two or thirty-three, yet he had about him the air of a bloom recently faded. He must have been spectacular-looking not long ago; already his light hair was thinning on his head and his plump midriff had lost whatever shape it once had. Kit, younger, clearly had not yet sacrificed anything to time.

Stanley pulled an empty chair forward. 'Actually, I've been too busy talking to my new friend, Nina. We will be friends, Nina, won't we?'

Nina saw a shadow pass over Kit's face at Stanley's words. He's jealous, she realized. 'Of course we will. I could do with a friend.'

'When will we see you again?' Stanley took a pen out of his pocket. 'We live in Crouch End.'

'Crotch End, as we call it.' Kit was sullen. 'Full of whores, lesbians and queers like us.'

Nina knew the remark was intended only to provoke her, so she made no reply.

Marietta stepped in. 'Don't be a bore, Kit. You ran off just to upset Stanley, and now you're cross because he's not in a dreadful state over you. Go and get yourself a drink and shut up. Everyone's having a perfectly happy day. How far out of your way must you go to spoil it?' There was a look of steel in Marietta's eyes.

Nina watched her, impressed.

'Here's our address and phone number, Nina.' Stanley handed her a slip of paper. 'And if you want to reach me at work, I work as a buyer in Jason's fabric shop.'

'Oh, I know Jason's. In the Haymarket?'

'That's right. Come by one day and we'll have lunch.'

'Yes, I must do that. Listen, I'd better get going now.' Nina looked at her watch.

'Why?' Gemma stared.

'Well, it's been a long day, and I really ought to go home. I've got lots of ironing to do, you see.'

'Are you always so highly organized?'

'Not always. Comes with motherhood, I guess. But I find it's now a habit. I'm like the white rabbit, running about looking at clocks and always in a panic, feeling I should be doing something useful.'

Gemma stood up. 'I'll walk you out to the car.'

'Goodbye, Marietta.' Nina put her hand on Marietta's arm. 'I'll telephone you, Stanley.' She gave him a smile. She glanced at Kit. There was no point in saying goodbye to him. He sat with his head bent over his pint of lager.

'What's the matter with Kit?' she asked Gemma when they were out of the pub.

'His mother and father were killed in a car accident when he was a child, so he was in care most of his life. Sexually abused, of course.'

'Why of course? There can't be that many sexual abusers around.'

'God, Nina, what planet do you live on? Just take my word for it. There are plenty. Anyway, he finally

179

got out at sixteen, met Stan at eighteen, and they've been together ever since. Poor Stan. What he won't accept is that Kit isn't really gay. He's just sexually delinquent, and when a better offer comes along, from either sex, he'll move on.'

Nina leaned against her car, feeling her face warm from the alcohol. 'Are you gay like Stanley, Gemma? I mean *really* gay?'

'Yes, I am.' Gemma's voice was quiet. 'I've never even entertained the thought of a relationship with a man. From as far back as I can remember, I always thought of myself in a relationship with a woman.'

'How about Marietta?'

'Marietta was married for years to a man who hit her and abused her. She lost her kids to him. She lost everything, even her home. She clings to me for now, but you can't be certain, at least *I* can't be certain, that one day she might not find another man and she'll leave me. The idea breaks my heart.'

Nina put her arm around the taut muscles of Gemma's neck. 'Oh, Gemma. Why does it all have to be so awful? I've lost Simon. You're afraid of losing Marietta. Stanley will lose Kit . . . What happened to us all? Is there no such thing as security?'

'I wish I knew.' Gemma hugged Nina. 'Drive carefully,' she said.

Nina left her standing on the grim pavement, a small determined creature with a white face. Pain.

Nina drove back down the streets. She had to concentrate until she reached the more familiar area around Hammersmith. The reason she left the pub she had not disclosed to Gemma. Gemma might not understand, but Stanley would. Nina very much wanted to get home to telephone Sonia and find out how Angela's dinner party had gone last night.

I wish getting a divorce were just like taking a sharp pair of scissors and cutting a ribbon in two. No, more like a worm, and each end crawls away forever. Why do I want to know anything about beastly Angela and Simon? I suppose – she put her key in the door – I suppose I hope they all had a perfectly rotten time.

Chapter 24

'It was weird as hell, that's how it was,' said Sonia down the telephone. 'There we were in this rather tiny flat with Simon sitting opposite Angela. Your kids were in the spare bedroom. Simon looked as if he'd been with Angela forever.'

Nina felt a pang. 'Did they say anything about me?'

'Noooo, not really. You were in the air, though. Everybody was trying so hard not to use your name, it was embarrassing. Susan was obnoxious, of course. She wants to live with them. I'd let her, if I were you. Angela tried to get her into bed before dinner, but no luck. That kid makes me glad to be childless. Was she born that way?'

'No. Well, maybe.' Nina lay on the sofa. She slipped off her shoes. She wiggled her stocking toes. 'I'm not sure. But from the start, she was horribly spoiled by Simon and his mother.'

'And now he's found the perfect little clone of his mother. I mean, you wouldn't have believed the hors d'oeuvres. Nasty bits of cheese pierced to the groin

181

by these awful cocktail sticks with coloured paper. The cheese was so heavily processed and pasteurized, it tasted like it never had anything to do with a real cow. The woman is tacky, I tell you. Downright tacky! But, listen, Nina. She's already talking about a four-bedroomed house. "A room for our baby," she said sweetly over the chocolate mousse. "And of course a room each for the children when they come to stay." That's the only time Simon snapped. "We'll see," he said. Angela withdrew the remark and mentioned that they really should have a granny flat for dear Enid. "Eventually she will come and live with us and we'll be one happy family."'

Nina laughed. 'She can try playing happy families with Susan around. Good luck to her!'

'She's got Susan eating out of her hand at the moment. She's taken the little bitch shopping today. And Hamish's doing the divorced child's day with Pop, while the two girls have woman time together. He's going to fly a kite with Simon on Parliament Fields.'

'But Simon doesn't know how to fly a kite, Sonia. He can't even tie a proper knot.'

'You didn't miss a thing by not being there, Nina. So don't worry at all. But you can rest assured that Simon's fallen into the hands of someone who's got his number. She's got him by the balls in her stubby little fingers and that rabbit tooth smile of hers. I wonder if she leaves lipstick on his prick?'

Nina looked at her feet. 'I don't know,' she said. 'And I don't care.'

'Hey, you sound terrible. You okay?'

'It's probably just that I've got four gins in my stomach and not much else.'

'Post-divorce drunkenness. Par for the course. Stay

away from the gin, is my advice. It's miserable stuff. Stick to wine instead.'

'Miserable stuff indeed.' The gin had given her a rolling headache.

'You know what?' said Sonia, as if arriving at a sudden revelation. 'You ought to read Kahlil Gibran. He wrote this great poem that begins, "Your children are not your children. They are the sons and daughters of Life's longing for itself." Something like that, though I'm terrible at quoting. But the point is you're hanging on too much to . . . to everything. If you don't mind my saying so. I mean, do you seriously plan to spend the rest of your life reacting to everything your ex-husband and his bitch of a secretary do? You ought to free yourself, or else you'll end up making yourself morbid.'

'What do you suggest I do instead?' Nina was not sure whether or not to feel offended.

'I'll tell you what. You should make plans for yourself. *Only* yourself. Where's the one place on earth you most want to go?'

'Greece,' Nina said without stopping to think, feeling herself free, if only momentarily.

'Greece? Fine. Greece it is.'

'What do you mean?'

'I mean we ought to plan to take a trip to Greece. You and I. Just the two of us. Why not this summer? Listen. Myles no doubt will do what he does every damn summer which is to spend the whole thing with his mummy. I sure as hell don't relish the thought of some gloomy English country house kissing Mummy's ass with Myles. I'd much rather disappear with you to some Greek island. That's the way you have to look at things from now on. Not shaping your life around everybody else's but making some plans of your own and let *them* do the accommodating for a change.'

'That's easy for you to say, Sonia, but what am I supposed to do with the kids?'

'Make them Simon's problem.'

'For the whole summer? I can't. Honestly, I just can't.'

'Promise me you'll think about it at least, will you?'

Nina ended the conversation and hung up the telephone without having promised anything. She roamed into the kitchen.

All alone on a Saturday night. She took two brown eggs from the fridge and marvelled at how odd it was to cook just two boiled eggs! Usually she made soft-boiled eggs for Sunday breakfast. Two for Simon, one for her, and one each for the children. Her two lonesome eggs lay forlornly in the saucepan. For four and a half minutes she stood at the counter waiting for the toaster to pop. She watched the eggs. If no cracks appeared, she told herself, she would take it as an omen that she would get to keep the house. If one egg cracked, she'd lose, but not too badly. If both cracked, she would face a disaster. The buzzer sounded and she turned it off with thankful fingers. Neither egg had cracked.

She noticed that, egg and spoon in hand, she was wandering unconsciously from room to room. Strange thing to do, she said to herself.

To fill the empty silence of the house she put on a record. Soon she was made to feel less alone by the sweet, reassuring sound of Beethoven's Archduke Trio, the music her only company. And suddenly she wondered if Jimmy Donleavy liked Beethoven. *That's my girl*, he had said. *That's my girl*.

Nina entered the kitchen again and looked at her

coffee pot. 'You,' she said to the pot, 'I intend to donate to the office at Latchmere House.' To make coffee, she added mentally, for Jimmy Donleavy.

Chapter 25

'Cal, what a surprise! I didn't know you'd be here.' Nina stood in the doorway puffing. The office for the homelessness charity in Latchmere House was up three flights of stairs from the street along Shepherd's Bush Road. 'What do you do here?'

'Just giving a hand. It is Nina, isn't it?'

'Yes.' Nina was amazed to find herself pleased to see a familiar face, even if the face belonged to Cal. She had learned her lesson from the conference, so today she wore plain jeans and a sweater. 'I saw Jennifer this morning, and she didn't mention you'd be here.'

Cal's brow creased. 'Yeah, well things got a little hot over there. Come in. Is that a coffee pot you're carrying?'

'Yes. I thought I'd donate it, if that's all right.'

'Much appreciated. We need *everything*.'

'What d'you mean everything got hot over at Jennifer's?'

Cal smiled grimly. 'Ah well. You see, Jennifer and Ziggy and I were kind of having a consciousness-raising session.' Cal swept a pile of newspapers and booklets to the floor. 'It got . . . well, we were all rapping about how we felt about each other. And I said I felt it was terrible that Ziggy was laying Neville because if we were all sisters, we wouldn't screw each other up.'

'You didn't! But, anyway, Ziggy insisted that Jennifer tacitly knew she was having an affair with Neville.'

'Yeah, well that's just it. She probably did sort of know, and that was okay with her. But she didn't actually want it out in the open. She got *unbelievably* pissed off with Ziggy and she chucked Neville out.'

'Really! Poor Jennifer,' said Nina.

'Poor George. He's probably the one who's been betrayed the worst. He never knew a thing about anything. And God knows if anyone will tell him what's going on now.'

Nina said, 'Hm. You're right. But I wonder why I'm surprised to hear you siding with a man in this situation.'

'It's wrong for people to betray people, whatever sex they are.'

For the first time, Nina began to think she had misjudged Cal when she met her at Jennifer's house. Worse still, Nina realized she owed Cal an apology for having been rude. 'You know, Cal, it looks like we'll be working together from now on. And . . . What I'm trying to say is I think we got off on rather the wrong foot when we met at Jennifer's. Some of what I said I shouldn't have, or at least I should have said it in a different way. But really . . .'

'No sweat.'

'I beg your pardon?'

'I said don't sweat it. All is forgotten. You and I met today for the first time. We're starting from scratch. Okay?'

Nina smiled. 'Tell me what I can do to help. And thanks.'

Cal looked around the dingy room. Along one wall were brown carrier bags full of letters. 'We'd better start dealing with some of the mail. Can you work a typewriter?'

'I'll try. I haven't typed for ages, though.'

'Right now, you're the best we've got, and that makes you pretty good.'

The door opened quickly. Several chattering young women came in. 'We got the posters for our rally, Cal . . . Oh, you've got someone with you.'

'Hey, come on in. There's someone you ought to meet. Sally, Virginia, and Ronni, meet Nina. She's our new sister. Nina, these women work downstairs in the Women's Liberation Front. I'm with them in spirit, but I spend my time up here volunteering for the homeless. In the other office is the group called We The People – a great gathering of leftist minds. All different branches of the same tree.'

'Hello,' said Nina. There was a moment's silence. Three frozen faces stared at Nina but she held her ground. She was very aware that she was wearing lipstick and mascara. They were not.

'Which group are you from?' Virginia had an imperious air about her.

'I'm not from any group.'

'Then how did you get here?'

'I went to a conference last weekend with two friends of mine.'

'Mind giving their names?'

'No, not really.' Nina looked sideways at Cal.

Cal shrugged her shoulders. 'She's okay, Virginia. I'll vouch for her.'

The three faces relaxed.

'We can't be too careful.' Sally grinned. 'The pigs keep trying to infiltrate. Mind what you say on the telephone. We think they've tapped the phones in all the offices in Latchmere House. Our office downstairs, yours up here . . .'

For a moment Nina thought the world had gone crazy. 'The pigs?'

Ronni had short dark hair and a pair of snapping turtle eyes. 'Police, you know? Where the hell have you been all your life?'

'Having babies,' Nina said humbly.

'Oh. That would explain it.'

'Surely you don't count having babies as a crime?'

'No, not in itself. As long as you don't have a boy.'

'Virginia is a militant feminist separatist,' Cal explained. 'She lives with the others in a squat in Islington. I crash there some of the time myself. I think of these women as my family. Do you all want coffee?'

'Yeah.' Sally bent over the pile of letters on the rickety typing table. 'Is Jimmy Donleavy, your office hero, coming by today?'

'In a couple of hours,' Cal said.

'Lucky you.' Expertly Sally flipped open several letters. 'Great! Somebody sent in a donation of fifteen quid. We needed that.' She put it in her pocket.

Nina frowned. 'Um. Isn't that for *this* office? I mean, whoever took the trouble of making that donation, didn't they intend for it to go to the homeless?'

'But I *am* homeless. We live in a squat. Close enough to being on the streets for you? Anyway, we don't have any of that bourgeois crap. Like Cal said, we're all branches of the same tree.'

'But do you *have* to squat? I mean, if you got a

188

paying job as well as your volunteer work down-stairs, wouldn't you be able to rent some nice place of your own so you wouldn't have to squat? And by the sound of it, I'd say you speak very well. Your voice sounds as if you must have gone to a good school yourself.'

'Beaudon, actually,' Virginia said stiffly. 'Terrible place. Ought to be blown up.'

'You can't be serious! Beaudon's an excellent school. One of the best. I've got two cousins who went there, and they both loved it. How about you, Sally?'

'Darlington.'

'Another wonderful school. And you, Ronni?'

Ronni made the face of someone caught out. 'St Anthony Girls.'

'So you're not actually homeless then. Not with your backgrounds. You *choose* to be homeless. That's very different.'

Cal unplugged the kettle. 'Yeah, if you want to look at things that way. I mean, I'm the only one here who really did come from a rotten background. My mom was *really* poor. We lived outside LA in a trailer park. But don't you see, Nina? We're all in this together now. We're here to organize as women. I'm commit-ted to helping the homeless, and I'll work with any-one to help that cause. Now if you three will kindly make yourselves scarce for a while, Nina and I have work to do up here. You can take your coffees back to your office with you, but don't forget to bring back the cups.'

Virginia paused at the door. 'I say, Cal. I'm sorry about last night, but Sally really needed me.'

'So I heard,' Cal said dryly. 'So I heard.'

Virginia waved her hand.

Nina heard the young women clatter down the stairs. She saw Cal's face flush. 'Is that your girl-friend, Cal?'

'Yep.'

'Is she unfaithful?'

Cal nodded. 'All the time. But I can't get over her. She's so cute when she wants to be.'

'And that's why you let them take money that's not theirs?'

Cal's fraught face seemed to go through many bewildering emotions. 'Look, Nina. Don't ask too many questions. You may not like the answers. Let's get down to business with the mail, okay?'

Reading the letters, Nina found her eyes filling with tears. *'God bless you, Latchmere House. I heard the good things Jimmy Donleavy had to say about you, and I just had to write and send a little something to help you in your work. I've listened to Jimmy on the radio for years, and his voice is like a friend to me . . .'*

'I am an old age pensioner and I remember the War when we was bombed out and had to live in the London Underground . . .'

'Dear Mr Donleavy, I saw you on the telly and enclose a cheque for ten pounds to help house the homeless. I know it's not much, but I was homeless, believe it or not, when I was in my early twenties. I had two young children and my husband was very violent. He beat all of us and abused us. He was a solicitor, so I did not stand much of a chance if I tried to take action against him. So I left, taking the children with me. Thanks to my faith in God and to a good social worker, I found a flat and then got remarried to a wonderful man . . .'

Tears were running down Nina's face. She felt a warm hand on her shoulder from behind. 'It does get to you at times, doesn't it?'

Nina sniffed. 'I haven't got a hankie . . . Oh! Jimmy! I mean, Mr Donleavy. Hello.'

'Jimmy. Please.'

Nina was embarrassed to be seen with her face messy from crying. 'You must excuse me,' she laughed.

'They say that if you smile through tears, somewhere else God makes a rainbow.' Jimmy grinned. He gave her his handkerchief. 'And ever since Noah, the rainbow is God's promise that He'll take care of everything. So if you smile enough, He'll make all your troubles go away.'

'I wish He would.'

No, I won't burden him with all my troubles, she thought, afraid of becoming a bore. When she had wiped her eyes, she said, 'It's nice to see you again, Jimmy.'

'And you. Nina, right? Yes, I like to drop by whenever I can, just to see how everything is getting on. So tell me, how is everything getting on?'

'Fine. I've only been here such a short while. But fine so far. Actually, Jimmy, I was thinking. It seems there are so many letters to answer, how about I take them home with me and I can do them at night when the children are in bed?'

'Now there's a good idea. But won't your husband object?'

'There is no husband.' Her voice very subtly left the door open to the question in his eyes.

'Oh. That's right. You told me at the meeting he was giving you a hard time. Well, that'll be grand then. Absolutely grand. Very good of you to try so hard. What have we made, Cal?'

Cal did a quick calculation. 'About seventy-eight pounds in donations so far this morning.'

Minus fifteen pounds swiped by the girls from downstairs, thought Nina. If I take the letters home, at least they can't steal from the homeless.

The telephone rang. 'Yeah?' Cal frowned. 'I don't know the answer to that one. I heard something about the Hampstead group threatening to fight the Leeds group if they carry their Trotsky banners on the march, but that's more the Women's Liberation Front department . . . Sorry. You'll have to ask downstairs. Virginia, Sally, and Ronni are down there now. Remind them to bring their cups back up here, will you?' She hung up.

Overhearing, Nina said, 'What was that all about? I thought the office downstairs was devoted to women caring about each other. Not about Trotsky and all that.'

Cal grinned. 'You're a baby in this forest, Nina.' Then she muttered, mostly to herself, 'She doesn't begin to understand.'

'Pay no attention, Nina,' Jimmy cut in. 'It's just rubbish, all that muck. Political in-fighting is all, and nothing ever came of that. Stick to thinking about the homeless in this office and you can't go wrong. That's all any of us need to worry about. It's the homeless who need our help,' Jimmy said shortly, 'not the economists or the political theorists.' He glanced at his watch. 'Look, I've got to run. Just thought I'd have a look in. I'm really pleased to see you're here, Nina. How much time can you give us?'

He has such lovely Irish blue eyes, she thought. 'Every weekday from about ten to about two-thirty.'

'That's great.' He put his hand back on her shoulder. 'Remember, however much the letters hurt to read, you are making an effort to get things changed. That in itself counts for a lot. I've got to dash off and buy some fireworks for my kids. I'll be picking them up from my ex-wife tomorrow.'

'Oh! I'd completely forgotten. Guy Fawkes! Bonfire night. I'll get some for mine and then they'll plan to go over to my ex-husband's for another firework party. It's all so odd! Suddenly you have one toothbrush instead of two. You pour one glass of wine instead of two. But now the kids will have to get used to two of everything. Two celebrations. My firework party, then Simon's. My Christmas, and then Simon's. Very strange.'

'Not after a while it isn't.' Jimmy's eyes grew sombre. 'After a while it's just a matter of staying afloat in your children's eyes. "Are my rockets as big as my ex-wife's?" That sort of thing. My ex-wife cleaned me out and is married to a millionaire. I can't offer my kids a weekend in his private plane in Deauville. The best I can manage is my service flat and an Indian takeaway.'

Nina smiled. 'I've still got the house, but Daddy is rapidly becoming the Prince and I'm the Ugly Witch that makes them tidy their rooms and do their homework. I think mine just feel sorry for their poor old Dad who has to do his own ironing. Which, if you ask me, is probably a mercy, because I was never any good at ironing anyway.'

'I really *must* run,' said Jimmy, his face revealing the fact that he would rather not leave at all. 'Bye, Cal.' He smiled at Nina. 'Bye bye, Nina my girl.' And he was gone.

He said it again, she thought, calling me his girl. For Nina, a light went out when he left the room. 'You know, Cal, I always assumed that Jimmy Donleavy was a secure, successful man. But his life hasn't been all that easy. No wonder he's so good with all those people that ring in. Whatever possessed his wife to leave him?'

Cal looked at Nina. 'I guess some women just don't get turned on by good guys. Don't let Virginia ever know I said that, will you? They hate him downstairs. They think he's just a bored celebrity who's only pretending to have a social conscience. They think he's only in this for the publicity. But I think his heart really is in the right place. He's not just a famous spokesman; he really cares. God, don't *ever* tell them downstairs I said that. But it's the truth. He's a good guy. And I guess my record's pretty terrible for teaming up with the wrong people. I always seem to pick women who look like my mom, and then I kill myself trying to reform them. My mom tried her best, but she was a drunk, and when she drank she chased after any man who'd have her. There isn't much I haven't seen. Or heard, for that matter . . .' Cal stopped herself. 'Hey, I'm talking too much. The point is, I guess, Latchmere House is a funny place. They say everybody in the charity world is really only there to sort out their own problems. Probably true. I guess I'm no exception.' She smiled. 'Good to have you aboard, Nina.'

Nina found herself liking Cal. 'Good to be here.' She started collecting the pile of unopened letters to work on at home. 'I'd better get moving, too. I've got to get to Hamley's and get some fireworks. See you tomorrow?'

'You bet. And I'll get some decent coffee to put in your coffee pot.' She stretched.

'You get the coffee, and I'll bring you some doughnuts. You like doughnuts?'

'Love them.'

'Then, it's a deal.' Nina stood up and realized she

194

was stiff from sitting on the spindly chair. She kissed Cal on the cheek. 'See you tomorrow.'

She ran down the stairs. Soon the Volvo was absorbed in the traffic streaming around Shepherd's Bush Green. I'm going to be a little late picking the kids up, she thought. Oh well. It's the first time I've ever been late. They can play until I get there. The traffic was dense all the way to Hamley's, but she managed to park nearby. Inside she chose ten very large rockets. We might as well have ten stupendous bangs rather than dozens of cheap little squibs. She paid and walked back to the car and put the rockets in the luggage space. They looked magnificently menacing. She laughed at the thought that Simon never would have allowed her to buy ten. Ten would make him throw up his hands in horror and deliver a famous Simon lecture about cutting back on expenses. Well, the hell with him. Jimmy would have been delighted to see her buy ten.

'Wow!' Hamish was ecstatic. 'Look at those rockets!'

'You're late, Mum. Everybody's gone home. There's just Hamish and me left.'

'Sorry, but I was working and I had to drive all the way to Hamley's to get the fireworks. Do you know, Susan, after all these years, I actually *forgot* all about November the Fifth! And it used to be my most favourite occasion. Get in, kids, and let's get home.'

'Daddy says he'll pick us up at eight.'

'Great, Susan. I've got such a lot of work to do tonight.'

'What sort of work, Mum?' Hamish was sitting at the far end of the car, cradling the rockets in his arms.

'I'm answering letters for the campaign for the

homeless. It's all very sad, but at least I'm doing something about it, so I don't feel so upset.'

'Are you getting paid for it?'

Trust Susan, thought Nina. 'No, I'm not getting paid at all. That's why it's called volunteering.'

'You do it for nothing?'

'I have time on my hands, and you're both at school. What do you think I should do?'

'Get a proper job like Jennifer. Jennifer's split up with Neville. Hortense told me today. It's still a secret. Jennifer says she won't put up with him impressing her any more.'

'The word is *oppressing*. Anyway, I know they've split up.'

'How did you know, Mum? Hortense said it was a secret.'

'Oh, I have my sources, Susan. I know I've been an apple pie mother, but now I get around. Poor Jennifer. It must be hard on her.'

'Hortense says Jennifer is fine. It's her dad who's very sad. He's moved to a bedsit.'

'Serves Neville right.' Nina took a right turn a little too sharply. 'He should have thought of that before he had an affair.' She straightened out the car. 'Do you want me to make baked potatoes stuffed with chives and sour cream? We can stand outside and the potatoes will keep our hands warm. And this year you can help me let the fireworks off, Susan.'

'Daddy usually does that.'

'Hamish, you can set the rockets up in the bottles.'

Hamish grinned. 'Okay.'

'We don't need the potatoes, Mum. Angela has a whole crowd of people coming around, and she's making food.'

'Her cooking is awful. Yuk!' Hamish stuck his

tongue out. 'She makes us eat meat with fat still on it. I'll have a baked potato.'

The rockets were marvellous. Hamish and Nina stood in the garden and craned their necks watching the explosions high in the sky. Susan declined to join them. She stood by the kitchen window for the first few and then sat in front of the television.

'I like the Screaming Tailer best, Mum.' Hamish was alight with joy. 'It's the very best I've ever seen.'

Nina had saved that rocket for last. She held Hamish's hand. The rocket climbed into the sky, its tail ablaze like a heaven-bound shooting star. 'It really screams, Hamish. Listen to it!' She wondered, as the rocket shot into oblivion, if Jimmy would also be alone tonight. Or maybe he had his children for the whole night. No, probably not, she decided. A small service flat can't compete with a millionaire's firework party.

The garden was dark now. In past years, Bonfire Nights had been a meeting place for their friends. Tonight, as she and Hamish walked back alone up the steps to the kitchen, she took from his hand the baked potato's leftover aluminium foil. There were crumbs of potato at the corners of his mouth and his lips were shining from the butter. 'Thanks, Mum,' he said. 'That was fantastic.'

She heard Simon's car door slam round the front of the house. She marvelled at the fact that she could recognize the slamming as Simon's. She also knew how many steps it took him to get up the path and how many times he would wipe his feet on the door-mat. And then . . . Yes. There was his cough.

She kissed Hamish on the forehead. He was

wrapped up in a coat and hat. 'Keep your ears warm, darling. The wind is bitter tonight.'

The car door slammed again and Nina's children were gone.

Chapter 26

A new routine formed in Nina's life, a routine that gradually came to centre more and more on Latchmere House. During the day Nina became adept at meeting all of the administrative needs of a project for the homeless. At night she devoted herself to answering the many letters from the public offering moral and financial support to the charity.

She had developed an easy, steady friendship with Cal. Sonia was always only a phone call away. Jennifer surprised Nina by turning up on her doorstep one weekend. She invited herself in for coffee and proceeded to pour out her sadness at just how much Neville and Ziggy each had hurt her by betraying her. Nina offered what sympathy she could, saying yes, she knew first-hand how deep the pain was when someone you thought you loved turned around and kicked your teeth in. The trick was to hold firm to your principles and not to be afraid to stay on your own, even if being alone often meant being lonely as well.

She said she was thinking of throwing a party, and Jennifer ought to cheer herself up by coming. Then, in an effort to make Jennifer feel better, she invited her to join Sonia and herself on their summer trip to

Greece, for the trip was taking firmer shape in Nina's desires. Jennifer thanked Nina for her time and for the invitation. She said she'd have to think about it.

Oh, and by the way, said Jennifer before leaving, she had heard from Cal – whom Jennifer had decided to bless after all for showing her the truth about Neville – that Nina was getting on very well indeed with Jimmy Donleavy during his regular visits to Latchmere House. 'Any chance of romance?'

Nina laughed and said she didn't know. What she would have said, if she could have given expression to her deepest feelings, was that she was very grateful for her growing friendship with Jimmy. It was almost inconceivable that a man of his fame should suddenly be her friend. She found him honest, open-hearted, and generous of spirit. She liked the way his bright face seemed to shine with extra radiance whenever he turned his eyes to her. And she felt herself glowing in return whenever she knew he was due to drop by. But . . . What was the but? Nina could not admit aloud that her nocturnal fantasies – when alone at night, sleeping or half-awake, her fingers found their way to seek soft satisfaction – did not include Jimmy. Her fantasies were in the exclusive domain of another man, a man who could be hers only in fantasy for surely, during more wakeful hours, her rational mind told her how impossible it was that she would ever be face to face again with Michael Morningstar.

From Jimmy Donleavy she received soothing, healing warmth. Her darker thoughts yearned for something more intoxicating. But these impressions were so shapeless, so hidden, that Nina kept them secret, even from herself.

*

The idea of giving her own party excited Nina and she enjoyed making the round of telephone calls to invite her friends. 'The kids will be away Saturday night,' she told Sonia. 'So I'll have the place to myself and Susan can't spy on us.'

'In that case I'd love to come. Anybody in mind for me to sexually cannibalize?'

'I was thinking of inviting Jimmy Donleavy, actually.'

'*The* Jimmy Donleavy? The radio presenter with the lovely Irish voice? Oh, do invite him, Nina. I'll wear my briefest dress.'

'If you really must.' Nina tried to stem the disapproval in her voice. 'I'll ask him.' Nina put down the telephone. Shit, she thought. I'm jealous. I only have to mention Jimmy's name, and already Sonia is planning to lasso him.

She picked up the phone again and dialled the number for Jason's fabric shop where Stanley worked. Yes, Stanley said, of course he remembered her. 'You were wearing a lovely cashmere jumper and your crocodile handbag was exquisite. Hermes?'

'Naturally,' Nina laughed.

He said he'd love to come to her party, and he'd bring Kit along, too. 'I'll be in my best frock,' promised Stanley.

Hanging up, Nina invited Cal when she walked into the office. Suddenly caught in a momentary panic, Nina feared what the neighbours along Angel Walk, Richmond would think if they suspected that the person in the dress was no woman at all but was Stanley instead.

'But what will the neighbours say?' Nina said, putting her hand over her mouth. 'I never thought I'd hear myself say that sentence. Simon said it all the time.'

Cal laughed. 'I think most neighbours could do with some healthy upsetting.'

'Who's planning to upset the neighbours?' Jimmy's voice floated across the room.

'Oh, it's nothing, Jimmy. Just a party I'm giving on Saturday. Cal's coming, and some people I know. You're welcome to come too, if you'd like. You know Gemma and Marietta?'

'Sure I do. They're doing a grand job volunteering at the night-time shift. I can get a babysitter for the boys, and I'll enjoy a night out. Can I bring anything?'

'Don't worry. I'll see it's all there.'

'Let me bring some Guinness. I get it straight from Dublin. It's as dark and frothy as the Irish Sea.'

'That would be great. I'll see if Porch's have some oysters.'

'You do that.'

Nina turned over a pile of letters with a sigh. 'Hundreds of letters still coming in,' she said. 'I can't understand it. Why is there still such a need, with all the money taxpayers pay? Things seem to be getting worse, not better.'

'For every person who is homeless, Nina, there are at least three busybody bureaucrats to take care of him. He has a social security officer paid to see he's not given enough money to get himself a decent room, a social worker to drive him to the Social Security office. If he gets into trouble trying to stay alive on the streets, he gets a probation officer who will have meetings with his social worker. And when the poor bugger gets himself into more trouble, the bureaucrats have a picnic, all getting together to talk about him in their endless case conferences. Then they stick him in jail or bung him off to a mental hospital. End of problem. For the time being

201

anyway.' Jimmy moved over to the coffee pot. 'Coffee, both of you?'

They both nodded.

'Same old story,' Jimmy continued. 'Bureaucracies and overgrown institutions thrive on the administration of human misery, and only seem to make themselves stronger at the end of the day. That's why it's so important for *us* to be different. If a family comes to us, we'll see that they are housed. You don't see most of the homeless. They aren't around at this time of day. Gemma and Marietta get them up here in the evenings, and boy do they fight to get them a place! The Salvation Army are our best allies. Aunt Sally's been around a long time. If I had my way, I'd hand over all the money for the homeless to the Salvation Army and let them do the job. Far better than most so-called experts doing nothing but getting into each other's knickers every chance they get at seminars, symposiums, and the endless circuit of useless conferences.'

Cal agreed with everything he said.

Nina took her mug of coffee from Jimmy's squat brown hands, so unlike Simon's long thin fingers. Jimmy's hands were designed to dig potatoes. Peasant hands, Simon would say, but Simon no longer had any say. Sonia will bag Jimmy, Nina thought resentfully. I don't stand a chance.

Briefly, before the lights changed on the way to school to collect the children, she wondered how his hands would feel on the inside of her thighs. She was amazed by the magnitude of her own desire, delighted to entertain lustful thoughts at last about Jimmy. She felt two bright burning spots in her cheeks. Well, even if Sonia does try to get him, I'll give her a run for her money. Sisterhood is powerful, she muttered to herself, but not powerful when we want the same man; that's when things turn competitive. I'm going out to get myself an outrageous dress. Stanley won't be the only one in a killer frock.

'Where are you going in that dress?' Susan was at her familiar post by the bedroom door that evening while Nina tried on her new outfit. 'You look like a tart.'

'Thank you, Susan, for the vote of confidence. But the fact is I don't look like a tart. You're just not used to me wearing a miniskirt. Anyway, I'm not going anywhere. I'm staying right here and giving a party on Saturday night. You won't be here. You'll be with your father.'

Susan lolled against the doorpost. 'Who's coming to your party?'

'Sonia and Jennifer are the only ones you'd know. The others are people I work with.'

'The people Daddy says are pinkos and bolshies.'

'Bolshies is a silly, old-fashioned word. Your daddy is a bit behind the times. My friends are merely trying to help homeless people to find a place to live. They don't just sit in offices shuffling pieces of paper. They get something done. Anyway, run off and do your homework. I've got some samosas to make.'

'Hortense isn't allowed to play with Emma and Cassandra any more, not since Jennifer isn't speaking to Ziggy.'

'Well, I'm not speaking to Ziggy either.'

'Does that mean I can't play with Emma and Cassandra either?'

'No, of course not. You can play with anyone you like.'

'Oh good. Cassandra had her first period and Ziggy

is giving her a party after school on Friday to celebrate.'

'Celebrate? What a strange idea!'

'Don't be silly, Mum. To celebrate being a woman. Cassandra can have babies now.'

'Don't call me silly, Susan. That's rude. I'm your mother. And Cassandra is not a woman at the age of eleven. Her period is her own business. It's something you discuss with your mother and no one else. Good heavens! Is nothing private any more?'

'Emma says in America children stay in their parents' bed and watch them make love.'

'I don't believe you. You just made that up.'

Susan crossed her arms. 'I did *not* make it up. Emma saw it in a book called *Show and Tell*. It teaches parents how to raise children who aren't inhabited.'

'Inhibited.'

'Ziggy has the book in her house, and I saw it.'

'You saw it?' Nina studied her daughter. 'Well, I want you to know that I think walking around naked in front of children is immodest and disgusting. I think the *Show and Tell* book ought to be banned. When you're old enough to find a man who really loves you and wants to marry you, *then* you're old enough to make love. Not before. Making love is not a matter of having period parties. It's a very sacred act blessed by God.'

Susan grinned. She frightened Nina. When she grinned like that, it was as if an evil demon lurked in her eyes, as if the child was not and never had been a child. 'Hortense says never trust anybody over thirty. So we'll just wait and see. Anyway, Cassandra gets to wear lipstick any time she wants. Can I?'

'Absolutely not. You're much too young to wear

make-up, even if you do insist on making friends with much older girls.'

'That's because my age group is so boring. All they think about is horses and hockey.'

'What's wrong with horses and hockey?'

'If you don't know, Mum, I can't tell you.'

'Listen, go and telephone your father and ask him to make the arrangements to get you to Cassandra's party. It's his job to pick you up from here, and it's my weekend off.'

When Nina was alone again in her room, she stared into the mirror to double-check the way she looked in her new dress. It *was* a very pretty little red dress. The décolleté bustline showed the smooth, round mounds of her breasts. The material fell from the bust to the tops of her thighs.

I've put on a bit of weight, she thought, but that's a good thing. My legs don't look like matchsticks any more. She decided Jimmy might well like her legs. Here I am, a thirty year old woman, feeling like a teenager again. The sad days are still there, but they come less and less.

'I must talk to you.' Simon's face was white.

'So talk.'

'Not on the doorstep. The neighbours will hear.'

'No, they won't, Simon. I don't think anybody's sitting beside their window listening.' Nina's teeth were chattering in the cold, late November air. 'What do you want?'

'I want a quick divorce, Nina. Angela wants the baby to be born legitimate. That means we have to divorce on the grounds of unreasonable behaviour.'

'Whose?'

'Why, yours, of course.'

'*Mine?*' Nina's teeth stopped chattering. A surge of rage brought the blood into her face. 'What the hell are you talking about? You left me for your fucking whore of a secretary, and I'm the one who's supposed to be unreasonable?'

'Please, Nina. There's no reason to yell like this.'

Nina could see various curtains twitching in the front windows of houses along the road. Good, she thought. They'll all have something to talk about. Even more after tomorrow night's party.

'You know I can't afford the stigma of unreasonable behaviour on my count, Nina. Not with my job. It wouldn't do. It just would not do.'

She could see both children's faces pressed against the car window. Susan hooted the horn loudly and called out, 'Come on, Dad! I'll be late for my party!'

'Think about it, Nina. Promise me you'll give it some serious thought.'

'Serious thought? Oh fuck off, Simon. There's nothing to think about. Absolutely nothing.' She walked back into the house and slammed the door.

Saturday morning Nina awoke in the quiet of the house. She could luxuriate in a leisurely morning of reading the papers. Slowly she walked down the stairs to the kitchen and put the kettle on. Doris had done a wonderful job of cleaning. The place was spotless. Nina opened the fridge and inspected plate upon plate filled with various delicacies. All that was left was to pick up fresh salad from Mrs Porter's greengrocers and the oysters from Porch's to go with Jimmy's Guinness.

Nina got to Mrs Porter's shop at two o'clock in the afternoon. Mrs Porter seemed glad to see her. ' 'e died, you know.' Her kindly face was suffused with sorrow.

'Who died?'

'Why, the old fellow you used to ask after.'

'You don't mean the music professor?'

'The very one. He was found in the park on his favourite bench. Stone cold dead, 'e was. All froze up. Stiff as a board, the park attendant said.'

Mrs Porter's husband came along and shook his head. 'It's a bad business when an old fellow like that freezes to death right out in front of all them big houses. But 'ere.' Mr Porter put his hand on Nina's arm. 'He 'ad ever such a happy smile on his face, 'e did. Even in death. The park attendant was quite choked up telling us about it, really, as if he'd seen heaven for 'imself. More likely got a glimpse of his dear old wife, I said, and he knew 'e'd be seeing her again.'

Nina felt her throat tighten. Her eyes filled with tears. 'How awful. How absolutely awful!'

''tis, madam. 'tis indeed. Didn't 'appen in my day, I tell you. We was all family round here in me young days. Me gran lived over there, and me aunts that never married. There was always a door open for me and the brothers and sisters. An old bloke like that'd have family to look after him, back then. It's all changed, though, hasn't it? Now that the council's moved all the people out of these roads and into the new estates in the countryside. A new life, they promise. Gardens for the children to play in. No crime, good schools . . . Most of them went, silly fools, and then in came the rich folk. Bought the old 'ouses cheap from the council. Good for business, though. Mustn't grumble. But they don't talk to the likes of me. "Half a pound of carrots,

Porter! There's a good chap!" That's all I ever get from 'em.'

Nina watched the old man and his wife with sympathy.

'I'm sorry the professor died, Mr Porter.' Nina chose her lettuce. 'I know it's a silly thing to say, but at least he's at peace now.'

Nina drove to collect the oysters. She did not know what to feel about the death of the old man. A vague sense of guilt lingered.

Chapter 27

'I thought I'd arrive a little early to give you a hand.' Sonia stood on the doorstep, smiling.

'Wow! You look stunning.' Nina welcomed her in. 'You know, I can't believe how nervous I am. Isn't that silly? And it feels so strange to organize a party without Simon hanging about, getting in the way. Usually by this time we'd both be shouting at each other. I'm afraid I haven't decanted the wine. It's just plonk. Simon took the decent stuff with him.'

Sonia walked into the kitchen. Nina followed, thinking I'll never in a million years look like Sonia. She always seems to have walked out of a fashion magazine. Not a hair out of place, her black high-heels gleaming, her lipstick . . . 'How do you keep your fingernails from chipping, Sonia? I did my nails this afternoon, and then I chipped that one opening the tin of cashew nuts.'

Sonia sat down at the kitchen table. She spread her hands. Ten immaculate, long, perfectly-sculptured fingernails lay on the table. 'Living with a man like Myles, darling. I have plenty of time to do my nails. And whenever I can at the magazine office, I get my secretary to do my typing for me. All you have to do is keep them out of water for sixteen hours after you polish them.'

'Sixteen hours? Seriously? But I don't think my hands are *ever* out of water for sixteen hours.'

'Hm. That's a problem. Well, the only other piece of advice is don't have kids if you ever expect to have long nails.'

'Sometimes I think that's not such a bad idea. I'm afraid I'm getting quite used to weekends on my own. The peace and independence feel almost dangerously addictive.'

'There's nothing dangerous about enjoying being on your own from time to time. Now, Nina, my hostess, what are you giving me to drink tonight? Do you have any vodka?'

'You're in luck.'

'Then I'd love a vodka and tonic. I'll pour. You have enough on your hands already. Can I get you one, too? Why don't you try a vodka with me, Nina? Makes a nice change from wine.'

Nina was glad that she had downed the rather strong vodka when the doorbell rang and she opened the door to see Stanley standing out front wearing a large fur coat and a great deal of make-up. He carried a large black handbag. 'Good heavens, Stanley! You weren't joking about your best frock, were you? Do come in.'

Stanley opened his coat and slowly twirled around. The dress was a 1950s shirtwaister with a black cinch belt. 'You don't see many of these dresses any longer, and more's the pity.'

Kit gave Stanley a shove from behind. 'Get indoors, you old queen. Poor Nina's neighbours will be having a fit. You should have seen him dressing up. He's been at it all day.'

Stanley leaned forward and studied Nina's face intently. Nina backed into the hall. 'Mascara's all right, love, but your foundation is much too yellow.'

'You think so?' Nina was embarrassed by her own lack of skill in putting on make-up.

'I know so. Let's go upstairs and we'll start again. Can't have your friends thinking you're suffering from jaundice, can we now? Stop primping in the hallway mirror, Kit. One should try to keep one's vanity a secret.'

Nina called Sonia. 'Come and meet Stanley, Sonia. And this is his . . . This is Kit.'

'His boyfriend,' Kit offered helpfully. 'How do you do?' Tonight Kit was in a good mood. His fair hair stood in a halo around his face.

Sonia smiled. 'Hi, both of you. What do you want to drink? I'm tending bar tonight.'

'I'll just pop upstairs with Stanley. He says my foundation is the wrong colour, so can you give Kit whatever he wants to drink? I'd love another vodka, please.'

'Sherry for me,' Stanley put in.

Kit ambled off into the kitchen. Nina hurried upstairs, while Stanley appraised all that he saw. 'Um. Nice place you have here. Must have cost quite a bit.'

Nina tried not to appear flustered. What if Jimmy arrived before she was ready? Sonia would let him in, and that would be that.

Finally, after she prised Stanley's hands off the damask curtains in the bedroom, he was ready to help her. 'Take it all off,' he ordered, 'and we'll start from scratch.' He opened his handbag and took out a large plastic cape. Nina smiled at him in the mirror of her dressing table. She sat on her accustomed stool, but felt very unaccustomed to having a man in her bedroom supplying what seemed to be a portable beauty salon. In a moment she was gazing at him from under a thick white mask. 'Where did you learn all this?'

'From me mum. When I was ever so little, she used to sit me on her knees and make her face up first and then mine. I love the smell of make-up. Reminds me of her.' Quickly and deftly he wiped away the cream and then seemed lost in a reverie. 'She was little, like you, with blue eyes, but you mustn't use blue eyeshadow with your colouring. It's too harsh. Here.' Stanley took out a soft grey eyeliner pencil. 'See how I draw around your eyes? Makes them look much bigger, doesn't it?'

Nina wondered how a man's huge hands could touch her face so delicately. 'Where's your mum now?'

'Oh, she died a few years ago. I never thought she would, you know. I thought she'd live forever. But she didn't.' His fingers were flying around her face. 'Now, I'll put some foundation on your cheeks. No yellow at all with your skin.' The bell rang and she started to move. 'Don't fidget, Nina. Your friend will answer the door for you.'

Nina strained to hear the sound of voices in the hall. It was Jimmy. She could hear the low masculine rumble. Oh well. There was nothing she could do. She watched Stanley's face. He could be either a man or a woman, she realized. In the lights of the dressing table, the lines of his face were soft and gentle. His eyes were outlined by eyeliner and his eyelashes were thick with mascara. Watching him work on her face, she felt completely at home with this Stanley, as at home as she had been with the Stanley in the pub.

'That's looking really nice now, love. You've got lovely cheekbones. It's bones in the face that counts. When you get to our age, the wrinkles are just starting out, God bless 'em, but it's the bones that stay and gradually rise out of the face and give it character in old age. Your friend downstairs, she looks great for now. But she hasn't got bones that'll last.'

'Hasn't she?' Nina hated to sound pleased. 'But she's so elegant. I'll never be able to be like that.'

'It wouldn't suit you to try. You're not that type of woman. You've got to be sharp and very hard to look like that. But you're like my mum, all soft and warm inside. Are those your kids in the picture frame?'

'Hm. That's Susan. And there's Hamish.'

'Lovely. See? You're a warm person, just like me mum. You know, I had hair down to me shoulders long before it was fashionable. Finally me dad took me mum's scissors and cut it all off. I felt dreadful. Really dreadful. Mum cried and cried.'

'Was your father always like that?'

'Oh, he was a bastard to us all. A drunken bastard. And I hate him even now. I hate him.'

'Is he still alive?'

'All too alive, for my tastes. I get these phone calls when he's drunk. Why don't I love him, he wants to know. Well, I don't. He drove me mum to an early grave. Now look up and don't blink while I do your mascara. Anyway, he beat her whenever he was drunk, and he beat all of us kids. I was the eldest and closest to me mum. He was jealous of us. Look down for a minute. I always remember sitting on her knee, smelling the smell of her powder. I still sit by myself in the flat when Kit's out with his lads, and I take out my make-up bag. Here, have a look.' From a pocket in the side of the handbag Stanley's finger fumbled with a powder compact. 'I bought that for mum when I was thirteen years old. I got the money delivering papers.'

Nina looked at the white compact decorated with a thin band of gold. Stanley flipped up the lid and they both stared down at the almost empty powder compartment.

'Are you two coming downstairs?' Kit's voice cut across the silence.

Nina looked up at Stanley. The cloying smell of the dead woman's powder filled her nostrils. 'I think I understand, Stanley. I do.' She felt very shaken.

Stanley clicked the compact closed. 'I need a drink,' he smiled.

'I'm your waiter for the evening.' Standing in the doorway, Kit clicked his heels. 'Not a bad place, Nina. Not bad at all.' He put a small silver tray down on the dressing table. 'I must just have a bounce.' He threw himself on the bed. 'Lovely mattress. Come on, Stanley, why wait?'

Stanley laughed. 'He's always at it, is our Kit.'

Kit stopped bouncing and looked at Nina. 'My,' he said, clutching himself in mock despair. 'You look like the mad witch of the moors! What a sight! Stanley, what have you done?'

'Don't be terrible,' Stanley scolded. 'I made her look beautiful, like she really is.'

Nina gazed in the mirror. 'Gosh, I really do look different, don't I? We'd better get downstairs and join the others. I can hear the doorbell. That must be Gemma and Marietta. Thanks, Stanley.'

Nina was aware that Jimmy stood in the hall looking up at the three of them as they descended the stairs carrying their drinks. Behind him Gemma and Marietta were struggling out of their coats. Beside Jimmy stood a silent Sonia. 'You look wonderful, Nina.'

She smiled. 'Thank you, Jimmy.'

'I've never seen you so radiant.' He took one of her hands in both of his, and he held it there.

Nina could feel the heat from his hands steal over her body. Thank goodness he hadn't picked the hand with the missing nail polish. 'It's lovely to see you.' She stood on the bottom step. Jimmy turned her hand over and kissed the palm. She felt the heat from the kiss rise through her arm and fill her chest.

'Well, Cinderella,' said Sonia, 'whatever your friend did upstairs, it sure is magic.'

Nina stepped down and moved towards Gemma and Marietta. She linked her arms through theirs. 'I've had two vodkas and I think we'd all better get something to eat. I'll lead the way.'

The guests meandered into the kitchen. Nina laid out the food from the warm stove. 'Um.' Jimmy sniffed. 'Samosas. How did you know I like samosas? There're the bottles of Guinness I promised you. If you're a good girl, I'll give you a glass.'

'And if I'm bad?' Nina was surprised by her own words. Had she really said that? There was a look of anticipation in Jimmy's eyes. She pulled back from answering the look too directly. 'Can you open the oysters for me, Jimmy? Oyster knife's in the left-hand drawer.'

She carried a tray of curried fish balls into the

drawing room and was suddenly filled with self-doubt for having dared to be provocative. I ought to give up, she told herself. I should just stick to typing letters for Jimmy. Sonia's more his type.

Gemma and Marietta were deep in conversation. 'Don't let me interrupt you.' Cal and Jennifer were somewhere in the night together, due to arrive shortly. Sonia was leaning on Jimmy, talking into his left ear while he was busy with the oysters. Stanley and Kit were both gazing at the paintings in the drawing room. There was a man-shaped gap at Nina's side. This was her first attempt at entertaining without Simon, and it looked as if it would be her last. Why, oh why, she wailed inwardly, was the world divided into pairs?

'You're not interrupting, Nina. Marietta and I were just talking about the lease on Latchmere House. It comes up for renewal in not too long, and it looks as if Sally and Virginia and their lot have found another place in the centre of London, which is much more suitable for them. And We The People from the other office crowd are moving out to Clerkenwell. So we could have the whole place to ourselves. If we got our negotiations right with the owner.'

'Who owns the building?' Nina handed the tray of fish balls to Marietta. 'Take several. The napkins are on the sideboard behind you.'

'A man called Michael Morningstar,' Gemma continued.

Nina felt her throat tighten. 'Michael Morningstar?'

'He's a very rich American over here in the property market. He mixes with the Great and the Good and gets invited to their charity parties because he's prepared to part with a lot of cash. A useful man to know. And we'll all get to know him, no doubt,

215

because he's the head of our very own homelessness office. And half the charity's advisory board are there simply for the thrill of being associated with the likes of him.'

'Michael Morningstar,' said Marietta. 'They say he's also a dangerous man to know.'

Nina felt a shiver of excitement mixed with fear ripple over her body as she sensed fate at play in her life. 'Dangerous?' she said. 'In what way?'

Marietta popped a fish ball in her mouth. 'I've heard, among other things, he's a demon with women. A real heartbreaker.'

Nina grinned. 'I've heard that before. But he looks quite charming, eye to eye.'

Gemma looked surprised. 'You mean you know him?'

'Yes. No. Not know him. I met him in passing. That's all.' She couldn't stop smiling.

Marietta shook her head. 'Don't ever go near that sort of man, Nina. I've lived with a man like that. They're not human. It's like living with Dr Jekyll, and then Mr Hyde turns up.'

'But at least it wouldn't be like living with Simon.' She heard the doorbell. Enlivened, she rose to her feet. 'I'll get that. It must be Cal and Jennifer. Help yourselves to some more food.'

She opened the door, glad for a gust of cold wind to fan her fevered cheeks. Michael Morningstar. Yes, she was sure she was fated to know him, to know him better . . . 'Simon?'

'Sorry to barge in on you like this, but Angela is not well. She really is not well at all. Susan's given her the most dreadful headache . . .' Simon stopped mid-sentence and stared over Nina's head. 'What on earth is *that*?'

Nina followed his gaze and saw that he was staring at Stanley. 'He's a *who*, not a *what*.' She reached for Hamish who was clinging to Simon's knee. The child was white and trembling. 'Susan, just what have you been up to?'

Susan stood innocently by her father's side. 'Nothing, Mum. Honestly, nothing. Angela started screaming and screaming, and Hamish cried and said he wanted to go home. That's all.'

'I'll deal with you later, Susan. It's all right, Simon. But you could have rung me.'

Simon's face was still frozen. 'You look different, Nina. Is that a new kind of make-up or something? I'm not sure I like you with that much make-up on. Maybe I do. It's hard to say.'

Nina ignored the critique. She pulled Susan into the hall and then she saw Cal and Jennifer walking up the road. Cal was wearing her labourer's trousers, big army boots, and a grey air force flak jacket. She had her arm around Jennifer's shoulders and was talking volubly. The next door neighbour's curtains were visibly twitching. Nina felt a moment of panic. Then she started to laugh.

Simon turned on his heel and bolted back towards the car. 'Hello, Jennifer,' he said as they crossed each other on the kerb.

'Hello, Simon. I didn't know you were invited.' Jennifer was swaying.

'I'm not, thank God.' Simon jumped into the car and was gone.

'So that was your old man!' Stanley stood in the hall with his glass of sherry. Nina nodded speechlessly. 'You must be Susan,' Stanley went on, 'and you must be Hamish. I saw your pictures in your mother's bedroom.'

'Are you a man or a woman?' Susan's blue eyes surveyed Stanley evenly.

'I'm a man, but I like dressing in women's clothing. Same as you probably wear trousers some of the time?'

'No, I never do. I don't like wearing trousers or anything that boys wear.'

Nina could see the hurt on Stanley's face. 'Come on, children. Up to bed. Sonia, could you take over for a while? I'll be down in a minute.' She rushed both children up the stairs. 'Give Cal and Jennifer a drink please, Stanley.'

She undressed Hamish quickly. 'What on earth happened?'

Hamish looked at his mother. 'Susan got bored. She said you had a party here tonight, and she told Angela that she was bored and didn't like supper. She wanted to eat samosas instead. And Angela said if she felt like that, she could go home right away. And Daddy said no, and Angela said it was her flat and then she began to shout and Susan shouted rude things back.'

'Rude things? Like what?'

'Susan said you told her that people who say *serviette* and *toilet* are common.'

'Did I really say that?'

Hamish nodded.

'Well, that was a long time ago. I'm different now. Very different.' She kissed her son goodnight.

'You won't tell Susan I told you, will you?'

'Don't worry.'

He settled down on his pillow. 'I like that man in the dress. What's his name?'

'His name's Stanley.'

'Is he a sissy?'

218

'No. He's a new friend. You go to sleep now, Hamish.'

'Night, night, Mum.'

Nina walked across the landing. Susan was sitting up in bed with her knees under her chin. 'I'm not going to ask you any questions, Susan. I just want you to know that I don't expect any nonsense from you. You are to stay in bed and go to sleep. Do you understand?'

Susan gave her a fish-eye stare.

Nina made herself kiss the child. There was a familiar triumphant look in Susan's eyes. She's won again, Nina realized as she walked down the stairs. Why can't I stop her?

'I'm guarding a plate of oysters for you.' Jimmy called to her from the sitting room. Jennifer and Cal were sitting on the floor, their plates heaped with salad and pâté. Jimmy patted the sofa and Nina slid gracefully beside him. 'Here. Try a glass of Mother's Milk.'

Stanley grinned. 'I'll drink to that. I was breastfed until I was four and a half.'

'You weren't really, were you?' Nina sipped the Guinness.

'Can't you tell?' Kit lay back in a big armchair. 'He's a right sod for the condensed milk. Says it's the closest thing he's ever tasted.'

Nina picked up an oyster and slipped it into her mouth. The Guinness tasted bitter and the oyster juice flooded her tastebuds, breaking the bitterness and catching the tide of the creamy froth. 'Delicious,' she said, smiling. 'Absolutely delicious.' She watched Jimmy's eyes. He's watching me watching him, she thought. But the trouble is that the moment of madness when the oyster explodes in the foam of the tide does not belong to him or to his hands or to his mouth. It belongs to the big man with the diamond ring and the high cheekbones. Michael Morningstar. Step by step, my fantasy is coming true. I will *make* it come true.

Nina's eyes faltered and she saw disappointment creep into Jimmy's expression. He can see I'm thinking about someone else. Damn, she thought. Why does he understand me so well?

By midnight Sonia stood up to leave. Most of the others had gone. Nina saw Sonia to the door. 'I didn't mean to spoil the evening, Sonia. But Mrs Porter told me the old music professor died. He was found frozen to death in the park. Isn't that awful?'

Sonia put on her coat and pulled it around her shapely figure. 'Yes, it is awful, darling. But I can't bear to hear about things I can't do anything about. I like your Jimmy Donleavy, though. He's a good guy. You go for it.'

'I don't want to go for it, Sonia. I like him as a friend. That's all.' Nina shut the door and walked back into the sitting room.

'I'll help you clear up.' Jimmy picked up two plates. 'This is always the loneliest part of a party given by one person when you are used to another person clearing up with you and gossiping about your guests.'

'Yes. I see your point. I guess it is lonely. This is my first time.' Nina was aware of Susan's form flitting up and down the stairs. She was determined not to notice her.

'I enjoyed talking to your friend Stanley. He loves Charles Dickens, you know.'

'I didn't know. I've only met him once before. He's

an old friend of Gemma's. I didn't see much of her when I was married to Simon.'

Jimmy laughed. 'I'll bet you didn't.'

'Gemma says the lease for Latchmere House comes up next month, and the groups from the other two offices want to move out.'

Jimmy was loading the dishwasher. 'Yes. I can see we're thinking the same thing. Of course I'm only a spokesman for the homeless office, but it occurred to me that we might try to persuade the committee that runs Latchmere House to let us use the other rooms and house people who arrive in the middle of the night, or women with children running away from violent men. I'd feel a lot better about what the office does if I knew everybody didn't just get treated as a housing problem. I mean, we often shunt people off to shelters when the shelter is really not suitable. Like young kids. If we could hold them for a day or two, we could perhaps find a more permanent solution. I think lots of good things could happen if Latchmere House became more than just a referral service.'

'Yes, I see what you mean. There are lots of possibilities. It's all very exciting, actually.' She was near the coffee pot. 'Another cup of coffee?'

Jimmy stood in the kitchen and smiled at her. 'No. I really mustn't. I've got to get back to the kids. They'll be up at the crack of dawn tomorrow, so I'd better get some sleep. But listen. There's a meeting of the board that runs both the building and the charity next weekend up in Birmingham. Let's go up, shall we? And see if we can put in our two cents' worth.'

'All right. Let's.'

'Gemma and Marietta and anyone else who wants

to come should go along too. The more voices heard the better.'

Nina followed him into the hall. She reached into the cupboard to get his coat. Jimmy pulled her towards him. He kissed her gently on the mouth. Nina heard a scuffle behind her. Susan, she thought. She pulled away. 'Here's your coat, Jimmy.'

He slipped his coat on and then looked seriously at her. 'You're not ready yet, Nina. I can see there's a lot you want to go through first. But I can wait.' He kissed her cheek and stepped out of the door into the black night.

Nina sat on her chair in front of her mirror. She wiped a make-up removing pad over her left eye. Imagine, Jimmy Donleavy is a little in love with me. And me?

He's kind and warm and caring. He loves children. He might even be able to cope with Susan . . . But no. I'm thirty years old and at last I'm beginning to live.

She went to sleep with a different name on her lips.

Chapter 28

Doris picked up the telephone. Why, Nina thought, did the telephone always sound so shrill on a Monday morning? 'It's 'im,' Doris said. 'And he sounds in a bad mood.'

Nina reached for the phone. 'Hello, Simon. Yes, the children are fine. I'm sorry Susan behaved so badly . . . That's not what you're calling about? No . . . Oh, don't be an arsehole, Simon.' Nina made a face at Doris. She put her hand over the mouthpiece. ' "How could you let those weirdos and perverts into our house?" ' she repeated the words to Doris who stood in front of the sink, laughing. 'Stanley is *not* a child-molester, Simon. Anyway, the children weren't supposed to be here. *You* were the one who brought them back. Remember? Anyway, those *perverts*, as you like to call them, are my friends. They can come to *my* house whenever they like. You don't dictate my social life . . . Angela thinks you should go for custody of the children? Don't be ridiculous! I'm a good mother. Susan is *not* out of control. She's just a spoiled little bitch. But that's thanks to you. You and your bloody mother made her into a monster.' Nina heard her own voice rising.

She took a deep breath. 'Look, Simon. Let's not fight over this. We both live very different lives. We like different sorts of people. We were both very young when we married. Too young. Don't let's fight now, after all these years.' She could hear the pleading tone her words had taken on. 'After all, we once loved each other very much.'

She heard a silence on the other end. Simon was in his office. She knew the room well. Big French windows looking over St James's Park. Now that Angela was officially Simon's pregnant bride-to-be, Simon had another secretary to carry in the coffee and biscuits. Did he still have two chocolate digestives at eleven o'clock? Did the new secretary cross her plump little legs when she took dictation? Did she have a moist little rabbit mouth like Angela?

'I'll have to talk things over again with Angela, Nina,' Simon said at last. 'She's really very upset. She

223

says you've become a hippy. You don't take drugs, do you, Nina?'

'Yes, and I sleep with black men. Six of them, all at once.'

'There's no need to be rude.'

'And there's no need for you to be insulting, Simon. You have no right . . .'

'Oh, yes, I have. I have every right. I don't expect my children to live in a promiscuous household.'

'How strange to hear the word *promiscuous* coming from your adulterous lips. Are you jealous, Simon? Is that what all this is about? It seems to be all right for you to bang your secretary in secret, without that counting as promiscuity, but you're saying it's not okay for me – as if you still think of me as your wife – to kiss a man goodnight?'

'It's different for a man, and you know that. Anyway, I always intended to marry Angela.'

'You're a liar, Simon. You always intended to live off me and my inheritance and keep Angela as your office wife. Only she sussed you out, which you hadn't counted on. She did the cunning thing: she got pregnant. That's the truth. And of course the clever bitch has an even better plan now.' Nina's mind was racing. 'Look, Simon, I'm late for the office. Let's talk some other time.'

Simon mumbled unhappily, 'All right.'

'You will be sure to pick up the children on Friday because I have to go to a work session for the office.'

She put the telephone down. Doris looked at Nina through a stream of smoke. ''e's upset you, hasn't 'e?'

Nina's hands were shaking. 'It's not him so much. He's just terminally weak. It's that bitch of a woman. I think she's worked out that if she can get custody of both children, she and Simon would "have to" take over this house, the scheming cow. Clever little bitch, isn't she? She'll claim I'm an unfit mother. She'll call in the social worker who'll call in a shrink. And no doubt Susan will give them all a fine story, how badly I've treated her her whole life. I know she will. I knew she was spying on me from behind on Saturday night. Jimmy kissed me at the door before he left.'

'Jimmy Donleavy kissed you? You told me he'd be coming here, but he actually kissed you?'

Nina smiled.

'Does he like you? I mean in a boyfriend–girlfriend kind of way?'

Nina slumped into her chair. 'I suppose you could say that. But . . . I don't know. Why does fantasy have to be so far away from the real world? That's my problem. It's always been that way for me. Even with Simon. In the beginning sex between us was fun. I enjoyed it. But it pretty much wore down with time. Making love with Simon never did fulfil all those promises you read about in books. No flutes or violins or earth-moving thunder. After the children, it was just something I did to keep him happy. Still, I've always had the feeling that I'm looking for something more . . . more . . . *extraordinary*. Does that make sense?'

'A leg-over's a leg-over. Mind you, if I have one pint too many on a Saturday night, I can't half make the bedsprings rattle. My Jim says I'm a right goer when I get going. But it's not so often any more, except for our weekend morning regular. I'm too fucking tired most of the time.'

'Yes, but I don't think it's just that I was too tired, or that I was bored. I just think that there is a part of me which I've never explored. Why, when a genuinely nice man like Jimmy Donleavy wants to love and take care of me, do I look at him and realize that half of me is thinking: Uh oh, more of the real world? Is it because I'm afraid of a man who seems too safe? Do I really want some awful bastard to mistreat me instead? Do I think that even if he is an evil bastard, I can change him? I wish I knew what I was feeling. But everything feels dead now at this time of year. The garden is frozen over.' Nina stood at the kitchen door. She could feel the frost through the windowpanes. 'An old man died out there in the cold a few days ago, and here I am dying of self-pity in a big warm house . . .'

'Well, I'm off to do the top floor.'

'Thanks, Doris.' Doris was so *very* down to earth. 'I'd better get to the office. I'll see you Wednesday.' Nina picked up her pile of letters, collected her handbag and her coat from the hall cupboard, and climbed into the Volvo. Next weekend she would meet Michael Morningstar. She looked forward to their meeting with a greater anticipation than she had felt for years.

Chapter 29

She watched Jimmy sign the letters she had typed. 'We have so many pamphlets and papers to take with us.'

'Yes, the preliminary committee meeting is when I will argue that we should extend our charitable status from just advising and referring the problems of homelessness to actually being given permission to take in cases. If we have two empty floors, we can have some temporary dormitory accommodation.'

Since the party, Nina had been aware of a certain distance between herself and Jimmy. No one else could see it or feel it, but she knew it was there and she felt sorry. The ravine was unbridgeable and she could not cross over into his promised land of simple love and happiness. She knew if she could, the sun would shine and the birds would sing. Always behind the sun and the singing birds was a road. Long and black, reaching . . . where? There were no hints, no answers in the chilly wind that blew down the road, just puffs of disturbed dust as her unwilling feet walked closer and closer to the edge . . .

'I've got to get back to the studio for my next show. Nina, would you please give this list to Cal? It would be great if she could come up with a breakdown of how many people have used Latchmere House this month, how they came, I mean who referred them, that sort of information. I'm interested to see how many came because they knew we were not officials of any kind. And she can note down where she sent them to, and if any of them are off the streets yet. Okay?'

'Fine.'

Jimmy, on his way out of the door, poked his head back in. 'We're still friends?'

'Of course, Jimmy. We'll always be friends.'

'You know what they say about friends,' Jimmy grinned. 'If you make your friend your lover, you end up losing your friend. Maybe you're right, Nina. I'd rather have you as a friend for life than risk losing you as a lover.'

'I need a friend. There's none I'd rather have more than you.'

Jimmy smiled. 'Right then. I'm off.'

'I'm standing in Fortnum's luggage department looking at briefcases, Sonia. I've never bought a briefcase before.' She could hear Sonia laughing.

'So why are you buying a briefcase all of a sudden?'

'Because I'm going to a big meeting in Birmingham at the weekend.'

'Well, if the meeting has anything to do with homelessness, I'd imagine most of the other people there will all be your socially-minded types, all shuffling around in love beads and serious shoes.'

'Hm. You're probably right. But I'd feel better with a briefcase anyway. I mean, really it's for the committee of the charity, and I hear the chairman, Michael Morningstar, will be there, and . . .'

'Oh I get it. You're going up there to chase *him*, aren't you, sweetie? I tell you, you're something else. A couple of quick glances in a crowded restaurant, and you're gone. Sounds like a lady who spends too much time in fantasyland, if you ask me. In your mind you've probably worked yourself into the love affair of the century.'

Sod Sonia. She was always so perceptive. 'Are you a mind-reader or something?'

Sonia laughed. 'Nearly. Don't forget, I *am* an Agony Aunt. And my diagnosis is you're heading for a bad dose of agony if you get yourself caught up with him. Sounds like you already have a pretty strong case of lust and addiction. Leave him alone, Nina. He's out of your league. He's way out of *my* league, and I'm no beginner.'

'Oh, you shouldn't even indulge me by giving any weight to my dreams. I mean . . .'

'Of course not. You'd be much better off hooking your fantasies onto someone like Jimmy Donleavy. He really cares about you, you know. I'm shocked that he spent the whole of your party not even noticing my existence. Can you believe it? I think he's hung up on you bad.'

'I've got to run, Sonia. Quick, what do you suggest?'

'Stay away from our man Morningstar. That's my suggestion.'

'No, I mean about a briefcase.'

'Oh. Crocodile. Get a really snazzy black crocodile briefcase and shoes to match. You're sure to get yourself noticed, if the animal rights extremists don't chase you out of the place first.'

'Well, if they did, Mr Morningstar would have to rescue me.'

'But you'd be safer getting caught by the animal rights extremists.'

Nina was hopping from foot to foot. 'Really, Sonia. I think we're both taking my fantasies a little too seriously. But thanks for the advice anyway. I'll telephone you next week.'

Nina wandered back to the rows of briefcases. 'That one, please,' she said, pointing to a large square case, the edges bound in gold. She closed her eyes as the shop assistant wrote out the bill. Thank God for the American Express card. She had overspent on her Visa and Mastercard. And of course she still had the shoes to get. I'll have to go down and talk to Mummy. She'll understand how expensive life is after a divorce, and we're not even divorced yet. To think, Simon and I used to spend so little. Well, at least I did.

She stood by the lift. The light blinked and then she stepped in. 'Shoe department,' she smiled. I do love this place, she thought. Behind her she saw a mirror. Now *there's* a woman with style, she congratulated herself. I'm no longer Simon's little country mouse. Now her make-up reflected the lessons learned from Stanley. Her wide blue eyes stared back at her. Her mouth was luscious and pink. 'Say *grape*,' Stanley had instructed. 'It makes your lips pout.' *Gra-a-ape*, she practised and then lowered her lashes like a drawbridge.

The lift stopped and Nina steadied herself as her stomach caught up with her chest. Now what I need is an utterly wicked pair of black shoes.

'Where did you get those shoes?' Susan from the back of the car was rustling in the shoe box. 'You don't wear spikey heels like that, Mum. You always wear sensible shoes. Look at this, Hamish! It's a suitcase.'

'It's a briefcase,' Nina corrected.

'It's not like Daddy's briefcase. His is all shabby and battered.'

'I know that, Susan, but Daddy's briefcase is very old. It belonged to his father.'

'Is that real crocodile skin?'

She watched Hamish run his fingers over the skin. Inwardly Nina cursed, knowing that all of this would be recounted to Simon. 'Yes, it is, dear. Just like my crocodile handbag, which used to belong to my mother. The good thing about crocodile skin is it lasts for ages and ages, so it's really very good value. Simon's briefcase must have been just as expensive when his father bought it new all those years ago. You see, Hamish, when I'm an old toothless woman, you'll be carrying this case around, like Simon does.'

'I bet it cost a lot of money.' Nina heard the hostility in Susan's voice. 'Angela says she is saving up to buy a pram.'

'Oh, that's ridiculous. Angela doesn't need to save up to buy a pram. Simon can buy her a pram any time she wants him to.'

Thank goodness I took the bill out of the box, she thought, or Simon really would have a fit.

Later, when the children were in bed, Nina tried the shoes with the dress she had decided to wear for the meeting. 'Marvellous,' she said, turning slowly. 'Absolutely marvellous.' She turned her back to the mirror and looked over her shoulder. 'Gra-a-pe,' she said, the air softly leaving her lips.

'Well, whatever you do, Nina, keep your knickers dry.'

'Thank you, Stanley. I expect that's very good advice.'

'Where are you staying?'

'In the Grand Palace Hotel.'

'That's expensive.'

'You guessed right, Stanley. But that's where our meeting is and I'll be sharing a room with Cal. Poor old Cal! She's miserable at the moment. Virginia is with that awful bitch, Sally, leaving one very hurt Cal. She takes care of Virginia like a mother.'

Stanley snorted. 'That's the problem right there in a nutshell. And it's me own problem, too. Here I am, cooking Kit's tea, and he's out with Hugo.'

'Hugo?'

'Hm. You'll come across Hugo if you work in the charity business. Hugo is Lady MacLaughlin's pet. He's from Honduras. He's over here being trained

231

for the revolution. She's put him in a flat in Eaton Square, and she knocks him off in between meetings of her various charities. Gordon Bennett, Nina! She's got wattles down to her waist and her fanny must be like climbing up the Khyber Pass. But Hugo is having the time of his life. It's true, you know, what they say about black men.'

'What's true?' Nina was lying on her bed with the phone to her ear. The phone bill was going to be huge, but she loved talking to Stanley.

'You *were* born yesterday. They've got bigger dicks, I mean.'

'How do you know that?'

'My friend, François, in Paris. He takes a plaster cast of all the dicks he's had and he keeps a collection. Name, date, everything. And he says blacks win, dicks down, so to speak.'

'Oh, Stanley. It could be just random luck. It doesn't sound like a proper experiment, with control groups and everything.'

'My, aren't you picking up a lot of social worker jargon!'

'And you're repeating stereotypical misinformation.'

'Well, yes, you could put it that way, I suppose. I saw a man on the Tube the other day . . . Showed me his dick. Must have been at least a foot long. I felt all funny for the rest of the day. Awestruck, like. And he was a white fellow.'

'Stanley, you're obsessed by dicks.'

'I know. I can't help it, but I'm feeling nervous. I've been waiting for dinner for two hours, and Kit hasn't come back.'

'Then you ought to go ahead and eat your supper and go to bed. If he thinks you're waiting up for him, he won't come home. Just pretend you don't care.'

'It's so hard, Nina. I miss him when I'm not with him. But he needs to get out and about with his friends. I'm no good with all those people. I like a quiet life. Me own home. Me own cooking.'

'What are you cooking tonight?'

'*Avocado au poivre noir avec saumon fumé, Gruyère et vin blanc.* I made it up for a friend of mine. Christopher le Petit. He's straight. More's the pity. Anyway,' Stanley's voice changed. Nina picked up a pad from the night table, 'you take a layer of smoked salmon, a layer of avocado, a layer of cheese. Sprinkle black pepper, crush fresh basil leaves, and keep layering until you reach the top of the casserole. Then fill the casserole with a bottle of good white wine. Cook for twenty minutes in a hot oven, and then remove the top and grill until the cheese is a little brown.'

'Wow! That sounds fantastic. I'm sure Kit will love it.'

'Most men can't decide which to do first: feast or fuck.'

Nina laughed. 'And most women just diet. That's why they're so boring.'

'Have you done your nails yet?'

'Yes, I have. They look perfect, if I may say so myself. So far I've managed to keep them out of water. Only Hamish doesn't get his back washed this way, poor boy.'

'You're a good mum, Nina.'

'I'm not really. At least Simon doesn't think so.'

'Don't worry about Simon. He doesn't know who he is or what he wants. He's just a mess. Everybody seems to have different ideas of what a mess is. That's

233

the problem. But don't worry too much. Go to sleep and have a fabulous time at your meeting.'

'You go to sleep too, Stanley, and take care of yourself. I'll tell you all about it next week.'

Nina lay back on her pillow and smiled. Who would have thought that I'd be lying here on this bed, which once was so boring, dreaming about forbidden sex with another man who isn't my husband? I have a friend who is a transvestite, but is like a sister I never had. I'll worry about the telephone bill later.

Cal, Nina realized as they stood in front of the reception desk, was having a difficult time feeling at home in the elegant lobby of the Grand Palace Hotel. Her big face was scarlet and she moved her big boots up and down in embarrassment. She stood wrapped in her thick parka, sweat running down her face. 'Dinner is at eight, madam,' the sleek woman at the desk smiled at Nina. Her eyes meticulously ignored Cal. 'Formal dress for dinner, of course.' Nina tried not to laugh nervously. The idea of Cal in a tight dress and high-heeled shoes was alarming.

'Thank you, but we'll be dining in one of your private suites. Could you check on the bookings? The board meeting and dinner in Michael Morningstar's suite?'

'Ah yes. His plane arrived this afternoon.'

'Thank you,' Nina smiled. 'Let's go up, Cal.' She put her hand on Cal's arm. 'Let the bellhop carry the bags,' she whispered in her ear.

Cal's mouth tightened.

After Nina had tipped the bellhop, Cal still looked strained. 'I'm perfectly capable of carrying my own bags, Nina. I don't need a bellhop to do it for me. I could carry him *and* both the bags, if I wanted to.'

'Yes, but it's his job and he needs the money. Look at it that way, not as an example of male domination.'

Upstairs Cal looked around the room. 'This sure is comfortable.' Cal took off her parka and put it over the back of the chair. 'Can I make a phone call? To Virginia I mean? Just to see she's all right.'

'Go right ahead.'

She took a scrap of paper out of her hip pocket and picked up the phone. 'Hi, it's Cal calling from Birmingham. Is Virginia there?' Nina watched Cal's hopeful face. What a waste, Nina thought. What an awful waste of a warm motherly woman, in love with a spoiled, conniving bitch. She saw Cal's face ease. 'Virginia? How are ya, okay? Yeah, we're here all right. Swell hotel.'

Nina spoke up a little too loudly. 'Tell her the capitalist bitch says she'd hate every square foot of the place. Tell her we're glad she's not here.'

Cal put her hand over the mouthpiece. 'Sshhh! I can't say that.'

'Then just tell her we're busy with a board meeting and you've got work to do.'

'Listen, Virginia, can I call you up later tonight? You'll be in, won't you?' Nina saw Cal's shoulders slump. 'Oh, I see. You promised Sally you'd take her out to the pub. Well, what about after that? I could still give you a call afterwards. Maybe if the pubs closed . . . You'll be back, won't you? All right. I'll try back later.' Cal put the phone down. 'I could hear Sally laughing in the background.'

'I've told you before, Cal. You're better off without that woman. And they're about to move their office anyway. Isn't it time to make a clean break?' She could see how distraught Cal was, but she knew there was no real help she could give. 'Listen, I'll have a shower and get changed. Jimmy should phone in any time now. Tell him we'll meet him in the foyer.'

Half the fun of an obsession, she decided in the shower, is that you've got something to think about all the time. Nina heard the telephone ring. That'll be Jimmy. She ran the soap over her nipples and she realized that she did not feel at all guilty about having one man on the telephone while fantasizing about another.

Chapter 30

'Good heavens, Jimmy! We could house half of London in this suite alone!'

Jimmy's face was grim. 'I remember just how much I dislike these occasions, now that we're here. I hate putting up with committees full of pompous busy-bodies. But it's part of the charity world, I guess. Seems to be the only way to get anything done. But still, the people on the boards can be really quite disgusting. Better prepare yourself for your first encounter with the Great and the Good, most of whom are neither.'

Nina looked about the room. The walls were patterned black marble. A huge bulbous fireplace with fake logs squatted against the far wall. Much of the furniture was rococo Louis Quinze; the armchairs and sofas looked comfortable.

Cal's workshoes looked incongruous on the thick plush carpets. Even Jimmy looked slightly shabby. Nina was glad of her crocodile shoes and briefcase.

She put the briefcase down and leaned back in her chair. 'Where is everybody?' she asked.

As if on cue, the double doors opened at the end of the room and a group of people strolled across the floor talking eagerly. An incredibly tall woman with a mauve turban led the crowd.

Anyone so outlandish, Nina decided, must be exceedingly important.

As the crowd advanced into the room, Jimmy got to his feet. Nina noticed that he was indeed nervous of them. She saw his fingers picking at his tie. His unease made Nina feel an unexpected wave of sisterly affection for him. Cal looked desperate. Nina smiled and confidently remained seated. Cal, intimidated by the approaching people, struggled to her feet.

'Jimmy! How super to see you again!'

'And you, Lady Phillips.' Jimmy took her hand and made a semi-bow in the direction of the company. 'Let me introduce you to my colleagues, Lady Phillips.'

'All right, everyone. Let's stop the gossip and get down to business.' Lady Phillips reminded Nina of her old headmistress. She could inspire fear in a pit viper.

All voices fell silent and many eyes stared with disinterest at the more humble group of three. Nina sat firm. They did not overwhelm her because she had seen collections of human beings like this before. At Devon hunt balls there was always a top table of men and women from London or the shires who arrived immaculately overdressed. They talked in high-pitched voices to each other or to their various chinless offspring. Lady Phillips looked down at Nina and put out a long be-diamonded hand. 'This is Nina

Stockton,' said Jimmy. 'Nina, Lady Germaine Phillips.'

'Stockton?' The face clouded. 'Stockton, you say? We don't know a Stockton, do we, Alison?'

A short fat woman double-checked some invisible register in her mind and then shook her head so that the artificially-coloured blonde curls bounced. 'No, darling. We don't know any Stocktons. Where are your people from, dear?'

'Devon,' Nina replied evenly.

'Good hunting country.'

'Let me introduce you, Lord Ben and Lady Bobo Radnor, in charge of our public relations,' Lady Phillips waved a hand. 'I'm Treasurer. This is Lady Alison MacLaughlin, our Secretary.' The fat woman with the dyed golden hair tilted her head. 'Mrs Antonia Hurst, a true dear who serves as our expert on homelessness.' At last, one face that looks nice. 'Of course,' said Lady Germaine Phillips, 'all we need now is our illustrious chairman, Michael.' She turned her gaze to Cal. 'And who might you be?' She raised her eyebrows quizzically.

'I'm from California,' Cal said, trying to smile.

'Ah, an American. There's a lot of you about these days. Come along, everyone. Let's go next door and get down to business. You, young lady with that exquisite briefcase, where did you get it? I love it! It's so very businesslike. Will you take the minutes?'

Nina looked sharply at Jimmy. He nodded his head urgently. Nina vaguely remembered a section on taking minutes in her secretarial days. 'With pleasure,' she said cheerfully. 'I bought the briefcase at Fortnum's.'

'At Fortnum's?' Lady MacLaughlin's voice rose and hung accusingly in the air. 'Did you say Fortnum's?

But that's awfully expensive, and you work for the homeless, don't you?'

'I do, Lady MacLaughlin, as does Cal.' And then it struck Nina that this must be the Lady MacLaughlin whose rent-a-boy Hugo was a friend of Kit's. Her smile widened as she heard Stanley's voice: '. . . *must be like climbing the Khyber Pass.*' She laughed. 'I work for the homeless and I also have an account at Fortnum's. And at Harrods. Some of us do live quite well above the bread-line.' Nina saw a look of intense loathing in Lady MacLaughlin's eyes. Damn, she thought. I should have kept my mouth shut.

The group trailed into a room which seemed to be by nature a dining room but was now in readiness for the board meeting. 'Nina, dear, will you sit beside our chairman?' Lady Phillips pointed to the chair on the left side of the table. 'Alison, you sit on the other side as Hon. Sec. And I'll sit beside you as Treasurer. That leaves Antonia next to Alison. Ben, you and Bobo sit opposite each other. Jimmy, you and . . . and . . .'

'Cal,' Jimmy offered quickly.

'Yes. You two can sit below the salt, as it were.'

Nina sat down at the table and thought, well, if we are to be patronized, we might as well look as if we know what we are doing. She put the briefcase on the table and pushed the latches open. Good. She did have a clean pad and two freshly-sharpened pencils.

'Oh dear!' Lady Phillips cried, a little too loudly. 'Where *is* that Michael? He's always so late.'

'I'm here, darling. I'm here.'

Nina was suddenly aware of a tall male presence. He had moved so silently across the room that no one had heard him come in.

'How Machiavellian you always are, Michael!' Lady

MacLaughlin's wattles swung and flushed with pleasure. 'Really, Michael. Are you ever on time for anything?'

'Only for one thing, my dear Alison. Only one thing. But don't be angry. I've been inescapably busy. Jimmy, good to see you again. And who is this? Ah!' he said, sounding surprised. 'It's you.'

Nina looked up at the eyes which, though dark and slanted, contained small amber lights in the bottom of both pupils. The eyes reminded her of a small collection of stones her father kept from his days in India. Tiger's eyes, she remembered they were called. There was a strange quality to the man before her, Nina sensed, a charismatic energy stronger than any she had ever felt emanating from any person. Was it his reputation or his wealth that made him appear irresistible? she wondered. Or was his power more integral than that? A glance from his eyes gave the impression that one was privileged to be within his field of vision. Nina felt herself sucked into the magnetic draw of his power, succumbing to the feeling that the most important task was to hold on to the attention of those eyes, that if only she could make herself special in his sight, then she would have achieved something rare and coveted. He was a personal moon and she wanted no cloud ever to pass between him and her, blocking out his vitalizing nocturnal light, keeping her in lonely, obscure shadows. She knew she wanted always to remain within his mysterious radiance.

Nina stared up at Michael Morningstar. He, his head slightly inclined, smiled.

'So.' His voice was like silk drawn through a velvet ring. 'We meet again.' There was a slight American twang in the voice, but it was very gentle. He tugged at his ear with the hand that held the large diamond ring.

Michael, Nina felt while looking at his beautifully-cut suit and designer tie, had left a lot of his life behind him. 'Yes,' she said. 'We meet again.'

Lady MacLaughlin heard the comment. 'You don't mean that you two know each other?'

Michael pulled out his chair and sat down. 'Indeed, Alison. Nina and I know each other very well.' He lay back in the chair and smiled at everyone around the table. 'And you must be Cal.' He leaned forward. 'Jimmy's told me about you. And about your friends. I'm very pleased and grateful for all your hard work. Let's get on with the agenda, shall we? Do we have the agenda?'

'Yes, dear, I do,' Alison MacLaughlin chimed in. 'Now we have Nina with us, I can thankfully give up the beastly boring job of writing all this stuff down. I usually jot it down and hand it to Germaine, and she hands it to her husband and he gives it to his secretary. But it seems her husband's secretary objects to doing my typing for me. Can you imagine? Silly woman.'

So now you've recruited *this* silly woman to do it instead, thought Nina.

Michael, beside her, smelled wonderful. Nina tried to concentrate on the agenda. She read the date of the last meeting. I was still happily married to Simon the last time they all sat down together, she realized, and now here I am sitting next to one of the most famous men in the world and he seems glad to recognize *me*. Simon and the children might as well be a million miles away. She looked sideways at Michael. On the back of his hands he had long, silky, black hairs that you had to be quite close to to see.

'Right.' Michael cleared his throat. 'Jimmy, you said you wanted to discuss the possibility of using some of the Latchmere House rooms as temporary housing.' He turned to Jimmy. 'This is your pet project, so let's scrap the tedious part of the agenda and get right down to the meat.'

'But, Michael.' Lady Phillips's turban shook. 'You always scrap the agenda. We are supposed to do these things in order. First you must hear my report before moving on to any new business. After all, I am the treasurer.'

'Darling.' Michael's voice contained a lilt of laughter. 'We don't *have* anything to treasure. Not yet, anyway. So far the charity is just rolling over, but this new plan sounds really exciting and worthwhile. After Jimmy's had his say, Bobo and Ben will tell us how they will go about raising money for the project, and then Antonia might have a moment to tell us about her forays into the world of the bureaucrats, and then after all that hard work, I have ordered a sublime meal for all of us. You'll have to hurry, Jimmy. The first course will be here in twenty-five minutes.'

Jimmy began. 'I've discussed this plan with Michael on the phone. The two other organizations that leased office space in the building are planning to move out. This will leave us with two empty floors. Now I've come to feel that, for all the good work Help the Homeless does now as a referral agency, I'd be even more proud lending my name to a residential project that could accommodate some of the more desperate cases, at least until we can find suitable places that can offer a long-term future. I'm thinking mostly of women with small children, or teenagers who are on the run. If we can offer more than just a roof over their heads, if we can give them also a sympathetic ear, then I think we might immeasurably increase our usefulness to the homeless. For many people coming to us, homelessness is just one symptom of an even deeper problem.'

Antonia Hurst nodded approvingly. 'How right you are, Jimmy. I agree with you wholeheartedly.'

'You mean you're going to actually let these homeless people live in the building and you're going to talk to them about their problems?' Lady Alison MacLaughlin appeared incredulous. 'Oh, I'm not sure I think that's a good idea at all. I mean, don't social workers do that sort of thing already? And don't you think it could be dangerous, getting ourselves mixed up in the lives of street people?' The blonde curls bobbed in Nina's direction.

'Isn't that what we're all about?' Jimmy asked. 'Involving ourselves in their lives in the hope of making a difference?'

'Well, who is to do this talking to them and listening to their problems?' Lady Radnor cut in. She turned to Nina. '*You*, I suppose? Are you qualified?'

'Well, I'm not a social worker, Lady Radnor. I'm just a housewife, really, but . . .'

'My point exactly.' Lady Bobo Radnor was triumphant. 'What could you possibly know about homelessness?'

Nina felt a strength, possibly born of irritation, growing within her. '*But* – as I was saying – I agree with Jimmy that this new direction for the work is vital. And though I've only been with the programme a relatively short time, I'd be more than happy to do anything I could to make it possible.'

She heard a small chuckle emerge from Michael's throat beside her. She turned and he gave her an encouraging nod and smile. 'Confidence,' he said. 'I love it.'

'*I've* been homeless.' Cal's deep voice came rushing up the table. 'It ain't easy being out on the streets. Not for a woman especially. I know more about being homeless than most any social worker I've met.'

'Oh, do you? How very nice for you.' Lady MacLaughlin's face registered disgust. 'And are you homeless now, dear?' Her long nose curled.

'Not for the moment, thank you. I live in a squat.'

'A squat?'

'Cal means she is living in semi-derelict housing which she and her group of friends are upgrading, don't you, Cal?'

'Yeah, Jimmy. If you say so.'

'But is that legal?' Lord Ben Radnor looked towards Michael with some concern. 'This isn't the United States, you know. Law breaking isn't very popular over here. In the States, on the other hand, you seem to have a wealth of long-haired hippies on the home front. We have our share over here too, no doubt, but we wouldn't want anything to do with that sort of thing, would we, Bobo?'

Jimmy stepped in. 'I promise you the project will be run properly, Lord Radnor. We've got Nina on the staff now. She's an experienced administrator, aren't you, Nina?'

'An experienced administrator, are you?' Michael stepped in with a teasing smile.

'Let's say eager to learn,' Nina smiled back.

'That's the spirit.' Michael looked very pleased with her indeed. 'I like people who bite off too much,' he said. 'They either choke or . . .'

'Or,' Nina interrupted with a grin as full of implication as his, 'they learn to chew.'

Michael hit the table. 'Decided. Nina can head things up. She seems to have all the tact and diplomacy required. She's certainly presentable.'

'Yes,' said Jimmy, wanting to be supportive. 'She'll do very well.'

Suddenly realizing how quickly her role was being decided, Nina blushed. 'Well . . . Thank you, Jimmy. And Mr Morningstar, but . . .'

'Michael.'

'All right then. Michael . . .'

'And where,' Lady MacLaughlin shot in, 'were you trained in your highly-prized administrative skills?'

'Well,' Nina began to feel caught out. 'I was at St Erwin's, but really I was trained in secretari—'

'St Erwin's? Really?' Mrs Antonia Hurst appeared genuinely delighted. 'How splendid! My sister went there.'

Lady Germaine Phillips seemed mollified. 'Well, if you say so, Antonia. That's all right, then. We are in good hands.'

Nina glanced down at her hands and remembered she should be making notes.

'Then it's all settled. The board resolves to open a residential unit for the homeless at Latchmere House.' Again Michael turned his smile towards Nina. 'Nina Stockton at the helm. We'll see how things go from there. And, Nina my dear, I'll make you a promise to sweeten the offer of leadership, beyond whatever reasonable pay schedule we work out later. My promise is this: You'll have autonomy in your running of the project. The board here will keep off your back. Won't you, everybody?' Everybody looked too startled to speak. 'They'll worry about their outside ring of order, while you get on with the important part of running things inside

Latchmere House. Anyone gives you any trouble, you come and tell me and I'll get them to back off. All right?'

'Thank you,' said Nina.

'Done. That's one thing I've learned in getting where I am. Too much deliberation is counterproductive. When you see something that's right, follow your instincts. And I've got very good instincts about you.' Michael took out a gold pen. He ticked off all remaining items on the agenda. 'Now, Bobo. Let's hear how you intend to raise money for this new adventure.'

'Well, Ben and I will have to put our heads together, really, but how about a ball?'

'A ball?' said Lady MacLaughlin.

'Yes, a ball.' Bobo warmed to her own idea. 'A homeless ball. We could use our London house and my son, Sebastian, could do the decor. He's just recently opened such a wonderful business doing this sort of thing. It's called "Just Parties", and it would certainly take all the sweat out of such events.'

'I know what!' spat Lady MacLaughlin. 'We can have an Alice in Wonderland costume ball!'

There was silence around the table. 'Why?' said Michael. 'What does that have to do with homelessness?'

Lady MacLaughlin's speechless face turned fuschia as the idiocy of her remark became clear, even to her.

'But the costume idea is good,' Michael put in when he had decided she had suffered enough. He threw her the small bit of reassurance as a beneficent master might toss a table scrap to a dog.

'Here's an idea,' said Lady Radnor. 'We can serve the food out of big vats, just as in *Oliver Twist*. Think what it will save on the catering! What do you say to

an *Oliver Twist* party? Homelessness, street urchins
. . . That sort of thing.'

Michael smiled. 'That's better. Sounds fun, and
appropriate, too. Does everyone like it?' But his eyes
looked only at Nina.

Privately Nina thought it to be an idea that bor-
dered on poor taste, wealthy people costuming themselves as impoverished to raise money for the truly
needy. But she could see Michael was keen and her
relationship with him was far too nascent for her to
risk contradicting him. 'If you think it's a good idea,'
she said. Immediately she cursed herself for not having taken a firmer stance. Already his will seemed
stronger than her own.

Michael returned her look. 'That's resolved then.
Nina thinks it's a good idea.'

And suddenly a feeling overtook Nina, a feeling
stronger than her self-recrimination. Nina had never
before thought of her name as sexual, but in Michael's
mouth the two syllables were sucked and licked and
then allowed to leave between the lips. Nina felt the
blood rise in her cheeks.

'Ah,' Michael said with delight in response to a
knock at the door. 'Dinner is served.'

Nina stood up to go and join Cal and Jimmy, but
Michael put his hands on hers. 'You sit next to me. I
deserve a beautiful woman as a companion. When I
first saw you at Joe Allen's, I knew we'd run into each
other again.'

'But how could you know?'

Michael put his face close to hers. 'Thought creates
matter. That's how I've got everything I have. I concentrate on something, and I will it into being.'

The word *will* sent a shiver through Nina's body.
Michael's will must be a fearsome force.

'And coincidence held out,' she said, recalling their encounter outside the Gay Hussar, 'so we *did* meet again.'

'Coincidence? I prefer to think of it as the manifestation of thought.' Michael grinned. 'You don't fully believe me yet. But wait until you know me better.'

Three laden trolleys were wheeled around the room. 'Quails' eggs!' screeched Lady MacLaughlin. 'How wonderful, Michael!'

'I do hope everybody likes them,' he said.

Lady MacLaughlin's eyes bored into Nina. 'Love them. Absolutely love them. I last had quails' eggs at my daughter's twenty-first.'

The conversation rumbled around the table. Nina leaned forward. 'Is it Miss or Mrs Hurst?'

'It's Antonia. May I call you Nina?'

'Please do. I'm a bit lost with all the titles.'

Antonia smiled. 'Listen, I've got Monday off, so I'll come down to Latchmere House and spend some time with you. If you're a newcomer to this game, you'll need some advising. We mostly raise money to keep Latchmere House going. I like to give a hand in Michael's charitable foundations, particularly the work with the homeless. He's called together some of the groups that invest in his interests, and tomorrow he will address them at a morning seminar.'

Michael was deep in conversation with Lady MacLaughlin.

'Interests?' Nina looked at Antonia. 'What are Michael's interests?'

Antonia sighed. 'Anything and everything.'

Nina lifted up her glass of wine. She hadn't even

248

noticed the wine waiter. No, Michael is all magic. Everything seems to come from nowhere. Nina sipped the wine. It was crisp and fruity.

'How are you finding this little get-together?' Michael asked, suddenly giving her the grace of his attention.

'Magical,' she answered before she could think. 'I always wanted to be magical. When I was a child, I used to sit in the apple orchard and talk to my fairies. I really thought I saw fairies, you know.'

'But you *did* see fairies,' said Michael. 'I'm sure of it. Where I come from, we saw spirits of old, long-dead ancestors. My grandfather was part-Navajo. I saw wolves running in packs in the arroyos. Only when I went to check where they had been, there were no tracks. They were ghosts. Long, grey ghosts. I could hear them howling.'

Nina looked into his eyes. Way down there was an ice cold cave and something moved in the cave. Something shuffled on its floor. 'Where do you come from, Michael?' She kept her voice even.

'Oh, here and there.'

'Michael is a man of mystery!' Bobo squealed. 'Nobody really knows anything about him except what we read in *Fortune* magazine.'

'Don't believe anything you read about me, or anything you hear.' He spoke directly to Nina. The trolleys were moving around the tables again. 'A little wild teal?' Michael offered, smiling at her.

Whatever was in the cave, she would help. If she could help the homeless, she could also help the damned. Michael for a moment had opened a window to his soul and she had glimpsed a man in torment. Whatever it was, Nina believed she could help that soul. Had Michael, like Faust, already sold his soul to the devil? Was it too late? Nina watched the waiter change the glasses.

'Châteauneuf-du-Pape, Nina.' Michael tapped his glass with his knife. 'To Nina and Cal, two important parts of our little family. May our work prosper with their guidance. To all the good people who help to run Latchmere House.'

Nina watched Jimmy raise his glass. Their eyes met. Jimmy signalled a warning, but it was too late. Nina was already in pursuit of her fantasy, trying to make it real.

Chapter 31

The next morning when she awoke, Nina found herself unsure for a moment as to where she was. Carefully she dressed. He stayed with me all through the evening, she mused in disbelief. And when I left with Cal and Jimmy, he kissed me on the cheek. The thought of his firm, smooth lips against her cheek made her eyes glow. He didn't kiss Cal. And he didn't kiss Lady MacLaughlin, the jealous, evil, old bag. He only kissed *me*.

All weekend long Nina kept catching glimpses of Michael. She sat beside Jimmy and a very silent Cal. They observed Michael's meeting with his colleagues and investors. She noted the graciousness with which he handled them and won them over to support his cause. He informed his investors of the board's decision to expand the functions of Latchmere House, and Nina was surprised to hear her own name spoken by Michael as the woman who would be heading up this new direction. Things are happening awfully fast, she thought.

Various other people gave talks on topics related to homelessness, for the edification of the investors. The man who caught Nina's attention was Paul Davison. He suggested that squatting was the way of the future. If the government owned a surplus of housing which for any number of reasons they chose to leave vacant, he argued, then why shouldn't the homeless exercise their rights as citizens by claiming those houses as their own? By squatting, the homeless could be housed, and the government could save itself the trouble of creating too much bureaucracy to oversee an already over-administered but inefficiently-handled problem. Nina agreed with what Paul Davison proposed. He, she promised herself, would be worth getting to know as a contact for the future.

By the end of the day, Nina was exhausted. She complained to Cal that she felt like an over-stuffed filing cabinet. Cal, too, was worn out. But Cal also looked miserable. It was Saturday night, and Michael had told Nina he had some important business to attend to, so she had no reason to push herself to be sociable with anyone else. She and Cal planned to stay in their room for the evening.

Cal took off her jeans, flopped down on her bed and stared at her naked legs. The tops of her thick thighs were melting with years. She had a varicose vein bulging in her calf. 'I feel my age, Nina. I'm nearly forty. The big four-oh. Virginia is only twenty-three. And the difference between our ages matters, let me tell you. In our case it matters a lot.'

'Why should it matter, Cal? You love people because of who they are, not because of what they look like.' An image of Michael swam past Nina's eyes: Michael with no clothes on, lying on a bed with clean blue water flowing nearby. 'At least maybe at first you're turned on by what they look like,' she hurriedly corrected herself, 'but then it becomes less important.'

'In pure theory, maybe. But Virginia's getting antsy. She'd much rather spend all her time with Sally and Ronni and people her own age. I can tell.' Cal forced herself to get up and she plodded into the shower. 'I need a slug of bourbon and a rocking chair.'

'Well, I can help you out with the drink at least.' Nina opened the bar fridge. She poured a miniature of Jack Daniels over some ice. 'Here,' she shouted through the haze and the steam of the shower in the bathroom. 'Have a drink.'

Cal pulled back the shower curtain. Nina stood frozen for a moment. She had never confronted a fully naked woman before. Cal's breasts flopped almost to her waist. The nipples were large and bulbous. Her pubic hair matched the red of the hair on her head. 'Thanks.' Cal took the drink. 'I'm a poor lonesome cowboy . . .' she started singing in the shower.

Nina went back into the bedroom and smiled. Cal's obliviousness to her own nakedness was strangely refreshing. It was natural, not a forced sexual sophistication, like Jennifer and Ziggy's, looking for innuendo in every comment. Maybe with Neville gone and the friendship with Ziggy ended, Jennifer might try to develop some real attitudes of her own.

'. . . and I'm tired of life,' sang Cal.

Nina winced. Cal's voice was loud and mostly flat.

Nina changed into a pair of tan slacks and a matching V-necked jumper. She took off her diamond earrings and rubbed her earlobes until they throbbed. If by any chance Michael should telephone, she wanted to be by the phone. Even if she was transcribing the notes of last night's meeting, at least she felt she was with him. Where was he tonight? She had no idea. Tomorrow after lunch, she would drive Jimmy and Cal back to London. But tonight Michael was either in his suite or somewhere in this big industrial city.

Cal roared through the bedroom, dressed, and then roared out through the door. 'Don't wait up for me, Nina. I'm going to have me a ball after all. No good moping around, I've decided. I'm off to see what Birmingham has to offer.'

'Night, night.'

Nina closed the door with relief. Should I telephone his suite? She walked around the telephone and sat down at the table under the lamp. She couldn't sit still, so she studied the room service dinner menu. The selection was excellent. I'll pretend I'm in Michael's suite and I'll order for both of us. I'll have the snails, and he can have frogs' legs. Let me see . . . A bottle of champagne. What does he suggest? The Perrier Jouët of course. I'd love that. To follow, um . . . Is that lobster fresh? Yes. Flown in from Boston. Is it? Couldn't be better. I'd love the lobster in a dressing made from its own roe. So pink and so fresh, tasting of the sea . . .

Upstairs in the suite the telephone was silent. It had been switched off. Michael was lying back across the big four-poster bed. A blonde girl with thick hanging hair had her plump lips over his penis. 'Slowly,' he said. 'Take it slowly.'

She extended her neck like a boa constrictor and then she rolled him over on his side.

'Now go straight down.' Michael smiled. Michelle knew what she was doing. Michael began to move, slowly at first and then faster. Finally, as he held his hips steady, he came.

'Get out,' he said, rolling away.

Michelle wiped her lips. 'That feel good?'

'It always feels good, you whore.'

Michelle took the money off the night table. 'Deep throat is expensive,' she said, gazing down at the back of Michael's head.

He was asleep, but before he dove down that big black hole, he saw the remembered image of a very young girl who had not been so experienced. She was lying on the floor at his beach house in the Caribbean. Her face was blue and her neck hung askew.

'Happens,' the Chief Inspector said. 'Badly taught. Neck broken. Shall we say death by misadventure?'

Michael nodded.

But the girl's eyes haunted him at moments like this. Oblivion was what he sought. Oblivion.

Chapter 32

Antonia Hurst surprised Nina. She arrived at Latchmere House, as she said she would, at eleven o'clock. 'Do come in. I'll take you round the building later on. But let's have a cup of coffee first.' Nina motioned Antonia into a chair. 'I'm beginning to get the feel of things around here. Between the lot of us, we have at least got a filing cabinet and a Rolodex for our letter writers and supporters.' Nina picked up a file from the desk. 'Here's the accounts. I know I'll have to submit them to the Treasurer. I hope this is what she wants. I must admit, I never thought I'd bless the day I took double-entry bookkeeping.'

Antonia smiled. 'Looks like you're doing a terrific job.'

'I'm glad you're pleased. But do explain to me, if you can, just what Michael is doing in the middle of all these groups? He doesn't seem the type of person who spends his time with people who quite frankly –' Nina paused, trying hard to articulate her confusion. 'Well, judging from the people I saw at the first meeting on homelessness in the town hall, quite a few of them seem to be cranks. Seems as if for every office such as ours simply getting on with straightforward work, you have many more other organizations all out for their own political ends.'

Antonia sighed. 'Yes,' she said, as Nina reached for the kettle. 'Lots of them are cranks. But there are enough people in the homeless movement who are doing a good job. Paul Davison and his group of squatters are actually doing a great service, even if others might say he's a bit of a maverick. My background, until I retired, was among the bureaucrats in the Elephant and Castle. I sat with paper pushers and watched the way a good idea could get memoed to death. I also walked home to my flat in Bermondsey past the ragged and the derelict. I took early retirement and then I decided to put my efforts and my experience into housing the homeless. I find Michael refreshing, even if I don't particularly understand him. He gives his money and his time very directly, especially if the recipient is a young, pretty woman. But I expect you knew that already.'

Nina could see that Antonia was watching carefully. She felt a thin wire of caution. Was Antonia here as a friend or was she sent by the committee to vet Michael's newly-acknowledged acquisition? 'I honestly don't know very much about him, Antonia. I've been a housewife for the last ten years. The biggest decision I had to make was whether the children should have baked beans and fish fingers or chops. It's been wonderful, since starting here, to sit at home in the evenings and write back to all the hundreds of people who write and send money for the homeless. It's given me some purpose to my life. Before I met Jimmy Donleavy, I was in the slow lane. My husband had run off with his secretary and I was a mess, a complete mess.'

'Oh. I am sorry.' Antonia moved in her chair.

'Don't be. I'm not. I don't want to live my whole existence pretending that real life happens at the theatre or in a book review. I was literally dying of boredom. Now there's not enough time in the day for me to get all the things done that I want to do. I'm afraid the kids get frozen TV dinners these days. It makes Simon livid, but too bad. I'm happy, and because I'm happy, so are they.'

Antonia finished her coffee and rose. 'Shall we have a look round the building? Have you got any idea of how much it will cost to make the other floors habitable?'

'Gemma – do you know Gemma? She and Marietta couldn't make the meeting in Birmingham, but no doubt you'll meet them. Gemma reckons we can do most of the work ourselves, but we will need about thirty thousand pounds, mostly to see that the place is fireproof.' The two women toured the building, discussing all the practicalities necessary for running a residential unit: rewiring, extra showers, commercial-sized water heaters and a clothes dryer.

When they finished Nina felt pleased to be able to demonstrate graciousness by taking Antonia out to lunch at her favourite Chinese restaurant. She enjoyed Antonia's pragmatic approach to making plans, but she could not resist looking for an opportunity to bring the conversation back to the topic of Michael.

Both women sat down in the restaurant booth. Nina relaxed. She was aware she had been nervous while showing Antonia over the building. The Women's Liberation Front rooms downstairs had been a disgusting dump. Upstairs, We The People had already left and their rooms were empty except for a torn picture of Lenin that blew around the floor.

'I think you could do a magnificent job for thirty thousand pounds.'

Nina released a sigh. 'I'm glad you think so. Gemma, Marietta, and I are all good at painting and decorating. We plan to roll up our sleeves and get down to work. And whoever is staying in the hostel can pitch in, too. My friend Stanley says he can get us donations from his fabric shop of curtains and covers. He's fabulous with a sewing machine. And even Kit, dear elegant Kit, has promised to tile the kitchen. So we should be set to open by the New Year.'

'It can't be soon enough, Nina.'

The thin wire of inner tension was still there, pulling at Nina.

'You like look at menu, Madam? I make roast duck Szechuan style for you today.'

'Oh yes, Ah Li. That would be wonderful. Do try it, Antonia. It's delicious. Simply delicious.' Ah Li bowed and slipped away.

Nina sipped her green tea and then said non-, chalantly, 'You know, we never quite finished our conversation about Michael, Antonia. Does he have a bad reputation? I mean, is it a deserved reputation, or is it just the sort of thing you hear about any rich and attractive man? After all, he is married. I would imagine Mrs Morningstar keeps quite a good eye on him.'

'I'll be honest with you, Nina. I'm not part of Michael's inner circle. I get whistled up for events that include his charitable work. I sometimes help with the accounts to check up on the money to see that it's not wasted. I can see that you and your friends genuinely wish to help the homeless, and I'll do everything I can to help you. As far as Michael is concerned, women fling themselves at him in droves. Quite why his reputation is so awful, I think, is in part that he gets bored easily. He has so much money, he couldn't spend it all if he tried. In a funny way, he's even bored with spending money. He has suites in all the big hotels all over the world, a mansion in Washington, an entire skyscraper in New York, a house in Greece . . .'

'Sounds lovely. The idea of a Greek house.'

'It is lovely. He flew us in there for a week last year, but he only stayed a few hours and then he was gone. I don't know what drives him. He had a tough childhood. Maybe that's it. I know for part of his young life he was homeless.'

'Poor Michael.' Nina liked saying the words. 'Poor

Michael,' she said again. She had never been able to say *poor Simon*. Simon needed no compassion or pity. Simon was perfect. Michael was far from perfect. Nina knew she could settle his restless feet and stroke his head. She could calm him.

'Um.' Antonia pulled the roast duck off its bones with chopsticks. 'Excellent. You were quite right. By the way, Michael says that if you sketch your ideas for a kitchen, he'll give it to his architects. He says the kitchen gives the feeling of homeliness, which is the most important thing you can offer.'

'Sounds like he was hungry once as well as homeless.'

'Here, have a fortune cookie.' Antonia reached across to an empty table where two cookies lay in a saucer. 'You choose, Nina.'

Nina chose and broke hers open. '*Beware desire caught by tail.* Oh. That's a bit ominous. What does yours say?'

'*Good joss comes your way.*'

'I don't suppose you want to swap. I could use all the good joss I can get.'

Antonia laughed and exchanged fortunes. 'You'll have much better joss if you stay away from Michael, I can tell you that.' Antonia's face became very strained. 'I was divorced myself years ago, at a time when divorce was still hush-hush. I didn't want to get a divorce. I thought we were very happy, actually. My husband wanted children, but I couldn't have any.' Nina saw the pain in Antonia's face. 'Finally he told me he had fallen in love with my best friend, and they wanted to get married. So I didn't stand in their way. He left the house and they did marry.' Seeing the question on Nina's lips, she answered, 'Yes. They had children. I saw the whole family once in Queensway. They were walking up the road. I saw my husband first. Isn't it dreadful? I still think of him as my husband. Anyway, I looked at their son. He must have been about six. It gave me such a pang of regret. He looked so like my husband. The girl resembled her mother more, but the boy . . . He could have been mine.'

Nina put her hand on Antonia's wrist.

'But I've got off the point. The point of the story is that after he left, I was so lonely. I had made him and our house my life. I baked my own bread, dug the garden, grew my own vegetables. I knew very few people . . . For the longest time I found myself very much on my own. And then I met this man.' Her face was bitter. 'He wasn't rich, like Michael, and he wasn't an international tycoon. In fact he was a house painter and decorator. He came in answer to a job I advertised. We got talking and he told me all about his wish to be a writer. I gave him the job doing some bits of decorating, and before long we were lovers. Sometimes I think he made me at times happier than I'ver ever been in my life. At other times I look back and I'm so ashamed of myself. I wanted to die.'

'But what did you do that made you so ashamed?'

'I made a complete fool of myself. I went out and spent money – an awful lot of money – on clothes I couldn't afford.'

A vision of crocodile shoes and the matching brief-case sitting in her cupboard at home made Nina wince. 'Yes, but he did help you get over the divorce, didn't he? And didn't he show you that sometimes there can be more to life than just . . . than just real life?'

'In a way, I suppose he did. But I paid too high a price for him, Nina. Much too high a price, both emotionally and financially. Naturally, Michael won't cost you a penny. But the time for you to pay your price is when Michael thinks he owns you. That's when he's dangerous. We don't even know each other very well, but I'm saying this because I like you. The Michaels of this world are dangerous to vulnerable women like us. Whether they are millionaires or painters and decorators, they live to enthral women and then cast us away. At last my painter and decorator got bored and went on his way with his manuscript under his arm, the manuscript I had typed for him. He left me broken, but alive to pick up the pieces. Michael is different.' She stopped herself. 'If Michael ever found out I had told you this much, he'd be enraged. He likes all his staff to keep his secrets. Michael survives by keeping all his secrets and his people apart from each other.'

'What keeps them so apart?' Nina tried not to laugh. 'Michael is only a man, Antonia. You make him sound so sinister.'

'Fear is what keeps us all apart. Don't laugh about Michael. He can be quite sinister indeed. He's very powerful, and he has friends bought off in all the right places.'

'Well, I guess he won't have to worry much about me. All I'll be doing is some volunteer work at Latchmere House. That's very little potatoes for a man like Michael.'

'For now, I suppose. I must get back, Nina. It's been lovely to lunch with you. Thank you.' Antonia got to her feet. 'Forget we ever talked about Michael, okay?'

'I've already forgotten,' she smiled. 'Not to worry.'

*

Driving back to collect the children, she realized that she was late in starting her Christmas activities. This year it was already too late to make her own Christmas pudding.

'Mummy,' she said that evening on the telephone, 'can I bring the children down at the start of the Christmas hols with your presents?'

'Certainly, dear. We'd be delighted to see you. How are you getting on? Daddy and I do worry, you know. Aunt Persephone wants to see you as well. Are you sure you're all right?'

'Actually, Mummy, I'm fine. I'm doing some voluntary work and making new friends. Susan and Hamish are looking forward to Christmas very much, especially as they get two Christmases this year. Children are such unsentimental beasts, aren't they? Hamish is trying to argue that he can burn two wishlists for Santa Claus even though he insists he doesn't believe in him. Anyway, I think I'll let them spend Christmas Eve with me and Christmas Day with Simon and Angela. I can't imagine sitting down to a Christmas dinner just the three of us. I'll probably spend the day at Latchmere House. We are cooking a meal for the homeless.' Nina knew she was chattering on, but she could feel her mother's distress at the end of the line. I wish I felt as distressed as she does. She heard her words pouring down the line, but in truth the idea of *not* having to cook a vast gluttonous meal for the first time in ten years was definitely appealing. Seeing other people with Gemma, Cal, and Marietta sounded much more fun.

'Goodbye, Nina darling.' Her mother's voice was faint. 'You will bring the children down though and spend some time with us, won't you?'

'Can't wait. Goodbye, Mummy.' Nina put the telephone down.

She lay back on the long sofa in the drawing room and smiled. The children were asleep. Her letters were done, and now she could lie there luxuriously thinking about Michael. Slowly she recalled everything Antonia had told her about him. What bliss to lie back and to rehearse the facets of a man's life! What she would do from now on was to put Michael together like a jigsaw puzzle. He was part-Navajo, so now she must go to the library and take out all the books she could find about the Navajos. He grew up in New Mexico. Another book. He had been in *Fortune* magazine. I must ask Sonia where to get back copies. Michael was going to be fun to track down. Everyone who knew him seemed to think they had a piece of the puzzle, but Nina was determined that she would finally complete the whole picture and ultimately put in the last piece that would make Michael Morningstar entirely understandable. For now, he had power over her, but on the day of the last piece the balance would change.

Chapter 33

Christmas Eve in London left Nina feeling confused. Blithely she had thought the children leaving the next day to spend Christmas with their father would mean the traditional exhausting Christmas Day cooking and cleaning would not be her expected lot this year. 'Will you be all right without us?' Hamish asked, his big eyes gazing at his mother as she served a very untraditional Christmas Eve home-made hamburger.

'Of course, Hamish. After you both leave, I'll go to work at Latchmere House. We have two families living there, and I expect some comers for our Christmas dinner. Gemma and Marietta will be there, and Stanley and Kit have promised to help. Jimmy can't come. He's hosting a new programme on television. You can watch it if you want.'

'Will you have television?' Susan asked.

'Yes. The chairman of the board, a man named Michael Morningstar, donated a colour television to the centre for a Christmas present. It was very good of him.' Nina was thrilled to be able to talk about Michael in her own home.

Susan pushed her hamburger around the plate. 'You talk about that man a lot, you know.'

'I do?' Nina felt her voice rising.

'Yes, you do. I heard you yesterday talking to Sonia about New Mexico. A place called Toes, or something like that.'

'Not Toes, darling. Taos,' Nina laughed. 'Taos is a town with an old Indian pueblo.'

Hamish looked interested.

'Yes,' said Nina. 'Real American Indians lived there. They still do, in fact. Also lots of famous writers and painters were attracted to Taos. D. H. Lawrence, one of England's most brilliant writers, lived there on a ranch, and that's where he's buried. Sonia's been there. She says it's very beautiful.'

'What's it like to be a real Indian, Mum?'

'Not much fun these days. The Indian way of life is almost gone now, thanks to white people. Anyway, Mr Morningstar is part-Indian.'

'Can we open our presents now?' Susan was plainly bored.

And why not? Nina smiled. 'Just let's clear away and wash up, shall we? And then we can sit down and have an opening session. Doesn't it feel odd, children?'

'Not really,' Susan said. She carried her plate into the kitchen. 'I like it this way. I have two families, two Guy Fawkes, and two Christmases.'

And two battlefields, Nina thought ruefully as she followed her daughter into the kitchen.

The next morning from the drawing room window she watched the children leave. Behind her was a pile of discarded wrapping paper and two separate piles of toys. Hamish had taken a hand-carved toy soldier with him. Nina was pleased that he enjoyed the puppet soldier. Susan left her pile of toys and books and clothes on an armchair. Not much had interested her, but then, Nina consoled herself, eight is such a difficult age. The Cacharel skirt and matching jersey had cost an awful lot of money, but in her heart, Nina had to admit that Susan much preferred the latest ethnic baggy jackets and beads look. We both want such different things out of life. That's our trouble.

The streets were silent and empty that Christmas morning. Passing Acton Green, she saw that the shops were unlit. She could see the cheerful Latchmere House sign on Shepherd's Bush Road, and she was glad to see the festive nativity blinking on the front steps. In the back of the car she had a sack of new toys. 'Goodness,' she remarked as she hauled the black bag out of the back seat. 'What an odd way to spend Christmas Day!'

Usually by this time, Simon, the children, and she

would be at Jennifer's house drinking champagne with Jennifer and various other school parents. The champagne had always given Nina a vague headache. And later in the afternoon, while she tried to sleep off the inevitable hangover, she had to dissuade Simon from making amorous advances. If she succeeded, she slept and awoke refreshed. If not – and it was usually not – Simon's body would labour above hers as she lay there mentally working out how many twenty minutes of oven time went into twenty-five pounds of deadweight turkey meat. Her maths were so bad, the calculations usually covered the time it took for Simon to reach his very prim climax. How can I expect to feel randy when I've got to dash downstairs to baste the turkey's gaping bum? It's all too visceral . . .

But her Christmas was not to be so this year.

Nina was smiling as she walked into Latchmere House. The smell of fresh paint hit her nose. Today I don't have to paint. I don't have to type. I can just enjoy myself. Gemma and Marietta were in the kitchen. Gemma was talking to a tall, thin, fair-haired woman. The woman had a baby in her arms. Gemma looked up at Nina. 'This is April Stevens, Nina. And here is Baby Derrick.'

The baby wiggled and tried to smile. 'He's just had his bottle,' April said, 'so he's about to go off to sleep.'

'You're lucky. Both of mine were screamers for the first three months.'

'I'm surprised, really. Even with the eviction and all that worry, Derrick never missed a night. Out like a light, regular. But then Ben is ever such a good dad. He changes nappies and everything.'

Nina watched the young woman's face soften at the mention of her husband's name.

'Who's talking nappies, then?' Ben walked into the kitchen, his voice echoing off the walls. So far the boards had all been laid for the flooring, but no carpet had yet been found.

'How's the other mother with the two children?'

Gemma frowned. 'She's up in the office with both children, and I can't get her to come down.'

'She won't leave the office?'

'She says she's too afraid.'

April nodded. 'She told us last night about her old man. He's ever so violent and dangerous. Even the police are afraid of him.'

'I'll go up and see her. I brought some Christmas presents for the children. Here's a rattle for Baby Derrick. Do let me hold him for a moment. May I?'

Nina stretched out her arms. The small bundle fitted her body in a well-remembered embrace. She lowered her face to breathe in the baby smell that Nina remembered was universal to all mothers. That smell, and the slightly off-putting smell of puppy breath, were the most well-remembered in her world. She looked down at the baby and then realized she was about to cry. The child that was to be born in a few weeks belonged to Simon and not to her. No soggy, sleepy baby mouth blowing bubbles at two o'clock in the morning. No fat little thighs to wash and powder as the sun rose. No more hours on a rocking chair singing *Ba Ba Black Sheep*. No. Those days were gone. And anyway, she reminded herself that men like Michael Morningstar were not interested in babies or in puppy breath. She handed the baby back to April.

'The food smells fabulous, Marietta. How many people are we expecting?'

'Father John says he has ten people who are in

need of a hot meal. He'll send them round at two o'clock. The turkey's doing fine.' Marietta was stirring something in a large saucepan. 'Cal will be here at two, and Stanley and Kit will make it a little later on.'

Nina walked up the unfamiliar stairs, unfamiliar because they were now painted gleaming white. Her feet creaked up the stairs and onto the third floor. She knocked on the office door. 'Can I come in?'

'Yes,' an anxious voice replied hesitantly. 'You can come in. Are you a social worker?' A squat woman sat upright at the desk. 'The other ladies aren't social workers, so I don't know what to do. My social worker is away for Christmas, and the emergency number doesn't answer.'

Nina put the sack of toys on the floor. 'I'm not a social worker. My name is Nina. I've got two children like you. And I'm getting a divorce.'

'Did the bastard beat you then?'

'No, not really. He got his secretary pregnant though.'

'Oh, so he did play around. All men are the same, that's what I say. My name's Janice. And these are my kids. This is Elsie and Ryan. How old are you, Elsie? Tell the lady then.'

'I'm seven,' Elsie said, lisping through two missing front teeth. 'And Ryan is six.'

'I've got some presents in the bag for you both. You've probably had to leave your own presents behind.'

'We don't get presents at Christmas, or for our birthdays.'

Elsie's face tightened. 'Dad drinks all his money. Especially Christmas. He drinks all the time. Can I open the presents?'

'Certainly. Take them over there, and you can both help yourselves.' Nina sat down. 'Did you sleep at all, Janice?'

'No, not really. That nice big American lady gave me that mattress over there with some bedding, and I put the kids down, but I couldn't sleep. Mind you, I'm exhausted.'

'Why don't you stretch out now, while the children play with their toys? I'll make us some tea, or would you prefer coffee?'

'Tea, please. I wouldn't say no to a lie-down, if you'll mind the kids for me. I'm so afraid he'll find us. Last time the social worker put us in a homeless family unit, just four roads away from where we live. He's a local dustman, and he kept going past in the dustcart. This sounds funny, but it's almost worse being away. At least I knew where he was when I was at home. This time I had to go. He said he'd kill me, and he's got another woman into trouble. It's not the beatings I mind so much, I can take them. But him going with another woman, you can never get over that.'

'I did. You have to.' Nina plugged the kettle in. 'You lie down and rest. You look absolutely knack-ered.' She sat down on the chair and watched Janice move over to the mattress. 'This is my first Christmas without my children. They're at their father's flat. Actually, it's *her* flat. Her name's Angela.' Why was she confiding in this woman? 'I really feel so odd. All my friends are at home with their husbands and children. Of course, my other friends are all going to be here. We're all sort of freaks, I suppose. If you're not a couple, what do you do?'

Janice was asleep.

Nina smiled encouragingly at the children and held

out her hands. The kettle whistled. Janice moaned and turned in her sleep. Nina switched the electric kettle off. 'Let me see, Elsie. What have you got?'

'A dolly with baby clothes. She's so pretty! And a hairbrush set. See?'

'I've got a red London bus,' said Ryan. 'Look, you can wind it up and it goes!'

'Can we stay here for Christmas, Miss?'

'You can call me Nina, Elsie. Of course you can stay.'

'You won't make us go back? Me and Ryan don't want to go back to him. Dad's mean and he beats mum and he kicks her in the stomach. Once he threw Ryan down the stairs and split his head open. He told the social worker that Ryan tripped. The social worker always believes him, not Mum. Anyway, I like it here. The big lady did drawings with us yesterday. Will she come back?'

'Yes. Cal should be here any minute, and then we can have our Christmas dinner all together. Won't that be nice?' The two faces shone. The hollow in Nina's heart filled. She was moved to great pity by Elsie's words. She hardly knew what to say in return, except to promise that she would help keep them safe.

She devoutly hoped Hamish and Susan were enjoying themselves. Of course they were. Angela was a good cook, and Enid would also be there to fuss over them.

Nina was surprised by how very much she truly enjoyed the meal. Stanley had organized four wooden sawhorses that had been used when sawing the floorboards. He made a trestle table and he donated two linen tablecloths with matching napkins. 'No need to look shoddy,' he said.

Nina kissed him. 'You're an angel.'

'What about me?' Kit was grinning. 'Don't I get a kiss? Look what I've made.' He pulled a glittering sequined miniature Christmas tree out of a carrier bag. 'It took ages to do, but it will look fabulous on the table.' Nina rewarded him with a kiss, too.

At two o'clock Cal arrived, puffing and stamping in the cold. Behind her, Father John led a motley collection of people into the converted dining room next to the kitchen. 'I'll go up and persuade Janice to come down with the children.'

Gemma nodded. 'See if you can, Nina. It will be good for her to meet some people, and for the kids. They've been cooped up there for days. They worry me, those kids. They never make a noise. They never fight or argue. It's not normal.'

'No, but it's not normal to watch your dad beat your mother. He sounds dreadful.' Nina climbed the stairs. 'Janice,' she said gently. She leaned over the sleeping figure. She put her hand softly on the woman's shoulder. 'Janice?'

Janice's body convulsed. 'Where am I?'

'Don't worry, Janice. It's only me. Nina.'

The two children stopped playing with their toys and watched. They're waiting for something bad to happen, she knew. She felt Janice's body shaking under her hand. 'You're quite all right, Janice. We were going to have a cup of tea, but you were so tired, you fell asleep.'

Janice stretched. 'That feels better. I guess I was tired. Have the kids been good?'

'They've been angels. It's time to eat. It's my first Christmas dinner on my own. Will you come down and sit by me? I can borrow your kids. I really am missing my two. Cal is downstairs, so you're not to

271

worry about your old man turning up. Let him try! Cal could deal with him.'

Janice laughed and the laughter shed years from her drawn face. 'She could, an' all. Okay. Let's go down.'

Nina watched the assembled guests fill their mouths with food. Stanley, wrapped in a big white apron, doled out roast potatoes and Brussels sprouts. Kit sloshed huge spoonfuls of gravy over the plates. 'The turkey is great, Marietta. Where did you get it from?'

'Michael Morningstar. He dropped by the flat the other night with all the food we could possibly want for the holidays, and the presents for everybody. He seems such a *helpful* person underneath it all, when he wants to be. I begin to think I misjudged him.'

'Presents for everybody?'

'Yes. All of us included. The presents are all underneath the tree in the front room. After dinner we can open them.'

Nina thought she saw a slightly quizzical look on Gemma's face.

'Typical Morningstar,' Gemma said. 'Everybody homeless, at least most of us are, and all the presents come from Harrods.'

Nina laughed. 'Why not?'

'He's very attractive, isn't he?' Marietta's dark eyes gazed sombrely at Nina.

'You noticed?' said Gemma.

Marietta nodded. 'Quite devastating. And he looks like a man who can do anything he puts his mind to. He . . .' Marietta interrupted herself, giving Nina the vague impression that she was stopping herself from saying something which perhaps was best not said.

Nina paused, unsure. Then she turned to Janice

272

and asked, 'When does your social worker get back?'

'I don't know. Most of the social services are on holiday until after the New Year.'

'By then, I hope, we'll have you settled in your own place.'

'You'll be lucky. My social worker says there's a queue a mile long for housing. Anyway, I don't live in this borough. I've got no rights.'

'Don't you worry about that now,' said Nina. 'I've got an idea.'

Nina opened her present from Michael. In a square box on a piece of cotton wool lay a miniature conch shell.

'How beautiful!' Gemma was standing next to her in the kitchen. Most of the presents had been opened and the guests departed.

'If you must be homeless, you might as well be homeless in Harrods socks and blankets.' Father John was delighted. He clasped a bottle of Balvenie in his hands. 'How did the man know this is my favourite Scotch?'

'I think Michael knows everything about everyone,' Marietta replied. Again she had the air about her of someone keeping a secret.

Father John left in high good humour.

Nina glanced down at her Caribbean seashell – Michael's gift. Marietta had a silver bracelet. She put it on her slim brown wrist. 'Isn't it beautiful?' she said.

'Very,' Gemma commented. She and Cal had thick Fair Isle sweaters. 'We'll have to rescue some socks for Stanley and Kit. They really did work hard.'

Stanley bustled in and out of the kitchen. 'Ow! Me poor feet! Kit, they're killing me!'

Cal sat protectively close to Janice. 'Don't worry,' Nina heard her say. 'I'm here for the next few days.'

Ben and April Stevens and Baby Derrick had gone to their room flushed with food and their presents.

On her way home, Nina realized she envied them. She was the only one that day to go home on her own. Father John had his homeless, Cal had the new inmates at Latchmere House, and Gemma and Marietta had each other. Or had they?

Nina put the shell on top of the television in the drawing room. She gazed at the perfect pink, fleshy lips. A promise, a hope for the future. Nina got herself a glass of wine and turned on the television. She smiled. *Climb every mountain*, sang Julie Andrews and her movie family across the Alps. The song faded away and Jimmy Donleavy's familiar face filled the screen. 'That's the end of our programme. To all those of you who have homes, a happy Christmas. And to all of you who don't, I'll be praying for you. Happy Christmas, everyone.'

Nina telephoned the studio. 'I just caught the last bit of your programme, Jimmy. You were excellent.'

'Thank you, Nina.' His now cherished voice pushed aside all trace of the loneliness she had started to feel since returning home. 'How did the dinner go?'

'Very well. Very well indeed. We had about fifteen people, and we still have the couple with the baby, and there's Janice and her two kids living in the house. It feels good to have the house open like that. They had a good time. Cal is with them for the next few days. Any chance of seeing you, Jimmy? I need a friend.'

'A friend you have.' Jimmy sounded tired but

comforting. 'And nothing would please me more than to come over and be with you right now. But I'm afraid I'm booked solid over the holidays with work. I found it's the best way to get over the pain. Missing the children, I mean. Sorry, but these plans were made a while ago. I can't get out of it now and . . .'

'Of course. Well, Happy Christmas, Jimmy.'

'And you, Nina. Your friend Jimmy sends you a big Christmas kiss.'

She put the telephone down. I am a fool, she thought. Why can't I love Jimmy and make life simple?

Chapter 34

'Mrs Dobbs is not homeless, Mrs Stockton. She has a perfectly good home to go back to. Anyway, Janice, Billy's been on the phone all morning, and he's making a perfect nuisance of himself. I have the car outside and I'll drive you back. You can't stay here in this place any longer.' The social worker sniffed. She wore an expensive tweed suit with a camelhair coat. She sat on a chair in the office, her nose wrinkled with distaste.

'We haven't finished decorating yet.' Nina was immediately furious with herself. Why the hell was she apologizing to this woman?

Elsie leaned against her mother's knee, her Christmas doll clasped firmly in her arms. Ryan stared at the social worker. 'I don't want to go back, Mum.' Ryan's eyes filled with tears.

'I don't want to go back,' Janice echoed. She looked at Nina.

'Don't worry.' Nina glared at the social worker. 'She doesn't have to go anywhere if she doesn't want to, Mrs Johnson.'

'But how long can you keep her here? Surely not for very long. And what on earth am I to tell Billy? Do you have any qualification to do this kind of work, my dear?'

Nina grimaced. 'You don't learn caring from books, Mrs Johnson. Obviously Janice is terrified of her husband, and so are the children. You know he hits the children, don't you?'

'Occasionally, I gather, he has been violent, but Billy is always sorry. I'm working with him on his little problem with anger-management.'

'Anger-management?' Nina muttered.

'I don't think you quite understand, Mrs Stockton. This family comes from a very low socio-economic group, and violence is their only way of expressing emotion. Why, I have one woman who gets beaten regularly on a Saturday night – says that's how she knows her husband loves her.'

'Do you seriously believe that? Or is that some apocryphal social worker story, Mrs Johnson?' Nina could see Janice was trying not to break down. 'Janice,' she said. 'Don't worry. You're with us now. I promise you, you don't have to go back.'

'You mean that, Nina?'

'You have my word.' She looked at the tired woman and the two children. Over the days that stretched between Christmas and the New Year, their faces had changed shape. Their cheeks had filled out with the good food. Cal's motherly bulk comforted them. Nina enjoyed talking to Janice. Above all, they were no longer afraid. Now this interloper had brusquely walked in and was about to let terror back into their lives.

'Are you saying, Mrs Dobbs, that you positively will not return to your home?'

'That's right. I'm staying here with my friends.'

Mrs Johnson sniffed again. 'Hardly your friends,' she said. 'Well, we shall have to have a case conference about this.'

'By all means do, Mrs Johnson. Have as many case conferences as you wish.'

Mrs Johnson pretended to ignore Nina's remark, turning instead to Janice. 'Billy will be awfully upset, you know.'

'You won't tell him where we are, will you?' Janice's hands were shaking. 'Please don't tell him where we are. He'd come round and smash the place up. He'd kill me, he would. He'd kill me.'

Both children were crying.

'I think you'd better go now, Mrs Johnson.' Nina stood from her chair in a gesture to indicate that the social worker was no longer welcome. 'If Billy does turn up, then we'll all know who told him, won't we?' Nina put her arm around Janice. 'It's all right. It really is.' She smiled at the social worker. 'You run along now and deal with Billy. We'll look after Janice and the children. Tell Billy his wife and kids are never coming back and he has only himself to blame.'

Mrs Johnson swept out of the office.

'Stuff that up your case conference,' Nina said after she had gone. 'Okay, Janice. Get your things together. We'd better get out of here. It shouldn't take her more than a couple of hours to get back to the East End and tell him everything, so we should expect a visit from Billy some time this afternoon.'

'Where are we going?' Ryan's eyes were fixed on Nina.

'We're going home.'

'Home?' Janice frowned.

'Yes. To my house. Simon's dressing room is empty, and you can stay with me until we get something sorted out.'

Elsie's eyes were sparkling. 'Do you have a telly?'

'Yes, and you will have Hamish and Susan to play with. I'll just run downstairs and tell Cal. Then I'll drive you home. Cal can deal with Billy when he shows up.'

Nina laughed, hearing Cal's report.

'I told him to fuck off, and if he touched the building, I'd brain him. He's a big guy, Nina. I've never been frightened of a man before, but boy is he bad news!'

'Well done, Cal. So, that bitch of a social worker *did* tell him where Janice was.'

'Yeah. Most of them will. It's no different in America. The guys terrorize the social worker so the social worker tells them where their wives are to get them off their back.'

'Any luck with rehousing Ben and April?'

'Nope. I telephoned the National Housing Shelter. They just said they don't take individual cases. But if you ask me, I'd say they only take donations, is more like it. I'm trying Paul Davison next. Remember him from the Birmingham conference? He's the one running the squats. He'll have somewhere for them. I'll telephone him tomorrow.'

'You brought these people home, Mum? But you don't even know them!'

278

'Of course I do, Susan. They need a roof over their heads for a while, and we have plenty of space. Janice and I have fixed up your father's old dressing room. It has a bed in there anyway, and I've borrowed two extra beds from your room and Hamish's room, so everybody's happy.'

'But they talk funny. They talk like Doris.'

'No. Doris has a Hounslow accent. Janice is a Cockney, born within the sound of the Bow bells. There's a subtle difference, if you listen carefully.'

'Well, they're not going to our school, are they, Mum? That would be *too* embarrassing.'

'You're a snob, you know, Susan. A real snob.'

'I am not. I just don't see why we have to live with people we don't know.'

'During the last war my grandmother took in children from London to get them away from the bombs. Everybody did it in those days. People helped each other. It's perfectly normal.'

'You're always talking about the old days. It's boring.'

Nina looked at Susan's dissatisfied little face. 'Living with Janice and her kids will be good for you. You take much too much for granted.'

'Like what?'

'Like food on the table. Like hot water in your bath. Like central heating in a bedroom that's all your own.'

'So what? Everybody has hot water.'

'Oh no they don't. If you'd ever bothered to read a book instead of watching television, you'd see that Dickens wrote about all these things a hundred years ago, and none of it's got any better. That's the horror of it all. Anyway, you run along and tell Janice supper will be ready in half an hour.'

She heard Susan run up the stairs and then she

heard the ping as Susan picked up the telephone in her bedroom. The little bitch will be telephoning her father . . . Nina pushed the pork chops under the grill. If that bastard did more housing and less fucking in his Ministry of Housing office, maybe there wouldn't be so many homeless people.

She heard the ping again as Susan put down the phone. She was about due for another assault from Simon. Still, she was getting used to social workers. If Angela thought the Mrs Johnsons of this world were going to run her out of her own house, she'd have another think coming.

After dinner the children lay on the bean bags and watched the television. 'You know, it's really nice to have company, Janice. I don't miss Simon, but the night-times are awfully lonely.'

'Yeah, I know what you mean. That's the worst time. Wherever we was hiding, I'd tuck the kids up and then sit by meself and I'd think. Any little noise and I'd start. It's him, I'd think. He's out there. After three days of no sleep and all that fear, I'd have to go back. Anyway, I'd sit and look at the four walls and I'd think to meself, What are you going to do with yourself and the two kids, Janice? They're both good in school. Clever kids, especially Elsie. Ryan is good with his hands, but my Elsie, she's a good little reader.'

'Let's give them the rest of the week off, and then we can put them both in the local primary school. I don't think Billy will check through the schools to find the children, but I don't trust that bitch Mrs Johnson. I think we'll have to change your name.' Nina laughed. 'I wanted to lose Simon's name, but I couldn't in the end. Susan objected, so I'm stuck with it. You have a chance to make a completely new beginning. What do you want to call yourself?'

Janice grinned. She had a glass of wine by her hand. 'Dunno,' she said. 'Something posh. How about Janice Telford? I saw a town on the telly once called Telford.'

'Fine then. Goodbye, Janice Dobbs; hello, Janice Telford.'

Janice giggled.

'You won't go back to him, will you?'

Janice shook her head. 'No, I can't go back. I love 'im though, I really do. God knows why. He's nearly killed me enough times, and he's 'orrible to the kids.' She looked into the fireplace. There was no fire that night. The coals lay grey and lifeless. 'We did love each other, before the kids was born. We used to lark about. He's ever so big, my Billy, and ever so 'andsome. All the other girls were after him. Mind you, I was the one that got him. I was the one he married.

'He always was moody, even in the early days. But, you see, I understood 'im, better than anyone else. He was a Barnardo's boy, from one of them children's homes. Number 79 was his number. They didn't have names in those days, just numbers. He'd buy me anything when we first met, but 'e couldn't tell me 'e loved me. "What's love, Janice?" he'd say. "I give you everything already." And then I got pregnant with Elsie, and the drinking and the kicking began. Poor little Elsie, she was nearly kicked out of me body, she was. It was Ryan he was really jealous of, mind you. He was meaner to Ryan than he was to Elsie. Always was. He used to say Ryan wasn't 'is, but the milkman's instead. I stopped getting the milk delivered. The milk wasn't worth the rows.

281

'So, I can't go back, Nina. For the kids' sake, I can't. Don't think I won't feel tempted. But if 'e does kill me, what'll happen to the kids? They'd go into a home. You can 'ardly call those places homes. They're like concentration camps. I was in one for three years when me dad died and my mum had TB. They sent her away to the sanitorium, and they split up me and my brother. He's somewhere in England, but God knows where. Then me mum died, and as soon as I was old enough, I left that awful place and got work in a shop. Not long after that was when I met Billy.'

Nina sighed. 'He must have felt like a knight on a white horse to you back then.'

'A black horse, more like.'

Nina laughed softly. 'There are those of us who seem to be drawn to black sheep and black horses.'

'Yeah, and the answer to them is no. From now on anyways.'

'Yes,' said Nina. 'The answer really ought to be no.'

Chapter 35

Michael, it seemed, was everywhere but nowhere. Billy was either on the telephone at the office or dancing with rage outside Latchmere House. 'Where's me fucking wife?' he screamed at Nina.

After a week of his antics, Nina was no longer afraid of him, just bored. 'Fuck off, Billy.' Nina stood with her hands on her hips. 'Fuck off and stay fucked off.'

Billy stopped leaping up and down. 'Yer not supposed to talk like that. You're a social worker.'

'I'm bloody well not a social worker.'

'What are you then?'

Nina paused. What a question! 'I'm a housewife, just like your wife. And she's fucked off and left you, and it serves you right. She's not coming back, Billy. You can rant and roar all you like, but she's safe now.'

Billy hung his head. Tears ran down his cheeks. Nina watched him with little sympathy. This was the same man who had made Ryan eat powdered mustard by the teaspoon, the same man who had kicked Janice's face black and blue. No, she felt no pity for him. 'I miss Janice and the kids. Look at me! I'm in rags. No one to wash me clothes or clean me shoes.'

'Do it yourself, Billy. Now get going, or I'll call the police again.'

'I'm not scared of the Old Bill. You can go ahead and call 'em. Doesn't worry me.'

'All right, Billy. Last chance. I'll go in and get Cal.'

'You bugger, you! Not her!' Billy was off up the road.

Nina walked into the house laughing. 'Where's Michael these days?'

Cal shrugged. 'I don't really know. I saw Gemma last night and she says he telephoned Marietta and asked her to go to Thailand. Apparently he has an orphanage out there. Wanted Marietta to pay it a visit for some reason. Anyway, there are more important things to worry about than Michael. You got an irate telephone call from Lady MacLaughlin. Seems dear Mrs Johnson's been creating hell.'

'What's it got to do with her?'

'I have no idea. Gemma took the call yesterday.'

'Then I'd better give Gemma a ring. What about Ben and April Stevens?'

'Good news,' said Cal. 'Paul Davison came through with a squat. There's a squatters' meeting tonight. Can you take them over to meet the group? They have room for a couple and a baby. The address is 12 Stoney Street, Notting Hill Gate.'

'Great! I'll enjoy the meeting. And, you know, now I have Janice at home, life is really much less lonely. She's lovely to come home to.'

'And I'm just discovering the joys of having no one to come home to.'

'How do you mean?'

'I mean I learned a lot from my night on the town in Birmingham. Didn't I tell you about that? Remember when I went out by myself that night? Nothing really happened. I went to a pub and drank a beer, and that was that. But what amazed me was that I had a good time, just sitting by myself. For once it was a huge relief not to have to put up with Virginia and all her hassle, or Sally, or Ronni, or any of them. And I thought, I don't need this shit. I'm better off on my own.

'So I'm going to ask Michael if I can move in here full time. I like looking after people. The telephone's been going all morning. We have a woman called Monica Ficus coming in. She's been in a mental hospital. Middle class lady. Alcoholic, they say. No one else will take her.'

Nina grinned. 'Well, we will. I'll get a cup of coffee, and I'll ring Gemma.'

But then the phone rang. Gemma had rung her first. 'What's the problem, Gemma? Cal says Lady MacLaughlin's been giving you a hard time.' She heard Gemma laugh. 'Where are you, Gemma?'

'I'm in the polytechnic teachers' sitting room.'

'Are you politicizing all those little sods?'

'Yes, if you really want to know, I am. The trouble is the students all like the idea of "Each according to his need", but they don't want to do the work to get the "each". They seem to think that everything comes to them on a plate. Jesus had the same problem with his disciples, come to think of it.'

'Anyway, Gemma, what does our dear Lady have to say?'

'Oh, a long boring lecture from the Great and the Good. Usual crap. "Don't upset the status quo. Let the working classes help themselves. They're really all scroungers, you know." I think the best thing is if you give her a ring and ask her about the tickets for the ball. Can you imagine all that lot dressing up as if they were homeless?'

'No, I can't.' But at least it means I'll get to see Michael.

'Lady MacLaughlin? I understand from Gemma that you were upset by a telephone call from a Mrs Johnson.'

'Indeed I was.' Lady MacLaughlin's magisterial voice filled the room. 'How *could* you, Nina? You're new at this game, I suppose. So I apologized to her on your behalf. You can't go round hiding wives and children. That's not what we collect money for. If you're not careful, you'll have all our names in the newspaper.'

'I'm not hiding wives and children, Lady Mac-Laughlin. I'm hiding one woman and her two children. He's terribly violent, her husband. Did Mrs Johnson remember to mention that?'

'She said something of the sort, Nina, but he's also truly sorry. They all hit each other from time to time, you know, people like them. It's best not to interfere.'

'I'm sorry, Lady MacLaughlin, but I . . .'

'Well, where is she now?'

'I'm afraid I don't know. I sent her to a battered wives refuge in Chiswick and they've probably moved her on already.' Nina surprised herself by the grace with which she lied.

'Oh, all right. You'll let Mrs Johnson know, will you?'

'Certainly. How are the tickets going?'

'Wonderfully, Nina, I'm happy to say. Homelessness is the latest in radical chic.'

'Where are you going, Mum? Dad says he wants to talk to you.'

'Not tonight, Susan. I've got to go to a meeting.'

'Well, he says it's urgent. He says he wants to talk to you this week.'

'Okay, okay. Janice will look after you.'

'I don't want Janice to look after me. She's rude to me.'

'No more than you deserve. She won't tolerate your sulks and tantrums, and why should she? Why should I, for that matter? Janice is a good woman, and Ryan and Elsie are lonely kids. The least you can do is try to be friendly.'

'I like them.' Hamish spoke from the back of the car. 'It's like having a brother and a decent sister.'

'Shut up, Hamish. You're queer.'

'I am not. What's queer mean, Mum?'

Nina looked into the driving mirror. 'Well, Susan? Answer Hamish.'

'Queer is what Angela says your friends are.'

'She says that, does she? Well, some are and some aren't. But they're still my friends.'

Susan no longer had the ability to bother Nina quite so devastatingly, but she still disturbed her a lot.

They arrived home and the children went upstairs to play. Janice helped Nina in the kitchen. She asked what was making Nina's face look so white. 'Susan's at it again,' Nina complained.

Janice, being there full-time, had come to the same conclusions about Susan that Doris had reached ages ago.

'She's a wayward bitch, Nina,' Janice said. 'You mark my words. I hate to have to say that about any kid, but it's the truth.'

'I wish I could disagree. She makes me feel so guilty and such a failure.'

'So she does, because she knows how to push your buttons. Don't let 'er get to you. If she wants to live with a slimy dad and that whore of 'is, well then let 'er, I say. She'll come to no good.'

'You don't think she'll grow out of it? I mean, I've always tried to think it's just a phase, but I don't know. She just seems to get worse. It's like living with a permanent Judas figure.'

'She learned all that from her dad. She's his blood, you see. Blood will out.'

'Oh, I hope not.' Nina laughed. 'Oh, do you mind looking after all the kids tonight? I've promised to rush and go to a meeting with Ben and April.'

'Go and have a good time. And don't you worry. I won't take no nonsense from Susan.'

'No,' Nina smiled. 'I'm sure you won't.'

'So you see, Simon wants me out of the house so that he can sell it. Angela did want to live there herself,

287

but if they give me my share of the value of the house, she realizes they can't afford to live there. Either way, we're homeless. I could squat, I suppose. All those people we saw this evening are doing it. It's just that I love my house. Now I have Janice living with me, I'm not so lonely. Goodness knows why I'm telling you all this, Michael. It must be the wine. It is absolutely wonderful wine.'

'Nina.' Michael's voice was urgent.

She looked up at him. He was standing over her. She was aware of his tall graceful figure. They were in the drawing room of his suite at the Savoy Hotel. In front of the crackling fire an empty plate that had been piled with moist smoked salmon reminded her that she had not eaten a full dinner. But the salmon had been delicious.

'Nina, let *me* take care of you. From the moment I set eyes on you in Joe Allen's, I knew I wanted to look after you.'

Nina felt confused. 'I don't quite understand.'

'Then let me explain. You put your house on the market. I'll buy it. Get rid of Simon for good, and you'll be safe forever.'

'Oh, I can't ask you to do that, Michael. I simply couldn't.'

'You can and I will. You're one of my best workers, and I won't have you upset like that. There is nothing worse than being homeless. Believe me, Nina. I know what I'm talking about.' Michael pulled Nina to her feet. He wrapped her in his arms. 'I promise you, I absolutely promise you, I'll never ask for anything in return.' He gently kissed her mouth.

She felt the tears trickle down her face. 'How can I refuse? But really. There's no way I can accept. Thank you, all the same. Things will work out. Somehow.'

Michael pressed a handkerchief into her hand.

'I'd better go,' she said.

He walked across the room to a telephone. 'Telephone Mrs Stockton at eight o'clock tomorrow morning. She wants to put her house on the market.'

'Michael, it's two o'clock in the morning. That poor person!'

He laughed. 'So? It's two o'clock in the morning. I'm still up, aren't I?'

Nina sighed through the tears. 'Thank you, Michael. I'm not sure I'm comfortable with this. I mean, really there's no reason for you to be so . . .'

'Think nothing of it. I'll telephone you when the deal is through.'

'Marietta's right. You are unbelievably helpful.'

'She said that, did she?'

Grateful, yet somewhat incredulous, Nina left.

Michael went to the telephone. 'Send Michelle,' he spoke softly. He put the receiver down. Catching his prey always made him randy.

Chapter 36

'That's really nice of him. If he meant it.' Stanley was meticulously applying paste to the back of a long roll of wallpaper. The trestle table took up much of the space in the office, but by now half the wall had been papered and the result was a cheerful design of fruit and flowers.

'Oh, the offer was genuine, all right. I got a phone

call from his solicitor. He's a very nice man called George Hicks. He says all I have to do is telephone Simon and say I've seen the light and I will put the house on the market. And then Bingo! They'll leap into action.'

'Who's *they*?' Stanley stopped brushing the paper.

'Mr Hicks, naturally. And Michael's accountant, a man called Robert Wallace. They'll buy the house immediately.'

'Hm. I see.'

'What's the matter, Stanley? You don't sound delighted.'

'Oh, I am, Nina. I am. But will the house be bought for you? I mean, will it be yours? Or will it belong to Michael Morningstar?'

'I didn't ask, actually. I should have, I suppose, but Michael promised me there'd be no strings attached. Absolutely none. I mean, I still can't get used to the idea myself. But his accountant assures me there're no problems at all, really.'

'Let's hope not. Here, help me with the rest of this paper.'

'Are things okay with you, Stanley? I haven't seen much of you since Christmas.'

Stanley lifted the wallpaper off the table. 'Move to the left, love. A little further over. Yeah, things are all right. Kit's around and about, so I'm not all that lonely. But I'm feeling me age. I'm hardly past thirty, but I can see already that what once was won't ever be again. I'm starting to make plans for a face-lift in a few years' time and maybe a chin tuck. Kit says I'm being ridiculous, but it's difficult being around Kit and all his friends. They're all so young. I don't want to turn into just another ageing poofter, paying out all I earn to keep a boy to have sex with me. I'm still a long way off that, but maybe not too long. I just want to be loved.'

'Don't we all . . .' Nina looked at his face. He must have been quite beautiful not long ago. 'Great wallpaper,' she said. 'Makes the room look clean and attractive. It reminds me of my aunt's garden.'

Time had just started to blur Stanley's features and to pull down the corners of his full mouth. His blond hair was thinning at the top of his head. 'D'you think I should have a face lift, Nina?'

She sat down at the desk. 'It's your face, so naturally it's up to you. But if you're thinking about having your face carved up just to keep Kit, I'd say no.'

'Oh, is that because you don't think Kit's planning to stay around much longer anyway?'

'I just meant . . . Well, if you honestly want to know, I think Kit will go, and you'll end up with scars behind your ears and a scar under your chin, all because of him. But if it's something you want to do for yourself, Kit or no Kit, then why not?'

Stanley climbed down from the stepladder. 'I'd just like someone in my life who'd love me no matter what.'

'Yes, I've heard you say that before.'

'I've been saying it all my life. The only person who really loved me was me mum.' He sighed. 'She loved me so much, I can never find that kind of love again.' Stanley smiled. 'But then, Nina, the fun is in the trying, isn't it?'

Nina's head still ached from last night's wine. 'If we don't get it right, we might end up like poor old Monica downstairs, awash with booze. Poor woman. She's a sherry drinker. And we had a woman come in called Valerie. She's a prostitute. Her pimp is looking for her. She showed me where he slashed her last year. She's got a scar from her belly all the way down to her thigh. Not a pretty sight first thing in the morning.' Nina picked up the telephone.

She dialled. 'Simon? Look, I've been giving the business of the house a lot of thought. I really think I should put it on the market, and then we can split the proceeds. This way you and Angela'll be free to buy a place for yourselves . . . Yes, I really mean it. You're delighted? Good. I do hope Angela will be thrilled. So, I have your okay to go ahead and telephone the estate agent? I've been given the name of an excellent agency. I'll let you know as soon as I hear any news . . . Okay. Yes. Pick up the children as usual. What's that? Don't be ridiculous. Janice is not a squatter. I love her company, and her children are a good example to our two. Susan *always* complains, so what's new?' She put the telephone down forcefully.

'Smooth move, Ex-lax.' Stanley grinned. 'You're getting to be quite a good little revolutionary, you know. Soon I'll get you a blue Mao suit and the "Little Red Book".'

'No thanks. I'd rather have a copy of the Bible and a good bottle of champagne. Imagine! Angela's going to have the smile wiped off her face when we sign the documents and I don't move out. Ha! Thank God for Michael Morningstar.'

'Amen.' Stanley applied more paste.

'Are we selling the house, Mummy?' Susan sat at breakfast a week later. 'Hortense said she saw the advertisement in *The Times*.'

'Yes, the house is for sale, but we already have an offer. Remember I told you last Friday that a man had telephoned from the estate agents?'

Susan nodded. 'I told Angela. She's ever so pleased.'

'Don't say *ever so pleased*, Susan. It's such awful English.'

'Anyway, Angela says now we can get a proper place of our own, and I can move in with Daddy and the new baby.'

Nina glanced at Janice who was suddenly absorbed in looking at her plate. 'Are you really sure that is what you want to do?'

Susan stared at her mother. 'Yes, I'm sure. And Angela says I can go to the same primary school she went to. She says that our school is out of touch with reality.'

'She would. Angela doesn't fit into . . . Oh, never mind. All right, Susan. If you really want to live with your father, I'll talk to him and see what can be arranged.'

'I want to live with you, Mum. I don't want you to sell the house. I don't want to leave my room.' Hamish was white and tense.

'Don't worry, Hamish.' She hated to shake his confidence. 'Leave it all to me, darling. It'll all be all right.'

'What do you mean it'll all be all right?' Susan's voice was as sharp as Angela's.

What a chameleon that child is! thought Nina.

'You *are* selling the house, aren't you?'

'Will you *please* stop asking me that, Susan?'

'How can it be all right then?'

'Faith. Good, old-fashioned faith. It can move mountains, you know.' And pregnant ladies, she muttered to herself as she carried the plates into the kitchen.

'I'm taking the kids down to the local school this

morning. Doris says it's ever so good. Her kids are there. Then I'll go down by the Social and change my books.'

'Okay, Janice. I've got to go to court with Valerie. She's charging her boyfriend with grievous bodily harm. I'm not much looking forward to it. He's going to be there with his friends.'

'Well, you'd better be ready to do a runner then. You'll not go far in those shoes, Nina.'

'You're right. I'll take a pair of flats with me. Just in case we do have to make a run for it.'

'I took in four families last night and we have two homeless men sent in by Father John. Monica's tippling away on the sherry, and Valerie is waiting for you in the office.'

'I must have a cup of coffee before I go off to court, Cal. Come up and keep me company. I like our Valerie, but sometimes she frightens me. I wish I smoked like you do. I feel I could smoke a whole box.'

'Valerie's up there puffing up storm clouds. She's nervous as hell. I can't blame her for being scared.'

Valerie was sitting behind the desk taking phone calls. 'Might as well make meself useful while I'm sitting here. Could be my last day on earth, today.'

'Oh, come on, Valerie. It can't be that bad.'

'You ain't never seen him, Nina.'

'Well, perhaps you'd be better off without such huge false eyelashes.'

'I can't take these off. They're me trademark.' Valerie's eyelashes were clotted with thick black mascara. Her full sensual mouth seemed to have been outlined in prune juice and then bitten until her lips were like tumescent grapes. Her tight jersey shaped itself around a very protruding pair of breasts.

And good heavens! thought Nina. If we do have to run, that tight, black shiny miniskirt will split. Nina decided to try out her new vocabulary. 'What happens if we have to do a runner?' she said.

Valerie crossed her legs and Nina very much hoped she was wearing knickers. Valerie ran a finger down her black silk-stockinged leg and then gazed pensively at her high-heeled shoes. 'Nah. He wouldn't chase us in court, not in front of the tipstaff. It's outside we got to worry about. He's got a Jaguar. His hitman drives it for him. He lost his licence last year. Ran over a man and killed 'im. Accident, he said. The judge believed him, silly old fart. But still, he can't do no driving for a while. Anyway, I'm going to nail 'im this time.'

A timid hand came through the door.

''Ere, Monica,' Valerie instructed. 'You take over the desk while I'm away. Answer the phone and make notes there. By the way, Nina. A bloke rang up and said you was not to worry. The deal's going through now and you'll be hearing from 'im at the end of next week.'

Nina smiled. 'Thanks, Valerie.'

'Wouldn't've thought you was into drugs, though.'

'No, it's nothing like that. Not that kind of deal. Just getting my divorce settlement finalized.'

'He shafted you then, your old man?'

'Yeah, you could say that. Listen, we'd better go. Are you okay, Monica?'

Monica dropped into the chair. 'I think so, Nina. I'm sorry I haven't seen much of you, but I seem to sleep all the time.'

'It's the sherry, love. Give it up,' advised Valerie. 'Sex is much better for you.'

Monica Ficus smiled.

She must have been quite pretty at one time, thought Nina as she waved to Monica.

Cal sat on the desk. 'We'll run the store until you're back.'

'*If* we're back.' Valerie clattered down the stairs with Nina close behind her.

'You sure we shouldn't change into flat shoes in case we have to run?'

'Stop worrying, Nina. If he gives us any trouble, I'll take off me shoe and let 'im have it in the face. He hates 'aving his face marked.'

'Well. *There's* a comforting thought.' Nina walked to the car. The idea of two women attacking a man with their high-heeled shoes did not give her much strength.

Chapter 37

Acton Magistrates' Court in no way lived up to any fantasies Nina might have had as to the august traditions of a British house of justice. Acton Magistrates' Court squatted on a mean street. The building smelled sour. Nina found herself being herded into seats in the front row. 'Cooeee!' Valerie waved her black pocket book handbag enthusiastically at a thin, bespectacled, worried-looking man. 'That's me solicitor,' she explained to Nina. 'Over 'ere, Mr Hunter!'

Seeing them, Mr Hunter's face cleared and he hurried over. All around the square room people were jostling each other for attention. Most were standing and conducting what seemed like impassioned operas. So great was the diversity of actions and of accents that Nina felt herself quite bemused. Sheikhs argued among themselves, their wives by their sides, silent and heavily veiled. A Jamaican family, the matronly woman surrounded by five children, could be heard across the room. 'Foolishness!' she claimed loudly. 'This man talks lies and foolishness!' A heavy-jawed man stood by her side. A property owner, Nina guessed.

'Nina, pay attention,' Valerie demanded.

Nina reluctantly withdrew from the fray and concentrated.

'That bastard Leonard is pleading not guilty to grievous bodily harm. Says I was drunk and attacked him first. Mr Hunter says he's likely to get off with a fine for disturbing the peace.'

'Disturbing the peace, when the complaint is as serious as grievous bodily harm?'

'It's domestic, you see, and the court don't much care if it's a domestic. They think it's all right for a man to beat 'is wife.'

'But you're not his wife, Valerie.'

'I know, Nina, but I'm not going to tell them up there that 'e's a pimp, am I? What will that do to my good name? Shit! I wish I'd never charged 'im.'

The door behind them opened. Three men walked into the courtroom.

'Oh m'God!' Valerie's hands were trembling. She snatched a Rothman's from her handbag and began to light it.

'You're lighting the wrong end.'

'It's 'im, Nina.'

Nina had very much hoped it wasn't him. Leonard was the best advertisement she had ever seen for a pimp. He was well over six feet tall. His sleek black hair was brushed back from a low primate forehead. Two suspicious eyes searched the crowd and then the deep-set eyes found Valerie.

'He has a solicitor and a barrister with him,' Mr Hunter said quietly. 'I think he means business.'

'He always means business.' Valerie was smoking and shaking at the same time.

'He may look awful,' Nina tried to sound confident, 'but we're safe here. This is the court, you know. Look at all the policemen. But why does he look so angry? After all, you've had rows with him before. I mean this isn't the first time you've charged him for beating you up.'

'Nah, but it's the first . . .'

'All rise,' a voice interrupted.

Nina glanced at Mr Hunter who gazed coolly ahead. A muscle twitched in Mr Hunter's jaw.

Nina sat down along with seventy other persons and watched the two men and one woman who now sat at the front. The panel of three looked down upon the court. They appeared a lot less benevolent than the Justices of the Peace who were friends of her parents. The two men wore business suits. One wore a truly dreadful striped tie and the other a pair of National Health spectacles. The woman was rotund, sporting a hat which resembled a squashed cabbage leaf.

Leonard's bulk filled the box. Three pairs of eyes stared at Leonard and he stared back.

'Ah, you have your barrister with you, Mr Pollard?'

'Yes, I do, yer honah.'

'No need to address me as your honour, Mr Pollard. I'm only a humble magistrate.' The humble magistrate was clearly delighted at his rise up the judicial ranks. He cleared his throat. 'Is the other side here?'

Mr Hunter stood up. 'Indeed we are.'

'Please step forward with your client.'

Nina squeezed Valerie's hand. 'Good luck,' she mouthed.

'We don't want to take a lot of time over this case, do we?' The other two magistrates shook their heads. 'The charge sheet, Mr Pollard, indicates that there was some kind of fracas in your home last Saturday night. You struck your wife, Mrs Pollard, it would appear.'

'Wife indeed,' Nina heard Valerie whisper under her breath.

The magistrate continued. 'She went to the police station and signed a complaint against you. Can you explain, Mr Pollard, why you should behave in such an extraordinary manner?' Nina caught a look of amusement in the faces of the other two as they watched their colleague deliver lines as if he were playing the part of judge in a local amateur dramatic society's production. 'What had she done, Mr Pollard, to make you so irate that you struck the young lady?'

The magistrate leaned forward from the dais and stared at Valerie. Nina was reminded of the lascivious judge from *Trial by Jury*. Good, Nina thought. He's going to be sympathetic. Valerie smoothed her hips with her hands and gave an appreciative wiggle.

'I came home on Saturday night. I was late, yer honah. I was working at the motor shop till half eleven, and when I walked in, she –' He pointed a huge trembling finger at Valerie '– said she'd thrown me dinner in the bin. Me dinner in the bin!'

Nina felt the earlier sympathy for Valerie vanish.

'And not only that, yer lordships, I went upstairs to change me clothes and I found she'd razored all

299

me suits to ribbons. So I go downstairs and I give 'er a good hiding. It was no more than what she deserved. Then she run off and laid charges. Never said nothing about me dinner, or me suits. She did a bunk, and I haven't set eyes on 'er till today.'

The three magistrates conferred. 'Case dismissed on the grounds of complicity.'

Nina waited for Mr Hunter to return to his seat, followed by Valerie.

'What's that supposed to mean?' Nina asked.

Mr Hunter shrugged his shoulders. 'It means they think she deserved the beating. "A woman, a dog, and a walnut tree," Mrs Stockton. That's how the old saying goes. "The more you beat them, the better they be." Nothing changes.'

Nina saw Valerie's frame droop. She turned to her. 'You didn't tell me about cutting up his suits.'

'I know, Nina, but he was drunk as a skunk, and I was fed up. Here, let's go.'

The three of them filed out of the court room. Outside in the bleak grey hall, Leonard was waiting. Mr Hunter nodded pleasantly to Valerie. 'Goodbye,' he said.

Nina watched him move swiftly out of harm's way. She and Valerie seemed to take forever before they stood face to face before Leonard and his legal counsel. 'Don't be such a fucking idiot, Valerie,' said Leonard. 'Go 'ome and get back to work. Business is lousy since you left.'

Valerie looked down at her shoes. 'No thanks, Len. I'm happy where I am.'

'Oh, give us a break. I was a bit worse for drink, I admit. But I'm sorry, lovebird. Really I am.' He put his thick fingers under her chin. 'Come on, then. Let's go home and take our clothes off. Or I'll take you to the club and buy you a little bubbly. I'll even take your friend here, if you like. Nicko likes them short and blonde.'

'No thank you, Mr Pollard. Valerie and I are going home. We have an appointment.'

'High class, your pal, Valerie. Moving in higher circles, are we? Come on, love. Forgive your old Lenny. Bygones are bygones, and all that.' Nina decided Lenny looked like a starving gorilla being threatened with the loss of his last banana.

'It's no good, Nina. I'll 'ave to go back.'

'You don't *have* to, Valerie.' Nina was appalled. 'Why?'

Valerie gave a sweet smile. 'If I knew why, doll, I wouldn't 'ave to, would I?'

Nina watched Valerie's back as she linked her arm in under Lenny's massive biceps. She was flanked by the barrister and the solicitor. She looked very young and vulnerable.

Nina had to swerve as she pulled out of her parking space and a white Jaguar screeched past her with a squeal of tyres. Her last glimpse of Valerie was of her face eclipsed by Lenny who was kissing her passionately in the back of the car.

'Shit, Cal.' Nina sat slumped in her chair in the office of Latchmere House. 'I feel an absolute failure. Valerie went off with him as if he were some Arab prince. All he is is a bully and a pimp.'

'But not to her. What would she be doing if she wasn't with him?'

'I don't know, but at least she could stay here and not have to prostitute herself.'

'It's not that easy, Nina. Anyway, she'll be in again. I'll bet you we'll be seeing her in here before too long.

Then you can ask her your questions yourself. By the way, you had a call from your ex. Oh, and a call from Michael.'

'Great. But I'm off men for the moment. I mean I just can't understand why a woman would be drawn to a man who is so blatantly bad for her.'

'Can't you? You've honestly never felt anything for someone you know you ought to keep clear of? I have. And maybe that's why I've sworn off women for a while. The wrong kind of women anyway.'

'No, I don't understand,' said Nina. Suddenly an image of Michael Morningstar came into her mind and she felt she knew very well how easy it was for Valerie to be pulled as if against her will towards the very man who promised danger. That's a stupid thing to think, she immediately scolded herself. Michael was a friend, a good friend. And he was being a help to her in buying the house, wasn't he? Certainly no danger . . . But even if the dangerous air about him ever did make itself manifest, thought Nina, she would *still* be attracted to him. 'Maybe I understand a little,' she said softly, not wanting to discuss her feelings openly. Then, to change the subject, she said, 'I'll tell you what, Cal. Why don't you come over for dinner. Janice would really like to see you, and it would be good to see Stanley, so I'll invite him, too. We can all drown our sorrows together. What do you say?'

Chapter 38

'Any news yet, Nina? Angela is getting impatient.'

'I'm so sorry Angela is impatient, Simon. Yes, there is news. My accountant says we have had a serious offer.'

'Really? That's marvellous! Who's your accountant?'

'Oh, a Mr Wallace.'

'Not Robert Wallace of Wallace & Cohen?'

'Yes. That's the one.'

'Good heavens, Nina! How on earth can you afford them?'

'That's my business, Simon, not yours. Anyway, Mr Wallace will be working closely with my solicitor, George Hicks. You'll be hearing from them soon. And, oh yes. I'm thinking of asking Mr Hicks to handle my side of the divorce.'

'But there's really no need for you to put yourself to that expense. Hicks & Morris are top lawyers. We can stick to the idea of a do-it-yourself divorce. Where did you meet all these people?'

Nina was dying to say the words *Michael Morningstar* just to hear the sharp intake of breath. Michael's face was all over the newspapers this morning. He had donated half a million pounds to a Cambridge college. 'I've made some friends, Simon, other than the people you called my freak-friends.'

'Do you have any plans to move yet?'

'Why, Simon? Why do you want to know my plans?'

'Oh nothing. it's just that Susan says she doesn't think you really intend to move out. And Angela's afraid this might all be a ruse on your part to keep the house.'

'But why should Angela care where I live?'

'I've no idea. I'll be blowed if I can understand her, but she seems to feel that as my future wife she should have the same standard of living that you and I shared when we were together.'

'I've already told you, when the house is sold, you'll have forty thousand pounds. We bought this house for twelve thousand ten years ago, so you're coming out of it quite all right. Tell Angela the facts of life. She'll be doing bloody well out of the deal, as it is. Pinching another woman's husband is an expensive business. Anyway, as you bring it up, Susan does seem determined to live with you, so I've said, provided it's okay with the two of you, you can have care and custody of her. Hamish wants to stay with me.'

There was a silence. 'Are you sure Susan wants to live with us?'

'You created her, you and your mother. She's taken to Angela, and she wants to go to the local primary, so you'll save on school fees. You have her, Simon. I've thought about it a lot. I think Susan and I will be much happier apart. She belongs far more to your world than she does to mine. Always has.'

'I really don't understand all this talk about different worlds. Life is quite simple. At least it can be. If only you didn't complicate it so much.' She heard a growing petulance in his voice. 'Yes, of course we'd be delighted to have Susan, as soon as we find a place to live.'

Nina was getting bored. 'Fine then. It's settled. Speak to you soon.' She put the phone down and drew a deep breath. She had not meant to have the discussion about Susan over the telephone.

Monica Ficus was in the room. She sat cross-legged on the mattress vacated by Janice. 'That must have hurt,' Monica observed in her fuzzy, sherry-besotted, middle class voice.

'Yes. You're right. It did and it does. But it's been a hurt for so many years, I feel it's time to make it stop. Susan will be much happier with her father and with Angela. Sometimes children just get born into the wrong family.'

Monica agreed. 'I certainly was.'

Oh shit, Nina groaned inwardly. She's going to unload, and I want to ring Michael.

Monica's thin hands picked at the sheet covering the mattress. Nina immediately felt guilty. She had talked to Gemma and to Cal; Monica had confided in no one.

'Until I heard you talking about your daughter, I didn't feel anyone would understand. My real surname is Foster, Monica Foster. D'you know the artist Sheridan Foster?'

Nina smiled. 'Of course I do. She's world famous.'

'Well, she's my sister. Do you know what it's like to have people say "Monica Foster . . . Are you related to Sheridan Foster the artist?" Suddenly you're a non-person. All they want to know about is your sister. I changed my name to Ficus a while ago, but I still feel bitter. My brother is a well-known barrister. My other sister is an actress. I didn't want to be any of those things. I just wanted to live in a little

305

house, be happily married with children, and have some roses growing over the back door. It's not much to ask, is it? But as things turned out, I'm an embarrassment to my family. I'm the black sheep. "Monica? Oh, poor Monica . . ." So I drink. It passes the time.'

Nina gazed down at her. 'Maybe if you had something more practical to do, you wouldn't need to drink. We have these new families in tonight. Cal needs a break. She's coming to my house for dinner. She'll probably stay for the night. Can you run this place until tomorrow?'

Monica laughed. 'Give me some responsibility and I'll clean up my act, is that the idea? Well, it sounds a jolly good one. Let's give it a try. I'd be happy to hold down the fort, and I'll just drink less. I like the office. It feels safe.'

'Well, thanks. That's a great help.' Nina checked her watch. She dialled Michael's number.

'Nina? Just a second.' She heard Michael push a button. 'Nina, I've just heard from George Hicks. He says he's taking care of everything for you.'

'Yes. I can't believe how fast it's all going through. He told me he was sending round some contracts to sign.' Still uncertain Nina dared to ask, 'Will it really be mine, Michael? I mean, in my name, sort of thing?'

'Oh, Nina. Don't you trust me?'

'Of course I do. And I'm very grateful, really I am.'

'So you should be.'

She heard Michael put the telephone down. She felt a moment of fear. Why couldn't she get a straight answer? Anything is better than Angela living in the house, she thought.

In his office, Michael leaned back in his black leather armchair. 'We're in business, my little lesbian,' he said, pulling Marietta onto his knee.

'Don't call me your little lesbian,' she said crossly, struggling to get off. 'I'm already regretting the fact that I asked you for help to get my children back.'

'But you did. You started working at Latchmere House and you took one look at the big man at the top and you thought, oh goody! It's Santa Claus Morningstar. And I have only to ask him for help and he'll do whatever I want. So now you're getting what you want, aren't you? I've told you I'm doing what can be done. And now you have the nerve to complain to me?'

'I didn't know the price would be so high,' said Marietta, lowering her head.

Michael took her chin in his left hand and pulled her neck back until it was painfully arched under his mouth. 'Nothing comes free.' He smiled and then he bit into the exposed throat. His other hand was over Marietta's mouth. It stifled her scream.

I have such sharp teeth, he observed as he watched the bright beads of blood. 'You'll have to wear a scarf,' he said, laughing as he let Marietta struggle out of his reach. 'What will Gemma think?'

'One of these days, Michael, I'll tell Gemma who you really are and how you really make your money.'

His eyes clouded. 'I don't think you will. In fact, I'm almost certain you won't. The waterways in Bangkok are pretty unhygienic, and you're not a very good swimmer, are you? Besides, you *do* want to see your children again, and you know I'm your only hope. So that makes me something of a saviour to you, doesn't it?'

'Hardly my saviour.'

'Nevertheless, dearest, a deal is a deal. And between the two of us, we have a deal.'

'What? That if I behave well enough as your

indentured servant, then some day, when you feel like it, you'll pay off my ex-husband enough money to buy me the right to have my children back? It's not a very good deal. And how do I even know my ex-husband would co-operate at any price? How do I know I'll ever get my children back?'

'You can only trust me. But don't worry. Everyone has their price. And your ex-husband is a man of such low principles that his won't be any more than I'm willing to pay.'

She stared at Michael. They both knew she had no choice but to carry on living under his conditions. 'What do you want from Nina? I don't see what you stand to gain from her.'

'Nothing. Absolutely nothing. Oh, a few practical things maybe. She's pretty. She's presentable. She'll look good in photographs. She's the right person to figurehead my London charity. Get some good attention and press and public support. Those things are always useful. Nina's perfect for that. But that's all business. That's frosting. No, Nina isn't business to me. She's a hobby. She's for the pure pleasure of it.' Michael picked up a slim, gold paper knife. 'She's so fresh, so uncorrupted, so idealistic. I can't resist owning something so pure. Don't you see her lovely innocence? It's like having something extraordinary as a pet. A white dove, a unicorn, a tame butterfly.

'When I was growing up in the desert, I used to watch my tarantula stalk the grasshoppers I fed him. I'd pick up a grasshopper, hold it over the tarantula's box, then drop the insect in. Grasshoppers have big iridescent eyes, Marietta. The grasshopper hit the bottom of the box and then he would see the tarantula. Those huge eyes would fill with panic at the mere sight of my pet. Then slowly, incredibly slowly, the tarantula would begin to move in on the grass-hopper, until it pounced with terrible speed.'

Marietta put her hands over her ears. 'I don't want to hear any more. It's too horrible. Why, Michael? Why do you need to trap people and then hurt them?'

'I've outgrown tarantulas and grasshoppers. It's far more interesting to collect people.'

'What ever happened to make you so cruel?'

Michael sighed. 'Darling,' he said, 'all those sociologists and psychiatrists just can't understand that some people are born evil.' He opened his eyes wide, showing the barefaced honesty of Eden's serpent. 'Yes, I say it of myself. It's no particular secret. Why should I deny the way I am? It's a foolish man who doesn't know himself. My mother said that when she saw me for the first time, she crossed herself. She swears I hissed at her. "Eee, holah! That one is cursed of the devil!" she said, a self-fulfilling prophecy, if ever there was one. But don't forget, "The wicked shall flourish like the green bay tree." And I would say I've flourished rather well, wouldn't you?'

'You'll rot in hell, Michael.'

'*Please*. Spare me your schoolgirl morality. Hell sounds like a perfectly entertaining place and we both know it. We'd be bored to death in Heaven. No, you'll probably wind up in the next fire pit along and we can have a wonderful time tormenting each other for eternity. Now why don't you go and do something about your throat? You appear to be bleeding.' He watched Marietta's slim back leave the room.

She wouldn't say anything. Michael smiled. In his briefcase he had a picture of Marietta's husband and her children. He had what she wanted literally in his hands. Women are their own worst enemies. They can't keep their private lives separate from their professional lives. It's her own fault for asking him to help. Michael's Mephistophelean hand had not taken long to locate Marietta's husband. For Michael there was no such thing as an Iron Curtain or a closed border. Marietta's ex-husband was happy for the extra money, and the children's letters to their mother could bring tears to eyes even as cold as Michael's.

Gemma, he decided, was not worth trying to possess. She would be no fun to play with and he had no real reason to want to control her. Gemma's devotion to Marietta was probably enough to keep her a safe distance from his own affairs. And he was not interested in seducing Gemma because she was truly indifferent to men or money. Gemma was too much of a simple sort. She had her relationship with Marietta and she had her love for Nina. Not a sexual love, but the love of friendship all the same. For the moment, Gemma was of no particular use.

Michael put his feet on his wide desk and gazed over Hyde Park. His wife was flying in from New York for Lord and Lady Radnor's ball. Lady Bobo Radnor and Michael's own wife, Titania, got along splendidly. How wonderful to have such a rich wife! How very lucky!

Michael's whole life was based on assumptions. The born-rich are all so very stupid. Rich wife keeps adoring husband happy spending her money. And that was the only headstart, years ago, that Michael ever needed. The rest of his empire he had built himself. Perfect.

He thought of Nina, like a beautiful butterfly, and he thought of himself as the tarantula of his youth. The tarantula, apparently, had developed a taste for butterflies.

Chapter 39

'The whole feel of the house has changed. It's *my* house.' Nina handed a plate of smoked salmon to Kit. Stanley hovered near the kitchen door. 'You carry the tandoori chicken, Hugo, and leave some of it for Cal and the others,'

Hugo grinned. 'You are the only white woman I know who can cook proper food.'

Nina laughed. 'Don't you get well-fed by our dear Hon. Sec., the good Lady Alison MacLaughlin?'

Hugo shook his head. 'English cooking is for children. No spices, no good smell, just lumps of rice pudding and meat surrounded by fat.'

Stanley finished whisking the mayonnaise. 'Are we celebrating your personal freedom from homelessness, lovey?'

'Yes, in a way. I stopped off at Theodorakis's and bought some goodies. The contract arrived just before you did, so I got the gang together to celebrate.

'Isn't it odd, Stanley? Before I got rid of Simon, I lived in this house as half of a married couple. In those days, the house only filled up with the children's friends or their parents. Now the house is full of all sorts of different people – people I've chosen because I like them. Simon thinks we're all freaks, and in a way he's right, you know. Outside this house on this street there's a whole raft of married couples leading perfectly pedestrian little lives. I can see all the lights go on in the road between six-thirty and seven in the morning. That means mother is up and getting dressed. Then she sees to the kids while father is standing in the bathroom shaving. Most people in this road have two children, sometimes three. They all have breakfast and Daddy leaves for the office and Mummy takes the children to school in the second family car. Then she returns home. Most of us have some other woman to do the housework. I used to be the wifey, just like that. I watch them return to their houses with that determined look on their faces. If they are rich enough, they fill their weekdays with coffee parties and exercise classes. The whole road grunts and groans from ten in the morning onwards. After work-out hours, they shower and then you see them go out to shop. Most of them have country cottages, so the boot of the car is filled on Friday for the trek to the country. We used to go and visit Simon's bloody mother. Thank God the awful woman's out of my life now! And thank God I'm not the poor, tired, soulless woman I used to be.'

'You're certainly not that at all.' Stanley stuck his finger into the mayonnaise. 'Needs more fresh lemon,' he said. 'But, you know, I'm worried about the house deal you've done with Michael. I don't know the man at all, but I've read all about him. I see your Michael Morningstar's picture all the time, and he looks odd to me.'

'Odd? What on earth do you mean?'

Stanley continued to stir the mayonnaise. 'There's something in his eyes that frightens me. I'll be honest with you, Nina. He looks as if he's been cut out with a pair of scissors and pasted into the magazines and newspapers, as if he really doesn't exist as a person. I'm usually good at finding out about people. I'm perceptive. It's just the way I am. I can read people quickly and tell you what they're like inside. But him?' Stanley shrugged.

The doorbell sounded. 'Let whoever it is in, will you?' Nina called to Hugo. When he had left the room, Nina stared sombrely at Stanley. 'I think I might know what you mean. I've felt the same thing, in a way. And this is something I wouldn't admit to anyone else, not even Sonia. But Michael does frighten me. And I can't help but think that's part of why I'm attracted to him. Does that sound too stupid of me?' She took the lid off the casserole and pushed the chicken pieces around, the smell of forty cloves of garlic filling her nostrils. 'I've always been able to control Simon. He's perfectly predictable. Oh, I know you're about to say he fooled me for those two years. In a way he did and in a way he didn't. I really didn't care enough to notice what he got up to. If I had cared, I might have bothered to say something about the smell of scent on his overcoat, or I might have complained about the late nights at the office. But quite honestly, as long as he left me alone sexually, I was quite content. You know, Stanley, it's hell on earth to have to have sex with a man who bores you. Feeling like I do about Michael, I can imagine why sex could be such fun.'

'It *is* fun between two people who really love each other. Otherwise it can be a dreadful trap. And if I can give you a truthful answer to the question you ought to be asking, the answer is yes, Michael could be a dreadful trap for you. But I also know there's no stopping you. I should know. I've made a fool of myself often enough. There's the door again. Is the chicken ready?'

*

313

Nina carried the casserole in her gloved hands to the dining room.

Cal and Janice were deep in conversation. Kit and Hugo were playing on the floor with Ryan's train set. Ryan sat back on his heels, grinning. Nina watched Hugo. Lady MacLaughlin's lover, she thought. He glanced up and saw that Nina was studying him. 'You thinking about me?' he said, his glossy eyebrows arched.

What perfect teeth he had, Nina noticed, smiling back. 'Not thinking exactly. Just wondering.'

'Don't wonder.' He stood up slowly. 'I'm the latest of the old gorgon's fads. Radical chic, darling, that's all I mean to her. Nobody else will get it up for her, so I oblige occasionally. And for my efforts I've got a pad in Eaton Square, the use of a Rolls, and I go to all the right places. You have no idea how boring the rich are in England. Absolutely ghastly! No sense of humour.'

'I am about to get a very good idea.'

'Does that mean you're coming to the ball thrown by the Radnors?'

'The only balls I've ever been to were the hunt balls in Devon. Those were really good fun. We all grew up together, so everybody knew everybody, and you were as likely to "strip the willow" with the local undertaker as you were to dance with the MFH's son.'

Hugo snorted. 'This will all be very different. I'll wear my Honduran rebel uniform. The New York Black Panthers will prowl around in their battle outfits. There'll be several African rebels wearing dashikis.'

'But I thought everyone was supposed to come in Oliver Twist costumes?'

'And no doubt lots will. But the rest of us will dress as ourselves, and that ought to scare the shit out of everybody. Anyway, please don't tell anybody that I went to Radleigh. They all like to think I just hopped out of a bush and caught the plane to London.'

Nina chuckled. 'And how about you, Cal? Are you going?'

'Not my scene, honey. You can represent Latchmere House for the rest of us. We're packed to the roof, Nina. You know, I bet we could organize a lot of good secondhand clothes and toys and even household goods from the schools round here.'

Janice helped herself to the chicken casserole. 'I was thinking that your school might want to make some clothes donations, Nina.'

'That's a good idea. I've been thinking that we really ought to get into our own squats. After all, we now have groups of people living at Latchmere House. We could move them on in a sort of extended family unit. Then people like Monica could be rehoused with people she knows.'

'Monica needs to stay with us for a while, Nina,' Cal put down her plate. 'That tandoori's terrific. Monica really likes organizing the office. She says in the other places she's been, all the staff made the decisions and ran the administration, so she just sat around thinking about drinking, bored to death. With us, she doesn't have as much time to drink, now that we're overcrowded and we've asked her to help out.'

'It's funny,' said Janice. 'I haven't thought about Billy at all this week. In the other homeless hostels, I was so lonely that even Billy was better than that. But now we belong to one big family, I won't need Billy no longer.'

But I need Michael, thought Nina. She watched the faces move and talk to each other. For all she enjoyed cooking for her friends, for all she enjoyed having Janice in the house, over-riding all those happy feelings was the deep ache she felt for Michael, an ache that had been growing so big as to frighten her lately. As the fantasy of him took on more and more molecules of reality, so too did her desire for him increase. She wanted to be with him – in his arms, in his bed, by his side. She watched Gemma at the end of the table. 'Are you all right, Gemma?' she said quietly. 'You look a million miles away.'

Through the chatter she saw Gemma's silent face slowly flush. 'I don't know where Marietta is,' Gemma said. 'Michael seems to have a lot of work for her to do. She sends her apologies.'

'That's okay. Come on. Let's go into the kitchen together and we can make the coffee.'

The two women stood together in the kitchen. 'Life's a bitch, my pretties.' Stanley stuck his head around the door.

'Go away, Stanley. We're having woman talk.'

'Count me in, then.' Stanley put his arms around Nina and Gemma. 'Silly cows, both of you! Marietta's a double-crossing little bitch, and Michael is more dangerous than a pair of rattlesnake boots. And here you both are, pining away.'

'It's all right for you, Stanley. You have Kit.'

'No, I don't. I just have a new philosophy. Nobody has anybody. Nothing ever lasts forever, so stop moping and start living. Nina, I saw just the very thing for you to wear to this indecent exhibition you're going to attend.'

'I *have* to attend. A whole evening of watching the idle rich pretending to be poor is a perfectly appalling idea, but it will raise money. I thought I might go as Oliver with a begging bowl, but I think I'd make a better Nancy.'

'Because you expect Michael to go as Bill Sikes?'

'I wish you'd stop reading my mind. How did you know that, Stanley? Maybe I shouldn't go as anything at all.'

'When you're gay, you're on the outside, so you learn very fast to understand people. And sometimes to survive in my world, you have to know your enemy. Personally I'd have cast Michael as Fagin, with his little band of beggars and pickpockets around him. And in no time he'll do more than make you beg, my dear. Don't say I didn't warn you.'

Nina shivered. 'Don't be such a spoilsport.' Gemma hugged Stanley. 'My, you're in a strange mood tonight.'

Stanley looked out of the window at the cloud-covered moon. 'Nothing good will come of this,' he said. 'Nothing good for any of us.'

'Oh, come off it, Stanley. You've had too much wine.'

'Perhaps I have.' He turned his bulky body and left the kitchen.

'I wish he hadn't said that.' Gemma wrinkled her nose. 'You don't think Michael could hurt Marietta, do you? She's been different lately. I can't quite say how, but she often seems lost in thought.'

'This is all getting silly. I don't see how or why Michael should hurt anybody. He houses homeless people because he's been homeless himself. It's as simple as that. I know he's got a few problems, but then so have we all.'

*

317

Much later Nina lay dreaming of a shipwreck and she found herself struggling in a warm dark sea. Far away she saw a hand waving and then it slipped under the waves and was gone.

Chapter 40

Nina was grateful to Antonia Hurst, the charity's homelessness adviser, for being a friendly face in an otherwise alien ball. They happened to arrive at the same moment, so together they walked through the imposing door of the Royal Crescent Hotel. Nina immediately became insecure as to whether or not she had made the right decision by not dressing up in costume. She had chosen instead her elegant evening dress. Now she could not decide which way she would have felt sillier: in or out of costume. All that she felt sure of was that she disliked costume balls.

Antonia, in costume as the Artful Dodger, wore a pair of scruffy trousers and a moth-eaten top hat.

Nina looked around at other people in costume and decided that, as everyone seemed in this together, she should have risked herself. 'My goodness,' Nina pointed, as they stood in the crowded lobby. 'Who on earth is that? I'd say she's pretty brave to come dressed like that.'

'That's Ben Radnor's pet, Jocelyn. She runs the Radnor Clinic. She recycles heroin addicts.'

Jocelyn made her way towards Antonia and Nina. 'Antonia, darling!' She air-kissed both cheeks of Antonia's face. Nina watched Jocelyn's pale pink nipples flash in and out of her slashed sequinned dress, evidently designed not to appear Dickensian but to make a strong impression nonetheless. 'Lovely little outfit, don't you think? I've shaved my pubes, so I'm quite hairless. Such a change for Ben! The poor dear has to put up with the hirsute clutches of bloody Bobo, so tonight I intend to make him a present of myself. Anyway, I'm having trouble with my car. I *need* a new one. And that's what charity patrons are for, isn't it? I absolutely must have a white Corniche.' She winked at Nina. 'Don't think I haven't heard all about *you*.'

'About me?' Nina was surprised. 'I wouldn't think there was very much to hear.'

'Oh. I see. You don't kiss and tell. But come now, Nina. We pets should stick together. It's a short life and a pet should get as much out of it as she can. Life with Michael is shorter than most.'

Nina watched Antonia's face change. 'Jocelyn.' There was a warning in Antonia's voice.

'Antonia, don't be such a stick in the mud. I call Antonia the Nun that has None. She gets furious with me. Truth is, I'm perfectly happy with my patron. I like an owner who's safe. Your Michael may be a lot of things, but safe isn't one of them.'

Nina was scouring the lobby. There was no sign of Michael or of his wife.

'Well,' Jocelyn twittered, 'I'd better go and scout out an utterly perverse venue for a furtive fuck.'

Nina watched Jocelyn shoulder her way through the crowd. 'Whew! Is she for real?'

'All too. She's one of the many hopeful young

women,' Antonia explained. 'In the old days, rich men had mistresses. Those were the days when divorce laws were strict and wives had no say. If they did divorce their husbands because he had a mistress, she lost everything. These days, with modern divorce laws, the rich men just tuck their mistresses away in their pet charities, and nobody says a thing. Sort of doing well by doing good. You'd be amazed just how many charities are nothing more than mistresses' playthings.'

There was a shuffle among the thronging crowd, then a collective gasp as three men walked into the lobby. Their shiny black skin was exposed to the waist. Figure-hugging black leather trousers gripped their bulging crotches. Black hats and very dark glasses reflected the frightened white faces. They strolled arrogantly through the crowd. Nina laughed as they came closer. 'Hugo,' she said, grinning. 'Not a bad entrance.'

He greeted her with a bow.

'What on earth have you got down your trousers?'

'Anticipation, sister. Some little rich white chick will ball the three of us together. Meet my brothers. Charlie, introduce yourself to Nina.'

'Hugo,' Antonia was chuckling. 'You are dreadful.'

Charlie inclined his massive head in Nina's direction.

'And Whiplash.'

Nina took Whiplash's extended hand. She stood feeling a little nonplussed. 'Hello, Whiplash,' she said uncertainly. 'What do you do in London?'

'Nothing.' He looked at her with warm brown eyes. 'I killed a man back home, so I had to leave.'

'Oh,' said Nina. 'I see.'

Fortunately the doors were opened to the dining

room and the guests seethed forward. Antonia pulled Nina with her as willing hands grabbed Hugo and his two friends. 'Catch you later,' he shouted over the crescendo of humans heading for the tables.

'How lovely to see you, Nina dear!' Lady Bobo Radnor fussed about the table. 'We're sitting twelve per table tonight. Michael's darling wife Titania is here from New York. You'll absolutely adore her, Nina. Antonia, you sit there and keep my dear Percy Cochran amused. He likes to talk about fly-fishing. The best salmon comes from his estate in Scotland. Though you know women are far better at salmon fishing than men. I don't know why, but it's a fact. Now where are you, Ben?'

Ben strolled towards the table. 'I've just been seeing to the drinks. Nina, you sit over there.'

Nina saw a trace of Jocelyn's lipstick on his cheek. She wondered if his evening with Jocelyn had already been consummated. Really, I always imagined the charity world would be dull. All those comatose pictures in the *Times*, all the announcements in the *Telegraph*, seemed to imply that the charitable sphere consisted of saintly Samaritans brought together by their philanthropic inclinations. She looked around at the guests. Their unashamed displays of their varied forms of decadence were quite unexpected. 'Has Michael arrived yet?' Nina tried to make her voice sound casual.

She saw the glint in Bobo's eyes. There were no secrets among the very rich, she knew. 'He'll be along in good time, darling. Our Michael does like to make an entrance.'

'After all, it is his ball and his wife's money,' trumpeted Percy Cochran. 'The man's a cad. An absolute rotter. Married money, that's what he did. Can't even cast a rod, y'know.'

Nina tried not to laugh. Percy Cochran reminded her of a character in a Whitehall farce.

Everyone sat down and Ben summoned the wine waiter. The glasses were just filled when a rush of fresh air seemed to enter the ballroom. The silver helium balloons along the walls quivered with electricity, and then in a puff of imagined smoke, Michael could be seen standing in the doorway. He had indeed come as Bill Sikes, his shabby suit a clever parody of hoodlum formality. His strong hands were covered in woollen gloves the fingers of which had been cut off. Beside him, elegantly swathed in a scant brown cashmere dress made to resemble a sack, belted by a silk rope, stood his wife. Nina at once felt very small and very silly in her own unremarkable attire. Titania apparently had dared to be more outrageous and was consequently more striking. Nina wished she had tried harder, but there was nothing she could do now.

An appreciative pause formed and then the room rose to its feet and people began to clap. 'Michael! Michael!' the voices brayed. The star had arrived among the planets.

Antonia stood beside Nina. 'The same lot would be shouting "Off with his head" under different circumstances,' she observed in an icy tone.

Nina felt startled. 'Surely you don't think most people are that cruel?'

'Not people, Nina. The rich. They don't have to care. Life for most of them is just one long party. Michael's secret is that he knows just when and where to throw his parties. Michael is *in*.'

'Radical chic?'

'You learn fast.'

Nina watched Michael and then their eyes met. She felt burned by the intensity of his gaze. All necks craned in her direction. She felt herself blush. Shit, she thought. Why do I have to light up like a beacon? Hundreds of pairs of eyes pierced her with a salacious gleam. I'm not even his mistress, she told herself. He's a married man. I just happen to work for him. Lady MacLaughlin was eyeing her from down the table. There was a sardonic grin on her face. You can grin, dear, thought Nina. You shrivelled old bag. You look perfectly ridiculous in your Fagin costume. Nina sat down. She cast a triumphant look at Alison MacLaughlin. Hugo's got a lump in his trousers that's not for you, she thought, you ugly old bitch.

Titania Morningstar slid into her chair beside Nina. 'I'm so glad we get to visit together, honey. All these classy English people frighten me.'

Nina was surprised. Titania's face was as hard as the multi-faceted diamond she wore on her hand, but the voice was breathless, like a bird fluttering.

Titania frowned. She put her hand over her glass as a waiter passed behind her. 'No wine,' she said. 'I never touch alcohol. It's too ageing, they say. Every drop shows on your face.'

Nina considered Titania's long upper lip. Somebody must have spent ages tweezing out the hair from above her mouth. The lip was beaded with moisture.

Titania sighed. 'You'd think that a hotel like this would have the class to serve ice with their water.' She clicked her fingers and several waiters ran forward.

Nina knew in a million years she could never click

her fingers and have a bevy of waiters rush to her side. It must take money to do that, she thought. It's the legendary smell of money that gives people like Titania their power. She breathed in deep and caught the aroma of her perfume. They smell different indeed, she decided.

Around the room the Great and the Good sat surrounded by their hangers-on. At a table she could see Hugo teasing Jocelyn. Whiplash and Charlie also seemed to have commandeered a debutante girl each. The two girls laughed pretty little laughs as sparkling as chandeliers. But Jocelyn didn't glow the way they did. Jocelyn didn't reek of the self-confidence those girls had. Her hair and clothes didn't shriek of Daddy's money. No. Jocelyn, beside the two girls, seemed desperate. She flung her head back too frequently to appear natural, and strains of her frenzied laugh could be heard through the increasing noise from the dining tables. She was not born to be one of them, however hard she might try.

'We got held up, Ben. The traffic was terrible. But then Michael's always late for everything, so I shouldn't complain. Now, Nina,' said Titania, turning in her chair. 'It is Nina, isn't it? Tell me about yourself. I understand from Michael that you work for his homeless charity. Quite why he has to have all these charities I'll never know. He's certainly not in it for the money. I suppose it keeps him busy. Still, we have even bigger social problems in New York, but no, he likes flitting all over the world instead of taking care of his own back yard. His latest escapade is a children's home in Colombia. Can you imagine? First it was Hong Kong, then Bangkok, and now Colombia. I think it's just an excuse to rush around in his private jet. I bought it for him for Christmas. Sort of his and hers. You've eaten all your first course, Nina. Really, you mustn't do that. Just a nibble, and then push it away. You'll put on weight if you keep it up, the way you're going.'

Only half-listening to Titania's words, Nina heard Jocelyn's voice. She saw Ben frown.

'Silly girl,' Ben said, shaking his head.

'She's awfully pretty.' Nina tried to placate Ben.

Bobo's mouth was tight. 'We can't have the Radnor Clinic's director known as a drunk.'

'Of course not, dear,' Ben said to shut up his wife. 'I'll talk to her, as soon as dinner is over. She's so worried about the overdraft at the Clinic. The running expenses are astronomical. Nina, you have no idea.'

'Actually, I'm beginning to, Lord Radnor. I've been doing the accounts for Latchmere House. And the proceeds from this fund-raiser are more than needed, particularly if we're to expand our work.'

'I don't know what this country is coming to these days. Bolshies running the place, bloody bolshies. And have you heard about the squatters? Thieves and vandals, taking over other people's houses and breaking in. It's unthinkable.'

'Yes, but I thought they only took empty houses belonging to the Councils.'

Ben stared at Nina. 'You're not one of them, are you?'

'Well, not exactly. Still, if a house is empty and no one is going to move in, I don't see what's wrong in a homeless family taking over and putting it to good use. It's better than having them on the streets, isn't it?'

With an almost flirtatious gleam, Ben Radnor leaned toward Nina and said, 'I'm not sure that when your true colours make themselves seen they might not be tinged with pink after all.' Fortunately Ben was distracted by another course of food. 'Roast pheasant! Lovely!' Lord Ben tucked his starched white napkin under his double chin. He tore off a leg and sat gloating over the dripping limb. 'So much for Mummy's table manners. A man ought to eat with pleasure, I say.'

Nina looked at Antonia. Around her the rich gobbled and snuffled. Antonia smiled at Nina. 'Oh well, if you can't beat 'em, join 'em.'

Sonia should be here, Nina thought. She'd get a kick out of this.

'What are you doing for the summer, my beautiful little butterfly?' Michael's arms were around Nina's body and she moved against him, lulled by the music. The evening was late and she knew she must go.

'Well, Mr Sikes, I'm planning to go to Greece with Sonia. I've never been to Greece. I've always wanted to go.'

'Then we will have to see what we can do. Won't we?' Michael was gazing down at her face, a slightly quizzical smile on his lips.

'I'd better go, Michael. I promised Antonia she and I would leave together in ten minutes and it's past that now.'

Michael's arms tensed. 'She can wait, Nina. This is our first dance together.'

'I know, but I do have to go.'

'No, you don't *have* to do anything. Have you signed the contract?'

'Yes. Simon and I have signed.'

'Good.' Michael's grip relaxed. 'You may keep your

midnight curfew. I'll waft you back to your kitchen and you can wait for me to arrive next time with a glass slipper. You can try it on and if it fits, you and your lovely little foot will be mine forever.'

Nina smiled. 'What happens to me and my lovely little foot if it doesn't fit?'

'Oh, it will fit, Nina. My shoes are handmade. They always fit.'

Nina was surprised that his normally humorous voice had lost its tone. He must be tired, she thought. It can't be easy being the central star in the charity world's cosmos.

Chapter 41

'The money's cleared into my bank account.'

Nina felt her stomach lift. 'Yes,' she said lightly. 'It must be a relief for you both, Simon. Now you can go ahead and buy a house.'

'Hm. But Susan says you have no plans to move out.'

'Actually, Simon, she's quite right. I have no plans to move out. Susan is the one that has a plan to move, as soon as you get into your new house. She's yours full-time.'

'Don't you think that's rather sad, Nina? Getting rid of your own daughter?'

'No, Simon. I've given it a lot of thought. Susan will be much happier living with the two of you than she is with me. So do hurry up and get a house.'

'Angela says she doesn't see how you can manage to stay in the house.'

'It's none of her business. Or yours.'

'Well, if this had been your plan all along, I don't know why you didn't tell me from the start. Why keep it a secret?'

'Because if you had known, you would have found something to object to, just to keep Angela happy. Now it's done and we can get on with our lives. By the way, I'm going to Greece this summer. You'll be taking the children to Spain, won't you?'

'You're going to Greece? Who with?'

'Sonia. Myles will be at his mother's for three weeks in August, and so she and I'll take off for a fortnight or so. Both of us could do with a break.'

'I'm not sure we'll be able to go to Spain this year.'

'Never mind, Simon. I'm sure you'll manage it somehow. But just make sure you're ready to have both children for the first three weeks in August, all right?'

'Angela feels you cheated us, you know. You said you were moving out of the house. I suppose your family came up with the money. But with my half, I can't buy Angela a house like in Angel Walk.'

'No, you probably can't. Tough titty. Hard times among the adulterous. I've got to go. Goodbye.'

Janice clapped her hands. 'Well done!' she said.

Doris was grinning.

Nina sat down at the table. 'That's that,' she said. 'No more Simon slobbering over the telephone, trying to get me to move out. Now it's my house and I can do anything I like.'

The telephone rang. It was Michael Morningstar. Janice handed the receiver to Nina.

'I need you to be at the Savoy for dinner tonight. I

have a crowd coming in from New York. I want you to meet Zelda Armstad. She's your American counterpart. Kind of. She heads up a homelessness research team in the sociology department at a university in New York. When America wants answers on the homeless, they ask Zelda. It's important for you two to meet, though I can't imagine how you'll get on.'

'After an introduction like that I'm suddenly nervous. But you say you think it's important that we meet?'

'Contacts are always important.'

'All right. If you say so.' Nina looked at Janice. 'Can you babysit, Jan?' Receiving a nod, she said, 'Okay, Michael. I'll be there. What time?'

'Seven forty-five for drinks and then dinner. Black tie and evening dresses. Get whatever you need in the way of clothes. I'll be doing a lot of entertaining in the next few months. Titania left yesterday for New York, so you'll have to take her place. Send the bills to my office.'

'That's kind of you. But for the moment, I don't need any new clothes.'

'It isn't kind. It's business.'

'Well, really. I'm fine for clothes. You've bought me the house, and that's more than plenty. See you tonight.'

Nina put the telephone down, feeling faintly taken aback by his tone which had not been entirely warm.

'All this social life gives me a headache. I can't understand how the rich think they are actually helping house the homeless when tonight we'll be spending the best part of a thousand pounds eating food. Crazy, isn't it?'

'Same thing in LA. They all eat in Beverly Hills, and the homeless get the leftovers out of the trash cans. If the Good Samaritan were alive today, he wouldn't be able to afford the cover charge at a charity fund raiser.'

Cal sat next to Monica in the office. The house was full of people. Small children scampered up and down the hall. Nina's nosed picked up the sour smell of the unwashed. 'What we need,' said Nina, 'is a plumber. I'm calling one in. It would appear the drains are blocked.'

Monica flipped through the telephone book. Nina was pleased to see Monica's face had filled out. She still drank, but not out of despair. 'We're packed to the gills, Nina. The Public Health Inspector has been in. He's a really nice chap. He left you some daffodils. Said he grows them all year round in his greenhouse.'

Nina put her nose into the yellow mist of trumpet-shaped heads. 'How lovely they are! It's like an early harbinger of spring.' She saw a note pushed into the flowers.

7 Abbey Court Road. Owned by Hounslow Coun-cil. Empty six years. Excellent condition. Back kitchen window open. Good luck.

'God bless you,' Nina whispered. 'A health inspector with a heart. Monica,' she said, feeling her voice tremble, 'how about we organize our own squat tonight? Ought to be a nice spot for some of the families we have packed in here. The committee will all be at the Savoy, so they can't stop us. I'll get Paul Davison to arrange a big lorry.' She looked at her watch. 'Cal and I can go off now and do a recce. Monica, you get everybody together. Telephone

Janice and ask her to collect Hamish and Susan from school, would you?'

'Righto.'

'Let's go, Cal.' She grinned at Monica. 'Keep the faith, Monica. We'll get this lot rehoused, one way or another.' She ran lightly down the stairs. 'Gosh, Cal. I hate to admit it, but this feels quite exciting.'

The car took a left turn off Chiswick High Road. 'Boy!' cried Cal. 'If that's the house, it's a great place.'

Nina parked the car. 'We'll have to be very quiet. The house is set well back and secluded. There's a huge hedge around it.' Nina pushed open the gate. Followed by Cal, she walked across the front lawn of a large and gracious stone home. Victorian, she guessed. 'I'll get in the window, if you give me a leg-up.' Nina pulled open the kitchen window and then scrambled inside. 'Hang on. I'll open the back door.'

When Nina had opened the door, Cal stepped in. 'Wow! Even bigger than it looks from the outside.'

Nina flipped the light switch. 'It's wired up.' She giggled. 'Now I know how a burglar must feel.' They walked into the hall. 'It's beautifully decorated, and there must be at least ten rooms. We could put four families in here easily.'

'Sure thing. Monica can organize furniture. All we need tonight are camp beds so everyone has something to sleep on.'

Nina climbed the stairs. 'The loo works.' She flushed the lavatory on the first floor. 'I wonder what the council planned to do with this house.'

Cal laughed. 'It certainly doesn't look as if they planned to have it occupied by the homeless.'

'Then they're in for a surprise. We've got plenty of blankets. The dear old Sally Ann can supply beds tomorrow, but tonight we have to move fast. I wish I were squatting with you, Cal, but I think it's important that we keep the committee busy at the Savoy. Lady MacLaughlin will create a huge fuss if she thinks we're up to something only marginally legal.'

'Well, we're not breaking the law, not if we get into the house first and put up a squatter's rights notice. Once that notice goes up, then squatters get to stay right where they are, or, if the council wants to move them on, it has to find them adequate rehousing first. Anyway, Hounslow won't want to rehouse four families. They can't evict them onto the streets by law, and they would have to explain to the press why they left a huge building like this empty for six years.'

Nina pulled the window shut. 'You can get in by the back door now. We'll leave it unlocked. The important thing is to move in quietly. Use torches for light, and everyone can carry their clothes in black bags.'

Nina gunned the Volvo around Hammersmith Broadway. She parked on Shepherd's Bush Road and ran up the steps of Latchmere House. She found most of the community in the dining room. An air of expectancy hushed the usual chatter. 'It's a fabulous house in a good area, and the schools are good for the kids. I reckon we can move in four families. Any of you up for it?'

A timid woman raised her hand. 'What happens if we get caught moving in?'

'Nothing much. The council might contemplate charging us for trespass, but I don't think they'd want the hassle or the public attention. So you'd only have to come back here again, which, as far as bottom lines go, isn't too bad. But we should get in if you all move quickly and keep the kids quiet. Cal will put a notice on the door claiming squatter's rights, and then you're safe.'

The woman looked satisfied by the answer. 'What do you think, Pete?'

Her husband beamed. 'I say let's 'ave a go. We got nothing to lose.'

The front door opened and Paul Davison walked in. 'Monica says you plan to squat tonight.'

'We need something for everyone to sleep on.'

Paul hugged Nina. 'Welcome to the fine art of squatting. You're learning, girl. Don't worry about the beds. We're moving out a squat in Islington, so we'll have extra beds in the van.'

'So, Pete, you're happy to go? Sheila and Brian and four kids . . .' Nina counted the hands that were held up. 'Great,' she said. 'That makes nineteen bodies.' She looked at Monica.

'No.' Monica was leaning against the door frame. 'I'm not ready to leave Latchmere House yet, Nina. I'm too attached to this place.'

'That's fine. We need you here anyway.' Cal stood in the middle of the room. 'Okay, everybody. Let's get out the black bags and start packing.'

'I'll be here with the van at midnight. The pubs will all be closed and the fuzz will be busy picking up drunks on Chiswick High Road. The neighbours will all be asleep,' said Paul. 'Where will you be, Nina?'

'At the Savoy, keeping the committee at bay. I'll talk my head off until you telephone. Ring Michael Morningstar's suite once the notice is up, and let me know everything went well. Then I'll make my excuses and head for the squat to say goodnight to everyone.'

Cal smiled. 'Don't worry. We'll get in.'

All around her, men and women were milling about the place. Nina watched the glow of happy hope on their faces. 'We can't let them down, Cal. But it's going to be tough once the committee get wind of this.'

'Too bad.' Cal shrugged. 'If you can't stand the heat, get out of the kitchen. They want to party – we'll give them a party. They want to conference, so we'll squat while they conference. You know this makes much more sense than all that crap Sally and Virginia put me through. Armchair revolutionaries is what they were, full of political theory and rhetoric and hot air, if you ask me. But tonight we get some real action.'

'I'm with you in spirit. I'll be sitting through a whole evening of Michael's New York friends who think they have all the answers. Anyway, it will be great tomorrow morning to come into a virtually empty house, knowing everybody is being set up somewhere else. I'll come prepared to scrub the place out.'

'Do that. And don't forget to doggy-bag me some Savoy food.'

Nina laughed.

Chapter 42

Nina handed the key to her Volvo to the doorman at the Savoy. Behind her she saw Hugo pull up in Alison MacLaughlin's Rolls-Royce. She leaned into the front window, knowing her voice was blocked from the back seat by a glass partition. 'Hugo,' she said. 'Get a few of your mates and go down to 7 Abbey Court Road in Chiswick. We're squatting it at midnight. Whatever happens, don't collect Lady MacLaughlin until after they get in, okay?'

Hugo's eyes widened. 'This is more like it. I'll take Charlie and Whiplash. Right on, sister.'

For once, Nina didn't find the sentence silly. She looked through the glass partition at Lady Alison MacLaughlin sitting in the back. Her wizened chest was covered in diamonds. Nina returned her glare with a demure smile. Nina shook out her full black taffeta skirt and walked confidently into the main lobby of the Savoy. 'Michael Morningstar's suite, please.'

'I'll take you up, madam.'

An impeccably black-clothed back led Nina up a small flight of stairs to a lift. Nina checked her watch. She was ten minutes late. About the right time for a social arrival, she thought. The lift stopped. 'To the right, madam.'

Nina followed the back to a door numbered 221. He knocked discreetly. The door was opened and Nina was ushered into a vast drawing room. In a corner she saw a grand piano. Sitting across from the door was a very fat woman wearing what Nina assumed must be a wig clamped to her head. She was smoking a cheroot and was surrounded by six young men all in black tie and clutching expensive briefcases. Behind the fat lady stood Michael and a rather tall man. 'You're late,' Michael said, his eyes hooded, his mouth frowning.

'I had to help Susan finish her homework.'

The fat lady rustled. 'Punctuality at all times, dear. You should know that. In our department, any

335

member of my research team who is late for anything gets two demotions. Discipline, discipline.'

One of the young men was busy scribbling furiously. Nina realized that he was writing down everything the fat woman said.

'This is Zelda Armstad, Nina. As I told you, she runs a highly respected think-tank on homelessness in New York. I thought she might be able to give you some advice. Zelda Armstad, Nina Stockton.'

Zelda gazed contemptuously at Nina. At the far end of the room Nina could see Antonia Hurst talking to Lady Bobo Radnor. Alison MacLaughlin was just coming in the door. At least Antonia Hurst's face was friendly. Nina felt intimidated by just about everyone else.

'What's your position on the homeless in England, Nina?' Zelda had a voice like a cheese grater.

'My position, Mrs Armstad?'

'*Mrs* Armstad? Don't you know anything about the women's movement? I'm Ms Armstad. Zelda to you. What do you mean you don't know? What don't you know?'

'All I know is that we have people coming to Latchmere House who have nowhere to live and we try and find them somewhere to live.'

'Yes, well I'm sure you think you're carrying out your work with the best of intentions, but what data have you generated? By which measures do you select your study group? Have you come up with any significant statistical evidence to support a theory of causality?'

The question came in a relentless bombardment. Nina said, 'I beg your pardon?'

Ms Zelda Armstad exhaled impatiently. 'Why are they homeless?'

336

'For lots of reasons, actually. Sometimes they can't pay the rent. Other times there is a fire. Fire victims are the easiest to rehouse because the councils have a statutory requirement to rehouse in case of fire.' Nina felt on firmer ground. 'Then there are women who are beaten by their partners and have to run with the children. And of course there are people who have been through other programmes, alcohol dry-out centres, mental hospitals, drug rehabilitation . . .'

Zelda waved her hand at Nina. 'No, no, no! That's all anecdotal. Quoting individual cases without having first set up a representative data base is meaningless. Don't give me anecdotes. What's your political position anyway?'

Nina paused. She frowned, beginning to feel her own anger. 'I don't have a political position.' She looked at Michael's face. He's enjoying this, the bastard, she thought.

'In that case, honey, you need to do your homework. The research my team's been doing is light years ahead of you. We've collected enough empirical data to start to confirm a hypothesis or two, which is more than it sounds like you've managed to do. And do you want to know what our research indicates? This, sweetie: Capitalism is the cause of homelessness. Don't you understand that?'

Nina shook her head. 'No, I'm not sure I accept that. I think that's an oversimplification. Besides, I've always thought of myself as pretty much a capitalist. I own a house. I send my children to a private school . . .'

'For heaven's sake, Michael! This poor child needs some lessons in social research and the scientific method! Send her to New York for a while, and we'll

337

see if we can't get her head screwed on the right way. She could start by processing some measurements, and then maybe work her way up to data analysis. That, and a bit of political re-educating, and we might make something of her. Where did you find such a quaint anachronism?'

Nina felt the colour rise in her face. 'The one thing I don't hear you saying about your own work, though you seem to think very highly of it,' Nina dared to say, 'is whether or not you've actually helped anyone.'

'*Helped* anyone?' yelped Zelda Armstad. 'Oh, you deluded little do-gooder you. You don't seriously think you're helping anyone by handling individual cases, do you? How does that change society in any way, particularly if you haven't gone through the requisite discipline of amassing figures to support your hypotheses in the first place? Surely you don't think you and your house of busybodies are really impacting anything, do you?'

'Impacting? Is that a word? But yes, as a matter of fact, I could give you the names of a number of people I think we've helped a lot. They have houses now and they didn't use to. They . . .'

'*Names*?' Zelda's cheeks shook with such rage that Nina wondered if the woman might not immediately suffer a paroxysm of some sort. 'What do *names* have to do with sociological research? It's populations that merit academic study. I can't believe I even have to tell you this. It's so basic, any lowly undergraduate could tell you that. Can't you see? Or is the truth too self-evident for your middle class inbred English mind to grasp?'

'Well,' Nina collected herself, 'I wish you the best of luck with your statistics and your data and your measures and your empirical evidence. The Latchmere House staff and I shall muddle along in our quaint, misguided way doing what we can to help real people with real names find real homes for themselves and their real families. We'll leave the important work to you and we'll see who comes out ahead on the human scale. Now, if you'll excuse me, I'm off to talk to Antonia Hurst, a fellow English-woman who still remembers how to talk like a person instead of a textbook. Zelda, meeting you was a rare experience indeed.'

She stalked across the carpet. She felt Michael's eyes on her back. She checked her watch. Eight o'clock. The hours were going to drag. 'Who the hell does Zelda Armstad think she is?' she whispered to Antonia Hurst.

Antonia looked across the room to where Zelda held court. 'The Queen of Homelessness, that's all. The shining star of the academic circuit. Her first husband shot himself, she was so promiscuous. But no doubt she blames his death on capitalism, too.'

Nina and Antonia were enjoying a laugh together when Lady Alison MacLaughlin intruded into their conversation.

'Well, Nina. I'm sure you're proud of yourself for the way you treated our honoured guest. I hope you'll listen with a little more respect to what she has to say in her after dinner talk and use some of her advice to help you run Latchmere House. You never know. You might even learn something. Such a fine, educated mind the woman has!' Alison MacLaughlin's face was aglow. 'And by the way, Nina, I saw a bill for toys from Hamley's. What on earth are you doing, buying toys for the Latchmere House children from Hamley's?'

'But I buy toys for my own children at Hamley's, Lady MacLaughlin. Don't you?'

'Of course, dear, but that's different.'

'Why is it different?'

Alison MacLaughlin shook her head. 'Toys for Latchmere House can be secondhand, or if you have to buy some new, you can get them from Woolworth's. But if you carry on the way you're going, next thing you'll be ordering food from Harrods Food Hall for the homeless.' She gave a short sharp laugh. 'The trouble with you is that you identify too closely with the people you are trying to help.'

Nina glanced at her watch again, wishing the minutes could pass faster. 'Oh, I'm sure you're right, Lady MacLaughlin. You're absolutely right.' Anything to keep the old bitch busy. The telephone rang. Nina picked up the receiver. She heard the international blip. 'Is Michael Morningstar there?'

'It's for you, Michael. I think it's your wife.'

Michael put a restraining hand on Nina's shoulder. 'Sure . . . Fine . . . I'm busy,' he said into the mouthpiece, and he put the telephone down.

More people were arriving. And in walked one tall man whose good-looking face was striking for the intelligent, open, friendly expression it held. 'Sorry, Michael, but my plane was late. Heathrow is a mess these days.'

'Never mind. I've reserved a room downstairs and we can all go down for dinner. Nina, this is Justin Agate, the journalist. And I'm pleased to say I've thought of him as my friend for years. You would describe yourself as my friend, wouldn't you, Justin?'

Justin gave a warm smile. 'Probably the best you have.'

Nina shook his hand.

'I'm here,' he said, 'to do a profile for the *New York Times* on Zelda Armstad, though frankly I find myself losing interest in my own story. My eyes are open for something else, if anything interesting comes along.' Justin looked at Nina. 'What do you think of Zelda?'

'What do *I* think?' With a member of the press at hand, Nina decided she ought to be diplomatic. 'I don't know her well enough to have formed an opinion.'

Michael laughed. 'Zelda intimidated Nina in her usual fashion.'

If Michael was clearly not concerned with diplomacy, then neither should she be. 'She didn't intimidate me, Michael. I just think she's frightfully vulgar. Stereotypical smartarse New Yorker. Cal warned me all about New Yorkers.'

'And Cal is . . . ?' Justin waited.

'Cal works with me at Latchmere House. That's the place where Zelda says we're foolish enough to try to help people. We just take in those who are homeless, and put them up until we can find somewhere for them to live. And for those who need more than just a house, but who have some deeper problems of their own, we do whatever we can to help. Give them a bed to lie on, food to eat, a sympathetic ear, our hearts. Love. Yes, that's it. We love them. No isms. No capitalism. No feminism. No communism. None of it. Politics is not what makes people happy. Love is.' Nina realized suddenly that it was precisely because of Zelda's opposition that she was forced to formulate her work at Latchmere House. She was pleased to see the shape her work had taken on when she described it in her own words.

'What a revolutionary idea, helping people without politics!' said Justin. 'This sounds like a story I could get my teeth into. I'd like to come around and see your place. Tomorrow, if I can? I'm here until tomorrow night. Excuse me, Nina. But I can see my photographer over there. Let's see if I can't do a story about your work as well, all right? I'm sure I could find a magazine or newspaper to run it. Excuse me for a moment.' And he went off to tell the photographer what shots he needed to get of the great Ms Armstad.

Nina was left facing Michael. 'I didn't think you'd like Zelda.' He was grinning like a naughty schoolboy. 'You handled yourself very well, by the way.'

'Oh, I don't dislike her, Michael. Not really. Why should I, poor old girl? She thinks she's important? Congratulations to her. I'm never one to take away people's illusions about themselves. Anyway, I'm hungry. Shall we eat?'

It was half past eleven by the time the group finally made it back to the suite. Zelda had given her little talk. The little talk was an excellent job in self-promotion. If God were a woman, Nina thought watching Zelda in action, she would probably be Zelda. She had mentioned the well-known names of leading American feminist social scientists and academics. Everyone in the room squealed and clapped. Nina tried to look interested. Apparently the cabal of powerful women thinkers lived up each other's knickers, drinking white wine and bemoaning the ways of men. Nina observed that, for a woman who professed to hate all men, Zelda was remarkably lenient with those around her. She largely ignored Alison MacLaughlin and Bobo Radnor who were sitting either side of her. She spent most of the time gazing ardently at Michael or issuing short asides to Justin.

Justin looked largely bored. 'I've heard all this crap before,' he lamented once he found himself a seat beside Nina. 'I'll have to write up my piece in the morning and get her off my hands. Then I'll be free to do some interesting work. I'd like to come over at lunchtime, if that's okay.'

Nina smiled. Of all the Americans gathered in the room, Justin was by far the nicest. 'What's wrong with all these people, Justin? They don't seem real.'

'That's because they aren't real. Zelda and her crowd are all aardvarks. She survived the McCarthy witch-hunt by snitching on her friends. That's why she drools over Michael. Most of the rich and careless won't have anything to do with her, except for Michael. And he doesn't give a damn for anybody.'

'I thought you were his friend.'

'I said I was probably his best, but I'm not sure he has any others. I admire him for the fortitude he has, but that doesn't blind me to the fact he uses people like Kleenex. Still, there are some people you just like *despite*. And I think he's one of those people to me.'

Nina looked at her watch. Ten past one. She saw Alison MacLaughlin shift in her seat. They should be in the house by now. The phone shrilled. Alison picked it up. 'It's for you, Nina. I think it's your nanny.'

Nina took the receiver. She heard Cal's voice. 'Squatter's heaven!' Cal cheered. 'Everybody in, safe and sound.'

'Oh, I'm sorry to hear that,' she said for the benefit of Lady MacLaughlin beside her. 'Hamish has a sore throat you say? Then I'd better come home at once. Thanks for letting me know.' Nina put the telephone down. She caught Michael's eye. 'I have to go home, I'm afraid. Hamish isn't well.'

343

'I'll see you to your car,' Michael offered.

'Goodbye, Justin. See you tomorrow.' She didn't bother to say goodbye to Ms Armstad. Zelda was too busy with her entourage.

'For a mother who has just heard her son's so sick you have to run home right away, you sure have a hell of a smile on your face,' Michael said on the way down in the lift.

'Do I? It's probably just that I'm glad to be out of there. Too many people in dinner jackets make me nervous.'

The car stood waiting. Nina felt her heart pounding. Every nerve in her body was screaming to get away. She saw Hugo pull up in Lady MacLaughlin's Rolls-Royce in the Savoy's courtyard. 'You're a deep one, Nina.' Michael pulled her into his arms and lightly kissed her cheeks. 'You're full of surprises.'

Nina looked at him briefly. 'As long as you like my surprises.'

'I always love your surprises.'

'That's all right, then.' She got into her car.

As she pulled away she saw Hugo's raised fist of victory through the back window. 'Excellent,' she said aloud in the privacy of her Volvo. 'Right on!'

Chapter 43

Sod Zelda! Nina drove down the Embankment. The cold moon hung over the River Thames. The familiar London bridges calmed her. Under those bridges lay the lost and the homeless. Zelda Armstad and her entourage would never see that world. They brought their New York arrogance and their New York spiteful edge with them. They were only too happy to forget that their statistics ever had anything to do with human beings.

Two Jamaican families were coming in from Battersea. Always new families coming in, no end to the ranks of the homeless in sight. Still, she comforted herself, the West Indian women were the best and strongest members of the community in Latchmere House. They left huge extended families back in their islands. Their homesickness was palpable. The women were clean and well-organized . . . Sod Michael! He enjoyed that little farce, but just wait until tomorrow when he and the board inevitably would find out about the squat. Let's see what they'll all have to say then.

The roads were empty and quiet. Nina put on a tape. *I am a rock*, Simon and Garfunkel sang. *I am an island*. I suppose I am, thought Nina.

She passed through Fulham Palace Road onto Hammersmith roundabout. *And a rock feels no pain. And an island never cries*. This one does, Nina observed. This one cries buckets. Why wasn't Jimmy Donleavy there tonight? Probably busy at the studio. He was a rock. Michael was an island. A dangerous island.

Nina stopped the car. There were lights on in the squat. Well, they were in and it was legal. She walked up to the door. A man moved out of the shadows of the hedge. 'Just a moment, Mrs Stockton.'

Startled, Nina jumped. 'Oh! You scared me!'

The man smiled. 'I'm Eddie,' he said. 'Eddie Saunders. I'm with the *Standard*. We had a tip about this

345

squat, so I decided to stake it out. I hope you don't mind.'

Mice were chasing each other in Nina's brain.

'Look,' Eddie said. 'Take my word for it. You'll be better off if I break the story. It's too late for the morning papers, but the *Evening Standard* will pick it up tomorrow during the day, which'll be all right because you'll get spared too many of the dailies. Anyway, I'd expect a lot of local people will be sympathetic. This house has been standing empty far too long. I'll do a really good piece. I'm all for the squatting movement. There's plenty of empty property all over the country. There's no need for anyone to be homeless. It's bloody politics that gets in the way.'

'Come inside, Eddie, and we can talk it over with the community.'

The vote was unanimous: Eddie should do the story. The four families had settled into their rooms. Paul Davison, still running about doing what he could to make everyone comfortable, had succeeded wonderfully. Mattresses lay neatly on the floor. Nina shared the thrill. Eddie prowled around, taking his photographs. Black bags, children asleep, their heads on the bags. Two of the women lay as if dead, exhausted by the pandemonium. There was a loud knock on the door.

Cal looked out of the window. Dawn was just breaking. Pink light streaked across the sky. 'It's the police,' Cal said.

Paul looked at Nina. 'You go downstairs and tell them that you are claiming squatter's rights. You'd be amazed how friendly they often are.'

Nina took a deep breath.

'I'll go with you.' Eddie's tall figure followed Nina down the stairs.

Nina opened the door. Two police constables gazed down at her. 'Squatters, are you?'

'Yes.' Nina pointed to the notice on the door.

The younger policeman looked at Nina, then at the notice, then at Eddie with his camera around his neck. The constable smiled. He touched his helmet. 'Wish everyone in the house a good morning. I don't like to see people homeless. You should try up by Wester Road. There's a whole row of pretty little cottages. Council's evicted all the old folk. Stuck them in those tower blocks. They plan to sell off the re-done cottages to young, trendy, investment banker types. Too bad my Nan was one of them that got moved out. They've moved her up to the nineteenth floor in a block of flats. No place for an old woman to live, if you ask me. Look into it, I would, if I were you.'

'Thank you,' Nina said gratefully. 'We will.' The constables tipped their helmets and left. 'Whew, Eddie! Life takes some funny corners.'

'Stand by the door and let me get a shot of the squatter's notice.' He shot a variety of photos of Nina. 'Good girl,' he said, putting his camera away. 'I'm off. Where can I reach you later?'

'At Latchmere House. The number is in the book under Help the Homeless. I must get home before my children wake up.'

Nina walked back alone into the house. 'Cal, can you organize breakfast?'

'Sure. We'll need to get everyone's social security books changed to this address, and Paul says he'll suss out the schools. The Salvation Army say they'll be here this afternoon with a truckload of additional beds and furniture.'

'God bless them.' Nina smiled at Hugo's friends,

347

Whiplash and Charlie. 'Thanks for your help,' she said.

'Any time. We'll stay to help unload the van.'

Nina drove home. By now a feeling of exhaustion began to creep over her. She walked into her silent house on Angel Walk and quietly went up to the bedroom. Had she done the right thing? Should she have allowed Eddie to take the pictures? Well, she thought as she soaped herself in the shower, she trusted him. He understood and sympathized with what she was doing.

She sat on her bed. She was too wired up to sleep. What on earth would her parents say? Thank goodness the *Evening Standard* was a London paper and probably wouldn't find its way out to Devon.

She picked up her Bible and let it open where it would. It fell open to 1 Corinthians. Nina read:

For now we see through a glass, darkly; but then face to face: now I know in part; but then shall I know even as also I am known.

And now abideth faith, hope, charity, these three; but the greatest of these is charity.

Nina let the book close and she was comforted, as if a special word had been given to her alone.

She heard Hamish moving in his room. 'Did it go all right?' Janice's face was at her door.

'Yes, it went brilliantly. The awful thing is, I really enjoyed the whole business. I think underneath it all, I'm a rebel at heart.'

Janice grinned. 'I'll get breakfast. You must be knackered.'

'I am. I'll take the kids to school, and then I'll come back and pass out for a couple of hours. Doris can take care of the telephone. Could you please go over to the squat and see that they have everything they need? Cal's taking them over to the Social Security. I guess they could do with a babysitter for the children.'

'I'd love to go over and see the place.'

Susan sat pensively at breakfast. 'Daddy says most people are not really homeless. They're just lazy. They don't want to work.'

'We were homeless, weren't we, Mum?' Elsie's face crumpled.

'Your mummy wasn't lazy,' said Nina, covering for Janice. 'Mummy worked very hard, and she did a very brave thing protecting you from your dad, didn't you, Mum?' Janice nodded. 'And I'm sure Susan didn't mean *you*, darling.' Nina felt too tired to take on Susan at breakfast, but she didn't seem to have much choice. 'Susan's just repeating what her father said. And we do have to remember that your father, Susan, is a fascist.'

'What's a fascist?'

'Oh, Hamish, it's too early in the morning to get into it, or too late at night, or whatever . . . All right, a fascist is someone who thinks that if everybody lived like they did, the world would be perfect. But if you don't live like they do, then they think you ought to be shot.'

'Daddy doesn't say anybody ought to be shot,' Susan defended. 'He just says they need a boot up their backsides.'

'Forgive me. Not shot, kicked then,' said Nina. She wearily acknowledged Susan's victory.

She watched Susan run into school without a backward glance. Really, she couldn't wait to get rid of the girl. What a terrible thing to think! she reprimanded herself. I'm only feeling this way because I'm tired. I'm tired of the endless *Daddy says*, *Daddy did*, *Daddy wants* . . . Fuck Daddy and all his world!

Once home, Nina passed Doris on the stairs. 'Whatever happens, don't wake me up, Doris. I plan to unplug the upstairs extension and make myself dead to the world.'

She threw herself into bed, fully clothed.

Through a haze she heard Doris's voice. 'Nina? I'm sorry to wake you up, but it's Simon. He's screaming and ranting down the telephone. Something about an article in a newspaper.'

'Oh no.' Nina put her hands over her eyes. 'I'd better plug in the telephone.'

'Would you mind explaining just what on earth you think you're doing?' Simon's voice was a waste-land of ice. 'Have you finally gone entirely out of your mind?'

'What are you talking about, Simon?' she grimaced.

'The article, the picture, the whole disgusting story.'

'What story, Simon?'

'You know perfectly well what story. Angela is in a dreadful state. She saw the headlines at the news-agent up the road. Whatever possessed you, Nina?'

'Are you talking about the squat?'

'Yes, I'm talking about the squat. I am, after all, a senior civil servant working for the Ministry of Housing. And now my wife . . .'

'Ex-wife, Simon. Don't leave off the ex. And the truth is I don't care what you or Angela think. It's my name in the paper, not yours.'

'But what will mother think? She'll be embarrassed

and humiliated. All the neighbours will talk. And I've been called to a special appointment to see the Minister at three o'clock, and he's always in a bad temper after lunch. With the press paying attention now, it looks like squatting could be the wave of the future, thanks to you, and that's one in the eye for the Ministry. I could lose my job over this, Nina. And it would all be your fault.'

'Oh, don't be silly, Simon. Just tell the old geezer I'm dotty and potty, as you've always maintained.'

'You've changed, Nina, I'll tell you that. Really, you have. Even your language has changed.'

'Has it? Well, maybe I'm becoming a bit more real, now I've escaped from your plastic lifestyle. What are the pictures like? Any good ones?'

'No, they're terrible, Nina, I assure you. The usual politically inflammatory set-up, the whole thing. That's what it comes out looking like. People pretending to be homeless, lying posed on the floor on mattresses . . . You should know. You were in on it. There's even a picture of you standing prettily in the front door pointing to a notice. It's unspeakably vulgar, Nina, this need for publicity.'

'I don't need publicity for myself, Simon, but the issue does have to be called to people's attention. And they really were sleeping on the floor on mattresses. That was no set-up. It's a bloody sight better than sleeping under the bridges.'

'"Queen of the Squatters", that's what the headlines call you. How low can you get?'

'Pretty low, if it houses the homeless. Now if you'll stop haranguing me, I've got to go to the office. Why don't you go ahead and ring your mummy and together the two of you can have a good old moan.' She put the telephone down. And hopefully, she said

351

to herself, Enid will have a heart attack and drop dead and the world will be one bitch lighter. But she's tougher than that, the old mare. No such luck.

The phone rang again. 'Darling?'

Oh no. It's Michael. 'Hello, Michael.'

'You've put me in a lot of trouble,' he said sweetly. 'The committee are after your blood.'

'Does that mean you're cross?'

'Of course not, Nina. I'd never be angry with you. And I promised you I wouldn't interfere with your running of things. I'm really finding it all rather amusing. I haven't seen Alison in such a state for years. Zelda is tearing out her hair.'

'Zelda? Why Zelda?'

'Because Justin Agate decided to scrap his profile on her and do you instead. He's waiting for you at the office.'

'Oh, Michael. I haven't done anything worth profiling.'

'You might not think so, but other people do. Besides, you're young and you're blonde and you're beautiful. Just the sort of head figure a good social cause needs to keep it in the public eye. The press will go for all of it. Wonderful shots, by the way. Simply wonderful. You look so woeful.'

'You will defend me from Alison MacLaughlin, won't you, Michael? I don't want her to descend on Latchmere House and carry on. I don't think our community would stand for it.'

'I'll keep her off for as long as I can, but I can't promise anything. She's a very determined lady.'

'Well, thanks for staying with me.' Nina leapt off the bed and ran down the stairs. The phone rang again, just as she opened the door. 'Tell whoever that is that I'm on my way to the office.'

'It's a man from *The Chronicle*,' Doris said in a hushed whisper.

'Tell him I've left already but he can get me in a little while at Latchmere House.' Oh dear. Nina drove quickly. *The Chronicle*, and I'm not engaged, getting married, or giving birth. I'm not even dead yet.

Chapter 44

There was a small crowd in front of Latchmere House. Nina approached hesitantly. She could see at least four men with cameras. They lifted their cameras to cover their faces and it seemed to Nina as if, when the cameras flashed in unison, they had taken her soul away. She pushed her way through the crowd who were gaping at her. ''oo is she?' an elderly woman in a brown-stained jersey asked her companion.

'I don't know. One of them social workers, I expect.'

Nina ran up the stairs and closed the door behind her. She was panting. Monica was in the hall. 'There's a man in the office to see you, Nina. Have you seen a copy of the *Standard*? Wonderful pictures. The phone's been ringing off the hook. "World at One" want to interview you. They'll send a car for you. Shall I say yes?'

'Interview me? About what?'

'About homelessness, I'd imagine.'

'Well, I suppose I ought to do it. Can you say yes

353

for me? How many people do we have in at the moment?'

'You'll never believe it.' Monica laughed. 'Four families went into the squat last night, and four new families have come into Latchmere House this morning. Oh yes. And Lilly.'

'Lilly?' Nina was on the stairs.

'You'll meet Lilly. She's in the office. With the journalist fellow from America. And Lady M. called. She sounds furious.'

'She probably *is* furious. I just hope she doesn't turn up.'

Children were darting up and down the stairs. Nina pushed the door open. 'Hello,' she smiled at Justin Agate. Over by the window a squat woman stood glowering at Justin. She held a suitcase up to her chest. Her fat fingers clutched at the handle. 'You must be Lilly.'

The woman's toothless mouth relaxed into an amiable grin. 'I like it here,' she said. 'I came in last night. No one made me 'ave a bath. I got clean sheets and a bite to eat. Gemma told me you'd be in. I need a room of my own, Miss. Just a room. It's not much to ask at my age. I'll be awfully handy round the place. You'll see.'

'Tell you what, Lilly. Would you like to make us a cup of coffee? Do you drink coffee, Justin?' He gave a little bow which said, *yes please*. He watched Lilly fixedly.

'By the way, Lilly, you can call me Nina. Okay?'

Lilly's delight was apparent. 'I'll get you coffee, and I'm good at cleaning. My vicar said I was the best cleaner he'd ever had. That was before he threw me out.'

'Why did he throw you out?'

'Because I had one of my turns.'

Justin looked pleadingly at Nina. She laughed and put her arm around Lilly and gave her a hug. Lilly's stale breath blew against Nina's cheek. 'We won't throw you out. Just give me fair warning before you have one of your turns, all right?'

'Fair enough. But I get ever so violent.' Lilly shambled happily out of the room.

'Aren't you scared of a woman like that?'

Nina sat down. 'I haven't been afraid of anyone who's come through those doors. I'm much more afraid of the people I was with last night. I can tell Lilly's been let out of a mental hospital.'

'How can you tell?'

'By her haircut. Looks like an upturned pudding basin. She's one of the many thousands that are left to fend for themselves. She'll stay a while, and then she'll go off if she feels like it. But there's a place for her here for as long as she wants. Her feet look sore from too much street roving, so we'll bandage them and feed her.'

Monica slipped into the room. 'I'll need to stay up with her at night, Nina. She's a smoker. If we don't watch her, she's likely to set her bed alight.'

'Can you take turns with some of the others?'

'We'll work something out. Listen, the car will be here shortly to take you to "World at One".'

'Go on telling me about what you have learned,' Justin asked.

'Well, I can usually tell if someone is just out of prison. There's a special pallor to the skin, and often a man will wear his shirt . . . I don't know. It's hard to explain, but you can tell by the way a man presses and wears his shirt, with the folds in the same regular pattern that they're forced to press their shirts in the lock-up. You get a sixth sense. Who's drinking, who's stealing, or whatever. Here everybody tells the truth. We don't need to hide anything from each other. We're not a local authority. We don't believe in punishment. We're just people who care.'

Nina heard Lilly lumbering up the stairs. Lilly pushed two cups of coffee onto the desk. 'There you are,' she said. Under her arm she carried a broom. 'Lift your feet, Mister. I'm getting down to work straightaway.' She brushed the floor with enthusiasm.

'Mind if I tag along to your interview with you?' Justin smiled.

'I wish you would. I've never done a radio interview before.'

The telephone rang. 'It's the man from *The Chronicle*.' Monica, clear-headed and sober in all the excitement, handed the phone to Nina.

'Hello, Mrs Stockton. I'm Andrew White, social services correspondent from *The Chronicle*. I saw your piece in *The Standard* and I wondered if I could ask you a few questions.'

'I suppose so.' Nina knew her voice sounded dubious.

'Which group do you represent?'

'Which group? I don't represent any group, really. I just volunteered my time since both my children were at school and . . .'

'Well then, what are your political objectives, Mrs Stockton?'

'Oh. Housing for the homeless, quite simply . . .'

'I mean what are your bigger political objectives?' The voice was getting impatient.

'Well, personally I think too much politicizing can

356

get in the way. I mean, I find most of the ideological issues irrelevant and boring.'

There was a silence down the telephone. 'Are you related to Mr Simon Stockton?'

'No. Not entirely. I'm his ex-wife.'

'I see. How old are you, Mrs Stockton?'

'I don't think that's any of your business.' Nina put the telephone down.

Justin shook his head. 'You shouldn't have done that. Most reporters think they're gods, especially reporters from *The Chronicle*. Incurring their wrath isn't always wise.'

Nina was flustered. 'Who the hell cares what he thinks?'

Lilly had finished her vigorous cleaning of one corner of the room and was now launching an attack on the filing cabinets. 'Fucking 'orrible ugly things.' Lilly whacked the cabinets with her broom. 'I'll knock some sense into your bleeding metal heads.'

Nina grinned at Justin. 'The car should be here in a minute. Lilly?' Lilly paused. 'Give the filing cabinets hell.' Nina stood up. 'I'll be back as soon as I can. The coffee was excellent. Just what I needed. Let's go, Justin.'

Nina sat in the taxi. 'I'm scared.'

'Don't be,' he said. 'Just say what you want to say. Don't let anybody intimidate you.'

The car pulled up in front of the BBC. Nina climbed out. 'You're the woman this morning's *Standard*, aren't you?' The taxi driver leaned out of his window. 'God bless you, ducks. I hate to see all those people in the streets.'

'Thank you.' Nina smiled. 'I need all the blessing I can get.' Her stomach felt as if someone had taken the corners and tied them tightly. Justin walked beside her into the large main lobby of the famous old building. '"World at One", please,' she said to the woman at the reception desk.

A man in uniform stepped forward. 'This way, please.'

Nina felt as if she followed for miles, up many flights of stairs, down many more, along lengthy corridors, all carpeted in the same dull shades of grey. The walls were painted institutional colours. Through windows she could see hunched figures talking, talking, talking into microphones, red lights winking over the doors. She, Justin, and the porter walked the tiring walk until, to her relief, they stopped in front of yet another anonymous door. A slim man with glasses greeted them. Nina looked around. 'I'm Duncan,' he said. 'The Minister is in at the moment. Bill is interviewing him. Come on into the control booth and have a seat till you're up.'

'Thanks. This is Justin Agate, a journalist from America. May he come in, too?'

'The more the merrier.' Duncan opened the door and led Nina and Justin into a room full of tape recorders and mixing panels. A producer sat beside a sound engineer watching the interview through a window made of several layers of sound-proof glass. The engineer turned around and gave Nina and Justin a smile and friendly wave. Nina decided she liked the happy atmosphere inside the studio control room. The producer stood up, introduced himself, shook hands, and asked Duncan to get cups of coffee for Nina and her guest.

Coffee in hand, Nina sat back and listened to the current interview which she could hear coming clearly through the speakers on the walls of the room.

'Yes, Bill,' said the Minister. 'I saw the pictures in the newspaper. This morning. I've had it on very good authority that this is just a publicity stunt. The poor woman is, well . . . I don't want to hurt her feelings. Let's just say she's not very stable. Only for the moment, of course.' He tried hard to sound concerned in a paternal sort of way. 'Suffered some husband trouble lately, you understand. He left her for another woman. Put her over the edge, apparently.'

Nina felt betrayed. Simon must indeed have put out word in his ministry that she was not of sound mind.

'Surely,' said the interviewer with a voice that sounded smooth and wise, pouring from the speaker, 'surely you're not suggesting that England has no homelessness problem, and that public attention has been created merely by one woman's husband troubles, are you? And from what I've heard of Mrs Stockton, who will be joining our discussion shortly, she sounds a very sensible woman indeed.'

Nina enjoyed watching the Minister literally squirm in his seat. 'Of course we have something of a problem with the homeless, but let's not forget that we do have the National Housing Shelter. They're due to release the latest figures on homelessness this afternoon. Actually, I'm on my way over there to make a statement. And only with well-researched figures can we begin to have a reasonable, meaning-ful discussion on the subject. All this that we've been reading in the press, therefore, seems rather premature.'

Justin saw the gleam in her eyes. 'Don't get mad; get even.'

'I'll try,' Nina smiled.

During a pause in the programme, the Minister rushed out of the interview room and careened into Nina. 'I'm Nina Stockton.' Nina tried to shake his hand.

'Can't stop, dear. Telephone my office, if you need to speak to me. My secretary will make an appointment.' The Minister went on out of the door.

'He didn't even hear what I was saying.'

Justin laughed. 'He's chasing his media image. No one likes the limelight better than your Minister of Housing, and you've cast a long shadow over him, little lady.'

Bill was a middle-aged, kindly, genial man. While talking into the microphone, he gestured Nina into a chair at a desk with a microphone stand in the middle. Nina stared at the microphone for a moment, then decided she had better try to ignore it. Instead she took Bill's outstretched hand and returned its warm shake. Bill was evidently used to carrying on a mimed conversation with someone else in the studio while speaking, without missing a syllable, into the microphone. Nina suddenly realized that, for all the rooms containing all the people doing all their talking in the entire huge building, this programme now was being broadcast live to listeners outside the building. What was said in this cosy room went out immediately and was heard far and wide. The microphone in front of Bill and the microphone in front of her own face were the two magic channels to the immense, silent, listening world. Nina felt her throat tighten. She knew she would be cued to speak in a minute, so she tried consciously to ease the muscles of her neck. She blocked out the sight of the producer and sound engineer and Justin sitting on the opposite side of the picture window. She tried to forget the microphone. Just pretend, she told herself, that you and this nice-seeming man Bill are about to have a conversation. And if a few million people happen to be eavesdropping, that's their business, not yours.

Bill said, 'Nina Stockton, spokesperson and head member of staff at the Latchmere House project for the homeless, welcome.'

Nina heard a momentary silence, and she realized that it was her duty to fill that silence. She said, 'Thank you, Bill.' To her amazement, her throat and vocal cords seemed to be working fine. Within the acoustically-designed room, Nina heard her own voice sounding clear and well-modulated.

'Mrs Stockton, the Minister of Housing has just described you as unstable. What do you have to say to that remark?'

'I think the Minister of Housing is trying to hide the fact that there are thousands and thousands of men, women, and children who exist without a roof over their head. His personal attacks against me are just a smoke screen.'

'Why do you think you can do anything to address this problem, Mrs Stockton? After all, we have social workers and we have the National Housing Shelter. If they can't make a difference, then how can one individual help?'

'I'm not foolish enough to imagine that I alone could make a difference. But the point is, it's not just me. There's Gemma and Cal and Monica and . . . Let's see, who else have we got?' She realized she was rambling and she felt a quick panic while she concentrated on steering her words back to the subject. 'We just take care of those who come to us. That's all. That's all we *can* do. We all take care of each other. Like a family. The National Housing Shelter doesn't actually take anyone in. They just give out figures and hold conferences. If the money wasted on such useless programmes was directed instead to groups that *do* accomplish something, like the Salvation Army and Latchmere House, society would see a change overnight.' She watched Bill's face and was pleased to notice his eyes twinkle. 'But what matters most is that each of us *should* feel individually responsible to do what we can. Things will get better by people helping people, not by everybody sitting back and counting on someone else handling everything.'

'Well. those sound like stable words from a sensible young woman.' He smiled at her. 'Tell me, how do you raise money?'

'We rely on donations from the public, and we have an advisory committee. Michael Morningstar is the chairman.'

'Ah! Michael Morningstar?'

'Hm. He's wonderful. He really is.'

'Nina Stockton, thank you. What we need are more people like you.'

'Thank you, Bill.'

'And we'll be back in a moment,' he said into the microphone. Bill flipped a switch. 'We're off the air for a minute. Well done, Mrs Stockton.' He took off his headset and let it rest around his neck. 'Just wanted you to know that we really do think you're doing a wonderful job. And any time you need some public support, you're more than welcome to come back on the show.'

Nina was delighted. 'That's really very kind of you. Thank you very much.'

The internal telephone rang on the desk by Bill. 'The National Housing Shelter are suing?' he said into the receiver. 'Let them sue.' Bill stood up. He put out a hand. 'Duncan'll show you out. Thanks again.'

'Aren't you upset that you're being sued?'

Bill laughed. 'The loony left sue all the time. If not the loony left, then the loony right. Let them get on with it. You take care of the people who need you, and never mind about the nay-sayers. Here.' He fished into his rumpled capacious suit. 'Here's a couple of fivers. Buy the community something nice.'

Nina smiled and thanked him. She was led from the room, just as Bill put his headset back on and returned his attention once more to his microphone.

In the hallway outside the studio, Justin slapped Nina on the back. 'You did well,' he said. 'You're a natural. Boy! You're going to piss off a lot of people in a big way!'

'Good,' Nina said shortly. 'They need to be pissed off. It'll give them something to talk about at their dinner parties and in their country cottages.'

Chapter 45

Nina heard the newspapers come through her front door's letterbox and hit the floor. She rolled over and tried to ignore a feeling of desperation in her stomach at the thought of what the papers might have to say about her. The telephone rang.

'I've just read *The Chronicle*.' Nina recognized Lady MacLaughlin's voice. 'What on earth did you say to the reporter to make him so cross?'

'I don't know, Lady MacLaughlin. I haven't seen *The Chronicle* article yet.'

'Bobo is extremely upset. Not only have you broken the law with your squatters . . .'

'Homeless people,' Nina put in evenly, glad that she was on the end of a telephone and not face to face. Her hands itched to wring the Lady's scrawny neck. 'And squatting's actually quite legal.'

'Yes, well. It's disreputable nonetheless. We shall have to have a board meeting about all this. We can't have you running around giving interviews without our permission. After all, Bobo and Ben Radnor are in charge of public relations. And squatting will do such damage to our image.'

'Lady MacLaughlin, I would like to remind you of Michael's own assurance that, for all the committee's value in fund raising for Latchmere House and our programme, the committee would never directly interfere with the internal running of the charity.'

'He promised you that?'

'He promised me that. You were present when he did. Remember? Therefore, you can have all the board meetings you want. It makes very little real difference. I'm too busy to attend them. I'll get on with the business of housing the homeless. Goodbye.' Nina slammed down the telephone.

Janice popped her head around the door. 'Trouble?'

Nina groaned dolefully. 'There's an understatement. You know, I was naive enough to think people would be grateful to us for wanting to rehouse the homeless. But I'm beginning to think it's not like that at all. Alison MacLaughlin and Bobo Radnor really just want to sit on a committee and give endless parties for their friends. They don't want us to actually *do* anything for homeless people. Maybe just keep a few neat, tidy families on the property, preferably ones with young children that can be photographed, and then leave it at that. Anyway, the piece in *The Chronicle* sounds horrific.'

'I'll put some coffee on and get the kids moving. Hopefully the papers aren't *too* bad.'

Nina was very conscious of the many pairs of eyes which turned in her direction as she walked both the children into school. Jennifer, who was dressed like a Third World refugee, at least had the grace to laugh. 'Well! You made a fool of yourself in *The Chronicle*.'

'I haven't even seen it yet.'

'Here, take my copy.' Ziggy helpfully pushed the paper into Nina's hand. 'Andrew White says you are either the most cunning woman he's ever talked to or the most naive.'

Nina sighed. 'I'm neither.' She looked back into the women's disapproving faces. 'I'm just doing my best to help take care of some homeless people. Come on, Jennifer. We talked about that at the last dinner party at my house. Don't you remember?'

'I do indeed.'

'But, sweetie,' Ziggy smiled, 'it's all right to talk about it at dinner parties. You can even make films about it, or write about it, but you really mustn't try to *do* anything about it.'

'Do you hear yourself, Ziggy? Why the hell not?'

'Because there're all sorts of people who are properly qualified to take care of our social problems.'

'Ziggy, I can promise you that there are hundreds and hundreds of well-qualified people all over England who sit in their offices every day, including your husband and Simon. And that's all they do: they sit. They have no intention of accomplishing anything real, so it's left to people like Cal and Gemma and me to get on with it. That's all I'm doing. Getting on with it. Fuck Andrew White at *The Chronicle*.' Nina hugged Hamish, waved to Susan, and stomped off to the car.

Simon's was the first call to the office that morning. He was barely able to keep his voice steady. Nina was unmoved. 'Why couldn't you simply say "no comment" like I did, Nina? Why do you always have to make such a fool of yourself in public?'

Cal looked up from a pile of letters. She waved a fist full of donations at Nina. Monica was smiling.

'It's worth making a fool of myself over something like this, Simon. You might not have liked the stories, but a lot of sympathetic people all over England put their hands into their pockets and have sent us contributions. Since the "World at One" interview, we must have made a thousand pounds, and I'd expect even more after today's press, whatever they say about me personally. People are awfully tired of being faced with the problems of homelessness and no solutions in sight. We are offering solutions at Latchmere House.'

'You'd better save your speeches for the press, my dear. But if you think squatting is a solution, you're quite wrong. You've really upset Angela this time.'

She smiled at Jean O'Malley, the mother of an Irish family who had just come in. 'Thanks,' she said.

Jean's big round shining face smiled back. 'They said you'd like a cup of coffee. No sugar, with milk.'

'Perfect.'

'What?'

'No, not you, Simon. Listen, Angela's not home-less, so I don't care what she thinks. Now if you'll let me go, I've got a lot of work to do.' Nina put down the telephone. 'That money can go towards the next squat, Cal, the ones the police constable told us about. Can you take the O'Malleys over to the row of cottages on Wester Road? They're all empty. See if you can find out if the electricity's been cut off. Ask at a nearby shop, or whatever. Anyway, just case the joint.'

'Sure. I'll take them over for you.'

Nina rifled through a pile of paper. 'An invitation to talk to the Women's Union at Maple Lodge in the City. How about it, Monica?'

'I can't talk in public, Nina. I'd die of fright.'

'If I can, why can't you? Give it a try. They're a powerful group of women, the Women's Union, and they'd be good friends to have any time we need to raise money.'

Monica picked up the ringing telephone and handed it to Nina. 'You poor old thing.' Jimmy Donleavy's voice was warm and concerned. 'How about coming onto my new television show tonight? And I'll buy you dinner after. I'm sure you could do with a sympathetic ear.'

'Jimmy, I'm really grateful, but I ought to go home and spend a quiet evening with the children.'

'There's no such thing as a quiet evening at home with the children, Nina. You're big news now. It's a moment to be seized. By tomorrow the wave might have passed. You're doing a fantastic job. I caught you on the radio. Time for you to try your hand at television. Shall I send a car for you?'

Nina hesitated. 'No, I'll drive myself. What time?'

'Be at the studios at six, and we'll do the interview at six forty-five. That'll give you time for make-up and a drink.'

'The drink I'm sure I'll need. Life is suddenly

so hectic. I'm in danger of splitting apart at the seams.'

'Join the rest of the world, darling. Must rush.'

She heard him put the telephone down. Suddenly she felt herself part of the strange world of the media, a world in which people say 'must rush' all the time. They're like the White Rabbit in *Alice in Wonderland*, thought Nina. Rush rush rush. And now I'm rushing too. I'd better telephone Janice to babysit. Again. Thank God for Janice.

Chapter 46

Friday night and the London streets were packed with cheerful people. Nina felt tired, but she enjoyed the bustle of a Friday evening – the night before two days of leisure. When she had been just a housewife, there had been no days of leisure. Taking care of Simon and the children had stretched through all the hours of the days of the week. Nina realized that time was elastic. It could be stretched to accommodate all those hours when she struggled to be a perfect wife and mother. Now sharing the house with another woman, the chores remained the same, but there were two pairs of hands instead of one. What started out as a few hours of volunteering at Latchmere House was now becoming a full and public career.

She was pleased that for her first appearance on television, she at least knew the presenter. After the hostile interview in *The Chronicle*, she realized she was nervous. Now she found herself talking to herself in a long internal dialogue, rehearsing defensive answers to offensive questions.

Guilt tugged at her. She would not be home to say goodbye to the children for the weekend. She was out gallivanting. She could hear Enid's reed-like voice. 'Neglecting the children!' Well, she didn't neglect the children. She took them to school every day and she mostly picked them up from school in the afternoons. Surely that didn't constitute total neglect, did it? Nina turned the car towards the river.

The television station was in the dockland area. Nina drove through the damp, dark streets. No busy people here. No warm coats or a pay packet stuffed in a jacket pocket. An old lady with a pram was caught momentarily in the beam of her headlights. The pram was piled high with newspapers and cardboard boxes. Now Nina knew from Lilly so much more about the collection-minded type of homeless woman. *I don't have any politics.* Nina practised her answer in her head. *I just volunteered to type because I had time on my hands and my mother trained me to be useful in my community* . . . No, no, no. I can't say that. Sounds too middle class, and that's unfashionable nowadays. But I *am* middle class. Why do I have to be ashamed of that? And why the hell do I have to have a pimple on the side of my nose today of all days?

Nina parked alongside a line of Porsches and BMWs down the cul-de-sac where the television station was. The building seemed an oasis of prosperity in the otherwise grim docks. The windows of the station were aglow with lights. There was an ebb and flow of people coming in and out of the double doors. Nina felt the pace at which these people seemed to live their lives. She envied them their apparent energy.

She climbed out of the car. I don't even have my briefcase. She stood outside the building and gazed, panic-stricken for a moment, at the door. Why am I here? Maybe I am failing the children . . .

She walked towards the building, but then she saw the woman pushing her pram in the bleak, sodden darkness of the docks. She remembered Lilly's stories of violent attacks from other alcoholic homeless people. She knew at once that she had no choice but to carry on doing what she was doing. And she would have to learn to live with the guilt.

She watched herself once removed as she pushed open the door and introduced herself to a man in the booth on the left. 'I'm Nina Stockton, and I'm here for the Jimmy Donleavy Show.'

'Yes. 'ello, love.' The man smiled. Nina, knowing she was recognized, felt a warm glow spread over her like sweet honey. 'I saw your face in *The Standard* the other day. Nice piece. You're the homeless lady.'

'Yes,' she said slowly, as if sealing her own fate. 'The homeless lady. But I'm afraid I didn't come out of it so well with one of the other newspapers.'

'Mustn't take it to heart. They're only selling papers, and they change their mind from one day to the next. This way then. Here. Pin this visitor's badge on your jacket and turn left.'

'Thank you.'

Nina joined the flow of people who effortlessly, like a tidal wave, ascended and descended the stairs. Some were by themselves, aristocratically oblivious of the other human beings around them, expensively dressed, insulated by wealth and privilege. Others looked like amateurs – in the glamorous world of television for the first time. They seemed to have agents nannying them along like worried sheepdogs.

Finally, a little flushed from nervousness and the long climb, Nina found herself in a square room. Comfortable chairs stood against white walls. Coffee tables sat piled high with magazines and a long table supported rows of flasks of tea and coffee. 'Not like the old days, I'm afraid.' A middle-aged man with a saddlebag of a face clutched his coffee cup and stared mournfully into its depths. 'In the old days they rolled in the entertainment trolley. Plates full of excellent chicken and ham sandwiches. Bottles of gin and whisky. Not like that now.'

Nina smiled at him. She recognized his face, having seen it for many years on television. He was an old school presenter, now apparently working the comeback trail. But, because he looked different in real life, Nina could not immediately put a name to the face. 'This is my first time on television,' she said shyly.

'Not to worry. I'm sure you'll do fine.'

The door behind her opened. 'Make-up for Mrs Stockton.'

'Well, good luck,' the man said. 'Welcome to our queer little world.'

'Thank you.' Nina turned to see a cheerful middle-aged woman in a blue overall.

'Hurry up, dear. We're all in a rush today. I'll get someone to bring you a coffee when I get you settled.'

Nina followed the woman's impatient back. They passed through a room jam-packed with electronic equipment. Nina was surprised at how chaotic it all looked. Men and women poring over television monitors, telephoning, typing . . . The noise was enormous. Nothing is as you expect it to be, she thought, running to keep up. At any moment the Queen of

Hearts might come rushing through the door screaming, 'Off with her head.'

She followed the make-up lady into a room with bright lights and long mirrors. Monster dental surgery chairs lined up in front of the mirrored wall. 'My name is Elizabeth,' the woman said. 'You must be Mrs Stockton. I know your face. You've been in the papers.'

Nina felt the same warm glow. 'Yes. It all feels like ages ago. Time goes so fast.'

'It does in here, dear. We do them all here in this little room. It's like the hairdresser's. We know everyone's private secrets. Who wears a toupée, who needs his nose hairs clipped . . . Let me see. You have a good skin, but we'll have to do something to hide the pimple on your nose. Tea or coffee, love?'

'Coffee, please.'

She asked for coffee from a younger woman who stuck her head in the door. 'Now,' said Elizabeth. 'How do you like your hair?'

'Oh. I hadn't thought about it.' Nina couldn't take her eyes off a woman further down the line of chairs. The woman, short with dark shiny hair, sat in her brassiere, slowly making up her own face. Nina remarked softly, '*She* really seems to know what she's doing, doesn't she? That's Judith Dearborn, isn't it? I recognize her.'

'Hm,' said Elizabeth. 'Always does her own make-up. Never talks to anyone.'

The famous face turned as its owner heard her name mentioned. She looked solemnly and blankly at Nina. The mask wrinkled into a caricature of a smile and then returned to the mirror.

'She thinks the suns shines out of her backside, that one,' Elizabeth observed in a whisper. 'She thinks she's too good to lick the jam off a spoon. Not like Jimmy. He's a darling. He'll be in in a minute to see you.'

Nina leaned back while Elizabeth put in hair rollers and performed the magic of her craft on Nina's face. Turning her eyes sideways she continued to watch the famous Judith Dearborn seal the make-up on her face with a spray of Evian water. Nina could not believe that she was the same woman she had watched on television since the children were born. The television show used to be a regular part of Nina's late afternoon ritual during the children's early years . . .

'Ah, Nina! There you are! I heard you were in the building and now I've tracked you down. You're in good hands with Elizabeth. She's one of our best.' Nina suddenly felt like an idiot to be seen by Jimmy with her hair in rollers. He sat down in the chair next to her. 'I'm sorry about the short notice. *The Chronicle* was unfair. They are usually so good about social issues. Andrew White is a well known radical extremist, so you didn't stand much of a chance. But we'll give you an opportunity to put forward your side of things on the air tonight. Keep it simple and straightforward. Let's just talk about how you started and see how it goes from there.'

'James,' Nina grinned, 'you are why and how I got started. Don't you remember?'

'Could I ever forget? You were a sweet innocent little Richmond housewife, and I changed your life.'

'You can laugh, Jimmy Donleavy. But you did just that. Think of the days – the years – I listened to your radio show. Then I met you. I offered to do a little typing, and here I am. You're the host of a new television series, and I'm about to do my first television broadcast ever. Can I telephone my mother? She was out when I tried to reach her earlier. I know she'd like to see the show.'

'Sure thing. We can do that in the studio.'

Elizabeth pulled the curlers from Nina's hair. The fair hair tumbled around her face. Elizabeth handed Nina a lipstick. 'Do your mouth, then blot it on this Kleenex, and do it again.'

Nina followed her instructions. She smiled when she saw her fully made-up face in the mirror.

'Even more beautiful than usual, if that's possible,' Jimmy said with real affection.

Judith Dearborn was getting ready to leave the room. Her packed handbag had reabsorbed the myriad bottles, brushes, and pots. She buttoned her shirt, walked past Nina's chair, and nodded stiffly at Jimmy.

Jimmy watched her leave the room. 'Such a pity,' he said. 'I hear in the old days she used to dance in here and chat to everybody. It's all gone to her head. It's a bitch, television, Nina. That's a lesson I've learned already. It takes you in, swallows your whole life, and turns you into something you had hoped you'd never become.'

'Aren't you afraid of that happening to you, Jimmy, now that you're on television?'

'I'll count on you to keep my feet on the ground.' His smile widened even more. 'Fame's an evil thing. Anyway, we're not here to discuss the Judith Dearborns of this world; we're here to talk about you. And I've booked a perfectly lovely table at L'Hermitage in Soho. It's my favourite place in the world. French name, Italian food. Perfect, don't you think? Now, if you're feeling nervous, take deep breaths and count to ten. And when we're on the air, just pretend we're

374

sitting by ourselves in the office at Latchmere House.'

Elizabeth wished Nina luck as she took off the apron and stood from the make-up chair. 'I'll be watching you on the monitor. Nice to have met you. I'm a real fan of yours, Nina. And so is my mum. She'll be ever so thrilled to know I've made you up.'

Nina smiled. Flocks of butterflies were fluttering about in her stomach. Her face felt clammy. She followed Jimmy down yet another corridor through many more packed rooms, until they came to a door marked *The Jimmy Donleavy Show*. He pushed open the door and greeted the two men sitting at a glowing console.

'Ginger, this is Nina Stockton, and, Nina, that's Ted. Okay, let's get right on with it. Nina, give your mother's number to Ginger. He'll get her on the phone and tell her you're on.'

He opened an inner door and they were in a spacious studio. At the back was a raised dais with two low armchairs. She recognized the set from having seen it on television. Somehow it looked smaller in real life. He pointed at the right hand chair. 'You sit over there, Nina, and I'll be with you in just a minute.'

Two television cameras stared impersonally at Nina. Shadowy figures were moving behind the cameras. She sat in the chair, her knees primly pressed together. *Nice girls cross their legs at the ankles.* Nina heard a voice from the past in her head. Nice girls don't have television cameras staring at them. Oh, Enid will be furious. It had always been Enid's dream that Simon should be on television. I hope the old bitch is watching tonight.

A man walked up onto the little stage. 'I'm just

going to put a mike on you, Mrs Stockton.' He handed her an object on a lead. 'Spark's privilege,' he smiled. 'Put the mike under your blouse and we can attach it to the inside of your jacket lapel.' His hands impersonally flitted about Nina's breasts. She felt herself going red. Don't be as ass, she scolded herself. He does this every day. But I don't, she reminded herself. I've never done this before.

Chapter 47

The lights of the studio grew brighter. Nina blinked. All of a sudden she could see the two television cameras clearly. 'Watch the red light.' Jimmy slid into his seat beside her. His eyes were raised to just above the machines so that he could read the words rolling by on a Teleprompter. Behind the machines, now mounted by two men, Nina saw a woman holding up her hands. 'Ten,' Jimmy counted. 'Relax, Nina. Take a deep breath. You'll be fine.'

Nina's heart went out to Jimmy. Somehow in command of his own studio, Jimmy had taken on a new confidence. This was the face behind the tender voice she had listened to for all these years. The studio lights behind his shoulders lit up his rust-coloured hair. His blue eyes sparkled. 'Five, four, three . . .' He nodded his head. 'Here we go.' He turned to the cameras.

'Good evening. Tonight I would like you to meet Mrs Nina Stockton.'

Nina sat frozen, her larynx shrivelled. She felt a

cold sweat rise on her forehead. The words out of Jimmy's mouth were a blur. 'Nina?'

That must be a question for her. She looked blankly at Jimmy.

'Do tell us how you started working with the homeless.'

'It started very personally, actually. I came to know about a man, a retired music professor, you see, whom I met in Mrs Porter's shop where I get my vegetables. One day I didn't see him any more. I asked Mrs Porter what had happened to him, and Mrs Porter said he'd been found frozen to death in the park. I was horrified. I thought there were people paid to look after the homeless – a whole system of social workers, and people like that – and here this lovely old man died alone. I couldn't believe a person could *freeze to death* in a so-called civilized part of the world like London.' The words came pouring out of her mouth, but she was relieved that at least she was speaking.

'What do you believe now, Nina?'

'I now recognize the appalling fact that we live in one of the richest countries in the world, yet we allow a significant portion of our population to have no roof over their head.' She heard her own words strengthening.

A subtle communication in Jimmy's eyes, fixed on her own, offered her encouragement. 'And whose fault is that?'

'It's everybody's fault. I was stupid to assume that you could ask or pay institutions to really care for anybody. My mother and her friends worked in their villages all their lives to help their communities. She helped with "meals on wheels". She pushed the trolley around the hospital. She knew who was having a baby and needed extra blankets or clothing. Helping each other used to be a part of English life. It used to be our second nature. I was brought up to volunteer my time, so when my children went to school full-time, of course I volunteered.'

Nina wondered for a moment if she sounded too shrill or too strident. But Jimmy was smiling at her. She began to relax.

The studio set slipped away from her thoughts and she sat comfortably talking to her old friend, Jimmy Donleavy. 'Are you aware,' he asked, 'that what you're saying will strike many ears as strange? Community service is hardly in vogue today.'

'Probably,' she smiled, trying not to sound bitter. 'In fact I'm sure lots of people are laughing at me right now, for many reasons. I didn't go to university. I don't have official qualifications to be in one of the so-called caring professions. But that doesn't worry me. I always wanted to get married and have children. I know that's not fashionable, but then I'm not fashionable. I'm just a housewife. Actually I suppose I'm more of a single-parent mother now.' Nina stopped, surprised by the starkness of her own description of herself.

'Do you think a person needs special training to take care of the homeless?'

'No, not really. Most of the work we all do at Latchmere House is practical, the same sort of thing you do in your own home. Clean, wash, make cups of coffee, listen to each other. You don't learn about people's problems from books, I've found. It's got to come from here.' She touched her heart.

Jimmy smiled widely. Nina felt the contagious warmth spread from him to her. She was amazed to discover how much she was enjoying this moment.

For an instant, she and Jimmy were suspended in space together. It felt strange. Jimmy had all the power: power to take her and introduce her to an audience of millions. The thought made her spine tingle. She had not previously thought of Jimmy that way, but Jimmy was indeed powerful sitting there, leading her through the interview.

'What particular message would you like to convey to our viewers tonight, Nina?'

'I'd like to ask them to dig out their attics and give away anything they feel will help keep the homeless warm. Whatever you have,' she said, looking directly at the camera, 'take it round to the Salvation Army. They do an excellent job. Tins of food, clothes, blankets, hot water bottles, anything you can spare. And don't remember the homeless only at Christmas-time; they're with us all the time.'

'Nina Stockton, thank you.' Jimmy turned to the camera. He crossed his legs.

How secure he looks, Nina thought. Close-up shots of poor people under the bridges slid up onto the monitor. Beggars, young people's dirty hopeless faces. Well, at least Lilly is warm in bed tonight, and the O'Malley family.

The lights went down and the programme's familiar signature music filled the studio. 'Excellent, Jimmy!' The producer ran up to the platform. Her face was flushed. 'Wonderful, Nina! Absolutely wonderful. Was this really your first time? I certainly wouldn't have thought so, by the way you handled yourself.'

Nina smiled. 'It went all right then? I didn't talk too much?' Behind her the sound man was fiddling with her microphone's cable.

'Well done.' A little hum raced about the room.

After the attacks in the newspapers, Nina needed that buzz of approval.

The director shook her hand. 'Good show, both of you.'

Jimmy looked at his watch. 'And now dinner.'

Nina stood up. 'I'm famished,' she said, her eyes shining. 'That was fun. I feel so odd, all lit up, and I haven't even had a drink yet.'

'This is a better high than booze,' Jimmy laughed.

The telephone rang loudly, disturbing the silence in Simon and Angela's sitting room. 'Yes, mother, we have been watching the programme. I think she did quite well, actually.' Simon crossed his legs to hide a half-erection. Damn, he thought. She didn't look like that when she was married to me. He gazed petulantly at Angela who sat bloated in her chair, her legs wide apart underneath her swollen belly. 'I know it's a terribly vulgar programme and you never watch it, mother, but to be fair, she wasn't too bad. Here. Why don't you talk to Susan?'

He passed the telephone to Susan who was sitting on the floor in front of his chair. He stood up. Stooping slightly, he went out of the room. 'Oh, it's just Mum showing off,' he heard Susan say. She might be showing off, he thought, but I'd better go outside and lift a car. A man shouldn't get blue balls watching his ex-wife on the telly.

For a moment, standing outside the flat in the privet-hedge, cat's piss-smelling night, he longed for the days when he lived in his big comfortable house in Richmond, the days when he and his friends sat around his dinner table eating Nina's excellent food. Let's face it, he said to himself, Angela's not much of a cook, and now she can't even fuck. Simon felt miserable. I'll telephone Nina and tell her she did a good job. That's the sporting thing to do.

He walked back into the confining flat and picked up the telephone. 'Oh,' he said, hearing Janice's voice. 'She's out, you say? Will she be back soon? . . . Oh, out to dinner. Ah, I see . . . No, nothing, really. Just tell her it's Simon calling to congratulate her, will you? She was really quite all right.' He put down the receiver. And now, he knew, Angela would sulk all evening, backed up by Susan. 'Come on, Hamish,' he said. 'I'll give you a game of cards.' Hamish was glad to accept the invitation. 'Women,' Simon said to Hamish. 'You never know where you are with them.'

Hamish smiled. 'Yeah,' he said, squaring his shoulders. 'You never know.'

'Shall we use your car, Nina?' They stood on the deserted, puddle-spotted streets. The human flow in the cul-de-sac where the studio was had largely subsided. The streetlamps glittered on the wet pavement. 'I've left my car at home.'

Nina handed him the keys. 'You drive. I'm too excited to concentrate on the road.'

Jimmy's driving was so unlike Simon's efforts. No stamping on the brake, waving fists at passers-by. Jimmy drove swiftly and confidently until they reached the warm lights of Soho. Nina still felt a sense of electricity, as if someone had pulled a long brass light switch and turned on a mega-watt bulb between her heart and her thighs. The car stopped and they found a parking space. 'A bit of a walk, I'm afraid.'

'I don't mind. I love Soho. The smell of it makes me happy.'

Jimmy took her hand and they walked in a comfortable silence. Nina gazed at the still open shops. Bulging bags of coffee beans, the smell of burlap mixing with the deep, dark smell of coffee, bottles of olive oil, green and yellow, Italian delicacies on countertops, Chinese ingredients on shelves . . . Soho was Nina's idea of an enchanted fairy land.

They turned the corner and Jimmy opened the door of L'Hermitage restaurant. 'Mama,' he said, taking a small, stout woman into his arms.

'My Jimmy!' she replied, and hugged him tightly, kissing him volubly on both cheeks. 'We have been watching you on the television. Very good, Jimmy. And this is the young woman you were talking with? Come in! Come in! Welcome."

'Nina, this is Mama Gina. She took me under her wing when I first came to London.' They followed Mama Gina's ample back as she pushed her way through the tables. 'I was a penniless lad off the Irish packet boat and she fed me. I'd wash up for her in return for a plate of spaghetti. Mama Gina, this is Nina Stockton.'

'I know! I know! What for you tell me this news? I saw her in the paper. You look much better in the real flesh.' She reached up and pinched Nina's face. 'We must put some weight on you. You are too skinny. Isn't she too skinny, Jimmy? You work too hard, young lady. You must take time off to play. To make love.'

Nina felt herself getting hot.

Jimmy hastily interrupted. 'Mama,' he said, 'how about something to eat? We really are starving.'

Nina felt very conscious of her knees pressed close to Jimmy's under the table. They were sitting opposite each other, wedged into a tiny banquette. The table between them was only sufficiently wide to hold two plates and two glasses of wine. 'What would you like, Nina?'

'I'd love a drink. I'm parched.'

'They have a great chianti here. Mama gets it from her own region in Italy.'

'That sounds perfect, something red and earthy.' The light in her body shone so brightly, she was sure everybody in the restaurant could see it. She could see it glowing out of Jimmy's chest. There was a strange electric connection between them – a dry, crisp, crackling, as if there were such a thing as human static. It lit up their words and flashed as they touched their hands, meeting over the wine glasses.

Nina ordered calimare fried in breadcrumbs. She watched Jimmy wolf down a plate of spaghetti. How unlike Simon he is, she thought. His table manners would make Enid wince, but he clearly enjoyed his food. Here was a man who could eat and would not spend his life dieting. But then Jimmy was not in line for a paunch, and Simon already had a soft belly and was balding.

Nina drank a great stretch of the prickly chianti. I'll have a hangover tomorrow, she knew, but what the hell? Tomorrow is tomorrow. Why think past tonight?

Chapter 48

Nina's head was not just full of the warmth of the wine. The shimmering between them seemed to reach out in tiny leaps of yellow flame. Nina watched

the bright cloud expand around their table. She put
out her left hand and she saw yellow bubbles dance
on her fingertips. Jimmy raised his glass and then he
took her hand and gently kissed her fingers. Nina felt
the bubble inside her grow bigger. It began to throb.

Even as they left the restaurant, she felt they both
hovered a few inches from the ground. For a
moment, the cloud enveloped Mama Gina. She held
Jimmy in one arm and Nina in the other. 'Good night,
children,' she said, watching them leave. 'Jimmy, he
is in love with that woman,' she remarked. 'But the
woman is not in love with him.'

'How do you know, Mama?' her daughter asked
her.

'There is affection in her eyes, but no longing.'

'Mama, you are too old-fashioned.'

'I always longed for your father. I still long for him,
even though he has been dead all these years. I miss
the sound of him, the smell of him . . . No, that
woman is pretty. She is good also. But she is not
wise. Jimmy would be good to her, but then who can
say . . . ?'

'Shall I drive?' Jimmy had his hand on the car door.

'Please do.' As Jimmy closed the door, Nina felt the
cloud settle about her shoulders. She wondered, as
Jimmy started the engine, if passers-by would see
the brightness of the cloud. She sat silent until they
reached Jimmy's house. No lights were on. 'Where
are the children? Don't they spend their weekends
with you?'

Jimmy smiled. 'I have this weekend off. Madam,
upon whim, decided that she wanted to take the children skiing in the Cairngorms, so I don't see them
until next weekend.'

'I'm so sorry, Jimmy. Do you mind very much?'

'Yes, I do mind. I put everything I have into my working week, and then, when the boys arrive on the weekend, I do all the normal things a father does. And more, of course. I wash, clean, and cook, but then I always did most of the housework, even when we were married. Madam was used to servants.'

'Shall I come in with you and have a nightcap?' The house looked so desolate, Nina felt as if she could take the cloud with her and light up the house. They walked up the path.

Jimmy went ahead and turned on the light. 'It's just a bachelor pad, I'm afraid. Upstairs I have the boys' bedrooms and a bathroom. I use this room as a bedsit, and then there's a kitchen in the back.'

Nina walked into the centre of the room. 'You know, this is exactly how I imagined a room of yours would look. Isn't that amazing? It's almost psychic of me.' She paused and gazed at the big king-size bed. The whole room was a geometric design in black and white. The bed was a convoluted Victorian brass bed repainted in matte black. The bed fitted into the left-hand corner of the room. Across from the bed she could see through a hatch into the kitchen.

'Take off your coat, Nina, and I'll put some coffee on. What'll you drink?'

She stood swaying slightly. 'I don't know. What shall I drink? Something to celebrate my first television show.'

He grinned. 'You were truly wonderful.' He was smiling at her through the kitchen hatch.

'So were you,' she said, taking off her coat and hanging it carefully on a black coat rack. 'This room works awfully well. How did you do it?'

'When you come from a poor Irish family, you're

used to small spaces.' He re-entered the room. 'I promised myself I'd never live with another stick of Edwardian furniture in my life. My mum had a three-piece suite that haunted me as a kid. It had shiny brown-varnished arms and a brown nubbly wool covering that smelled of peat bog and old cigarettes. I *still* have nightmares about the old sofa from time to time.' He laughed. 'My dad used to take off his shoes and pass out on the sofa, after he'd come out of the pub.'

Nina watched a shadow fall over Jimmy's face. She put her hand on his arm.

'They were the bad days.' He shook himself. 'Enough of that. I have a not very good bottle of champagne in the fridge. If I doctor it with some brandy and a dash of angostura and a sugar cube, we can have champagne cocktails. Shall we? And we must drink a toast.' He disappeared again and Nina sank gracefully into a thick black leather sofa.

The glow was beginning to fade a little. The white stark walls were hung with stark photographs: harsh valleys, deep black ravines. Nina felt the deepness of the ravines and wondered if they could reach out and pull her into holes of black despair.

'Here you go.' Jimmy's voice intruded on her thoughts. 'Have a drink.'

She sat up and took a blue crystal goblet from his tray. 'To you and to television.' She raised her glass.

'To Nina,' he said.

She sipped the champagne cocktail. Almost immediately the cloud brightened around her head. 'That's wonderful. Perfect.'

Jimmy moved over to the phonograph. She waited with interest. Would he play the same music at home as he did in his studio? James Galway's magical flute soared through the air. Nina smiled. 'How appropriate,' she said, taking another sip.

Nina was never quite sure how she ended up lying naked in Jimmy's arms. She opened her eyes slowly. Her head was spinning. She lay on her side, curled into Jimmy's body. For a moment she was stunned. I must have had too much to drink, she thought. Did we?

Jimmy's eyes were closed. He breathed peacefully. She looked at his body. He was compact and well-made. The area around his pubic hair was dry: maybe they hadn't. She tentatively pushed her hand between her thighs. She smelled her fingertips. No, it didn't appear as if they had. She could only smell herself. She looked over Jimmy's sleeping head at his clock. Three o'clock. Good heavens! She would have to get back. 'Jimmy?' She put a hand on his shoulder.

His eyes flickered then opened wide. 'I just had the most lovely dream.' He sat up. Nina put her arms across her naked breasts. 'We were back in Ireland. Together. The hills were green and mossy. I was showing you a bird's nest.' He looked so young in the lamplight, his hair redder than usual. The glow was gone though, she realized.

'Jimmy, did we?'

He bent down and kissed her lightly on the forehead. He lay back on his pillow. 'I very much wanted to, but we didn't.'

'Did I very much want to?'

He paused. 'In a way you did, but not for the right reasons. Television can really go to your head, you know. You sit there with your interviewer, and the two of you share a time together when you are in an entirely exclusive relationship. Somehow the lights and the cameras and the knowledge that millions of people out there are looking at you create a sort of union, especially if you click with the other person. And we do click, Nina, in so many ways. I'm tired of the women I meet. They're boring, self-conscious, over-dieted creatures. All they think about is their calorie count, so they're no fun to take out to dinner. They don't cook, they don't even like making love, if truth be told. Anyway, we both had too much to drink, and I wanted to make love to you. I know what I feel for you. I also know what you feel for me; it isn't enough. That's why we didn't. But I loved holding you. You're calm and cuddly, like a soft, warm, little puppy.'

'I'm sorry, Jimmy. I wish . . . I don't know what I wish.' She sighed. 'I suppose I don't really know what I want.'

'I do. You want Michael.'

Nina shivered. 'Yes. I think you're right. But why do I want something that's not good for me? It's like owning a Sabatier knife and deliberately running your finger on the edge. I can see the blood beginning to appear, even now, but I'm helpless to do anything to stop myself. I don't love Michael. I don't think love is like this awful obsession.'

'No, what you are feeling isn't love, Nina. Believe me. What I had with my ex-wife wasn't love either. Love is kind and empathetic. Love is passionate but secure. There is no cruelty when you love the beloved, none at all. No need to twist or to wound.'

'But maybe you have to know obsession to appreciate loving,' she said.

'Could be. I've certainly known one. My ex-wife is an evil, dangerous bitch. She lives only for herself. She is eternally on show. Freud called people like her narcissistic exhibitionists. She lives in this solipsistic, self-serving cocoon. I was duped into agreeing with her image of herself, but only for a while. And now she's found herself a man who can afford her. Good luck to him! Mama Gina used to say, ''She's just a show off, that wife of yours.'''

'Do you think Michael is like that?'

He looked at her. 'I hope not, for your sake.'

'But we'll see, right?' She sat up. 'I'd really better be getting home. Thanks, Jimmy. It was a lovely evening.' She kissed his soft lips.

He lay still and watched her walk across the carpet and dress herself. There's no point in warning you, Nina, he thought. No point at all. The pain he felt was unbearable as he saw her pull on her coat and turn and smile.

'Goodbye, Jimmy.' The car keys were in her hand.

The woman Jimmy had loved ever since the first day he saw her was about to leave his arms, his bed, and his house, 'Goodbye,' he said. 'Nina.' His voice was urgent. 'I'll always be here when you need me. You know that, don't you?'

'Thank you.' She gave a breathless laugh and was gone.

Chapter 49

'Daddy's found a house.'

'Great.' Nina was tired and not in a good mood.

'It's not as big as this one, but it's right near

Richmond Park, and I can go riding. Angela says I can move in next weekend.'

'Hang on a minute, Susan. First of all, they'll have to sign contracts, and that all takes time.'

'They're not buying it, silly. They're renting it. Angela says they don't have enough money to buy anywhere decent yet. So after the baby is born, she is going to get an au pair and go back to work.'

'Are you really sure you want to go and live with your father and Angela?' Nina watched her daughter's small, determined face. It was so like Enid's that Nina thought the child must be a snapped-off branch that had grown to mirror the original tree.

'I'm sure. I like going shopping with Angela at the weekends. I like going out to dinner. You never take us out to dinner. And your friends are all boring. You talk about poor people all the time. Angela never talks about poor people. She says people are poor because they're too idle to work.'

She even sniffs like Angela now, Nina observed. Nina lowered herself onto the sofa. 'We don't go out to eat very often because I prefer to buy fresh food and cook it myself. And eating out is so terribly expensive. Really, it's a total waste. But if you move out, Susan, won't you miss Hamish?'

'I'll see him when he comes to visit every weekend, and then there's the new baby. Angela says she hopes it will be born next week. So if I move in next Friday, I'll be there when my new brother or sister comes home.'

'Half-sister, don't forget, or half-brother.'

'Well, anything's better than Hamish. Daddy says you spoiled him.'

Nina stood up. 'Fine then, if you're absolutely sure.' She extended her hand. She gently let it fall on Susan's tense shoulder.

Nina walked through to the kitchen by herself and sighed. Only the beginning of the week and already Susan was able to poison the days. Why should she give up her daughter? But then, even as she opened the fridge door, she knew she must. This child felt like no child of hers. The Stockton genes carried an immutable desire for bourgeois respectability, an ability to dislike that which the Stocktons could not comprehend. The world of classical music, literature, and art was closed. Mantovani, dance music, women's magazines, and vague paintings depicting seascapes and little girls in frilly bonnets filled the minds and the walls of their serialized houses, houses that reminded Nina of the rows and rows of brand-named cereal packets stacked up on top of each other in the supermarkets.

Maybe it was better to let Susan go now, even if the sorrow bit deep into Nina's heart, than to let her grow into a bitter, rebellious teenager. Maybe Angela could handle the dirty room, the constant fights over homework, the filthy fingernails, and the endless attempts at provocation in public. Above all, Nina wanted to get away from the searching, probing, blue-eyed contempt for all she was and all she tried to be. 'Maybe it's for the best,' she whispered as a comfort to herself.

She heard Janice at the front door and she blessed the day that Janice moved in with her children. Hamish would not be alone in the house without Susan. And, Nina had to admit, it would also be a relief not to have to watch over Hamish all the time in fear that Susan was quietly torturing him in some hidden corner. They would both be free of Susan's relentless bullying.

Nina attempted to smile as Janice walked through the front door.

'What's the matter, love? You look as if a train's struck you.'

'That bad?' Nina put a pizza into the oven. 'Looks like Susan really is about to go and live with Simon and Angela. They're renting a house up by Richmond Park, and she can move in on Friday.'

'Good.' Janice gave Nina a big hug. 'The sooner you get rid of the little bitch the better.'

'It's not as easy as that. I feel such a failure. I tried with her. Really I tried.'

'My Dad used to breed bull terriers, Nina. He always said you don't just breed for the build of the body, you breed for the spirit as well. Right? So I figure, if dogs can get their temperaments from their parents, why can't people? Susan's just like her father, by the sound of it. You don't get on with 'im, so what makes you think you'd get on with her? And that doesn't make you a failure. There's nothing to fail about. She'll get on lovely with Angela. They can tart about together and paint each other's fingernails and gossip over the fence with their nextdoor neighbours. She'll be much 'appier living with them, Nina, and you know it.'

'Yes, you're right. I do know it,' Nina said bleakly. 'Still, it's a hard truth to accept. All my life I wanted a girl and a boy. But it's difficult to have a daughter, and for her to be such an awful disappointment. We're both disappointments to each other, I suppose. I'm not at all the kind of mother she would have wanted, but I just can't be.'

Janice shook her head. 'You're too educated, Nina.

You think too much. Get her packed up and you'll see. We'll all be much happier. She gets you down with all her spying and her whining. Anyway, this bloke I met Saturday night telephoned today and asked me out. Can you babysit?'

'Glad to, Janice. Is he nice?'

She wrinkled her nose. 'Yes, I suppose so. But I'm all out of practice with men. I mean, Billy was my only man. But Ray is kind. I told you yesterday, he's divorced and a policeman. Imagine, me going out with a policeman!'

'I can imagine it. You look really happy.'

Janice left Nina alone in the kitchen. Nina had a warm memory that had stayed with her all weekend, a memory of lying snuggled close to Jimmy. His body and his presence were threatening to fade. Why does life have to be such a struggle? she wondered.

Nina pulled a lettuce out of the fridge. She chopped hot pepperoni onto the green leaves in the salad bowl. She sliced a fat, juicy tomato and then added some capers. A crumble of salt, some feta cheese, and sliced onion rings. Perfect Greek salad, she thought. And I'll be in Greece this summer with Sonia. Nina tossed the salad and watched the vinaigrette spread over the green leaves of the lettuce. Her thoughts turned to fantasy, to images of one body melting into another, of . . . The telephone rang. It's Michael. Nina knew it was Michael. How did she know? It must be love after all. She picked up the telephone.

'Nina?' Michael was in a hurry. 'I've had a telex from Justin Agate. They're running the story he did on you in *Time* magazine next week. He also says you ought to know a big confab is happening on homelessness in Washington. I think it's a chance you can't miss, Nina. Get to know some people over there, get yourself known. Meet with various other people who head up homeless projects on the East Coast. Press conference in the Press Club, the works. What do you say? I'm leaving for Washington myself next week. I can fly with you in my plane. All right?'

'Wait a minute, Michael.' Nina was flabbergasted. 'I don't know if I can leave the children.' *Of course you can*, an inner voice urged. *Susan will be gone, and Janice can take care of the house and Hamish perfectly well.* 'Anyway, I don't think I know enough about homeless people to go travelling around giving out advice on the subject. They'll all be experts with degrees and things like that.'

'That's precisely why Justin thinks you should go, and I think he's right: you'll keep the conversations real.'

'Can I think about it and ring you back?'

'You can think about it, and you will say yes. There's an excellent restaurant I frequent in Washington. It has the best stone crab you'll ever eat. I have a house in Georgetown, and you'll love the cherry blossom trees. They're at their best now. And London is so dreary this time of year. Hear from you soon.' And Michael put the phone down.

Well. Nina carried the salad into the dining room. She put the old walnut salad bowl in the centre of the table. The bowl was a wedding present from Aunt Persephone. After ten years, it was stained with oil, and the two wooden servers were encrusted with rime like the boards on the pier at the seaside. Nina wandered, distracted. I could pack my cashmere sweater and the blue dress . . . What on earth does one wear to public press occasions in America? I'll have to ask Sonia.

She pulled open the oven door. A waft of hot,

steaming dough flushed her face. She pricked the rim of the pizza with a fork: it was cooked. Making pizza particularly pleased Nina. Something about the symmetry of the pepperoni in a great wheel over the sausage and the cheese. The casual melt of the oil in the pepperoni despoiling the pristine whiteness of the mozzarella cheese, and then the sharp bite of the fresh parmesan. The faintly dirty-knicker smell of the cheese reminded Nina of the malodorous wash baskets at school. 'Supper,' Nina called up the stairs.

'I've been packing, Mum. Angela says she thinks she's having contractions. But Daddy says it's just practice.'

'About time, too. She's been pregnant for ages.' Nina ran a pizza cutter down the crust.

'Yum!' Hamish slipped into his seat. He pulled his napkin out of its silver ring. 'I love pizza.'

'It's better when it's shop-bought. Angela says it's silly to make homemade pizza. It's much better to order it on the phone.'

'It probably is, Susan, but I love making my own pizza.'

Janice walked into the room with Ryan and Elsie. 'I could smell the pizza on the landing. Smells lovely.'

'You look wonderful, Janice.' Indeed, Janice did look very pretty, dressed for her date. Nina stood for a moment, lost in thought. If I've managed to do anything at all while I've been at Latchmere House, at least Janice and the kids are a success. Janice stood over her two children. All three faces had lost the fearful shadow that had so marked the little family when Nina first saw them. 'Michael's asked me to go to Washington next week for a discussion with a group of people who run shelters for the homeless in America. What do you think?'

Janice sat down and handed Nina Ryan's plate. 'I think you should go. I think it would do you the world of good.'

Left unsaid between the two women was the knowledge that Nina would spend time with Michael. Nina was conscious of Susan's searchlight gaze.

'Who would you stay with, Mum? You don't know anybody in Washington.'

'I'll be staying with Mr and Mrs Morningstar, darling. Now everybody eat up. I'm babysitting tonight.'

Janice smiled at Ryan. 'I'm just going out with a bloke called Ray for a quick drink. Okay, kids?'

Ryan said, 'He's not like dad, is he?'

'No. He's not at all like dad.'

There was a knock on the door, and Janice gave Ryan and Elsie a quick kiss. 'See your brother washes behind 'is ears, Elsie, will you? I'll be back in not too long.'

Nina watched Janice dance into the hall and get her coat from the cupboard. 'Ready for pudding, anyone?'

'That's my favourite.' Elsie slipped off her seat. 'I'll carry the salad bowl for you.'

'Good of you, Elsie. Thanks.' Nina's mind was fertile with plans.

Before kissing the children goodnight, she telephoned Sonia. Sonia pointed out to Nina that, as her mind was probably already made up, she shouldn't torture herself by pretending she didn't know what she wanted. Of course Nina would go to Washington. And besides, Sonia added, Nina could have fun animal-watching among all the Washington species: ferocious feminists, far-out lobbyists, fascist right-wingers, pinko left-wingers, hawks, doves, fat-cats, bigwigs, warmongers, peaceniks, bra burners . . . Everyone.

Anyway, said Sonia. Since the two women were planning to visit Greece in the summer, and seeing as how Michael Morningstar was known to own a gorgeous villa on the island of Zakinthos, Nina ought to set herself the task of hustling from Michael the use of his house.

'Hustle Michael?'

'Why not? If you learn to hustle Michael Morningstar, you'll be the first. He's the master hustler of all time.'

'Well, I'd be happy to try.'

'Good luck, honey, and catch me when you get back.'

Nina put the telephone down. The idea of a villa on a Greek island sounded entrancing.

Chapter 50

Gemma seemed strained and tired when she came to have supper with Nina mid-week. April made Nina's back garden feel swollen with the trees sprouting tight green buds. Daffodils waved their tender, yellow, trumpeted heads. Close to the ground, crocuses opened their fragile, purple, vaginal throats.

Nina watched the pale yellow watery sun sink behind her garden wall. She had just cut a handful of fresh parsley and a few strands of chives. In the kitchen a pot bubbled on the stove, a thick, rich cassoulet made from a duck buried in pâté Vienne, lima beans, awash with white wine and a substantial piece of pork. The smell of the cassoulet drifted through the open kitchen door into the garden. How I wish it were Michael coming to dinner! Standing in the late April sunlight, Nina felt a fierce need to hold Michael, to pull him to her.

All week long she tottered between feeling sad and hurt at Susan's defection, and then she teetered back to the realization that both of them would be happier apart. Susan had no such compunction, as far as Nina could tell. She talked to Angela every day and repeatedly packed and unpacked her many suitcases. She is just a child . . . Nina also consoled herself with several more pairs of silk, lacy underwear and an exotic black nightdress with a vamp negligée. Absolutely Over the Top, or OTT, as Aunt Persephone might and indeed would say of anything so outrageously sensuous. Nina stood in Harrods, pressing the negligée up against her slim body. The black froth that fell about her was liberally laced with wide red bands of ribbons. 'I'll take it,' she said, and now she stood in the garden and very much wished she was not spending the evening with Gemma.

These days she realized she either wanted to be with Michael or she wanted to be alone so that she could think about Michael. There was nothing, utterly nothing, that could take away her obsession with the man. Neither a good book, nor as many glasses of wine as she could consume in one evening. Nor telephone conversations with Stanley, who didn't mind long, rambling, incoherent calls at all hours of the night. Well . . .

Nina walked slowly up the path and climbed the stairs into the kitchen. If this trip to Washington with

Michael doesn't exorcise me of him forever, nothing will. We will have a whole week together, so it's kill-or-cure time.

She chopped the herbs with a sharp knife. She watched her fingers sprinkling the green parsley over the white beans. If only she could get into bed with Michael! If only they could spend the night making love. If only her tired body could lie slaked beside him. Ah yes, but Michael was a married man with an awful reputation . . . Nina shook her head. Who said love was ever easy? Look at Romeo and Juliet.

She was interrupted by the doorbell. Gemma. Blast.

Nina wiped her hands on a tea towel and opened the door. 'Gemma,' she said cheerfully. 'Long time no see. Do come in.'

Gemma looked even thinner than usual. She smiled her characteristic half-hurt, crooked smile.

'Here. Let me take your coat. You look worn out. What on earth have you been doing?'

'Oh, just working hard.'

'Come into the kitchen and I'll pour you a glass of wine. How's Marietta?'

Gemma made a face. 'I don't see her much. She's travelling all the time.'

Nina poured two glasses of Pouilly Fuissé. She held up her glass. 'Here's a toast to you both.'

Gemma did not pick up her glass. 'Don't, Nina. It's all rather a farce. I mean, you toasting us. Michael, I now find out, has promised to bribe Marietta's ex-husband with a huge amount of money to eventually return her two children to her, or so Marietta says. For ages she didn't tell me about this, but she believes Michael can do it. Apparently she asked him for help just before Christmas, when he came by the flat to drop off the presents for Latchmere House. But there is also one proviso. Her ex-husband, despite the money he'll be getting from Michael, says the only way he'd ever let her see the kids again is if she and I don't live together. He says we can't even *see* each other again, or she won't ever see her kids. He doesn't approve of "perverts" like me. Seems he's afraid I might infect his children.' Gemma's face was bitter. 'And in return for helping get her kids back, Marietta has to run errands for Michael to all his charities around the world, not that I ever know exactly where she is. Michael swears to secrecy everybody who works for him. He's paranoid, as far as I'm concerned. I never know where Marietta is or what she's doing. She seems to criss-cross the world on endless business deals for Michael. Sometimes I start to wonder if he's really as straight as he pretends to be. A pillar of the charitable community, and all that. Sometimes I wonder what I'm doing every night up to my elbows in this homeless shit. Lilly had one of her temper tantrums last night. I had to calm her down. One of the black women called her a white honky. I pointed out that this white honky was keeping a roof over her head, but she didn't seem impressed. I don't know, Nina. I really don't know. I end up wondering if I'd be better off going back to university, helping with a blueprint for a fairer, more just society. Maybe that's where I belong. Seeing Marietta with all those disgustingly rich people upsets me. She travels first class, for fuck's sake! She has to buy elegant clothes.'

Nina's eyebrows rose. 'Does Michael pay for her clothes?'

'Naturally. He pays for her clothes, her hotels, always the best. Raffles in Singapore, the Peninsula

in Hong Kong, the Four Seasons in Beverly Hills, the Plaza in New York. That's what she says. The list is endless.' Gemma walked across the kitchen floor. 'I tell you, Nina, it's killing me, the ache of being without her so much of the time.'

Nina put an arm around Gemma. 'Gemma. I'm off to Washington with Michael next week.'

'Yes, and to tell you the truth, I feel a little like saying "Et tu, Brute?" Be careful, Nina. I can't lose you to him as well.'

'You're not losing me. Never. We've been friends for yonks. Nothing would ever come between us. Listen, let's fill our plates with stew and we can go and sit in the drawing room. Janice is at the cinema with the kids.' Nina plunged a serving spoon into the stew. 'After a good meal and a bottle of white wine, we'll both feel better.'

Nina raised the subject of Susan's leaving on Friday. Gemma listened to what Nina had to say, and she added her own reassurances that it was probably for the best this way, but clearly her mind was not very much on Nina's troubles. 'Nina,' she said suddenly, 'you don't think Marietta is having an affair with Michael, do you?'

Nina's heart stopped beating. 'Of course not. What on earth makes you say that?' She felt her throat constrict and her stomach clench with rage.

'Nothing really. Just a feeling of distance between us when she is home. We don't make love much. I miss holding her in my arms. She rolls away. She's always preoccupied or too tired. I wondered. That's all.'

'Well, I can try to find out, if you like, but I really can't believe Michael is having an affair with her.' Nina found it difficult to swallow her mouthful of

beans. She'd better not be fucking Michael, the calculating little bitch, said a voice in Nina's head with a jealous intensity that surprised her. She could see Marietta's high cheekbones and blue-black hair. 'Don't worry, Gemma. I'll do what I can, but I think you're just worrying yourself over nothing. Reading too much into the situation.' Nina realized the words were more for her own comfort.

'If Marietta and I ever did split up, I think I'd probably go up north. There's a place at Durham University. I like Durham. I'd be with my students again. I don't seem cut out for the real world. I'm safer in the ivory towers of academia where the theories sound plausible. The ideas still seem fresh and new. Out here, they lose their revolutionary flavour. The homeless, as far as I can see, vote Tory and their liberators, people like me, vote Socialist. They've never heard of feminism, and if they knew I was a lesbian, it would empty the shelter overnight.' Gemma sighed and Nina sighed with her.

I wish my heart would stop beating so quickly, Nina thought. All she wanted was for her trip with Michael to come quickly. She knew she should be sitting here feeling sorry for Gemma, but really her mind was elsewhere.

When Gemma left, Nina watched her walk alone down the street. Her brown macintosh matched her russet hair. She remembered the day both women arrived together behind Stanley in his dress, both laughing affectionately with each other. Poor Gemma. How awful for her.

Nina closed the door on a perfect April night.

Chapter 51

Try as she might, Nina found it almost impossible to fill the days leading up to Friday with exciting commitments. Friday would arrive in its own good time, but on Friday Nina knew she would lose her daughter forever. 'It's not as if all my memories of her are bad,' she told Stanley.

Stanley was sitting in the tiny sitting room in his flat. Nina sprawled on a pillow on the floor. She was aware that she clutched the pillow to her chest, just as she had held Susan a few moments after she was born.

'It's amazing, but Susan was actually born angry. She shrieked all the time, and when she wasn't shrieking, she'd moan. Hours and hours of moaning. All I could do was carry her about. She made me so desperate. I visited doctors and pediatricians. Everybody. There was absolutely nothing wrong with her.'

Stanley's moist brown eyes brimmed in sympathy. 'Don't cry, love. I'll get some tea. Ever such healing stuff, tea is. Lipton's all right? I never drink Earl Grey after ten o'clock. Do you?'

'I can't say I've given it much thought. I'm too worried about the effect Susan's moving out might have on Hamish. How will he feel with his sister gone? And bloody Angela's baby is due any day now. So Hamish's father will be living a proper life that doesn't really include him. Hamish and I will exist in a separate world of our own.'

Stanley crossed his legs. He was wearing a plain brown silk tea gown. Nina recognized the dress. Aunt Persephone owned something similar. The kettle on a small hob over the coal fire in the black leaded grate trembled in the heat.

'I'm off to Washington next week. That means Hamish will be on his own.'

'He won't be all on his own. He'll have Janice and her kids. If you ask me, I think Hamish is lucky. He's got lots of options. If my dad hadn't been such a violent old bastard, I could have got to know all my family. Maybe, if I'd had a gran or an auntie who'd have stopped by the house and said, "Here, Nora –" That's me mum's name, Nora. "– Here, Nora. Let the lad play out. And take that daft make-up off him and throw away the skirts," well, maybe then I wouldn't be such a mess now.'

'You're not a mess, Stanley.'

The kettle whistled. 'Yes, I am. I want a family. I want to have kids of me own, but I can't. Hamish has choices. He's not trapped. If he wants a straight life like Susan, then he's got Simon and Angela. If he wants more freedom, then he's got the likes of me and you. And don't worry. I'll pop over and keep an eye on him while you're away, Nina. I'm good with children. It comes from being one of the ones who are different. We know how it hurts and why it hurts. Here. I'll pour the tea. And you'll see. All things that hurt have a way of not hurting in time. I should know.' Stanley blew into his teacup.

'Where's Kit?' Nina realized she had monopolized the conversation with her own problems.

'Oh, you noticed something missing, did you? He's gone, Nina. I decided that what I was really doing was bribing him to stay with me. We're still friends, and we always will be, but my life came down to doing everything for Kit. I would walk round the shops looking for just the right piece of salmon that I knew he'd like. I'd buy the stuff I couldn't afford – just to keep him. I'd buy booze for him and his friends – lots of it – just to watch him drink like a fish and pass out. Then there was the waiting. The never knowing. I'd start checking his hankies and his knickers to see if they were . . . You know what I mean. Evidence. Signs. The other day I looked in the mirror, and I said, "Bugger it, Stanley. You're becoming an old queen before your time." I'd be better off on my own without a relationship. So I explained it all to Kit. Told him he was welcome to stay until he found someone else or someplace else.'

'How did he take it?'

'Quite well, really. Probably too well. He seemed relieved. Anyway, he moved out at the weekend and I had a phone call the other day. He's okay. Funny, you know. I'm quite enjoying my place to meself.'

'Gemma came round. She's having a bad time with Marietta. You're on your own. I'm losing Susan . . . Life doesn't always run in a straight line, does it? Still, Janice has a really nice boyfriend, so maybe there's hope for us all.'

'I hope so, Nina. I don't want anything complicated. I just want to be loved for myself.' Stanley stroked his blonde wig. His thick mascaraed eyelashes fluttered. His blood-red mouth pouted and then he grinned. 'But which of my selves wants to be loved? I should coco, darling. Listen, let's lighten up. You sit up, and I'll show you a dance I used to do with the girls when we were hoofers. Never knew that about me, did you? I was just a kid then. Eighteen or so. And for a while I had a job in a club doing all the old dance hall favourites.' Stanley pushed the tea trolley to one side. Nina picked up the cushion and sat on the plump sofa against the wall.

He went over to a chest of drawers and pulled out an old 78 record. On the chest of drawers was a gramophone. The familiar terrier with a cocked ear gazed at the trumpet as he did in Nina's house when she was a child. Stanley wound the handle and then lovingly placed the needle on the first groove. The sound of the steel needle sawed through the music and Stanley began to sway. For a moment Nina could see the Stanley of fifteen years ago, the tall slim boy with the handsome face and long slender legs. Stanley swung his legs higher and higher. The music filled the room. Raucous and bawdy, the music reminded them both of the ghostly, golden time before they were born, a time they had only heard about, a different era, before two wars tore Britain apart, a time when music halls and pubs were filled with people who hoped for a new age. Jazz, cigarettes, and a pint of beer . . .

Nina found herself laughing and clapping her hands. All of a sudden the music stopped and Nina saw Stanley staring at her upside down. His bottom was cradled in a ruffled pair of red pants. His head hung between his knees. 'See?' he said. 'I made you laugh.'

'You certainly did.'

'Oh, love. I'm already too old for this game. Me back's stiff.' He straightened up. 'I'd better adjust me boobies.' He peered down the front of his gown. 'All there, shipshape and Bristol fashion, as this wonderful sailor I used to know used to say. Sun's over the yardarm. D'you want a drink?'

'No thanks. I'd better get home. This is Susan's last night. So I'm letting her order her favourite take-away.'

When Nina was ready to leave, she hugged Stanley. 'I feel safe in your arms,' she said. 'You don't want anything from me.'

'Just want you to be my friend.'

The simplicity of the request brought tears again to Nina's eyes. 'Why is friendship so difficult?'

Stanley paused. 'Because there's no sex. When there's sex, there's power. Someone has something you want. With a friend, you just want them as they are. You don't have to give me anything. And that's why it's hard, because the rules of wanting and get-ting aren't there. Instead it's more like knowing and loving and those don't really have rules. Anyway, maybe it's something like that. I don't know.'

Nina left the flat feeling refreshed. I will get over Susan leaving, she thought. It won't hurt forever.

Chapter 52

It was when Susan's suitcases were actually sitting on the pavement beside Simon's car that Nina thought she could no longer bear the pain. In the days before Susan left, Nina tried to make the experi-ence a positive one. 'You can always stay with us whenever you want. You know that, Susan, don't you?' The offer was received by Susan with a disdainful smile. Nina felt the child counted the hours until she could be free of her mother and what she perceived as her mother's madness.

Nina stood beside the car shivering. Hamish held her hand tightly. Nina knew Hamish felt her anguish. There had always been a psychic bond between them from the moment he was born. It was as if God, sensing her loneliness and isolation in Simon's orbital relationship with his mother and his daughter, had sent Hamish as her consolation. 'Goodbye, Mummy.' Susan stood in the lamplight, her pale blue anorak highlighting her even paler eyes.

'Shall I kiss you goodbye?' Nina said lightly, feeling her breath struggle through her strained lungs.

'Don't be soppy, Mum. I'm much too old for that sort of thing.' Susan disappeared into the car.

'I'm not.' Hamish turned his face. He gave Nina a big hug. 'I'll see you on Sunday, won't I, Mum? I'm not staying with Angela and Dad forever. You will be here, won't you?'

'I'll be here, Hamish. Promise. Now get into the car and I'll wave goodbye.'

So far Simon had added nothing to the conversation. He busied himself piling the four suitcases into the boot. Various paper bags filled with toys and books went into the back seat. 'Well, cheerio, old thing.' Simon slammed the boot shut. 'It'll take a bit of getting used to, having Susan around permanently. Angela's looking forward to it, though.' He sighed. 'I'll be glad when the sprog is born and life can get back to normal.'

Yes, Nina thought, looking at Simon. Then you can stay long hours at the office and leave Angela to do all the work. How on earth, she wondered, did I ever marry the creep, let alone sleep with him? The lamplight shone on the shiny bony beak of his nose. 'If I'm not back in time, Janice will be here to take care of Hamish. Goodbye, children.' Nina waved a hand in the direction of the car. 'Be good, Susan,' she advised and then she turned and ran up the path through the front door and on up to her bedroom.

Beside her bed were two photographs in silver embossed frames. The first was Susan in her christening gown. She switched the table lamp on and examined the pictures. How could it happen that eight years after this photo was taken the little girl had packed all her belongings and left her mother for a strange woman? Did one of the fairies at the birth substitute a changeling? Had gypsies encamped unbeknown to Nina outside Susan's window and run away with her, leaving behind a wild child filled with anger and hatred? Was this the same baby that said her first words when she was nine months old? Or had Enid added some substance into her rock-hard buns that stole away a child's natural love for her mother?

Tears were running down Nina's face. No, it was not any such magical excuse. It was more the slow drip, drip, drip of disapproval over the years. The always conscious but often unsaid message in the air between Enid and Susan: 'You mother is different from normal women.' Normal women love to polish their nails, paint their faces, gather in groups with other women to discuss their husbands' sexual secrets, go shopping, strolling up and down the aisles. Normal women loved their mothers-in-law, telephoned them constantly, visited most weekends. Normal women worried about how they looked.

Were they sufficiently well-dressed to please the mother-in-law? Were their children also properly dressed? No, Nina was a source of continual irritation both to Enid and to Simon and finally to Susan. Susan yearned to be like other people, to giggle and gossip with Angela, to live a tight-cocooned life in an English suburb.

Well, Nina wiped the tears off her cheeks, I'll have to let her go. It was time to let go.

Nina wandered about the bedroom. Here was a picture of Susan playing Puck when she was six. Her laughing face mocked Nina. There was another picture of Susan as a Brownie. A furious Susan on a horse – furious, because she hated horses. Nina knew Susan would never ride horses in Richmond Park, for all her promises.

Nina gathered up the photographs and put them face down in the left-hand drawer of her chest of drawers. That part of my life with Susan is over, she said firmly to herself.

She knew Janice and the children were waiting for her downstairs. Thank God she was not alone in the house tonight. As she walked down the stairs, she glanced into Susan's room. It was a mess, as usual, but the ever-open drawers were empty of clothes. Susan had only taken her father's presents from over the years, leaving behind anything Nina had given her. On the floor beside the bed lay a teddy bear that Nina had chosen when Susan was four. The eyes had been gouged out. An arm was amputated. Next to the bear a doll lay on her face: the fifth birthday present from Nina. Doris can clean all this up on Monday, Nina told herself, her throat straining. She realized at once that if she did feel herself rejecting her daughter, she did so only defensively because,

410

since birth, Susan had always rejected *her*. She shut the door and went on down the stairs.

'You okay?' Janice was at the kitchen stove. 'I've fed Ryan and Elsie. I've just made us an omelette. Here.' Janice poured Nina a glass of wine.

'God, it hurts.' Nina's voice sounded as if it was strained through rice paper.

'I know, love. It must hurt something awful. But she's like a cuckoo's egg born into the wrong nest. She'll be much happier over at Angela's place. You'll get over it. Really you will. I never thought I'd get over my Billy, but I have.'

Nina sipped the wine. 'I'm sure you're right, Janice. I hope I do get over it.' But Nina knew she never would. In her heart there would always be a vacancy with a light hanging over it. *Welcome home*, the light would blink until the day she died.

Chapter 53

Michael's Rolls-Royce took Nina to Heathrow Airport in London. The heavy, puffy leather seats were as soft as the sigh that escaped Nina's lips as she slid into the back. Janice, Hamish, Elsie and Ryan waved goodbye. Hamish's face beamed at her, thinking of the promise of an American baseball bat. Even the pain of losing Susan lessened. Her heart was light and fluttering in her throat. In no time at all she would be with Michael. What would they say to each other? Nina already felt shy. In her suitcase were her new nightdress and several sexy cocktail dresses,

dresses easily removed in moments of passion. She knew her IUD was in place. A shamefaced visit to her doctor told her all was well. Now, with a small plastic device secreted away in her body, Nina was ready for her adventure. Bottles, tubes, oils and unguents travelled with her. Under her arms, she felt, lay tingling pits of pleasure. The soft down between her legs beaded with drops of anticipation. A small throb beat in her thighs and she felt her face and her chest redden with the lust for sex.

The limousine slid down the road like a cold ice cream down a raw and needy throat. How different the world looked from under a soft blue cashmere blanket in the back seat of a chauffeur-driven Rolls-Royce!

Soon the airport was visible. No need, Nina discovered, for the usual tourist scurry from car to air terminal. No need for the push and shove of the tired angry traveller. For Nina, it was a quick glissando into Michael's phallic, black-nosed private airplane. On the tarmac, at the bottom of the steps, she was greeted by a stunning blonde with impossibly taut breasts and very white American teeth. Her smiles stretched across the perfectly even face like bubblegum. 'Have a nice day,' the voice entreated.

'Thank you.' Nina ascended the stairs feeling a sudden sympathy for Elijah who must have at least experienced a moment of perturbation upon stepping into the fiery chariot on his way to meet his Maker. The inside of the airplane appeared to contain no discernible members of the human race. Nina paused.

The cockpit door opened and a broad-shouldered man extended his hand. 'I'm Captain Ellison. Mr Morningstar's private pilot.'

Nina took the warm hand. 'Hello,' she said. The man gave a crinkly-eyed smile. His face obligingly fell into friendly wrinkles. But somehow the wrinkles stopped before the smile reached his eyes. They, grey and sea-bleak, did not share the mouth's happiness.

'You must be Nina Stockton. I saw your story in *Time*. But you're a lot prettier than your picture.' He checked his thick gold Rolex watch. 'Your things are already in the cabin. Mr Morningstar will be along shortly. Lunch is served at one. We ought to be in Washington by five or so, unless we get stacked up. But that's pretty unlikely, since it's Mr Morningstar. Air-traffic controllers tend to give him landing priority.'

Nina walked down the centre of the plane. This is how the rich travel, she thought. Big swivel chairs. Large bar. Must be a kitchen somewhere. She walked to the end of the airplane. At the far end of the plane was a closed door. She pushed it open and gasped.

Behind the door was a bedroom. A circular bed greeted her. She ran her hand over the black bedspread and wondered whether or not it was real mink. It certainly felt real. The dressing table was pure Hollywood.

Nina sat down on the round stool by the dressing table and gazed at her face in the mirror. Her lipstick was still in place on her lips.

'Like what you see? I do.'

Nina jumped. Her eyes met Michael's in the smoky, azure-coloured glass. 'You surprised me.' She sat transfixed.

Michael walked up quietly behind her. His two large hands descended on her shoulders. The hands began to knead away the tightness. Their eyes remained in a passionate embrace. She felt the hot

413

thick push of his demand on her back. The hairs behind her neck bristled. She leaned back. A moan escaped her lips. Then he lifted her bodily from the chair and turned her round, bringing his mouth down on her lips. Fiercely he kissed her. She felt a thin red line of lava run from his lips down her throat and then spread out into liquid chaos. As she waited for the moment of chaos to explode into anarchy of the senses, she was aware of him pushing her away. 'First we lunch,' he said, his black eyes agleam with amusement. 'A good bottle of Taittinger is always the perfect way to begin the joys of fucking.'

Nina was startled by the raw word.

'I see you have a lot to learn, my little English rose. And I have all the time in the world to teach you. Come. Let's go back to the main cabin and feast ourselves on quails' eggs and then a little Peking duck. Afterwards, I've ordered a Durian fruit from Singapore. It's an aphrodisiac, you know. The smell is appalling, but the taste is divine. It's also addictive, and I intend to addict you to me in more ways than one.'

He took Nina's hand in his and gently pulled her back up the plane until she found herself sitting in a black leather chair.

'Fasten your seatbelts.' The hostess was now in the cabin.

'I'm not the addictive type,' Nina said, when she was settled and buckled in her seat.

'Everyone is,' said Michael.

'No really, I don't believe in addictions.'

'But some are good,' he protested charmingly.

'I don't think so. And I won't let myself become addicted to anyone or anything.' Why, she wondered, did her own words sound like a lie?

414

Michael took a proffered chilled bottle of champagne from the hostess's willing hands. 'Wanna bet?' he said.

Nina glanced at the young woman's face. Were her eyes offering Nina sympathy? Nina did not know. She didn't need sympathy anyway. She could handle Michael. The cork exploded.

'Sure,' Nina said, gently mocking him. 'I wanna bet.' She gazed steadily at his face. She picked up her glass and watched him as he sat secure in his chair. 'Here's to us,' she said. She raised the glass.

Michael bent his black head to taste the champagne.

Nina felt the liquid leak down her throat and unexpectedly the coldness of the champagne spread throughout her body, sending ripples of goosebumps down her spine. She shuddered.

'What's the matter?'

Damn! The man reads my mind. 'Nothing. It must be the air-conditioning.'

Michael laughed. 'A coyote crossed your grave.'

'No.' Nina shook her head. 'I'm sure it's just the air-conditioning.'

Chapter 54

Nonchalantly, Michael picked up the quails' eggs in his fingers and swallowed them one by one. Nina's thoughts, liberated by the champagne, wandered down paths of their own choosing: well, what's sauce for the goose or gander in this case. A horrid image of a gander mounting a goose formed in her brain. Do stop it, idiot, she scolded herself. She attempted to think herself back into the romantic world she had left in the bedroom. And suddenly she felt shy and embarrassed. The hostess and the crew would all know what was about to happen behind the bedroom door. How many other women had lunch with Michael and then 'got laid', as Sonia would put it, on that same mink-lined bed? Nina swallowed her eggs without much enjoyment.

The best way through this mess is to get plastered, she told herself. *Stinko*, she heard Aunt Persephone hooting gently in the background. Absolutely stinko.

The champagne bottle was upturned in the ice bucket. The table was piled high with plates. Two bottles of wine, also empty, witnessed Nina swaying slightly as she followed Michael back to the bedroom. He opened the door and she took a deep breath. 'I've been waiting for this moment for a long time, Nina.' Michael swept her into his arms and carried her over to the bed. Nina lay passively, watching him undress. Michael stripped off his clothes. He was tanned all over. He stood towering over her. His long fingers pulled her pants down her legs and over her high-heeled shoes. She could feel the electricity from his fingers running along her thighs. Then, with a practised move, he parted her legs. His obvious excitement showed Nina that he fully intended to enter her immediately.

Nina lay for a moment astonished. She had expected soft, sensuous overtures and tender introductions. Instead he seemed prepared to proceed without invitation. 'No,' said Nina, closing her legs.

'No?' Michael's eyes widened in real surprise.

Then, sensing she might be teasing him, they assumed an expression of flirtatious amusement.

'Not like that,' she said, marvelling at her own confidence.

He stood over her, puzzled.

She reached up from her lying position and put a hand behind his neck, feeling the strength of the muscles beneath her fingers. She raised her other hand to his chest and pulled him down to the bed, turning him as he let his large body be lowered. When he lay beside her, she elevated herself slightly and looked into his eyes. She was aware of an unaccustomed wild force within herself, but it was more than mere desire. Michael, left to his own way, might be savage and wilful. A sensation of nearly competitive pride asserted itself in Nina: she would not let herself be overwhelmed by Michael's spirit in any contest of power. She had a spirit of her own that *he* must reckon with. She intended to create a mutual seduction that would be a meeting between them, not on Michael's terms alone. 'Wait,' she said.

Michael recognized the challenge in her eyes. He did not shrink from her gaze but smiled and lay back. He waited while she undressed herself. Then he permitted her, naked, to take him.

She held his face between her hands and slowly kissed his mouth. She licked his lips with her tongue. Impatiently he reached with his mouth to give her lower lip a tantalizing bite. She pulled back, as if in insistence that her tempo would not be quickened.

She pinned his wrists with her hands and straddled him. She lowered her mouth to the hollow of his armpit and gave him a slow, lingering lick that made him shiver. He released a gasp of pleasure when she showed her own teeth by biting him on his sensitive nipple.

When she was ready, not letting herself be rushed, taking as long as she wanted to taste him, to let her lips become familiar with the texture of his skin, she lowered herself onto him. He let out the resonant grumble of a bear. She liked the way he felt inside her: strong and masculine.

His hips began to move beneath her. He started to set the rhythm. She tried to hold him, to contradict his motions by the undulations of her own hips, but his muscles were stronger and she found the sliding, penetrating of his pelvis irresistible. Inside her he created a *friction*, a friction that enticed every nerve ending, enlivening her body with a chilling heat. In the end she gave herself over to the rippling tingles of sensation that his movements created within. In the giving over of herself she allowed him to pleasure her. In the giving over of herself she opened herself to his will. In the giving over of herself she freed the uncivilized passion that she had always suspected lived inside her. The passion took possession of her and she experienced to the full all that in the past she had hoped for in fantasy alone.

Recognizing her pleasure, Michael laughed a laugh of triumph, a laugh of delight. In one motion he rolled her over and was on top of her. He continued his movements while she, abandoned, flew to an oblivion of unprecedented pleasure. She bit the inside of her own cheek. The sensations were overpowering. She was lost in a world of dark ecstasy.

She opened her eyes in time to see his face frozen above hers. Nina watched. The face, momentarily horrifying, was a mask. No emotion showed. The eyes were hooded, impenetrable. For all her pleasure,

Nina was startled and frightened, for Michael seemed out of reach.

He lowered himself onto her for the last time and he shuddered several silent shudders. After the last spasm, he rolled off and lay beside her. She waited for him to speak. She waited longer. Then she was astounded to discover that he was asleep. She did not know what to feel about his quick flight to unconsciousness. *Selfish* was a word that formed in her thoughts, but she dismissed the word, for too much had been felt before he slept for her to see him as only selfish.

What had she felt? Nina lay on the bed, confused. Released from within her was her animal side, and the vision, the experience of her own darkness, scared her. She had expected to be overcome by the warmth of love. Instead she had been stirred by feelings no less intense than love yet considerably less reassuring. Together she and Michael had travelled not through a pleasant, fruitful garden but through a dangerous and unknown wilderness of shadows. And the look on Michael's face left the lingering question of whether indeed they had journeyed together at all.

Awake, alone, Nina lay, full of questions. She felt Michael's warm semen drip down the inside of her thigh. She put her hand between her legs and touched her clitoris, still alert and sensitive. She put the tips of her fingers to her nose. The smell of Michael and me together, she observed. It takes semen to make that distinct sea smell. Simon and I together used to smell like buttered lobster. But Michael and I smell more like brine, a faintly acrid smell.

Nina retrieved her pants from the floor and quietly

slid off the bed. She walked to the bathroom. Once inside, she sat astride the bidet. How did she feel? Exposed. Raw. Satisfied but disconcertingly jagged. Yet she had found a well that she knew she would have to drink from again.

Maybe, she comforted herself, maybe Michael was nervous about his upcoming business in Washington. Maybe that was what gave ferocity to his movements. No doubt, she was sure, he could also be gentle. She wanted to feel the tender side of him, too. Later, when they were alone and would have more time, they would really make *love*.

After cleaning herself, Nina went back to the bed and lay down. She watched Michael as he slept. The long black lashes were at rest on his high cheekbones. Nina felt the fumes of the wine swirl in her brain and she, too, slept.

Chapter 55

'I'm sorry. I should've stayed awake longer.'

Nina smiled shyly. 'Don't be sorry.' She leaned forward and kissed Michael on the forehead. 'You were just tense and tired.'

He sighed. 'I'm always tense and tired these days. I guess I've been working too hard. I ought to take a vacation.'

'Why don't you come to Greece? Sonia and I have decided to spend some time there this summer. I've always wanted to go to Greece.' Michael lay silently beside her. Nina was very aware of his long strong body, his slim waist. She liked the way his pubic hair curled lasciviously around his defenceless penis. Nina, watching his deep black eyes glitter, ran her hand across his chest. 'Would you like to come with us? It would be such fun.'

'Funny, you know, I happen to have a house in Greece.'

'Do you really? What a coincidence.'

'Yes, remarkable.' He smiled, making Nina unsure whether or not he had worked out that she knew about his Greek house all along. 'Anyway, I haven't been there for a long time, but it's beautiful. The villa's on an island called Zakinthos. One of the few places on earth where the world doesn't seem terrible.' His mood seemed to darken quickly along with his thoughts.

Nina continued to stroke him, as if by her stroking she could gentle him back from the edge of a black abyss.

Michael brightened. 'You have good hands for making love.' He took the other hand and brought it to his lips. He kissed the five fingers individually. He checked his sleek black watch. 'Time to get ready to land soon. I'll have to get up.' He took Nina in his arms. 'I'm glad we'll have our time together in Washington.'

'Will Titania be there?'

'No,' he said shortly. 'She's my wife in name only. We have no children. She stays in New York. Her patch is Morningstar Tower. The hotel part of it, anyway. She plays with the usual New York crowd. You wouldn't think a woman could spend all day doing her nails, but *she* can. Going to her exercise class, shopping . . . That's all she does all day long.'

Nina felt pity tear at her heart. 'How awful, Michael! It must be very lonely for you.'

'Lonely? Yes. You could say that. It's strange, you know. When I was a kid in New Mexico, what family I had was at least close. My grandma raised me. She was a good woman, but she could be fast as hell with her fists. My dad drank, but he was a kind old drunk. He'd just sit around and chew tobacco with all the other drunks. At least he had some warmth to him. What I have now is cold. Titania and I have a cold marriage. I was raised on all the old Indian myths. Titania reads nothing. She goes to the theatre and sees nothing. As for the opera, she thinks it's nothing but a lot of screaming. But me, I love opera. I love Puccini. I know you're supposed to say Wagner is the big guy, and Mahler for the symphony and all that, but give me Puccini and Tchaikovsky any day. In fact, the New York crowd know I'll always finance performances of works by either of those composers.'

'I'd love to go to New York some day.'

'That's an easy wish to grant. After Washington, you must come up to New York. You can come and party. See how high the high life can get.'

'Really, Michael? New York? Fantastic! And can we go to the opera in New York?'

'That might be a little harder, with Titania lurking around. But the hell with her. We'll do what we want.'

'Oh, I've always wanted to go to New York! But I mean, can we be seen together?'

'I can do whatever I want. I'll have you on my arm, and I'll load you with diamonds.' Michael smiled.

'Hm. I'm afraid I might come to feel like a kept woman.' Nina found herself laughing.

'You *are* a kept woman. From this moment on, you'll be the best kept woman in the US of A.'

Gone, thought Nina, was the elegant, suave, indolent Michael Morningstar. Here, lying on this bed, approaching his own country, was an eager Michael, his face alive and his voice exuberant with his plan.

'Wait till you see my house in Washington! It's fabulous. An old Georgetown mansion refurbished. Mimi van Durden did it out for me.' He raised himself on one arm. 'Tell me what you want. You can have it.'

'I have enough,' she said. 'I have you.' She kissed him deeply on the mouth.

Pulling away, Michael sprang to his feet and walked across the room. Nina watched his broad shoulders swing. He walked so silently, he moved so sinuously, she wondered if she would ever get used to feeling such love for this man. To the rest of the world Michael was a terrifying cipher. To her he was like a diamond dug from the depths of a deep black crater. In her hands he was a gem, the person she saw as a loveable childlike boy. Her heart went out to the boy-child trapped in his lifestyle, isolated among the beautiful women that flung themselves at him, the houses, the jets, the whole charade. Nina was certain she could take care of him and kiss away the face that so blankly and absently had hung over her. I'm not a faceless woman throwing myself at him, she vowed. I've truly fallen in love with him and I can help him.

The house in Georgetown, Washington, DC was indeed an exquisite mansion. The gates were a marvel of curlicue wrought iron madness and the ancient red bricks shone brightly in the April air.

The mahogany double doors were opened by a butler. Several servants surrounded the black Rolls-Royce and fluttered about Michael. He sat beside Nina as the car pulled up. He looked bored. The old Michael was back, a covering like the expensive suit he put on before he left the airplane. Nina, her body still charged and electric, smiled. She knew the real Michael, she was sure, the boy-child. Now Michael gazed at her, one eyebrow cocked. 'The house really is beautiful,' she said. 'It's huge. Who lives in it?'

'Only me and a posse of servants. This is the Jeeves in my life. I call him Bertie, after Wooster.'

Bertie loomed over the car. He was making discreet commands to the other servants with little flicks of his fingers. He had a big, bald, wide, domed head. Nina felt he would be better employed as a professional mourner at other people's funerals. He greeted Michael with dogged emotion, his round brown eyes filled with loyalty. 'Hello, Bertie.' Nina took the proffered limp hand. She saw her suitcase disappear into the maw of the house. Michael was deep in conversation with Bertie.

'I'm Mrs Ennals, the housekeeper, dear.' A warm friendly woman walked beside Nina up the front stairs and accompanied her into the house. 'We get such a lot of visitors,' she said. 'You're a fellow Englishwoman, aren't you?'

Nina held out her hand. 'I'm sorry Michael didn't introduce us. I'm Nina Stockton.'

'Hello there.' Mrs Ennals enthusiastically pumped Nina's hand. 'As I was saying, we've had so many visitors from England just this year. And we had Mrs Luscova here last week. Do you know her, dear?'

Nina paused. 'Yes. I know Marietta. I thought she was in Thailand.'

'Well, she is this week, but she travels backwards and forwards like a cuckoo clock. But I really shouldn't gossip. The Master hates it when we say too much. Mum's the word in this house. Come along. I'll take you to your suite. Mr Morningstar told me to put you in the suite next to his.'

Michael had disappeared, and Nina stood at the bottom of a vast marble staircase that reached upward in a magnificent curve in space through a high, grand hall. How on earth can one person live in such a massive house?

'This is Dumbarton Avenue, as the residents call it, but it's really Dumbarton Street. A local quirk. The people who live here are quiet, moneyed families, but we have a few known names, too. The Kissingers live several doors up. Of course, we have a lift in the house, but I thought you might like the walk up.' Mrs Ennals smiled. She had a bright, fat, happy baby's face.

Nina's hand rested lightly on the heavily carved newel post at the top of the stairs. 'And when Mrs Luscova is here, does she stay in the suite next to Michael's?'

'No, she has a room in the servants' quarters, dear. We don't see much of her. She keeps herself to herself. She's looking awfully thin these days. The chef tries to tempt her with his wonderful food, but she eats very little. Never smiles, really. Such a pity. What a beautiful woman she is, too!'

'Yes. She certainly is,' Nina agreed fervently, glad to believe that Marietta, relegated to the servants' quarters, was no threat.

Mrs Ennals chirped all the way along the upstairs corridor to the door of the suite. 'Here you are, dear.' She pushed open the door and Nina stepped into a warm, comfortable drawing room. It could have been an English room, for the furniture was based on English designs, but the absolute lustiness of the fabric and the absence of wear and tear belied its antiquity. Nina felt as if her feet were sinking into the fitted carpet, so thick was the pile. The curtains, still opened, were swagged as were her own curtains in Richmond. But again, there was a luxurious amount of curtaining here that showed itself to be more lavish than English. 'This really is quite extravagant,' Nina said, feeling the old English sense of guilt. Outside, the April trees were blowing papery thin in the new budding of spring.

'Well, the Americans have so much more money than we do, dear, and they do know how to live comfortably without shame. It's all central heating and bathrooms over here, you know. They shower every day in America. They're ever so clean.'

'Thank you, Mrs Ennals. I'll go and change. What time is dinner?'

'Eight o'clock. Just the Master and you. Drinks at seven thirty in the library. The library is on the ground floor. Second room to the left, as you come down the stairs.'

'Lovely. Thank you.' She wondered if she should tip Mrs Ennals. She should have asked Sonia. She didn't want to seem provincial in Michael's eyes.

Mrs Ennals left and Nina wandered into the bedroom. She wondered if she and Michael would make love in the big four poster bed. She went on into the bathroom where she saw a silver-backed hairbrush and comb laid out neatly by one of the hand basins. Two wash basins in one bathroom! It all seemed terribly elaborate. The black square marble bath was sunken into the floor. Beside it was an enormous black marble shower room. I could put three families into this one room, Nina thought. She kicked off her shoes and felt the thick black carpet under her feet.

Chapter 56

Walking down the sweeping staircase, Nina was fully conscious of her warm, glowing skin. Her face, recently checked in the mirror, reflected the happiness she felt being alone with Michael. Her feet seemed to float at least an inch above the floor. The blood throbbing in her veins made her tingle. She felt very much alive, in tune with the whole world. We *are* the whole world, she whispered to herself. When we are together, there is no one else in the universe. Just Michael and I.

At the bottom of the steps, she saw Michael leaning against a big, heavily carved door. He stood, smiling at her and saying nothing. She moved towards him. She had seen Michael in a dinner jacket before, but this time the dinner jacket was for her, not for Lady MacLaughlin or for any of the other adoring women. Only for her. She exulted in the swishing sound of her newly-acquired, black taffeta dinner dress. Her cleavage was well-perfumed as were her wrists. Don't forget behind the knees, was Aunt Persephone's long ago advice. She smiled at the thought of having remembered to make herself fragrant behind her knees as she reached up and kissed Michael gently on the mouth.

Michael took her shoulders. 'You look wonderful.'

427

He pulled open the door and they entered what was obviously a very well-stocked library.

Nina breathed deeply. 'I love the smell of books.' She ran her fingers over the spines of a bound collector's edition of *The New Yorker*. Above the fireplace were original drawings by James Thurber.

'What would you like to drink?'

'A gin and tonic, please.'

'I have tonic from London, if you prefer. The American bottlers have a way of making tonic too sweet. Awful habit. They tend to put sugar in everything.'

'But aren't you American?'

Michael grinned. 'Not entirely. I'm also Mexican, Indian, and a bastard in all senses of the word.'

'Don't be silly. You're nothing of the sort. You do more for people than all that rich committee put together. Without you, they'd just sit about and gossip.'

'Promise,' he said, with a smiling face full of candour. 'I'm a bastard, all the same.' He handed her the gin and tonic. 'Try it with a thick wedge of fresh lime,' he said. He poured himself a Macallan whisky. He let out a contented grunt as he sat down in his comfortable library chair. 'First Scotch of the day. Always a satisfying moment.'

'How's Marietta?' Nina watched his face. She wished she had not asked. Michael's eyes burned like those of a great eagle about to kill its prey. The eyes glowed and penetrated Nina's soul. 'I have no idea how she is.' His voice was strained. 'Why would I? Why do you ask?'

'Oh, no reason. I just haven't seen her for a while. Gemma doesn't see much of her, and I thought she was in Thailand, that's all.'

'Has anyone told you any different?'

'No. I'm sorry, Michael. I shouldn't have asked.'

His face changed to a more relaxed expression with alarming speed. 'Well, it's a perfectly innocent question.' His eyes lost their look of bleak paranoia. 'Marietta's okay. She's working hard for me, and I'm trying just as hard to help her get her kids back out of Hungary. Costs big bucks, though. Her ex-husband is an evil son of a bitch, but we're negotiating and I never like to lose.' He gave a sharp yelp which startled Nina. She realized it was more of a strangled laugh, strangled at birth by so much innate anger. And seeing him suddenly making such an unpolished sound, Nina felt immediately endeared to him. For all his newfound wealth, he was still the boy from New Mexico who at times did not know how to express himself gracefully. She loved him for his very awkwardness.

A telephone rang. 'Thank you,' he said. 'We'll be in in a minute.' He put the telephone down. 'Shall I phone Justin Agate about the meeting at the Press Club now or after dinner?'

Nina felt a heatwave beginning to build. 'Now,' she said, eager to have real-world concerns out of the way.

'Indeed,' Michael smiled, catching her urgency.

Nina felt her pulse quicken. After dinner, they both knew, there would be no time to talk to Justin. There would be time only for making love.

Dinner passed in a golden haze. Nina felt she was really standing behind a television camera, filming herself sitting at an elegant dining table and talking and laughing with Michael. Who was the poised, beautifully dressed woman? This woman threw back her head and laughed. This woman gazed at Michael with misty intensity. This woman touched Michael's hands. These were the hands that parted her legs so firmly only hours ago. This was an abandoned, flirtatious woman whom Nina did not recognize. She watched herself change courses. Dover sole in a champagne sauce came first, followed by a curl of red lobster with its own roe, a line of sliced black truffles marching down the spine. 'Delicious,' she heard herself. Well, it's a long way from baked beans and fish fingers, her doppelgänger remarked from behind the camera. Go away, the wanton in her instructed. Don't talk about baked beans now, not at a time like this. There is no time like this again. It is a precious time, not to be confused with reality. Go away. The doppelgänger gave up, turned out the lights, and switched off the camera.

Nina felt the split heal. She was of one mind, pushing away any lingering thoughts of children, domesticity, safety. She relished instead whatever sensations, pleasures, tastes, and smells could be extracted from tonight alone.

Michael leaned over and took both her hands. 'Listen, Nina, we don't *have* to make love tonight. We have all the time in the world. You're probably tired.'

'But I'd love to make love.' Her voice shook with passion. 'Really, Michael. I can think of nothing better than lying all night in your arms.'

'In that case, I suggest we forget about the coffee. I'll bring the rest of the wine, and I'll see you after you've changed.'

They rose in unison and again Nina felt they were now both wafting up the staircase. No one ever told me that being in love was like flying, she thought. You really do feel as if you are walking on air. Michael had his arm around her waist. Every few steps, they would stop and kiss. She walked into her room and quickly slipped out of her clothes. As she lay waiting for him, she felt her nipples harden under her searching fingers. She felt her body eager to arch beneath his weight.

When he came into her this time, she was relieved that there was no struggle between them. Like the ripple of a boat on a lake, she began to move and then the motor turned to a roar. She let go of years of sexual frustration. She heard herself first catch her breath and then – to her astonishment – she heard herself scream out with pleasure. She was beyond embarrassment. There was no going back. Over the deep shuddering edge she went and for a moment there was just blackness.

'*La petite mort*, the French call it. "The Little Death."' Michael was lying beside her, looking amused.

'I'm usually much quieter.' She wondered if the servants had heard her.

'Don't apologize. You were beautiful. You are a passionate little English girl!'

Nina felt the blood run through her cheeks. 'I haven't had all that much experience. I mean, I was a virgin when I married Simon, and he made it all unthinkably boring, something you did after the washing up, and with about as much pleasure.'

Michael poured Nina a glass of wine. 'Well, we don't ever have to wash up,' he said. 'Now, I'll let you get your beauty sleep. You have to look bright and chipper for the Press Club. Justin'll be here to pick us up at ten thirty. Goodnight, my creature of passion.' He left the room.

Nina lay in bed wondering what had happened to

431

her dream of spending the whole night in Michael's arms. She saw the light under the door of the adjoining room go on. She did not hear his telephone call.

'Are you still doped to the eyeballs, Marietta?' Michael's voice was sharp. 'Tell me. Who knew you were in the house last week? Nina's been asking after you . . . She was lying to me? Ah, yes. It *would* be Mrs Ennals. We'll have to get rid of the old gossip . . . Yes, the stuff is moving tomorrow night. Okay. Tell Hong Kong and then go back to your base. And, Marietta, some day your kids will thank you for this.'

He put the telephone down. Marietta had been easy to hook. Once she switched from simply being a courier to using the drugs herself, she fell even more under Michael's power. Now she was mainlining heroin. But then, he had suspected that Marietta would be easy to control. All the women who moved his stuff were highly educated, very elegant, and completely inconspicuous. No one would ever question them as they sauntered on and off their first class flights across the world. The rich associates and the charitable fronts covered for Michael. If some suspected him, they didn't ask. Many a blue-blood in London, Paris and New York had track-marks. Michael's inventory included designer drugs of the highest quality, guaranteed to provide the ultimate buzz.

And Nina was of use to him. She did do a good job running his London charity, and that gave him inarguable respectability. More importantly, he got from Nina the perpetual pleasure of toying with her innocence. It was as if she were a woman who could be freshly deflowered again and again.

Michael stretched. A good fuck always made him sleep better. And Nina was a much better fuck than he had expected.

Chapter 57

Nina stood next to Justin, nervously holding her sheets of notes. She had written down facts and statistics, but now, looking at a largely bored assembly in the Press Club, she felt trapped and unreal. What had the world of the homeless to do with her naked body under Michael Morningstar? She felt herself divide: there was the professional Nina who, compassionately and boldly, ran an effective programme in aid of the homeless; there was the private, sensual Nina who wanted still to be in bed. There was no question that it was the professional Nina that needed to be summoned to the fore to address the Press Club, yet, so recently rocking in passion with the man she loved, the private Nina could not be put aside. Nina felt like a naked impostor, quite sure that everyone about to listen to her socially minded words could see how that same mind was now consumed by sexual thoughts.

Talking into a battery of microphones was an earnest middle-aged woman whom Nina had hardly noticed upon entering. The usual platitudes about homelessness fell on Nina's ears. The sentences plodded on: '. . . an outrage and a disgrace . . . more than just individual efforts are required . . . the government's responsibility to *all* the governed . . . duty best executed by funding programmes that really can make a difference by doing scientifically accurate research.'

Nina realized how familiar the phrases were. Glancing at the programme, she saw that the present speaker was none other than Zelda Armstad. Zelda had evidently opted for a new hairstyle since her trip to London. Now permed curls hung around the flat, pudgy face. But the woman was definitely the same, and Nina felt her pulse quicken in terror at the thought of a public confrontation with the adversarial likes of Zelda Armstad.

Nina was slated to speak next. She looked at the bland faces of the journalists who gazed at the speaker as if they had heard all this before. And indeed they had. For the most part they were an expensively dressed group of people, far better dressed, Nina noticed, than most English journalists. Many of the men looked as if they spent hours 'doing lunch', as Sonia put it. They had broad, alcohol-reddened noses from years of hard drinking. The women, even more intimidating, wore business suits and sat superciliously on their chairs. Zelda Armstad finished her speech with what was intended to be a rallying cry. 'We must all lobby the government to study the homeless. It is our duty and moral obligation to do so. Ignorance of their plight is cruelty in disguise, and ignorance can be defeated by knowledge born of research. Sending money to research programmes such as my own is our only hope. Making donations to small-scale direct access programmes is well-intentioned but misguided. Each and every one of you I implore to sit at your typewriters and send forth the message.' Her voice was thick with an effort to squeeze out tears. 'Tell your readers that they must pressure the President and their Congress so that the government will take up its rightful responsibility and start putting money where money ought to be – research! Go to it, my brothers and sisters! We are one.'

There was a pause and then came the splatter of unwilling hands slapping together. Zelda Armstad bowed her head and walked off the platform.

Nina looked at Justin. 'Tell them how it *really* is,' he said. He smiled. 'Forget where you are, and just talk to the press as if they were ordinary human beings.' He laughed. 'All right: *pretend*. Go ahead. We're human.'

Nina stood almost immobilized by fear. She felt Justin's firm hand push on the small of her back. She walked toward the microphones. 'My name is Nina Stockton and I've come here from London to talk about our housing project, Latchmere House.' She took a deep breath. To hell with the written notes, she decided. 'Actually,' she said, 'I'm afraid I don't agree with um . . . with . . .' Damn! What was the wretched woman's name?

'Zelda Armstad,' Justin prompted in a whisper.

'Yes. Thank you. Mrs Armstad . . . I mean, Ms Armstad. I wish to make clear the plain truth that social research alone, unless it accompanies real hands-on compassion, is useless. No, it's worse than useless. It burns up money that could be better employed helping people, money that could be *given* to people to find them houses. In the same way, institutions that are too big inevitably fall into the trap of growing alienated from the very people they aim to help. Ms Armstad is quite wrong in her condemnation of small, grassroots, direct access groups, such as my own at Latchmere House. We are nothing more

435

than a collection of caring people who hold out our hands to other people. Directly. What could be simpler? What could be more natural?' Nina's sentences at first sounded clumsy to her own ears. She heard herself slipping perilously close to using jargon phrases. She felt herself floundering to speak succinctly. But as she spoke, she sensed an ease and a confidence setting in. She could see on the faces of her audience that they valued her remarks.

'Granted,' she continued, 'many of the homeless we see have problems underlying their homelessness. The lack of a house is sometimes only the symptom of deeper troubles. But when you commit yourself to *helping* people, without being bound by party-political rhetoric, or institutional policy, then you can hear what kind of help each individual is asking you for, and you can do your best to address those specific needs. More and more, we at Latchmere House devote ourselves to simple yet vital work such as conversation. Yes, conversation. Talking to people, listening to what's gone wrong in their lives, putting our human hearts into it, and seeing if together we can't come up with some individual solutions. Person to person. Heart to heart. That's the only way I can imagine anyone ever hoping to make a difference.'

Nina realized that she had captured the press corps's support. 'Homelessness is a classless tragedy,' she continued. 'We found, as we began working in Latchmere House, that what the homeless most wanted to do was to be part of the team that rehoused themselves and their families. More and more we came to see that we were just the enablers passing on what skills we had. And in turn we learned skills that the homeless taught us.' She smiled at her audience. 'We have taken the unusual step of "squatting". That means self-elected groups who wish to be rehoused finding empty property belonging to the government. We simply move in. It's quite legal, and the boroughs in question must then rehouse the families, or allow them to stay on in the houses they've taken over. Morale among our squatters is high. Self-supporting groups help each other. So I go into work knowing that our people are moving forward in their lives.

'Anyone can become homeless. It's important to remember that. Any time we see someone sleeping rough in the streets, it is our own challenge to say, "There, but for the grace of God, go I."' She remembered hearing a similar statement from Jimmy Donleavy's lips a long time ago. He always did know what he was talking about, she thought. 'The first homeless man I knew was a music professor from our Royal Academy. He died because no one personally took the trouble to care for him. In a way . . . Thinking about it now.' She blinked. 'Yes, I see my own guilt. Perhaps that's what caught me up in this work in the first place.' She was amazed to find herself fighting a genuine tightening of emotion in her throat. 'You see, I met him in a shop, but I gave him no food. I asked after him from time to time, but I never went looking for him myself. I was horrified when I learned he had frozen to death, yet I have to live with the fact that I never found him out on the park bench where he slept to give him a blanket. If I had . . .' Nina stopped and swallowed hard.

Her voice clearing, she said, 'I've met Ms Armstad before, and she accused my recounting of my work as being too anecdotal. Yes, clearly it is anecdotal. But I fail to see what's wrong with that, if an anecdote means an individual story. We mustn't forget: it's

437

also a *real* story. It's nothing that can be dismissed by the social science study because the person involved wasn't part of a statistically significant control group. The music professor had a real story, and it was a tragic story. Come to Latchmere House and you will meet many stories, many of whom, please God, we try to help have happy endings.'

A burst of applause interrupted Nina. The approval was so unexpected that Nina was not sure what to say next.

'In conclusion,' she spoke again when the room had returned to silence, 'I just want to say that it's not good enough to point a finger at the government, taking no responsibility ourselves. Real help is made up of individuals, and no government on earth can ever make a difference unless the public conscious-ness comes to demand more from the private con-science. We all should do what we can to help, help people help themselves.'

A hearty ovation followed, but was quickly inter-rupted by Zelda Armstad who hopped back on the platform and pushed Nina aside. 'Noble sounding sentiments,' she hissed, 'but I think our visitor from England is a little naive. I have a question for you, Mrs Stockton, since you would have us believe that you speak with the voice of authority. Please tell us: What are your qualifications for doing this work? Are you a social worker?'

'No. I'm a housewife and mother.'

'I see. Well, Mrs Stockton, I think you are experi-encing homelessness at a politically unaware level. It is the government that must be held responsible.'

'Naturally they should help, Ms Armstad, but they can only offer money. You need hands and feet for this work.'

438

There was a spontaneous burst of applause.

'No, I won't let you get away with that. The point is . . .' Zelda's voice took on a shrill quality as she tried to make herself heard.

But she was shouted down. 'Come on, Zelda. Give the woman a break!' screamed one voice.

'Sexist pig!' Zelda Armstad shot back.

Nina looked over her shoulder at Justin. He smiled and nodded his head. 'No doubt Ms Armstad is sincere in her denunciation of me,' Nina said sweetly. 'But I would ask her in return something I've never been able to grasp about her work: Ms Armstad, how many homeless families have you actually rehoused?'

Zelda glowered. 'You know full well I'm involved in the academic side of the question, and that's where the answers really lie. I conduct my studies, and analyse the evidence, and . . .'

'I see.' Nina stepped back from the microphones. 'I think you've answered the question.'

In the crush of photographers that surrounded her, she could see Zelda Armstad making her furious way out of the room. 'Boy, kiddo!' a kindly middle-aged man said. 'You've upset the queen bee here in America. But apart from her, what do you think of our country so far?'

'I think it's wonderful.' Nina felt her cheeks glowing. 'I'm in love with it already.'

Flashes were exploding in her face and she felt an enormous sense of power. She felt proud of herself in her own right, and proud of her work, but she could not fully fight away a feeling that, if Michael read some favourable write-ups of her appearance today, he might be proud of her, too. When she smiled into the cameras, she smiled for him.

*

'She was incredible, Michael!' Justin crowed. 'What a find! She's a natural.'

Michael stood in his library, his face alight. 'Yeah,' he said into the telephone. 'I kind of thought she'd handle herself all right. There's an innocence about her that the press ought to lap up. Makes a change from all those old batty war horses whinnying around. And if I didn't know better, Justin, I'd swear it sounds like you've fallen for her.'

'Sounds like that, does it?' He paused. 'She's yours, Michael. You got to her first. Besides, I think she's so crazy about you, I'd never stand a chance.'

'Then everything is as it should be,' Michael gloated.

'Yes, though God knows how you'll balance things, between Nina and your wife. But I guess juggling two women has never been a problem for you before.'

'Am I in danger of confessing something I shouldn't to a member of the press?'

'We're friends, remember? I know how to be discreet where friends are concerned. But promise me one thing. You won't hurt her, will you? She's not in your usual league.'

Michael grinned. 'I wouldn't dream of hurting her. You watch, she'll take Washington by storm.' He put the telephone down.

Lights were blinking from the other telephone lines. He picked up the phone again and punched a button to receive an incoming call from Colombia.

'Why are you calling me at home?' Michael's voice was instantly tense.

'We're out of here in a hurry.'

'You're busted?' Michael knew this phone was safe from wire taps. All his houses were constantly scanned for bugs. But he still disliked any direct calls.

'Yeah, there's been a leak somewhere.'

'Shit.' Michael drummed his fingers on the table. 'You know what to do, and do it fast.'

'Okay.'

Michael hung up. He paced restlessly around the room.

Nina pushed open the library door. She ran across to him. 'Oh, Michael!' she said. 'You should have been there! You'd have loved . . .' She looked at Michael's stony face. 'What's the matter? Has something awful happened? You look as if someone's died.'

'Someone will die.'

Stunned, Nina was made silent by the rage in the words.

Michael took both her wrists in his hands. He kissed her quickly. 'I've got to go. Business, I'm afraid.' His eyes were miles away.

Nina almost felt as if he had forgotten last night when they made such passionate love. She wanted to hold him, to keep him, to demand to go with him. She re-experienced the moment they had finished making love and something seemed to click inside him, as if he turned off this huge magnetic light that shone from his eyes and he became a robot, a velvet dark shadow of his former self. 'All right, Michael. I expect Mrs Ennals can look after me.'

'She's been fired, Nina.' He looked sharply at her. 'She talked too much.'

'Damn it, Michael, she was a nice woman!' The words came out on their own. Nina was shocked by the immediate look of almost uncontrollable anger on Michael's countenance.

'It's not your concern.'

She could tell he would allow no reasonable

441

discussion. That's my fault, she thought. I mustn't step into the parts of his life that he wants to keep private. 'When will you be back?'

'I don't know. I'll tell Justin to take you out to dinner this evening, and I'll get back when I can.'

'You don't have to *tell* Justin or anyone else to take me out to dinner. I'm tired and I'd rather stay in.'

'Fine then. I don't like the tone of this conversation anyway.' Then, as if nearly relenting, he gave Nina a quick, professional hug. 'I'm out of here. Catch you later.' The door slammed behind him. But his apparent gesture of reaching for her was enough to leave Nina feeling at least in some way needed.

Life in the fast lane, thought Nina. Seems to entail a lot of exits.

She had a list of appointments for the next three days, but Nina wondered when she would see Michael again.

After a solitary lunch in the dining room, Nina went upstairs to her room. As she walked in, she heard the telephone ring. She picked it up and heard Susan's excited voice. 'Angela's had a boy, Mum! He's a whopper!'

'Congratulations, Susan. And how *is* Angela?'

'Oh, she's fine. Shut up, Hamish. I'm talking. Anyway, the baby's name is Julian.'

'Jolly good, Susan. Can I talk to Hamish?'

'All right.'

'Mum?' She heard the hesitation in Hamish's voice. 'It's a boy, like Susan said.'

'I know, darling, and I expect you're upset, but we talked about it before, didn't we? You're still your father's first son.'

442

'I know. I miss you, Mum. When are you coming home?'

'Very soon, I promise. Not long. And this afternoon I'm going to hop into a taxi and I'll go and buy you your real American baseball bat. Where are you calling from?'

'We're at Dad's. Grandma Enid is looking after us and she says I have to eat all my carrots.'

'You don't have to eat them if you don't want to, Hamish. You tell her from me. All right?'

She heard the relief in the child's voice.

'I'll ring you tomorrow, darling. I love you very much.'

'I love you, Mummy.'

Nina hung up and sat on the edge of the bed. Why can't I ever say that to Susan? Nina knew the answer. Any attempt at giving love to Susan was always met with a rebuff. Simon was similarly lacking in warmth. Giving a gift bought him sexual favours in return, but affection did not figure in the formula . . .

The very act of talking to her children while sitting in Michael's mansion was for Nina a painful pull between two disparate worlds. To soothe herself after encountering Michael's harsh mood she tried to lose herself in thoughts of her family.

How did she feel about the new baby? She felt numb. A joint mutation of Simon and Angela. Probably a child that would grow up in the deadly embrace of suburbia. No doubt the Reverend Simpson would pour a drop of holy water on the screaming infant's forehead, and Angela and Enid would incline their awful hatted heads together. The blank in the faces in the following photographs would be Nina. She had been expunged from the holy circle. *So sad*, her epitaph. So very sad, the relatives would say. Poor Simon had to put up with that awful woman for so many years . . .

I refuse to be miserable, she thought. I'll go out and shop, as the Americans say, till I drop.

Chapter 58

The next day for Nina was filled with giving evidence before a governmental task force assembled to investigate homelessness in America. The task force panel met in a spacious, private conference room at a modern Washington hotel and listened to prepared speeches delivered by international experts in the field and to the personal first-hand accounts of people who had been or were currently homeless.

The giving of evidence before the task force was not quite such an ordeal for Nina as had been the conference at the Press Club. Nina marvelled that she seemed forever destined to follow Zelda Armstad, for upon Nina's entry into the hallway outside the conference room, Zelda and a group of her research cronies stepped from the meeting room door and walked straight past Nina in the carpeted corridor. Justin Agate, accompanying Nina, smiled sympathetically at her as they swept by. 'Every group has its star,' he said, 'and Zelda and her cohorts feel they are the luminaries in the constellation of homelessness. I guess you'll have to get used to the fact that in this world you can't do anything without opposition. Take a step in one direction, and you're bound to have someone on your heels telling you it's the wrong step to take and you should be going in the other direction anyway.'

Nina acknowledged the comfort in his friendly voice, but she was fretting about something that had nothing to do with Zelda Armstad. Where was Michael? Why hadn't he telephoned? That morning the mansion had been mostly quiet, yet she was aware of doors opening and closing, people moving about. 'Do you know where Michael is?' She was unable to control herself. 'He left suddenly after I got back from the Press Club yesterday, and I haven't heard from him since. Not a thing.'

Justin took her hand. 'I wouldn't take that too personally. Michael is a law unto himself. He has his own agenda. You'll see him when you see him. You'll have to get used to that, if you intend to stay with him. Listen, you'd better get your thoughts focused on what you're about to tell the task force. Representatives from a Dutch project are in there now, and they'll be finishing up soon.'

A small handful of people filtered up the hall. Nina recognized several of the workers from the National Housing Shelter from London. Oh shit, she groaned. Mindless English bureaucrats. Well, I have Hamish's baseball bat and glove packed away, several T-shirts for Susan, and stuff for Janice and the kids. In order to quell her nerves at addressing the panel, she went through a checklist of presents to bring home . . .

But where, oh where, was Michael? What happened to the days and nights of ecstasy she had promised herself? He had made no such promises to her, but surely he must feel the great sense of sexual liberation he had given her. For the first time in her life, she knew why God had granted the ever-consuming pleasure of sexuality to be celebrated between two people who loved each other. Her female opening was designed to fit and enclose his offering, the deepest and most hidden side of her female nature created to extract from him all that is male and different. Such a sweet communion, to fulfil each other and to enthral each to the other! Here she stood, alone and waiting, an invisible antenna searching space for her beloved . . .

'Your turn's coming up, Nina,' Justin said.

The group from the National Housing Shelter pushed past her and noisily took the seats vacated by the Dutch contingents. A Swedish man pulled Justin aside, evidently deciding that he was the most important person in the universe to speak to. 'We in Sweden do not have such many problems,' the man boasted to Justin.

'But you do have the highest suicide rate in Europe. Why do you think that is?'

Nina felt Justin mentally take out his reporter's pen. She grinned. 'I'll see you, Justin. After this is all over.'

The conference room was long. Nina stood at the back of the aisle between the many rows of the audience chairs, waiting for her turn. The task force sat in a faintly embarrassed silence. All of them were well-dressed and all of them carried titles pinned to their executive lapels. In front of the raised front table, from which the panel looked out over the whole room, was a chair and a microphone on a square table. A tall woman had just finished speaking and was collecting a substantial pile of books and papers. As she turned to walk down the aisle, an ebullient member of the committee called out, 'Just a minute, please. You're telling us that your agency needs three times the present funding it's already receiving in order to research the causes of homelessness? And at the end of all that, you still plan to house nobody directly?'

The woman walked back to the microphone and said clearly, 'As even the most cursory glance shows us from the framework of dialectical materialism, the roots of homelessness lie deeply embedded in the infrastructure of a fundamentally paternalistic socio-economic system, descended with only little alteration from the medieval model of feudalism, so naturally no amelioration in the distribution of communal resources can be considered before statistically significant empirical data are collected and analysed. I think that goes without saying.'

The committee sat looking stunned. Nina had heard similar statements before. No wonder, she thought, Zelda Armstad enjoys such popularity in the field if everyone else spews the same sort of rhetoric.

Nina realized she was the next to go on. She walked down the aisle toward the table facing the task force with nothing in her hands. No notes, no statistics, no empirical data. All around her, heads were nodding and the tall, departing woman who had just spoken swirled by to the joyful clapping of her friends.

Nina drew a deep breath. She remembered a passage in the New Testament: Now, Jesus says, is when one should let the Holy Ghost take over. You're my only hope, she prayed fervently. Without you, I'm sunk.

Then she heard herself begin to speak.

Finally there was a silence and she realized she had finished speaking. How awful not even to know what she had said! But she could see the task force members themselves all clapping enthusiastically.

447

She gazed behind her. There was row upon row of other experts' faces sullen with disapproval. Justin alone among the audience was cheering. He pretended to throw a baseball. 'Well done!' he yelled, quite beside himself.

The chairman of the committee leaned forward. 'Thank you, Mrs Stockton. Let me congratulate you on the first serious attempt to give this committee an idea of how self-help shelters such at Latchmere House do make it possible for the homeless to help themselves. We have for far too long listened to self-interest groups instead, all battling for funding that will offer the homeless nothing, not even a bowl of hot soup. But you are to be applauded and thanked.'

'Thank *you*,' said Nina. She slipped out of the seat and walked back up the aisle toward the exit.

'Revisionist,' she heard the whispered insults. 'Media cult figure,' Zelda Armstad hissed at her.

Justin pulled her out of the door. 'Whew!' he said. 'You must be glad that's over.'

A lined-faced, bulky woman came up to Nina who flinched, expecting an attack. But the woman said, 'I listened to what you had to say in there. You're right. I'm a displaced homemaker myself.'

'What's a displaced . . . Oh, I see. Don't use their jargon,' Nina said. 'You're homeless. You don't have to hide that fact.'

'Okay. I'm homeless. And you got me thinking. If we took over an abandoned old building I've seen – it's been empty for years – my friends and I wouldn't have to hang out at the airport any more. We could make a place for ourselves.'

Nina thought for a moment. 'Why don't you go and do a deal with the Port Authority? They give you a sufficient sum to do the repairs on the old building, and in return you agree to send a patrol of your people to redirect the homeless to the empty building. It could work.'

The woman grinned. 'Now you're talking.'

Nina smiled back. The woman walked off, her back straight and purposeful.

Justin took Nina's arm. 'You know, you'll never learn. There's a whole room full of so-called experts in there who aren't really looking for solutions. They all live off the problem.'

Nina felt dismayed. 'It can't be that cynical, can it?'

'You wait and see. Meanwhile, how about dinner? I'll take you to Le Chevalier. It's a fabulous restaurant.'

Nina shook her head. 'Thanks, but I can't.'

'Oh, I get it. Waiting for the telephone call, huh?' He sighed. 'Well, we've all done it ourselves, made idiots of ourselves in relationships. But if you won't come out with me, you ought to let me come and have dinner with you in the sprawling mansion. At least I'd be company for you.'

Nina conceded with a smile.

Actually, she thought as she got ready to change for dinner, I'd much rather be alone. To sit or to lie or to wander . . . The pain of separation was such a physical thing. There was no release. Having been taken over the edge and beyond the possibility of ultimate ecstasy with Michael, she felt abandoned emotionally and sexually. The conjoined self was now forever in search of reunion. Will I feel like this for all time? she wondered as she pulled a dress over her head. Will I ever be free of this bonding or this desperate need to be with Michael, to see his face, to hear his voice? She hoped not. She could not begin to understand how obsessed she had already become.

She sat staring at the telephone, willing it to ring. Ring, damn you, ring! But the telephone sat in obstinate silence, refusing to oblige.

In an orphanage on the outskirts of the city of Bangkok, Marietta sat on the side of a rusty army bed. The mattress was thin and stained. Outside the room she could hear the sound of the orphans playing in the dusty field. Mice scrabbled under the tin roof. The walls were made of dried mud. Beetles scuttled around the floor. Marietta was also waiting for a telephone call. By her bed she had two photographs of her promised children. The heroin she injected was free, supplied by Michael as a bonus for her work as a courier. But tonight she had to fly, so she used cocaine instead. Not the warm buzz of heroin to lull her to oblivion on her lumpy mattress, but the jolt of the coke hitting the brain cells, sending the synapses wild, lighting up the eyes and putting a surge of omnipotent power into her emaciated body.

She was waiting for instructions to leave for London. Her briefcase at her feet looked incongruous in the shabby hut. London, she sighed, and Gemma. This time she must tell Gemma it was over for good and make it sound like she meant it. When she got the children, she would not risk Gemma. She must take the children and hide, hide from her ex-husband in case he ever changed his mind, hide from Michael in case he ever insisted upon using her again. Maybe she'd try Australia. Who knows? The telephone rang. 'Okay,' she said.

She put the telephone down and picked up a shard of a mirror. First one nostril and then the next. She waited. Then she smiled.

Chapter 59

The days swirled by and Nina received only a message from Michael: she must take the airplane up for a final fundraising party in New York. She could not help but find herself immediately caught up in the fantasy that she and Michael would go all around New York together. He would take her to the opera, as he had said he might. He would take her to the museums. He would walk proudly with her on his arm . . .

Finally, on her last night in Washington, she agreed to dine out with Justin. Obviously, with a message from Michael left on the answering machine, he must have little intention of talking to her personally, so she might as well fill her last lonely night with Justin's company. The restaurant was full and noisy. 'What sort of people come here?' she asked.

'Oh,' said Justin, 'mostly people from the Capitol.'

Nina was aware of glances of recognition. She found herself blushing.

Justin eyed her, amused. 'You don't really enjoy the fame you're starting to have, do you?'

'No, not really. I mean, I can understand being famous as an actor or a painter, or even as a writer. But being famous for talking about homeless people makes no sense at all. There are thousands of people like me all over the world taking care of the homeless. Why aren't they famous?'

Sometimes, Justin found, Nina's innocence could be quite unnerving. 'Listen to me,' he said. 'The media are like a hungry lion. The belly is the insatiable public. They clamour to be entertained, to be told something new and different. They sit on the subway on their way to some dead end, boring job, or they live in cramped apartments just above the poverty line. They want to read about the rich, the bright lights and the glitter. They don't actually want to see pictures of the homeless, except at Christmastime when they can feel at least there are people on the rung below them. Zelda understands that game better than anybody. She surrounds herself with her legion of academic but attractive-looking young men. She speaks with authority. *Displaced homemaker*. That was her invention. So much nicer than "homeless", a lot less crude. And then you come along. You're young and pretty. You speak with passion.' He laughed. 'And that makes you flavour of the month. So Zelda's nose is out of joint. Besides, Michael has chosen you as his "pet", and that's sure to get some attention. He's smart, Michael. Ruthless and smart.'

'Pet or no pet, I haven't seen or heard from him for the last three days.' Nina buried her nose in her glass of wine. She toyed with her grilled swordfish.

'He'll be at the Morningstar Tower bash. You'll see him there. Men like Michael are different from the likes of us. They don't have human relationships with anybody.'

'I don't believe that,' Nina said sharply. 'I refuse to.'

Justin cut into his steak. 'Well, you'd better believe

it. I'm an old newshound. I've followed Michael ever since he first shot to power. And for some reason or other, I can't stop having misguided feelings of friendship towards him. Maybe it's his charisma. Maybe I'm as much of a sucker for it as anyone else. But he *is* interesting to be around, even if he plays rough. He bought Morningstar Tower and then he took the ball and he's still running.'

'And, I suppose, you're waiting to see what happens when he stops running? Just like a game of your American football, is that it? Who will tackle and who will block him?'

'You're catching on.'

'Hm. But no one will bring him down, ever. He's too clever.'

'People have tried, you know.'

'What happened to them?' Nina watched Justin closely.

'No one knows. They get paid off. They disappear.'

'Like Mrs Ennals?'

'Yes. Like Mrs Ennals.'

'Are you *truly* a friend of Michael's, Justin? I mean, do you really like him?'

Justin contemplated a tiny new potato which sat skewered on his fork. 'I don't know if anybody *likes* Michael, any more than he *likes* anybody in return. He's a life-force. He's an energy. He explodes into a room full of dull, overdressed people and somehow they all come to life. They feed off his energy and the excitement of being with him. And then he leaves. The lights go out. The party's over. Everyone goes home. Michael *is* a perpetual party.'

Except, Nina thought, when she saw his face when he first made love to her. That was no party. All his energy had been black and negative, his face a blank, his body momentarily a robot. Who was Michael? Well, at least she would see his precious face again. She decided to change the subject, afraid to have Justin do too much damage to her love for Michael. 'You don't realize how impoverished England is until you come to America. I went shopping for the children, and the choice here is enormous. And then I went into a supermarket to get Hamish some really crazy breakfast cereal. You have hundreds of different kinds.'

Justin laughed, sensing how consciously Nina was trying to change the subject. Well, he thought as he talked, I've done my best. I've sure as hell tried to warn her.

He left Nina on the steps of Michael's house. 'I'll catch the plane with you tomorrow. We can be in our rooms at the Tower in time for a good English cup of tea.'

'Great.' Nina kissed him briefly on the cheek.

As she got into bed she realized that she would be very glad to be back in her own home with her arms around Hamish. Yes, Washington had been exhilarating, but now she wanted to get back to everyday life, taking Hamish to school, going to Latchmere House, being with Cal and Gemma, having a cup of coffee with Monica, getting visits at the office from Jimmy – funny how much she missed Jimmy – hearing the familiar sounds of Lilly mopping furiously, seeing Stanley again. She had picked up a funny Mickey Mouse model for Stanley. The last few days felt as if she had been out of the real world for months.

God bless you, Michael, she said at the end of her nightly supplication, wherever you are.

*

Washington DC, apart from that bitch Zelda and her cohorts, had been a new adventure. Even then, as she strolled around the cobbled streets of Georgetown, peering in at the mullioned panes of the cottages with their bow-fronted bay windows, Nina knew that close by lurked the very poor, the starving, the murderous masses who faced the television cameras which greedily reported the latest bloodstained mayhem. The Capitol building, like an elegant white truffle fringed with pink cherry trees, sat above the inferno, the corridors of legislature perpetually buzzing with the latest scandal. And up the road from it all sat the White House, radiating complacency.

Nina drew her breath as the plane took off. Beside her in a carrier bag from the F.A.O. Schwarz toy store were the baseball and the bat for Hamish. Soon she would be home. Michael really had no home to go to. He had a wife who clearly did not love him. His marriage vows were in shards. No, Nina decided. He had nothing. Poor Michael, she thought – a favourite private phrase. Poor Michael.

Justin was asleep, stretched out in his chair on Michael's airplane. Nina had eaten a sparing lunch. She wanted time to think. Time to clear her head. She walked back to the room where she and Michael had first sampled each other's bodies. Now, at the memory, she felt a renewed yearning for more time to be spent anywhere with Michael. She lay down on the mink-lined bedspread and she slowly slipped into a dream that she was in his arms. His tongue lingeringly explored her skin until he found the softness between her lips. She moaned and thrashed in her dream until whirlpools of motion woke her. She gasped and then she sat up and smiled. Even long distance, Michael had that hold over her.

She stood up and pulled down her tight black skirt. She walked across the room and sat before the dressing table. She ran a comb through her ruffled blonde hair and she reddened at the thought of facing Justin. Her neck was still flushed with colour and her eyes were shining. It's the excitement, she told herself. Excitement at the thought of being in New York.

She had expected to be thrilled by New York. Sonia had talked so nostalgically about her city that Nina felt guilty as the limousine that awaited their arrival drove through a human crowd of misery which left Nina appalled and shaking. 'Justin, how can people get so excited by a city that looks like a slum? The streets are all broken, and it's filthy.'

More people shuffled in front of the limousine as it drew up at a stop sign. Justin looked out of the window as if he were used to it all. 'New York is either your city or it ain't. Simple as that. I was born and raised here. I love it. I can't help myself. I love the buzz, the crowds, the people doing their thing. New Yorkers are a special breed. We have vicious tongues, filthy minds, and hearts of gold. New York doesn't run on oxygen; it runs on sentiment. Say "I love New York" to a New Yorker anywhere in the world, and he'll bawl like a baby. And I'm no different.' Justin opened the window. 'Smell that? New York, New Yorkers, stale pizza, cigarette smoke, beer, car fumes, and sweat. Best smell in the world. Best place in the world.'

Nina watched an old woman pushing a shopping cart. Her mind went back to the homeless in the docklands of London. It's no different, she thought, anywhere. Homelessness is homelessness. Street life has a song of its own.

The old woman bent to pick up a discarded newspaper and a recumbent figure said something to her. The old crone laughed a crazy one-toothed smile and Nina felt her heart warm. I must find something for Lilly. She had the same smile when she was pleased. So little ever went well for Lilly that when it did, her smile was like a sunflower in full bloom.

The car moved forward slowly and Nina sat lost in thought. The fashionable, well-dressed New Yorkers pushed their hurried way through the crowded streets, elbows jutting, pocket purses and briefcases carried like weapons. They forced each other off the sidewalks and into the gutters. The homeless, or those that were at home in the streets, mostly sat with their backs against the walls between the storefronts, their hands outstretched with the warm April day ahead of them.

Justin, watching Nina's eyes to see what she was looking at, said in answer to her thoughts, 'The problem is a moral problem. No one gives a shit about *anyone* any more.'

'But that's just it, Justin. I think Michael really does care. I don't know what made him such a caring person. I mean most wealthy people don't devote themselves to charity nearly as much as Michael does. But that's one of the things I find admirable in him. I know he had a rough time growing up, and maybe that's why he's inclined to helping others, but most of his life is still such a mystery. Do you know if Michael has much family?'

'He had a grandmother who was good to him.'

'Yes, he mentioned her.'

'Then you know as much as anyone does about his

past. Except that after Korea he had some business dealings in the Far East.'

'Yes, I know he has an orphanage in Bangkok. Marietta visits it. And I think there's one in Hong Kong, too.'

'Does he now?' Justin looked interested. 'Funny. I never heard about the Bangkok orphanage. He's a strange man, Michael. He tells little things to various people, but he never tells any one person everything. He's like the military airplane manufacturer who keeps each worker busy on one tiny bit of the whole machine, in the hopes that they'll never make sense of the big picture. And no doubt his great fear is that all the workers might get together and swap notes and start to see what the whole plane looks like and the secret would be out. Bangkok, you say? Another interesting piece of the puzzle. Another part of the plane. I tell you, that man has more fingers in more charities around the world, you end up feeling he must get *something* out of it, aside from philanthropic satisfaction.'

'Maybe I shouldn't have said anything. You're right. Michael doesn't like us to talk about his private business.'

'It's okay, kiddo. I can keep my sources to myself.' In the steel cabinet at the back of his mind, a little file went click. Factoid: children's homes/India; orphanages/Bangkok and Hong Kong . . . Just lately, Michael moving into Colombia. Click, click . . .

Chapter 60

The glittering ballroom at Morningstar Tower left Nina speechless. Here were the American rich – the very, very rich – at play. Here Lady MacLaughlin and her English crowd would appear completely out of place. The English rich always managed to look shabby, their fur coats moth-eaten and their diamonds set in Victorian settings crusted with mould. The Americans, however, still possessed a sparkle new enough not to have acquired the corroded patina of age.

Until the double doors of the ballroom opened before Nina's astonished eyes, she had not imagined that such money existed. Justin pushed her into the throng. Hands reached out to her. Men's eyes widened with lust.

'For heaven's sake!' proclaimed a high, feminine voice. 'Saintliness come into our very own midst!'

'I beg your pardon?' said Nina.

'No, it's no use being modest. You're the Saviour of the Needy, the woman who puts our decadent indulgences all to shame.' Nina detected an American Southern accent in the voice. 'Admit it, sister. I've seen your face every place! You're in all the magazines. I'm Marsha, and my husband over theah is Billyboy. We're from Charleston, South Carolina, in case you hadn't guessed. And I must say it's a pleasure meeting the likes of you.'

Nina, still dazed, shook the proffered hand.

'Titania is so *good* at giving parties, don't you think? Hers are always the best.'

Nina could find no reply.

'Now, Billyboy,' Marsha called out, 'you just see that I get my raffle ticket. They're raffling off the sweetest little sportscar. Alfa Romeo, I think. And it would look so cute alongside my uthahs. At a thousand dollahs a ticket, it's a gift!' Her voice wobbled on words, flowing and flushing.

The thick Southern accent reminded Nina of Miss Scarlett O'Hara. She quelled an impulse to scream 'Lawsy, Lawsy! I do declare!' At first she could not decide if Marsha was authentic or not. The accent and the Southern act were *so* heavy, they matched too closely Nina's expectations of what a Southern belle would be, so closely that Nina suspected they were put on for show. But then she recognized that the air of plantation wide-eyed charm that hung about Marsha, whether an assumed gimmick or the real thing, worked. It enabled Marsha to get away with a lot. It was a way of engaging someone else in immediate conversation. It was powerful. Somehow she could not help liking the woman. And Marsha seemed so in control in this room. Here, the five hundred people in the ballroom all seemed to know each other. Voices were raised and a perpetual frisson of sexual signals linked men to women, women to women, and men to men. The atmosphere was incestuous and conspiratorial.

'You see, this is the biggest and the best, honey. Billyboy and I'd come out of the sticks for Michael and Titania any time. And isn't she just the most beautiful woman you ever did see? I don't know how she puts up with him and his wandering ways. But you must know all about that, now don't you?'

'No. I can't say that I do.' Nina's tone was short. 'I only work for him.'

'Only work for him? Why, you're too humble. You're the chef's special on his menu this month! You made *Time* magazine. Your name and Michael's name are everywhere. And *Time* magazine can't be the only covers you two have been between together. Oh! There I go again with that big old mouth of mine.' This she said with the most charming semblance of ingenuousness. 'Billyboy always did say my mouth's the best part of me, but it's sure to get me in all kinds of trouble!'

'Let's go and find a drink,' Justin interrupted. He pulled Nina behind him. 'Don't worry about Marsha. She's wacko. It's the South. Makes the ladies tough as overcooked chitlins.'

'She's all right. But does anyone ever do anything else except talk about Michael?'

Justin collared two glasses of champagne. 'Not really. What else do they have in their lives?' He raised his glass. 'Here's to the five hundred richest people in the world.'

Nina went white. 'And I've got to give them a speech, Justin. What on earth am I supposed to say?'

'Tell them off, girl. They loved to be told that they're fascist bastards. Kick them where it hurts. They get off on it. Let them all have one big *mea culpa* thrill. Tell them they're debauched and pointless.' Justin grinned. 'I'm glad I've been poor. I'm grateful that I still get a kick out of a decent steak and don't take it for granted. I even enjoy coming here and realizing that most of these people will never enjoy the food they can well afford from anywhere in the world. They're all at fat farms sipping soup. That's where they are.'

There was a sudden bustle and the crowd by the main door kept craning their necks. 'He's coming!' The words swept through the packed room. The door opened and the master of ceremonies boomed out 'Mr and Mrs Michael Morningstar.' Michael, with Titania on his arm, walked down the centre of the ballroom, the crowds falling away at their feet. Nina had to admit they looked fabulous together. Michael, tall and dark in full tailcoat, was only two inches taller than his wife. She, her blonde hair piled high on her head, wore a tight-fitting white lace ballgown. The bodice was deeply cut to show off a superb pair of creamy breasts. As Titania approached Justin and Nina, she could see that there were telltale signs of ageing on that seemingly perfect body. A little frill of skin was evident at the armpits. Two lines of worry appeared around the nose. Nina felt comforted by Titania's flaws. Titania stopped in front of Nina. 'Ah, Nina! How well you have done for our cause, my husband tells me.' Titania's voice deepened on the word *husband*. Nina felt the tether around Michael's neck jerk.

Only for a while, you bitch, Nina thought. She stared impassively at Titania. 'Yes. It's all gone very well. I'm glad you're pleased.' And by the way, she longed to add, why don't you book yourself in for a face-lift? Let it slide another week, and you'll be overdue.

Michael smiled at Nina. 'Speeches are at nine. You'll speak for ten minutes, then it's my turn. Between the two of us, we ought to make quite a killing.' Michael stood next to his wife, looking and feeling to Nina as if he had never held her in his arms all night, as if she had never lain naked, en-twined with him housed deep inside her body. He looked at Nina as if she were just an able, amenable employee.

'Certainly, Michael,' she said briskly. Inwardly she was raging. Jealousy had not been an emotion much explored by Nina. She had never been jealous of Angela, more relieved that Simon was gone. Yes, perhaps she had been somewhat irked that Angela could relate to Susan and indeed supersede Nina in Susan's affections, but there had almost been a relief in those feelings, too. Now the jealousy she felt was sharp, a razor's cut that tore deep and drew blood. The pictures of those hundreds of dancing people in their fashionable gowns and coats were splattered with the rage. Don't be so stupid, she warned herself. You knew Michael would be here with his wife. It's their annual ball. What did you expect him to do? Wrap his arms around you and say, 'Hey, everybody! This is my new mistress, the woman I love!'? Not that the news would be a surprise to anyone here anyway. There were no secrets among these five hundred people. Even past gossip, the servants saw to that. Whoever changed their love-stained sheets in Michael's mansion would be sure to tell Titania's maid within twenty-four hours. And Titania's maid would make it her business to inform her mistress. The huge batallion of maids that took care of these expensive women kept the phones ringing and the diet of whispered information bubbling. Next week *People* magazine, *The National Enquirer*, and *US* would be full of pictures of these partygoers dancing the night away. Secrets sold magazines, as did photographs surreptitiously exchanged. The wrong lips on the wrong cheek, hastily explained libel suits, public slanging matches . . . All part and parcel of this life. Well, Nina thought as she swayed in the arms of yet another drink-sodden mogul, I might as well make them all pay.

She stood feeling alone and very vulnerable at her place on the top table. Michael sat watching her through narrowed eyes. On his other side was Titania, her cold eyes waiting for Nina to fail. *I've been through all this before*, the eyes said. *He'll play with you for a while and then he'll get bored. I can wait you out.*

Wait on, bitch! Nina's thoughts sounded harsh even in her own head. 'I have never been homeless,' she began. 'But some of you may have known first-hand that unhappy state.'

A shocked ripple ran through the crowd of gaping faces. Well, at least she'd got their attention.

'What you're doing tonight is all in aid of a good cause, but a party every day of the week won't solve the problem of homelessness. All human beings have a right to a roof over their head. How ironic, that man had caves in prehistoric times, and now, in the twentieth century, even a cave would be a welcome shelter for many homeless people here in America, in England, and all over the world. To be homeless means you have no one who loves you enough to take you in. Homelessness is often not a problem that originated all by itself; it can be a symptom of a deeper disease. Simply taking a person off the streets and putting them into an apartment is not always a remedy. Increasingly at Latchmere House, we devote ourselves not only to handling the financial issues at hand, but also to counselling the emotional problems. What first caused the homelessness must be addressed. Dysfunctional families live dysfunctional lives, and I know, as I look at you, that some of you have children out there on those streets.'

The audience was still.

'Yes,' Nina continued. 'Not even your money – least of all your money – can stop your sons and daughters from drinking and taking drugs. I will not ask for a show of hands, but it would be an over-whelming sight, if those of you who are addicted to drugs or alcohol had to admit that the only reason you are in this room tonight and not out in the filth and squalor of Times Square is that your money is your cushion. But even money cannot lighten the dark night of your soul. And surely some of you know such loneliness that you might well covet the comradeship of the night-time camps where the homeless sit by their fires. Remember that you can only live in one room, sleep in one bed, and watch one television at a time. Life is about human relation-ships, not the endless quest for acquisitions. Without human relationships, the quality of life vanishes.

'On this, my first trip to America, I am struck by the kindness of the nation and by the vastness of your resources, by the affluence that you take for granted. But,' she paused, 'I am also appalled by the fact that you have hundreds of thousands of children sleeping rough at nights in this fabulously wealthy country of yours. I hope tonight you have not just come here to eat and drink and dance, but also to donate a sizeable amount of money to Michael Morningstar's charities which stretch all over the world. Every dollar you donate goes to the homeless and the hungry, to people less fortunate than yourselves. Tomorrow my job as ambassadress is over and I return to Latchmere House, Michael's project in London. I'll get back to my normal way of life, washing the homeless,

cleaning and cooking for them. God bless you all.'
Nina sat down abruptly.

'How did I do?' she whispered to Michael.

He squeezed her hand hard. 'Well done.' He stood
up and said, 'I have nothing to add to Mrs Stockton's
speech, except to say that, although you have already
paid for your plates, and your sportscar raffle tickets,
I would be grateful if you wish to add to your contributions. Please give what you want to Mrs Stockton.
And now let's thank a great little lady for doing an
excellent job.'

There was a burst of hysterical applause. Justin
leaned over from his seat on Nina's far side. 'It was
the bit about their kids that really got them. I mean,
half the rich little brats must be in therapy or in drug
abuse programmes.'

'Was I all right?'

'Sure, you were all right. I knew when I first saw
you. You're a natural communicator, Nina.'

She sat back and smiled.

All through dinner people came up to the table.
Soon the centre of the table was piled high with
dollars and cheques. As Nina stood up to dance with
Justin, an anorexic woman approached her. 'I have
something to tell you. I've never told anybody before.
I told my husband that my uncle raped me when I
was a child. All my husband said was, "What did
you do to encourage him?"' The pain in the woman's
voice was bottomless.

Nina could see and hear those pitiless words falling
like stones down a disused well. 'Tell him all children
are innocent. And so were you.' Nina instinctively
put her arm out to hug the suffering creature. 'Tell
your husband that your uncle was a paedophile, and
paedophiles prey on innocence.'

The woman drew back from Nina's offer of an embrace as if she felt herself leprous from that awful event.

'If he doesn't listen,' said Nina, 'divorce the bastard. He's not worthy of you.' Nina stood looking at the woman. What am I doing here? she thought, sensing her own futility. Who am I to give advice? Is there anything I can say that is adequate to help this woman? The woman's eyes filled with tears and then she was lost in a whirl of men in white gloves serving coffee.

'I'm tired, Justin. Do you mind if I slip away? I'll check with Michael. But we leave for England in the morning, and I'd like to get a good night's sleep.'

'Of course, Nina.'

They walked back to the table. 'I'm going off now, Michael. I need an early night. I'm very tired.'

Michael checked his watch. 'But it's only half past twelve. The folks will expect to have time to talk to you.'

'The *folks*, Michael, have already been talking to me. What time will the car leave for the airport?'

'Seven-fifteen.' She could hear his irritation. 'Anyway, I won't be going back with you. I've got a business meeting tomorrow morning.'

'Oh!' Titania leaned forward. 'Does this mean you'll have to miss tomorrow's lunch? It's Marsha's famous lunch at the Castaways. It's always such fun. She has all this Southern food flown up from her mansion. Fresh stone crabs, deep-fried catfish . . . You know. Things like that.'

Nina smiled at Titania. 'Sounds wonderful,' she said. 'Shame I'll have to miss it. Eat a catfish for me, though, would you?'

Michael sat unsmiling in his chair. Nina longed to

push him off his self-made throne. You're spoiled, Michael, she wished she had the nerve to say to him. Bloody spoiled.

She kissed Justin on the cheek.

'I'll see you to your room, Nina. Can't have a beautiful woman like you roaming the lonely corridors of Morningstar Tower this time of night.'

'That's good of you, Justin.'

'What are you going to do with all this money and cheques on the table?'

'Could you ask someone to send it upstairs to my room please? Thank you, Michael. It seems to have been a very lucrative evening. Goodnight, Titania.' She took Justin's arm and whispered in his ear. 'Come on. Let's go and get properly plastered. I've got an excellent bottle of brandy upstairs.'

She turned on her heel and walked away. Wow, thought Justin. She handles herself well.

Chapter 61

Nina sat alone on Michael's private jet. She ignored the sympathetic smile on the stewardess's face. She restrained herself from asking the stewardess if Marietta had ever been on the plane. Already Michael's need for subterfuge was beginning to dictate her actions. She had disobeyed him by wanting to leave his ball early: all right, he would pay her out by his absence. Instead of making luxurious love in the bedroom of the airplane, she was sitting by herself. 'Take care of yourself,' were Justin's last words to her before leaving her hotel bedroom last night within Morningstar Tower. 'For all the years I've known Michael, I still don't really think I know him.'

Nina sighed in her airplane seat as she pretended to busy herself. I don't suppose any of us will ever know anything about him, she decided. Beside her was the carrier bag filled with toys. For Lilly there was a small sphere of plastic with the outline of New York skyscrapers. When it was turned upside down, snow fell on New York City.

The little Nina had seen of New York bewildered and frightened her. How could such awful poverty and depravity exist so close to those amazingly rich people who danced a lifelong waltz only a few hundred feet away from the worn, unwashed bodies of the street people?

Marsha and Billyboy would soon be chomping their way through bowls of stone crab and mud-filled catfish, pigging out yet again with their friends. The homeless to them were nothing. But to Nina the homeless had names, like Lilly and Janice and Monica. She had T-shirts for Gemma and Cal, and hopefully one day she would hear from Valerie – the prostitute who had chosen to remain with Leonard, her pimp – and be able to give her a bumper sticker which she picked up that said, 'Wedlock is a padlock when you're married to a no good man.'

She was not pleased to see Simon's face sticking out of a sea of people waiting to collect their friends and relatives at London's airport. 'What on earth are you doing here, Simon?'

'Dad says you're a celebrity, and he wanted to have his picture taken.' Susan presented her cold little cheek for a kiss. 'What did you bring me, Mum?'

'Don't pay any attention to Susan. She's been difficult all weekend. I just thought I'd give the kids a run to the airport.'

'How did you know I was coming in?'

'I told Dad, Mum.' Hamish flung himself into Nina's arms. 'I'm glad you're back. We had a horrid weekend. Angela's in an awful temper. The baby screams all the time. I want to go home. I don't want to stay there ever again.'

'I say!' Simon said. 'Steady, old chap. Give poor Angela a break. She's just had a baby, and there's you two going at it hammer and tongs.'

A camera flashed and then another. Nina looked up, temporarily blinded. 'Do take your arm off my shoulder, Simon. We're not married. Remember?'

Simon smiled. 'We'll always have been married, Nina. Pity you won't be my mistress.'

Nina was rushing and pushing through the crowd. She stopped. 'Simon! You are the most boring lover any woman could ever have the misfortune to encounter.' A hush descended on the passers-by. Nina felt her words float across a quiet lake of mute astonishment. 'Oh shit.' She put her hand over her own mouth to stop herself from saying anything further. Please, Lord, let there be no reporters within earshot. She could see the headlines now: CIVIL SERVANT IS LOUSY LOVER, SAYS HOME-LESSNESS CHAMPION. And the down-market newspaper market would report: NIX ON SEX WITH EX, SAYS NAUGHTY NINA!

The noise resumed and Nina was out of the terminal into the grey, slimy fog of an English day. Feeling guilty for her outburst, she accepted a ride in Simon's car, but she sat mostly silent. She could tell the children in the back seat were watching her. New York, she decided as she gazed out at the sad, dirty streets of Hounslow, was frightening and awful, but inevitably thrilling all the same. London just appeared poor and mean. The streets were cleaner, but the people were bored and boring.

In her bag she had a present for Mrs Theodorakis at Theodorakis's shop along Chiswick High Road. It was a jar of Cypriot honey. She knew it would raise a smile from Mrs Theodorakis, always homesick for her native Cyprus.

Already Nina was bored by Simon. She missed the smells and the bustle of Washington. A visit to the Theodorakises and a takeaway from the Chinese restaurant would reconnect her to her former English life.

She waved goodbye to Simon and took the children inside her home on Angel Walk, Richmond. 'You can collect Susan at eight o'clock,' she said firmly.

'Can't I stay the night?' Susan whined.

Nina studied her daughter's face. And sit on the end of my telephone and listen to my conversations? she thought. No, thank you. 'Susan, you live with Simon and Angela now. I certainly wouldn't want to interfere with that.'

Susan sulked.

Nina handed her a skirt and a T-shirt. 'There wasn't much time to shop, and you say you're too old for toys, but the I LUV NEW YORK T-shirt is what everybody's wearing.'

Susan put the clothes on the sofa.

Hamish and Ryan ran out into the garden to play with the bat and the ball. Both Ryan and Elsie were pleased with their T-shirts, and Janice put hers on immediately. 'We missed you, Nina,' said Janice. 'Really we did. I've cooked your favourite, spaghetti Bolognese.'

'I was going to save you the bother and order a takeaway.'

'Live in sin,' Janice said. 'Let's do both. You order the takeaway and we can have the spaghetti for the main course.'

Nina hugged her. 'It's *great* to see you again,' she said. 'Is everything okay at Latchmere House?'

'Yeah, they did the squat at the row of cottages. Went like clockwork. Stanley went with them. He said when the police got there, they read the notice, knocked on the door, and said, "Oh, it's you," and scampered off.'

Nina laughed, feeling a bubble of happiness rise in her heart. 'I guess they're getting used to us.'

'Guess they are,' Janice beamed. 'Oh, and Sonia rang last night. I said you'd give her a bell.'

'Indeed I will. I'll get Susan off and Hamish to bed, and then I'll talk to her.'

Nina was in her own kitchen. She was surprised at how much she had missed her own food, her own salad bowl, well-oiled with years of use. 'I learned one thing out of all this, Janice.'

'Oh yeah? What's that?' Janice was boiling the spaghetti.

'I learned that I don't want to be rich. I mean, I've never been really poor or homeless, like you have, but I always thought how wonderful it must be to have anything you wanted. This trip taught me something very valuable.'

'Go on. What?'

'Well, the very, very rich – the super-mega-wealthy

– are awfully boring. Nothing excites them. I was turned on by Michael's mansion for the first few days, and then I was lonely and bored. I missed Stanley's sense of humour. I missed you and the kids. Those people over there have never kicked off their shoes and sat with no make-up on. The women I met were born with make-up plastered onto their faces. It was all a bit of a nightmare, in a funny way.'

'But you look wonderful, Nina! I've never seen you look so good. You kind of sparkle.'

'Oh, that's Michael, Janice. Nothing to do with the rest of it. He's impossible, but I'm afraid I do love him. Funny,' she said, 'when I'm not with him, half of me feels as if I'm not there at all. He's cross with me for the moment, but he'll come back. At least I hope he will.' Nina looked out into her beloved garden. It was dark now and the boys were inside watching television.

'Well, I'll say this, Nina my love. You've got it bad. Anyone can see that. If he's the disease, you've got yourself a heavy dose.'

'Isn't it silly? You spend all your life reading about the earth moving and breasts heaving and thighs lusting, and then it happens to you. I feel all of those silly, trite things. Here I am, a fully-grown woman making a perfect fool of myself over a man who's already married and probably has every intention of staying that way. I know he's no good. He's secretive. He's spoiled . . . But I still can't help myself.'

Janice nodded. 'I know just how you feel. I felt the same way for Billy. I let him beat me, torture me and the kids, everything. Now I look back and I'm shocked at what I let him do. It's so different with Ray. We're calm together. We just have fun. We sit and talk for hours. I cook his meals and he cleans his car. We go to the pub or maybe a dance. He's gentle with the kids. A while ago I'd have laughed in your face if you told me I'd fall in love with a man like Ray. Now I think different. With Billy, life was one big roller coaster. You never knew whether you were on your way up or down. But with Ray it's like the sea. It's warm and it's happy, and it'll go on forever and ever.'

'Do you ever miss Billy?' Nina very much wanted an answer. She wanted the answer to be yes.

'Truth?' Janice stirred the pot. She watched the spaghetti boil. 'No,' she said. 'No, I really don't miss him at all. And if I was to see him in the street, I'd probably not even recognize him, that's how I feel. Maybe I would, and I'd think "Janice, you silly sod! Why'd you ever let him do the things he did?"' She shrugged. 'Maybe I thought he was a frog, I could be a princess and kiss him better. Remember the old fairy tales? Turns out, you kiss a frog, you get a bigger frog.'

Nina heard the doorbell. 'That's probably the Chinese takeaway,' she said. Damn! she scolded herself. Why couldn't I fall for a man like Ray? Then she remembered Jimmy Donleavy. Why not Jimmy? she asked herself. Or even Justin. Why did she have to love Michael – moody, jealous Michael?

Chapter 62

'So did you?' Sonia's voice was amused.

'Yes,' Nina heard herself say, despite the fact that she didn't want to talk about it. Making love with

Michael was too precious. 'But listen, Michael says his Greek villa on the island of Zakinthos is ours for the asking. We can use it for our holiday. So you see? I did manage to hustle him after all.'

'Bravo! Will he be there?'

'He says so, but he's so unpredictable.'

'All men are unpredictable, the little pricks.'

'You can't say that about all of them. Jimmy Donleavy isn't unpredictable. Ever.'

'Then why aren't you with him instead?'

'God, Sonia. I wish I knew. I suppose it's like having two bottles of champagne in the fridge. One you know will always be worth drinking, and the other is iffy. But once you've tasted the iffy one, you can't settle for anything less.'

'That good, huh?'

'That good.' Nina laughed. 'Oh, I don't know! When I'm with him the world is a special place and everything glows brightly. And then when I'm back at home, I just wish he'd get out of my life and leave me alone. He's sulking for the moment. I upset him, so I probably won't hear from him for a while. But tell me what you think. Should we accept his offer for Greece?'

'Are you crazy to have to ask? A free villa is *always* a good idea, particularly when it's owned by one of the world's richest men.'

'I was thinking, we could take Stanley with us.'

'Suit yourself, Nina. I have every intention of finding myself a Greek god of a lover, so you might as well bring along someone to amuse you, if Michael decides not to turn up.'

'Shall I take my frocks?'

'Somehow I don't think they'd go down terribly well in Greece, Stanley.'

'But Greek men look so lovely in their pretty white tunics, don't they, dear? And they have such shapely legs. My answer is yes. A thousand times yes! Only, what? Ten or eleven weeks away? I can't wait. I'd adore to come and float about in the Ionian Sea. I've always thought the word Hellenic is so much nicer than gay.'

Nina laughed. 'Sonia's given herself the quest of finding the perfect Greek lover. While she's out searching you could keep me company.'

'I'd love to, darling. I'm very chaste these days. As pure as a monk. There's a nasty virus going round. Nobody's talking about it yet because it's only killing off the poor. And of course *we're* being blamed, as we are for everything else. But no matter. Just wait until one of your committee comes out in purple polka dots, and it will all become very fashionable. *Très* trendy, a virus that gives you street cred. No, Nina. You've changed my life, my darling. I've given up sex and taken to squatting as a man might take to his outside toilet. Keep your furtive fucks against back alley walls; give me the thrill of breaking and entering the council's property any day. The tingle of acquiring houses illicitly is really quite habit-forming. I wish you'd have been on the last squat. Basset Council were all set to rip up the old electrics. The men were actually digging up the wires when they pulled the plug. And that arsehole of a councillor – you know, the one with three warts behind his ears? – he looked up and saw lights shining in all our windows anyway. Well! The lovely Irish workmen set up a cheer and we all waved at the silly bugger of a councillor. We *knew* ahead of time they'd be cutting us off, so we got in there first with our camping lights and torches. It was marvellous!'

'Oh, Stanley. I'm so sorry I missed it. But I did raise a lot of money.'

'You know, Nina, you're an anarchist at heart, that's what you are.'

'I don't think I'm any sort of "ist" in particular. Listen, I've got you a super T-shirt and a fun little gift. Can't wait to give it to you. But I'll absolutely collapse it I don't get to bed in a hurry. This globetrotting's all a bit too much for me. Why don't you come by tomorrow and collect your prezzies from the office?'

'I'll be there. I suppose this means you won't be going to the squatters' rights meeting tomorrow night, will you?'

'They'd have to wheel me in, I'm so worn out. Can you take notes for me? And I really ought to spend some time with Hamish. He's really missed me. I've missed him. I'll stay home and we can watch telly together.'

'My dear, I'd be delighted to be your personal secretary and note-taker. There's a really good squat going in Notting Hill Gate. A whole row of houses has been empty for ages.'

'Sounds too good to pass up. I'll see how many families from Latchmere House are ready to move on when I get in tomorrow. Goodnight, Stanley.'

'Night, night, love. And thanks. I can't wait for Greece.'

'Hm. Me too. I've always dreamed of going with someone I love.'

'Well, I love you, dearest.'

'And I you, Stanley.' There was a moment of shared silence. Nina sighed. Why, she asked God in her unbidden prayer, can't I love someone who will love me back? There was no answer forthcoming to her prayer. Absolutely no answer at all.

Chapter 63

Nina realized she had forgotten how noisy Latchmere House was. Before she left, she was unaware of the sound of continual hammering and the incessant whine of an electric saw, the counterpoint of never-ending house repairs. The men and a few women – all new faces – greeted Nina with shy smiles. 'We saw you on the telly,' a young strained-faced woman whispered. 'Can't believe we're actually meeting you in real life now. You look different.'

Nina felt embarrassed. 'Well, yes, people do look a little different from being on the telly when you meet them.' She recalled having felt the same thing the first time she met Jimmy and the first time she met Michael. She was still unused to people seeing *her* that way. 'It's only the telly,' she said cheerfully.

Cal ran down the stairs and enveloped Nina in a warm bear-hug. 'Lilly is banging the hell out of the filing cabinets. Come and distract her. She'll be thrilled to see you.'

Nina laughed and she realized she was more than just glad to be back; she was home, among real people facing real issues. After the silence in Michael's mansion and the frenetic gatherings of the American rich at play, Latchmere House, for all its overcrowding and non-stop pace, seemed a welcoming oasis. 'Lilly darling.' Nina stood in the doorway of the office. 'I've brought you a present.'

Lilly paused for a moment from her assault on the filing cabinets. 'Where've you been?'

'I told you, Lilly. I had to go to America to raise some money for you to live here.'

Lilly's expression softened. 'You bought me a present?'

Nina took out a little package from a carrier bag. She walked over to Lilly and gave her a hug.

Monica was sitting at the desk, smiling. 'Lilly's done a wonderful job of keeping the office spotless.'

Lilly took the small parcel in her hands, her toothless mouth widened into a grimace of pleasure. Her hands shook. 'Look,' she said. 'A real ribbon and a bow.' Her fingers gentled the ribbon apart. She stared at the glass dome sitting on a black plinth.

'Shake it, Lilly.'

Lilly turned the skyline of New York upside down. Then she held the object in her hand and watched the snowflakes drift downward and settle on the skyscrapers. 'My!' she said. 'Nina, it's beautiful!' Again came the cracked, agonized smile that so tore at Nina's heart.

'It's for you, Lilly. I chose it specially.' Nina took out the T-shirts for Cal and Monica.

'I'll make coffee.' Lilly stuffed her present in the capacious pockets of her much-patched jersey. 'What's for lunch?' she said, evidently having forgiven the filing cabinets. 'I'm starving.'

Nina pulled up a chair and examined a sheet of paper. 'What's this?'

'A directive from on high, dear,' Monica answered. 'It's Lady MacLaughlin. She's been by a couple of times to patronize the children. She took a bunch of kids to her house and then, after she got Hugo to return them in her limo, there was the most hysterical phone call. Seems she showed some of the girls her jewellery and the little beasts pinched a few pieces. But, really, what did the silly cow expect?'

'Oh no!' Nina tried not to laugh. 'I can't say I blame them. If my family were homeless, and some rich bitch decided to flaunt her wealth, I'd probably do exactly the same thing. Did you get any of it back?'

'No.' Monica suppressed a chuckle. 'Actually some of the kids turned out to be trained thieves. We didn't get a thing back, but they're all in the new squat and their mums suddenly have a great amount of terrific new gear. I don't know if it was the jewellery that bought it all, or maybe the stuff came off the back of a lorry.'

'Yeah,' said Cal, 'but whatever, I think it's a damned stinking letter for the stupid bitch to send us. She insists she wants to see you. And she's heard all about the latest squat and she still can't accept the idea that we are within the law. Just.'

Nina shrugged dismissively. 'Well, she ought to get used to it. She's likely to hear about many more. If only she'd get so upset that she'd resign from the committee!'

'We should be so lucky,' Cal muttered.

'Hm. I think she'll never resign because she's too fascinated by Michael.' Nina made her tone sound casual. 'Any telephone calls from him, by the way?'

Monica shook her head. ''fraid not.'

Lilly came through the door with a tray of coffee mugs. 'I've done one extra,' she announced. 'Young Stanley just come in.'

'Young and handsome, if you please,' Stanley sibilated behind her. He kissed Lilly on the forehead as he walked past. 'One of these days I'm going to kidnap you, Lilly, and take you over with me to one of the squats. We'll be a right pair together.'

Lilly giggled and turned bright red. 'You are a one, Stanley!'

Nina felt herself at peace. She said to Stanley. 'Michael's probably still in New York, but the offer still stands for Greece.'

'You bet it does!' He grinned. 'I already got meself a little Greek yachting cap, but I can't make the weeks pass quick enough. Imagine, Nina! You and me sitting in a Greek taverna, a glass of ouzo in our hands, and Michael off brooding in the distance. Brood, brood, brood.'

Nina felt a wave of annoyance, but not at Stanley. Why the hell don't I just telephone him? She knew she couldn't. Compartments again. Always compartments. Michael kept his life neatly divided into different compartments and for her to peek around the corner of the one she was relegated to and poke herself uninvited into another would be tantamount to treason, according to Michael's rule book. Well, there was a board meeting in a week's time, and she'd be sure to see him then.

Nina turned her attention to a pile of letters. 'We'd better get on with the post.' She picked up a stylish news sheet. 'I see the National Housing Shelter is putting out more glossy crap at the taxpayers' expense.' She read a few sentences to herself. 'Really! Is it absolutely vital that we be told that the results of their two-year study prove beyond a margin of statistical uncertainty that homelessness can, in many cases, lead to an impaired sense of self-esteem? The amount of time and money they waste, doing endless research to prove the most minute self-evident truths, while doing no real good to any person in the mean time . . . It makes me sick. Wads and wads of bumf. That's all they ever produce. The hell with them.' She screwed the paper up and sent it sailing toward the dustbin across the room. 'Do you have the house register, Monica?'

Monica handed her the record of who had come in and left Latchmere House in Nina's absence.

Nina ran her eyes over the list of families. 'Twenty-eight families this month from all over England. Well, that's twenty-eight more families than the National Housing Shelter have housed.'

Monica smiled. 'It's not just housing people,' she said. 'A lot of people need to change their lives, not just their address.'

Nina smiled with heartfelt admiration. 'You've done well, Monica. You look like a completely different person from when you first came.'

'I *am* completely different. I feel like a real human being for once. I'm not a nothing any more. I have my job here, and I take care of other people. I help house families. I look at children now that I helped rehouse months ago, and they come back to see me. I used to look in a mirror and you know what, Nina, there was no one there. It was frightening. Just an empty blank. When my children were young, I spent days when I felt I was a non-person, so all I could do was drink. Now I look in the mirror and I see my face. I put lipstick on my mouth, if I feel like it . . .'

Cal cut in. 'This is the first programme I worked in where make-up counts as a triumph.' But her teasing was gentle. 'No, seriously. This is the first place I've worked that really *works*. People living in the project run it themselves.'

'Yes,' said Nina. 'I think that's very important. I

spent too many awful years being bullied by my ex-husband and his bloody mother. It seemed absolutely natural that anyone coming here should want to feel in control of their future. I was considered such a fool that I had to be furnished with a shopping list before I was let loose on the world. If you tell someone enough times they're bad, mad, and difficult, they will indeed become all those things. Look at you, Stanley. You've taken to a life of crime with perfect grace,' she laughed.

'Guilty as charged, m'lord. I've become a squataholic. And it's all the fault of that woman over there.' He pointed at Nina with both arms outstretched.

Monica looked up at the clock. 'Oo. We'd better go downstairs. Time for the house meeting.'

'I am not fucking violent!'

Cal sat on the floor beside a new arrival in the community. 'Sure you're not, honey,' Cal said sweetly in her warm Californian tone. 'You don't *think* you're violent; you just scare off people. They say you're violent; and then you feel left out.'

'Aren't you scared of me then?'

Theresa's behaviour was under discussion. The night before, she had come in drunk and she threw milk bottles through the dining room window. Nina guessed from looking at the girl that she had spent time – a lot of time – in prisons. She had that lonely look of solitary confinement. 'If you get drunk and throw milk bottles, Theresa,' Nina said, 'it's not the end of the world, you know.'

'No?' Theresa turned her desperate dark eyes towards Nina. 'You mean you won't boot me out?' She looked around the room.

Everybody was shaking their heads. 'Nah.' A

gentle, smooth-cheeked young man leaned forward. 'We were in the same children's home together,' he said, 'Theresa and me. Remember, love? We were talking about it last night. Dreadful place it was. The Social took me away from me dad 'cause he buggered me. They put me into a foster home where it was worse. My foster-mum used to stick her long fingernails up our bums. She tried to say she was giving us medicine, but really she did it just for kicks. And someone found out and I went to the children's home instead.'

'Yeah,' Theresa interrupted. 'That's when the home was all right. A nice house it was. But the milk-man interfered with me, and the staff didn't do nothing. They laughed when I told them. They said I had a filthy mind. But I paid them out all right.'

'What did you do?' Nina asked.

She gave a short laugh. 'I set fire to the place and good riddance to them! Then they bung me into Holloway. I like Holloway, though. It's the best prison to be in. The governor's a good enough woman. Very fair. And the swimming pool ain't half bad.'

'How about we ask our milkman to deliver the milk in cartons until you're over these episodes?' Nina suggested.

Theresa had to smile. 'Good idea. It's not just milk bottles, you know. It's when I see a whole row of lovely unbroken windows. Yes, I says to meself. Them windows could do with a bit of sorting out. And suddenly I get the urge to smash things. Just comes over me. Uncontrollable, really.'

'All right, then.' Nina's voice was practical. 'Maybe it wouldn't be wise for us to fix the windows right away. Might make them too tempting. Why don't we just board up the broken ones and leave them like that for a while?'

Stanley grinned. 'Perfect!' he said.

'Theresa?'

Theresa made her eyes into slits to better consider the windows. 'Yes,' she said. 'Board them up and don't bother to fix them. That ought to do the trick. I might just stay a while in that case. Don't see why I shouldn't.'

'Then it's decided.' Nina breathed in deeply. 'Mm. I smell lunch. Anybody else hungry?'

Agreement spread around the room, as did relief that Latchmere House and Theresa could exist in a state of mutual peace, at least for the moment.

'Before we go to lunch,' said Nina, 'let's do a quick check. How many familes feel ready to move on into a squat?'

Five hands shot up.

'Fine,' said Stanley. 'I'm going to a squatters' meeting tonight. Any of you want a lift?'

The men nodded.

'Good. It's a great place we're looking at. Been empty for years.'

Nina sat on her sofa at home with Hamish beside her. They were watching *Panorama* on television. Janice was out with her children. The doorbell went. Fighting off a feeling of mild irritation at having her evening disturbed, Nina opened the front door. 'Oh,' she said. 'What's this?'

A man in a chauffeur's uniform put a square box into her arms. Across the box lay a bunch of flowers.

'Who's this from?'

'Mr Morningstar, madam.' The man tipped his cap and moved away.

Nina shut the door and walked back into the sitting room. The box was from Fortnum's. She opened the soft white tissue, which rustled so expensively in her hands. 'Good heavens, Hamish!' She pulled out a gleaming fox-fur coat.

Hamish looked horrified. 'Are those real dead foxes?'

'I'm afraid so. But isn't it beautiful?'

'Must have been. When it was alive.'

Nina sighed. 'I know. You're right.' She took the note from the box.

Thank you, Nina, for doing such a wonderful job in America. See you soon. Michael.

She took the flowers through to the kitchen. She arranged the summer mixture in a vase. Shit, she thought. How on earth can I tell him I don't wear fur coats? She remembered the days when she used to go to hunt balls wearing Aunt Persephone's mink. Even though the animals involved had been dead for fifty years, Nina felt guilty. Try as she might to convince herself that minks were not the earth's nicest creatures, she still felt guilty. And though she told herself the coat succeeded wonderfully in keeping her warm in her boyfriend's draughty jalopy, she could not help but have a conscience.

I'll have to find a way to tell Michael, she decided. I wonder where he is. And how do you go about finding Michael when he could be anywhere in the world?

She picked up the telephone and dialled. 'Gemma?' It was Marietta. 'Gemma's not here.'

'Oh well. You might be able to help, Marietta. Do you happen to know where Michael is?'

'No.' The voice was lost and helpless. 'All I know is that I'm leaving for Zurich on another of Michael's missions tomorrow morning.'

'Where's Gemma then?'

'She's gone to Durham to see about a job up there. She's trying to decide whether or not to keep her flat on St Stephen's Street. One way or another, I'm moving out. It's over between us, Nina.'

'Marietta, I'm so sorry.' There was a silence on the line.

'I need a place for my children. If I ever get them back.'

'But you will get them back.' Nina's voice was full of unassured reassurance. 'Michael promised.'

'Yes, he did. But all his promises have strings attached, Nina. You will find out.'

'He doesn't have any strings on me.'

'He owns your house. Don't you think that counts?'

'That was a favour from him. A gift. But Michael would never hurt me.' She paused. 'We've become lovers, you know.'

'I know,' Marietta said bleakly.

'How do you know?' She laughed self-consciously. 'I guess there are no secrets in Michael's house. Is that it?'

Silence.

'Look, Marietta, I'm awfully sorry about you and Gemma splitting up. I just needed a word with Michael. That's all. But I'll probably reach him at his office tomorrow, or wherever. Could you leave a note asking Gemma to give me a ring when she gets back from Durham, please?'

'Of course. Goodbye, Nina.'

Nina put the telephone down. After a day at

Latchmere House, she just wanted to spend time with Hamish. She knew she should have listened more to Marietta and asked some interested questions, but she had promised Hamish her time and he came first.

Had she seen Marietta's white ghostly face and her hollow cheeks, she might have realized just how much Marietta needed help.

Nina returned to her sitting room and to Hamish. He had put the coat back in the box and shut the lid. 'I'm scared of the dead animals,' he said.

'Then we'll just have to send them back tomorrow.' Nina sat on the sofa, her arm around her son. She became aware that for once she was not missing Susan at all.

Chapter 64

Nina spent a frustrating day trying to find Michael. The staff at his office were tight-lipped. 'Mr Morningstar is not in London.' Mr Morningstar was also not in New York, nor was he in Washington. His Birmingham suite was empty. Nina felt restless and anxious. Obviously she would have to wait and see if he turned up for the next week's board meeting. Until then she concentrated on working as hard as she could at Latchmere House.

But for all her work, the pull toward thinking about Michael was never far away. She felt wretched in her need for him. Why can't I say no to him? Why do I put up with his idea of a celebratory fur coat and a bunch of flowers?

One day Gemma came by the office. 'I've come to say goodbye.' She hugged Nina. 'I've got a placement up in Durham.'

Nina held her friend's thin shoulders and looked at her pinched face. 'I'll miss you, Gemma.'

'No, you won't. You're a media cult figure now. Everybody knows your name.'

'Cut it out. I'm not like that.'

'No, you're not. But there are other people in the homelessness movement who bitterly resent you and all your public support. Be careful of them. When I hear things being said, I listen but I don't say very much. You know, there's a lot of money – millions – invested in the bureaucracy of administering to the needy. And a lot of people in that bureaucracy have a vested interest in seeing you're not too successful in providing an alternative that might put them out of business. And they don't like you criticizing them in public. At the moment you're in a safe position because you have the establishment pitted against the bureaucrats, with Michael and his board on your side. That's all very well until the board decide they're tired of you, and they join up with the bureaucrats to get rid of you. What will you do then?'

'Say my prayers, as I always do. Come on, Gemma. You're getting paranoid on my behalf. I think some time spent in your ivory tower at Durham will do you good. Basically all souls are potentially divine, it says so in the Bible.'

'A high ideal, but do you mean it? You think it even applies to Lady MacLaughlin?'

Nina rolled her eyes and laughed. 'In theory, I

guess so. Even Lady MacLaughlin is potentially divine, God help us. Funniest thing happened the other day. She let one of the kids here named Bobby see her Rolls-Royce when she took a load of kids off to her house, and then she looked out of the window and saw Bobby driving the car down her magnificent driveway. She'll never learn.'

Gemma smiled. 'Bobby got to drive a Rolls, though.'

'You mean Bobby got to crash a Rolls.'

'Seriously?'

'Hm. It's all hushed up. I don't think Lady M. wants too many people to know about it.' Both women shared a chuckle. Then Nina looked at Gemma with concern. 'Have you seen Marietta?'

'She's gone,' Gemma said with finality. 'She's probably back from Zurich by now, but I'm not sure where she'll be. Last time I did see her, though, just before I went up to Durham, she looked awful. Frightening really. But I've come to the point of feeling there's nothing I can do. I can't reach her and I can't help her. The problem is, I still love her. She's shied away from me. She's single-mindedly obsessed with getting her children back.'

'I understand that. It's hard enough to let one go willingly, but to have both taken forcibly . . . I can't imagine my life without Hamish.'

'How do you feel about Susan now?'

'Strange. I feel quite comfortable, believe it or not. She and Angela fight like fishwives together, but they seem to get along all right in their terms. I just can't live like that. And Hamish is so much more outgoing now. He doesn't have to live with her constant bullying.'

'I'm glad.' She hugged Nina again. 'Well, I'd better

be off to the train station. I'll telephone you soon.'

Nina smiled. 'Oh, did I tell you? I'm going to Greece with Stanley and Sonia.'

'And Michael, I'll bet.'

'And Michael. How did you know?'

Gemma looked sadly out at the golden afternoon. 'I see the way you look now, and I remember I once looked the same way over Marietta. But it's gone. Not for me. My love will never go. But I've lost her all the same. The best thing is to move on. I've no choice. Keep an eye on her for me, will you?'

'I'll try, but she's very secretive, and Michael's just as bad.'

'He probably has reason to be,' Gemma said shortly. 'Goodbye, Nina.'

When Michael finally telephoned it was the weekend. 'Thank you for the coat, Michael. It's really lovely. But I don't wear fur.'

'Don't tell me you've turned into a loony animal activist.'

'I'd like to think I'm not a loony anything. But the point is I just don't believe in killing animals unnecessarily. I shall return the coat to Fortnum's. But it was a very sweet thought. Thank you.'

'It was a hell of a lot more than a sweet thought, Nina. I'd expected you to be a bit more thankful.'

'I *am* grateful for the generosity, Michael, but . . . My God! You know for a moment you sounded just like Simon, telling me off.'

'I . . .' She heard him pause long enough to collect his voice. 'I don't appreciate comparisons with your ex-husband, thank you very much. I'm sure I'm not even remotely like him. Go ahead, return the coat if you want. Do as you please.' Michael's voice was bored. Then it switched tone with alarming rapidity as he said, 'Let's have dinner tonight.'

'I can't tonight. Hamish is at Simon's for the weekend, but I've promised to go down to Devon to see my mother and father.'

There was a silence. 'That must be nice for you.'

Nina could not discern the meaning of his inflection. She could not tell whether or not he was being sarcastic. Instead she decided that she heard a genuinely wistful note in Michael's voice. Nina's heart went out to him, thinking how much he must miss being part of a loving family. Poor Michael. 'I could have dinner with you on Sunday night, though,' she relented. 'I could leave Devon a little early.'

'That would be good.' His tone was again different, now softer. 'All right. I'll send the car for you at eight o'clock Sunday evening.'

'Eight o'clock, then. Oh, and Michael? The flowers were beautiful.' She put the telephone down. The world was again alight. Nina found herself laughing joyously for no reason at all.

A hazy early summer day with tea in deckchairs under the big horse chestnut tree reminded Nina of the years when she had sat as a small child, her shoes not touching the ground. The cup against her lips was the same cup she had sipped from in childhood. The teapot bespoke years of tea. Her father, stooped and growing older, smiled at her. 'So, you're off to Greece for your summer holiday. Wonderful place. The great magnet that drew Keats and Shelley. Oh, and Byron, of course. You must read them again before you go.'

'I wish I had the time.' Nina stretched out in the sunlight.

'Do take plenty of kaolin and morphine, darling,' said Nina's mother, Mrs Tolmadge. 'You don't want your holiday ruined by gippy tummy.'

Aunt Persephone reminisced. 'I once knew a gel who ate an iffy piece of pork. Tapeworm, they told her. Tremendous thing, it was. Yards and yards of it.'

'*Please*, Persephone,' said Major Tolmadge.

'Promise me you won't touch the pork, Nina.'

'I shan't,' Nina promised her aunt, wishing that worms were all she would have to worry about for her trip to Greece. However much she could not wait for the trip to start, she could not help but feel a queer fear at the thought of being entirely in Michael's world once again. What she felt overall was a sense of anticipation, though anticipation of what she could not say.

She left her parents' house on the Sunday morning. Her mother was up pottering about the kitchen. 'Gemma is starting work up North now.' They sat at the pantry table, drinking a cup of tea. 'Susan seems to have settled in perfectly. It's odd, but everything's turned out rather well. I like her much better, now I don't have to live with her. She's really much more Simon's child. She's so like him. Always was. And she seems to get on a bit better with me. She comes over and we do something together and then she goes back. Simon and Angela have an entirely suburban life, and Susan flourishes amongst that. I'd die if I had to live like that again.'

'You always were adventurous, Nina. You like to take risks.'

Nina was for some reason impressed by her mother's perceptiveness because, by setting out for a time in Greece with Michael, she did indeed sense that she was taking a risk. 'Well, if the worst comes to the worst, I'll end up like Aunt Persephone. All alone in a cottage with a treasure chest of memories.' She finished her tea and said goodbye to her mother. 'I'm having dinner tonight with Michael.'

'The man we see in all the newspapers?'

'The very one.'

'But he's married, isn't he, darling?'

'Yes, but in name only. She's an awful wife to him.'

Mrs Tolmadge looked sideways at her. 'They *all* say that. I'm surprised you believe him.'

'I believe him because in Michael's case it's true.' Nina hugged her mother and hurried away. She wanted nothing to spoil her day.

Hours later – hours which had transported her to a world light years away from Devon – Nina lay quietly by Michael's side in his bedroom. She contemplated his long, dark body which was softly illuminated by a Lalique lamp on the side table. 'I must go in a minute,' she whispered.

'Don't go. Stay the night.'

'I can't, really. I have to be there tomorrow morning for Hamish when he wakes up.'

'No, you don't. You have a housekeeper. She can take care of everything.'

'Janice isn't a housekeeper, Michael. She and I share the house . . .'

'Then that makes her *my* housekeeper, since it's my house.'

Nina sat up and stared hard at Michael. 'That's the first time you've ever used it against me, that you bought the house for me. And suddenly, I'm not at all comfortable with . . .'

He could see how earnest she was. 'I was only joking, Nina.' He kissed her mouth before she could speak further.

'No, Michael.' She pulled away. 'As you bring it up, it is something we ought to talk about. Why *did* you buy my house?'

'It's my generosity of spirit,' he smiled charmingly. 'I can't help myself.'

'*Seriously*, Michael. Some of my friends keep saying things that make me start to ask questions. And I wonder myself sometimes. This isn't some strange way of you wanting to own me, is it?'

Michael rolled over and held her wrists to the bed. He kissed her neck. Lifting his face, he smiled with what she took to be pretend wickedness. 'There. You've figured me out. I want to own every molecule of you. I want to keep you and possess you like a treasured pet.' He kissed her again.

After the kiss, her arms still pinned down, she said, 'Michael, I'm serious.'

'So am I.' His boyish enjoyment of the conversation would not let up. 'Why is it that when I'm telling you the truth, you don't believe me? Ownership is sexy, don't you think?' He kissed her naked breast, taking her nipple between his teeth. 'And don't you think every woman secretly wishes to be possessed?' He nuzzled his mouth into her soft armpit, giving her a slow, tingly, wet lick.

'You're *impossible*,' she said, half-laughing, squirming ticklishly, unable to fight off the overpowering sensations that electrified her body when he kissed her underarm. Then she decided he was joking with her. A sense of humour is proof of warmth and intelligence, she knew. His teasing seemed affectionate. Yes, it must had been what he said in the first place

495

– generosity of spirit – that made him buy her house for her. He was such a good person at heart. And with a man so good, she felt secure enough to let herself enjoy the inarguable thrill of being possessed. Yes, Michael knew how to read her fantasies, and how to fulfil them, but she believed she could trust a man of such philanthropic goodness never to do her any harm.

He moved his mouth to her other armpit, and she let herself become lost in the pleasure the mouth gave her. It was safe to take from Michael.

She made one last effort to stop him, 'I really *have* to go. But just think. In not too long we'll be in Greece, and then we can have two heavenly weeks together. All day and all night.'

Michael frowned. 'Well, you and your friends can stay in the villa for as long as you want, naturally. But I'll have to catch up with you once you get there. I think I'll be a couple of days late.'

'Michael, no!' Nina's voice rose. 'I've been keeping Greece like a dream in my imagination.'

'It will be everything you've dreamed of. Our time together will just start a few days late, that's all.' He soothed her, stroking her back and her legs.

Nina breathed deeply as he entered her body, a body which was now entirely familiar to him. They made love as do lovers who no longer fear awkwardness at the touch of strangers. Their bodies swayed and soared, lit for Nina by the hope of bright Mediterranean sunshine.

Chapter 65

But the questions would not leave Nina alone. At Latchmere House the weeks before August were still punctured with sounds of sawing and hammering. The weeks clotted into months and Nina realized that her relationship with Michael was a continual source of confusion. Sexually he enthralled her, making her feel loved and wanted. Then he would disappear for days without contact, as if she meant nothing to him. At times it appeared to her that the time they spent in each other's company had degenerated into feeding and fucking. He did not seem to want anything else from her.

They were in a suite at the Savoy hotel. In consequence of what Michael claimed to be a spontaneous desire on his part, Nina found herself with her wrists secured to each other by Michael's leather belt and her feet tied together by his Liberty silk necktie. For Nina this was a moment of particularly heightened puzzlement. She could not understand Michael's need to enslave her physically. Was this affectionate and loving? Did his pleasure spring from a perverse need to control her? But the most disconcerting thought of all was that she, too, was receiving pleasure. He's giving me no pain, she told herself. This is harmless play-acting. He's not hurting me at all. Why shouldn't we get pleasure in tampering with fantasy? It's not as if I was unwilling to let myself be tied up.

If I really didn't want him to, surely he wouldn't have. And the feeling of it . . . The sensation was incredible.

Michael's powerful hand held her two bound arms straight out on the bed above her head. He was a large man and his weight kept her body helpless. With her ankles tied together, she could not have spread her legs if she had tried. Instead, she felt like a high diver poised to slice the water, her form taut and stretched in one perfect arrowlike line. Michael's legs were outside hers, the muscles of his thighs pushing hers even tighter together. It was with an effort that he pushed himself inside of her. 'The friction,' he said upon entering her, though his legs would not relent in their grip on her own, stopping her from making the more natural movement of opening herself to him. 'You wouldn't believe what the friction feels like.'

'Yes, I would,' she said, unable to catch her breath. She clenched her eyes tight as he moved within her, his chest pushing heavily against her breasts. Again, she was lost in the world of sensation that she shared with him. Again, in climax, she experienced the paradoxical feelings that had become an inevitable part of her communion with Michael. Momentarily she felt the unspeakable intensity of the pleasure, yet, so soon after as to make the two feelings almost simultaneous, came an inescapable sense of self-recrimination that her pleasure had not been found through some gentler, softer means. And, in the return of her senses to more mundane reality, she could not help but wonder if she were doomed to have her pleasure always tinged with guilt when release was a fruit that grew from her own dark side.

They both had climaxed, and they both lay breathless, he on top of her. He rolled off. Her arms remained over her head. Suddenly, in the moments of detumescence, she felt almost ridiculous to still be tied up. 'Untie me, please,' she asked, and she felt silly for having to ask.

He untied her, threw the belt and necktie off the bed, and quickly engulfed her in a strong embrace, the two bodies lying on their sides. Ambivalence was pushed away from her mind as his hug proved to her that what they had just shared together was nothing but the amorous play of two real lovers.

When they had rested a while, she spoke first. 'Let's go for a walk together. All right?' She felt romantic. And she wanted further reassurance that their united joy did not always have to be sexual. 'We can walk along the Embankment.'

'But why would I want to walk along the Embankment when we can be doing this?'

She looked down and saw that his erection had returned. Without pause Michael moved on top of her and pushed his way deep into her. Unprepared, Nina noticed that she was sore inside. What was worse, she felt a powerful and immediate sense of boredom in the activity, and her own boredom irritated her greatly. 'Michael!' She rolled out from under him, amazed at how angry she felt. 'I'm not just some whore. You could pick up one of those and screw any old time, and you can pay for it. If you like, I'll send one of our homeless prostitutes and for a fiver she can pee on you, or whatever you're in the mood for.'

Michael lay on the bed, his eyes bright and gloating. 'Sounds good to me,' he said.

'I'm being serious.' Nina sat up, facing him. 'Look at this fabulous suite,' she said. 'We've just had a long luxurious bath in the most beautiful bath in Europe and just made love. It's wonderful, but all you want to do is to hump some more until you fall off exhausted.'

'Is there anything else?' He grabbed her by the ankle and pulled her foot to his face, resting it on his cheek. He paused, and she noticed with marvel how it felt to have his cheekbone – the same sharp, smooth cheekbone that had captured her imagination since the first time she saw him – pressed beneath the sole of her foot. He stared into her eyes all the while. He moved his face and bit her little toe.

'Oh, do stop it.' She pulled her foot away. 'You're being obnoxious on purpose. Yes, of course there's something else. How about warmth and affection? That's what gives sex its meaning. Without those feelings . . . I've had enough for one day. I'm going home.'

'Shit, Nina. I really don't need this. I've been working very hard and I don't need you to nag me. I've got old Alison MacLaughlin and Germaine Phillips, your honourable secretary and treasurer, on my back over you squatting everywhere, and now you're being a perfect bitch to me.'

'I'm not being a bitch. All I'm saying is, if you can't make love lovingly –' The feeling of self-reproach crept into her mind while she spoke. '– then maybe we ought to wait until we get to Greece and then you might be more relaxed. But already you've shaved two days off our precious two weeks together.'

'Look, don't forget I'm supplying you and your friends with an airplane and a place to stay. What more do you want?'

'I want you. I want to walk on a Greek beach with my hand in yours.'

'Seen one beach, you've seen them all. Frankly I hate the sun, and I hate getting sand on my feet.'

'Then I'll brush the sand off your feet for you.'

'Oh, get out of here. I don't want to hear you whining.'

Nina was stung, but in a way she felt she had brought his dismissiveness on herself by showing him her own anger. 'Fine, Michael. I'll go. I'll expect to see you in Zakinthos in three weeks' time.'

'Maybe.' Michael shrugged. 'Maybe not.'

'Anyway,' Nina tried to laugh. 'If you won't or can't turn up, I'll at least have Stanley.'

She drove home with tears running down her face. It's not the first time I've cried over Michael, she thought. Her heart was torn into small strips. She put on her tape of Simon and Garfunkel singing *I Am a Rock*. That's all very well, she whispered as she drove through the empty streets. But I don't want to be a rock. I want to be on a Greek island with my Michael. I want us to be happy.

She crept up to her bedroom after peeking in at Hamish. He lay obliviously and innocently on his pillow. Nina knew that Hamish would much rather be in Greece with her during the holidays, but she felt she must give her relationship with Michael one last try. She could not continue to feel like a fucking machine, a thing to be fed, watered, and bedded. Granted, the feeding was the Savoy, the Ritz, the Connaught, and the watering was done with champagne, and the bedding happened in the most sumptuous of suites. Still . . . She sighed.

Tomorrow Michael would be sorry. He would send his chauffeur round with a goody or two from

501

Fortnum's. Michael was always sorry tomorrow. One day, tomorrow would be too late. Nina wished she really believed that. She wished she had the power to sever the emotions that bound them so close together.

Was she fooling herself? Was Michael at heart a vulnerable, warm man who had shot into the rich stratosphere of the great and the good? Did hanging on in the midst of the rich playing their games conceal other games? Where was Marietta? Why did she always sound so desperate? What were the guarded sounds of Michael talking in the drawing room of his suite? The ticker-tacker of telex machines, making the nights sinister? The time she innocently picked up the long sheet of paper and said, 'I didn't know you owned ships . . . ?' 'There's a lot you don't know,' was the gruff answer. 'And the less you know the better.' Was there a warning in those tones? Something she should know about? Or was it just too-late-at-night, champagne-induced paranoia? At least it's a first-class paranoia . . . She fell into bed, her doubts giving her mind no peace, yet not strong enough in themselves to push her to any definitive action.

Chapter 66

'I don't *believe* this!' Stanley settled his large, puffy body into the black leather seat on Michael's jet.

Nina grinned. It was a hot August day. She had spent the last two days stretched out in her own back garden, giving her tan a head start. Hamish, bribed by Nina's promise of a super present from Greece, left quite happily for Spain with Simon's new family. Nina also gave Susan and Hamish ten pounds each as pocket money. 'Buy yourselves something really nice.'

Angela sniffed disapprovingly, her revolting, ugly baby now beginning to show a promise of developing his mother's rabbit teeth. 'You're bribing the children, Nina. You shouldn't do it.'

'Don't worry, sweetie. I can well afford it. I'm off in a private plane, and the view from the villa is said to be the best in Greece. And you're going to . . . Trek Tours sun-splashed hotel in Benidorm, is it? Sounds like just the sort of thing to make you feel right at home.' She hugged Susan goodbye. 'Have a wonderful time, darling.'

'I will.' Susan's face was alight. 'We're going on a coach tour when we get to Benidorm and the brochure says the waiters squirt wine down your throat from a goatskin bag.'

'Lovely,' Nina smiled. 'Bye, Hamish.'

'I don't have to have wine squirted down my throat, do I?' Hamish looked at his father.

'Of course you do,' said a jovial Simon. 'You'll have a marvellous time.'

Nina's heart ached, but it would do Hamish good to spend time with his father and with Simon's wife. He might see for himself just how far apart her world had always been from Simon's.

Nina put aside all thoughts of the beastly Angela and her wretched lack of taste. She settled into her seat just as Sonia sauntered into the plane. 'Not bad, Nina. Not bad at all. Beats Myles's little aircraft.'

'I shan't ask where Myles is. No doubt it's too depressing.'

'He's with his dear mama all this month, so I'm off to Greece to play.'

Nina envied Sonia's long, svelte figure. She wore a white silk suit. It was a man's suit, but on Sonia it looked feminine. She had a Pucci silk scarf around her neck.

Sonia kissed Stanley on the top of his head. 'Ready to party, Stanley?'

Stanley looked around with a slightly stunned expression. Nina smiled. Stanley was enjoying himself and when he was happy he folded his hands in a prayer of supplication. 'I can't *believe* it,' he said. 'We're actually off to Greece.'

The pilot came on board with a different stewardess than the one Nina had met before. 'We will be leaving shortly,' he said. 'Good morning, Mrs Stockton. I've been given orders to take you to Zakinthos.'

'Then where's your next stop?' Stanley asked like a curious boy.

'I am not at liberty to say, sir. The whereabouts of this aircraft is restricted information.'

'Oh, I'm sorry. I didn't mean to pry.'

The Captain grunted and walked into the cabin.

Nina gave Stanley and Sonia a little tour around the plane. 'And this,' Nina said nonchalantly, 'is the master bedroom.'

'Oooh!' Stanley walked across the deep pile carpet and ran his hand over the mink-covered bed. 'Very, very nice.'

Nina pushed open the door of the bathroom.

'Have a shufty at this, Sonia!' Stanley's voice rose with excitement. 'And a bidet as well!'

Nina walked back into the bedroom. She sat on the

bed and remembered making love to Michael for the first time all those months ago. She had seen the same utterly impersonal look on his face only twice since his orgasm that day, but each time it disturbed her. When he looked like that, she imagined there was nothing he wouldn't do. Except hurt me, she thought.

She saw a flash of gold glinting on the floor by the bed. She reached down to pick it up. Her fingers found the object. Studying it in her hand, she remembered where she had seen the heavy gold earring inlaid with lapis lazuli – on Marietta's earlobe, the night they first met at Gemma's flat. So, Marietta *had* been on this airplane before her. But why hadn't Marietta noticed the loss of a very expensive earring? She must have been in a hurry.

Nina slipped the earring into her pocket. I'll send her a postcard from Greece and tell her I've got it. Some instinct made her refrain from the thought of telling Michael.

The island of Zakinthos lay embraced by the blue Ionian Sea. Nina looked out of the airplane window. 'Look, Stanley!' She pointed downward. 'That horseshoe-shaped bay must be the Porto Roma beach and the headland.'

They both gazed out of the same porthole. Stanley's arm was around Nina's shoulders. 'I *still* don't believe this is happening. I'd pinch myself, but I'm afraid I'd wake up in the flat alone.' He took a large piece of skin between his fingers and squeezed. 'Ouch!' he yelped. 'That hurt.' A big grin broke his face in two. 'I *am* here. This *is* Greece! Oh, give me another ouzo. It has the most lovely liquorice taste, don't it?'

'You'd better go easy. You've had half a bottle

already, and you've done a good job on the retsina.'

'I intend to be as drunk as a coot.' He stood up. 'You'll never know what you've done for me, Nina!' His eyes were bright with tears. 'See? I've been prac- tising my Greek dancing.' He stood in the middle of the aisle while Nina and Sonia watched. He was wearing his Greek fez-like hat and a large splendidly striped blue and white T-shirt over a pair of royal blue slacks. He swayed and swung his right leg across his left, his arms outstetched. The two women giggled wine-induced giggles.

'If I were a rich man,' Stanley sang. 'Pidda pidda pidda pidda pidda pidda pidda pum . . . '

'That's Jewish,' Nina laughed, 'not Greek.'

'It's all the same,' he cried joyfully. 'It's celebra- tion!' He threw back his head and tried to stand the ouzo bottle on his forehead.

'Careful, Stanley!' Sonia said.

'Oops,' called Nina, but she found herself laughing even harder as the bottle crashed to the floor.

'Sod it,' Stanley muttered.

The stewardess came out of the front cabin. 'Fasten your seatbelts, please,' she said, a frown on her pretty, pert face. 'We're preparing to land.'

Nina sat back, feeling like a naughty schoolgirl. She rested her head on the window and watched as the plane flew over the airport for its final approach. I'm home, she thought. After all this time, I've made it at last to Greece. She very much hoped Hamish and Susan had had a safe trip to Spain. She took Sonia's hand and pressed it, while the plane touched down. 'Aren't you excited?' she said.

'Not yet,' Sonia growled. 'Not until I size up the action on the man scene. But I'll keep you posted.'

Chapter 67

Nina sat on the terrace of Michael's villa. The setting sun was a smouldering red ball, just above the sea's horizon. The air was scented with pine and wild thyme. The thyme grew around the terrace that wrapped the villa in a warm, spacious embrace. Nina breathed deeply. She missed Michael. He should be here, she thought longingly and with a trace of resentment.

Sonia had gone for a walk and Nina could see Stanley floating about in the sea below the villa. The bay was in the shape of a small horseshoe. The sand was white and the water a deep, unrelenting blue. Now the rays of the setting sun reflected on the water. Nina sat in peaceful solitude and ached for Michael. Now, here in his house, away from the rest of the world, she had time to think. Behind her the cook and the maid were preparing the evening meal. The smell of lamb cooked on hot charcoal on a bed of freshly picked rosemary prickled her nostrils. She sat in her new black bathing suit enjoying the last warmth of the day. Rolling over plumply in the water, Stanley was clearly enjoying himself.

'Telephone,' said the maid. A gentle black-garbed figure, she came onto the terrace. She handed the telephone to Nina.

'Just checking to see if you're settled in.'

'Oh, I am, Michael. And it's fabulous. When are you coming?'

'I can get down in three days. I've got a meeting in Zurich, and then I'm free.'

'Where are you now?'

'New York, and it's sweltering here. What's it like there?'

'Unimaginably gorgeous. Stanley is playing at being a hippopotamus, and Sonia's gone on a man-hunt. I'm sitting by myself on the terrace with an ouzo in my hand, wishing you were here.'

'I will be soon enough. Three days isn't long. Then we'll have all the time we want together. Listen, I've got to run. I'm being dragged off to a boring opera.'

The telephone clicked. Then a second glance of a thought occurred in Nina's head: I thought he always went on about how much he loved opera. Couldn't be he was just trying to make a good impression, could it?

Story of your life, Michael – must rush, got to go . . . She looked at the sun, which was up to its waist in the sea. How can anyone own such a beautiful villa and not want to live in it for the rest of their life? She stood up and stretched. She could see Stanley getting out of the water. She walked back into the villa, her bare feet warm on the cool marble tiles. The air flowing through the villa was filled with sounds, mostly the buzz and whirr of crickets singing in the wood behind the house. She walked past the kitchen.

The cook beamed at her. 'Meat very good. Very fresh. Deaded yesterday.'

Nina wrinkled her nose, but she said, 'Wonderful.' There was a markedly visceral quality to life here. Good thing, probably, that Hamish wasn't around to be upset by the thought of an animal being killed.

She missed Hamish nonetheless. He would have loved the beach and the wild headland beyond it.

'I *still* can't believe I'm here.'

Nina had showered in the expansive white marble bathroom attached to her suite. She had changed into a simple white linen dress. Stanley was sitting at the dining table in an alcove off the drawing room. His hands were resting on his stomach. He hadn't yet changed out of his bathing suit, and his stomach rolled over the waistband. He sighed noisily.

'Must be nice to be rich, Nina. I could soon get used to it. Once upon a time, and very long ago . . .'

Nina pulled out a chair and sat down. 'Do tell, Stanley.'

'Well, I had a lover. This was a couple of years before I met Kit. I was gorgeous when I was in my early twenties . . .'

'Hang on. That wasn't long ago.'

'It *feels* it, Nina. And ten years isn't a short time. Anyway, I was saying. Me and my friends used to go to these parties. The Chelsea Arts Ball was one of the best. I went all sprayed in lavender paint, even my hair, and I wore the tiniest G-string. I caused quite a stir. And I had this rich lover.' He rolled his eyes.

Nina watched his face. Oh, Stanley, she thought. Those were his golden years, when he was untouched by time. But now age had started to prod him with a gnarled finger. Nina saw through the coquette in Stanley, endlessly playing to the gallery for his mother's approval. His mother was long since dead, but she hung like a putrid corpse in the air beside Stanley, even in Greece. 'It's okay to be rich, Stanley. But how much did you see of your lover?'

He hesitated. 'I know what you mean. Rich people don't have time for love. They're too busy making money. My memory of him is lying in bed watching him on the telephone to his brokers with a fag dangling from his lips dripping ash on the lovely linen pillowcase. Such a shame! Pretty linen, it was.'

Nina heard Sonia's voice. She saw Sonia enter the main door of the house, followed by a very tall man. 'Nina, this is Pakis. I found him in the forest, so I rescued him and brought him home. Pakis, this is my friend Nina, and this is Stanley.'

Stanley eyed Pakis. 'Very nice, Sonia. Very nice indeed. Any more like him?'

Pakis gave a wide smile. 'Is Michael's house. I am friend of Michael. We drink together.'

'Michael will be here in a few days.' Nina pushed out a chair. 'Will you join us for dinner?'

'Okay. I join you.'

The maid came in carrying a tray. 'Pakis!' she said, and then proceeded to talk to him in Greek. It sounded like the stuttering of a machine gun to Nina.

'My Aunt Suko,' Pakis explained. '*Biera, paracalo.*'

Nina looked at the Greek salad which the woman had put before her. The feta cheese was sprinkled with fats dots of black pepper. The lettuce was green and tender. Thick rings of raw white onion sat on top of red juicy tomatoes. The whole plate was bathed in a yellow olive oil and punctuated with shining blue-black olives. Nina reached for a chunk of thick coarse Greek bread. She dipped the bread into the olive oil. 'Perfect,' she said. 'Absolutely perfect.'

Stanley looked at her. 'Well, not quite perfect.'

'Hm. All it needs is Michael, and he's too busy making money, as you say. Still, we'll have fun.'

Pakis was talking urgently to Sonia. Her head was

bent, and her eyes were wide. 'Tonight,' said Pakis, 'we go to town. You come?' he asked Nina.

'No, but thank you,' she shook her head. 'I didn't come to a Greek island to go to town. I'll stay here in the peace and quiet.'

'I'll come.' Stanley grinned. 'Where are we going?'

'We go to night club and dance. All-night dance on the sea.'

'Will you be all right if I go? I mean, I won't leave you if you'd rather not be alone.'

'But I'm happy to be alone. Go and have a wonderful time, Stanley. You can chaperone Sonia for me.'

Sonia giggled. Even a single day away from London softened her face. She looked years younger. She wore a sleek blue bikini.

I wish I looked like that, thought Nina, feeling a familiar envy at Sonia's height and her surprisingly full breasts. She further envied the fact that Sonia was going out dancing with Pakis. She was jealous, she realized, because she had only half of her dream. She wanted to wait on the headland for Michael. When she did go into town, she wanted to see it with Michael. When she did dance by the sea all night, she wanted her partner to be Michael. Already she was forced to be in his house without him. The house was beautiful but anonymous, as were all of Michael's places. Designers, decorators, and architects created the stages to be peopled by the cast of servants. They created the seamless luxury for and around Michael, but none of the houses reflected Michael himself. Here, in this serene, cool villa, there were no signs of Michael's personal life. Not a picture or a photograph of Titania or Michael. Nina felt as if he blew like a wind through the places he owned. And once he passed through, there was a hush and a falling of dust. Until the next time.

'The lamb is excellent.' Sonia smiled at Pakis.

'Good Zakinthos sheeps,' he said. He picked up the wine bottle. 'Zakinthos wine. Good wine.' He filled the glasses. 'Drink!' he said. 'Happy holidays.' There was something clean and wholesome about Pakis. He sat relaxed at the dining table as if he had known his three dining companions all his life. Why not? Nina mused. It's his island. We're the intruders, the strangers at the gates of this paradise.

After cups of very black grainy coffee on the terrace, Pakis, Stanley, and Sonia roared off into the night in Pakis's red, rusty, old Cadillac.

Before he left, Pakis hugged Nina. 'You are all okay, pretty lady?' His golden eyes filled with concern.

'I'll be fine. Maybe I'll take a walk a little later on. I love being by myself. Really.'

'Okey dokey.' Pakis shrugged.

Nina watched the back lights of his car disappear into the night.

Later, much later, Nina changed into her bathing suit and walked down the honeysuckled path to the beach. The sand was crisp under her feet. Small crabs gave notice of their presence by scurrying away from her approach. The cicadas struck up a choir, and the frogs oompahed in the swampy bushes. Nina stepped into the water. It was warm around her knees. Slightly afraid of the dark and the night, she shivered. Was there anything out there to hurt her? Of course not. She was living in Michael's charmed circle. Nothing could hurt her. She plunged in and parted the water with her breaststroke. The water closed behind her.

She swam towards the full, pregnant moon. The beams lay like a gleaming highway on the water. She saw the night-variegated light of phosphor outlining her arms and her shoulders. She lifted an arm and watched the glow as she plunged it back into the water. She was joyous but alone in the blue-black wine of the Greek sea.

The days passed slowly. Achingly slowly. Nina stretched out in the sun. She swam and she walked each day. How can three days take so long? Michael did not telephone, nor by now did she expect him to. She knew he used the telephone only if he had information to impart. The idea that the telephone was an instrument to while away idle social hours was foreign to him.

The meals came and went. Pakis was happily installed in Sonia's bedroom. Nina envied them. Sonia was gentler, softer, and Pakis teased her unmercifully. 'New York Woman,' he called her when she tried to issue orders. 'Yes, New York Woman,' he said.

Stanley drifted about, reminding Nina of Pooh Bear with his tub of honey. 'Everybody's so kind here,' he said. 'You see fellas walking hand in hand and they're not even gay. Men can hug and kiss each other.'

Nina was lying on her designer deckchair. 'I haven't seen anyone noticeably homeless or hungry,' she said. 'I've walked all over the headland. The children come back from school in their overalls. They look clean and well-fed. Wherever I go, women invite me into their houses and pour a glass of ouzo. They don't have much, but all the houses are spotlessly clean.' She shook her head. 'Where did the rest of us all go wrong?'

Sonia looked up from her beach novel. 'Small communities work,' she said. 'Pakis must have a hundred relatives. And those are only the ones who seem to be in walking distance.'

'You really like him, don't you, Sonia?'

Sonia blushed. 'Well, it's only day three, but he's kind of funny. He doesn't play any head games.'

Nina sat up. 'Michael will be here in a few hours. Seems like ages since I've seen him.' She felt fidgety. Her feet tingled. 'Might as well go for yet another walk.'

Sonia laughed. 'Only three hours to go, and you're still impatient. The naughty Michael Morningstar. Gracing us with his presence.'

'I'll send off my postcards,' Nina said decisively. 'That's what I'll do.' She left the sunny beach and walked into her bedroom.

She looked at the bed in anticipation.

The postcards were of the headland, but they were flat, conventional pictures, unable to capture the golden sheen and the ever-present smell of the wild thyme. Nina wrote a few cards, then decided she really was too restless to write any more. She would take a walk after all.

She walked past the taverna at the end of the road. She lifted her hand to pick a yellow bulbous lemon off a tree. Behind the lemon tree stood rows of oranges and pomegranates. Around her feet chickens clucked. Pakis was cooking lunch at the taverna. Ducks and geese waddled and squawked as she walked up the dusty road. She smelled the sharp smell of the lemon.

She walked past the taverna until she came to the front of a little shop. The outer wall contained a postbox for outgoing letters. She re-read the card she had written to Marietta: *I have your earring. Don't worry about it. Having a wonderful time. Love, Nina.*

She slipped the card into the postbox, along with cards to her mother and father and Aunt Persephone. On Gemma's card, she had written 'Wish you were here,' and she realized she really meant it. It would have been nice to have had the last three days with Gemma. They so rarely spent time together now.

An old lady came out of the shop and cackled a friendly welcome to her. Nina smiled and nodded. She stepped up to the woman's terrace. 'How's your husband's knee?' she mimed. 'Any better than yesterday?'

The old woman bobbed her head. 'Good, good!' she said. The two of them sat in a companionable silence at a rickety table on the terrace. Nina sipped the ouzo which the old woman poured for her. She had added half a glass of water, making the ouzo turn white and cloudy.

On the table lay a plate full of ripe green figs which the old woman had put out. Nina bit into one plump juicy fig. Just like sex, she thought as the seeds gushed into her mouth. She swallowed the rich, thick juice and she thought of Michael.

Chapter 68

These were golden, precious days. Mostly.

Nina and Michael made love in their pristine white bedroom. Nina climaxed on their first night together, her soul leaving her body, pulled by the Greek wind tugging at the long lace curtain. Once her soul was free, she was able to soar up into the Greek mountains, the magic taste of honey on her lips, the stars her close companions. Inevitably she was forced to return to her all too human body. She lay gasping for breath, but she felt a calm, a sweet, languorous calm.

For the next two days she kept Michael busy. He was quite unable to relax. They swam in the glassy sea. Nina watched her toes, pink against the sand. They made love in the surf in a deserted horseshoe bay, the waves rippling over their entwined bodies. Michael complained about the sun. Nina only laughed and dragged him into town.

But the mixture of people in the villa was often awkward. Michael seemed incapable of simply enjoying the company of her friends. Stanley, with his easy-going, camp good-humour, seemed to irk Michael. It was clear that Michael never wanted to be left alone in a room with Stanley.

Things were hardly more comfortable with Sonia. Nina could not help but notice the way Michael flirted with Sonia. Whenever Stanley said something, Michael would roll his eyes and try to catch Sonia's glance, as if to imply that she alone shared in his disregard for the strange creature that Stanley was. And Michael made no secret about the way he watched Sonia move in her revealing bikini. At the table Michael would stare unashamed at the deep sensuous concavity of her navel. Nina never told Michael not to stare. How could she without sounding petty and jealous? Besides, she knew she had no cause for jealousy. Sonia behaved as if she did not notice Michael's interest in her, so entranced was she by Pakis. Sonia really is falling in love, thought Nina. She felt quite safe, though mildly annoyed, to let Michael's straying eye have its meanderings.

Seeing his attentions unreturned, Michael soon decided that Sonia was a bore. Stanley, he deemed, was not worth discussing in any serious context. In private moments he asked Nina how she could tolerate such pedestrian people, trying to entice her to betray her friends by sharing in his disapproval. Always Nina was quick to defend them. So Michael grew tired even of their mention. He can't cope, Nina realized in the end, when a group of people aren't disloyal behind each other's backs. He doesn't know the rules of friendship, perhaps because of the loneliness of his childhood. Poor Michael, she thought again, basking in her favourite feeling of compassion for him. In a group of real friends he seems completely at sea.

Then, in a whimsical change of mood, he was suddenly friendly, as if having found something new to amuse them all. One day Michael said he had a surprise for everyone. He assembled the little group on the terrace of his house just as a magnificent apparition could be seen rounding the corner of the headland. It was Michael's yacht, which to Nina's eyes seemed more like a moderately sized cruise ship than a private boat. Michael explained he never really had time to float about on it, certainly not enough to use it as a means of transportation between, say, England and Greece. But he thought it might help pass the time more quickly to play around on board for a day or two, so he had called up his captain and issued orders that the ship be brought down from her usual anchorage in the south of France. Nina loved the yacht and wished she could live on it forever. Stanley and Sonia, always accompanied by Pakis, sunned themselves on the deck and dived into the sea as, during the day, the boat took them around the island, exploring miraculously beautiful beaches and grottos all along the shore.

Stanley watched Nina and Michael together, his own face sad, his eyes sympathetic. Michael often disappeared into town on his own.

Pakis knew where he was and what he was doing. 'Michael bad news,' Pakis told Sonia, sitting on the side of her bed.

Sonia shook her head. 'But that's for you to know and for Nina to find out.'

'He meets with other women.'

'I know, Pakis. But what can I do? She won't listen to reason.'

'Then it is sad.' Pakis put his arms around Sonia. 'You I love,' he whispered in her ear.

'I'll bet you say that to all your tourist women,' she teased.

'You are not a tourist woman. You are *my* woman.'

She smiled. 'That's sweet,' Sonia said. 'We'll see.'

'No.' Pakis was adamant. 'You and me, we get married.'

'Really, Pakis. you've only known me for a few days.'

'Forever. I know you forever. From before I am born. Always.'

Sonia hugged him. 'Let's just wait and see. We don't have to take anything too fast, all right?'

'What fast? I want to make Greek babies with you.'

Sonia could not help but laugh. 'I think this is all a little impractical. Aren't you forgetting my job at the magazine? And I'm not used to all this. I mean, American and English men aren't exactly tripping over themselves to get married and have babies. They have other things on their minds.'

'American and English men are silly peoples. You and me give my mother a grandson, a little boy. We show that my water is strong, yes?'

'My God, Pakis! Do you hear yourself? Do you know what a sexist statement you just made?'

'Yes, Sonia, you are very sexy woman.'

'Not sexy, Pakis, *sexist*.'

But he was kissing her, and her mouth became more engaged in returning the kiss than in trying to formulate explanations.

'You know,' Stanley was sitting beside Nina in a car borrowed from Michael, 'I'm accepted here. I'm not frightened to walk about the town by myself for fear that some gay bashing yob will jump me. And there's quite a few gay men in town. They're open about it. No one objects. Seems like once you step outside England and take a look at Europe, you see that in other places not everyone has to be a clone of each other.'

Driving, Nina negotiated around the hairpin bends. 'Why do Greek drivers think I have x-ray eyes? They all shoot around the bends as if I can see them coming, and then they hoot once they've already passed. Shit!' She swerved to avoid a very fat taxi driver's car. He grinned and hooted at her. She waved back. 'You can't be too cross, I suppose. Hm, I know what you mean, Stanley. Gays have an awful time in Washington or in New York. Justin says they get beaten up all the time.'

'Tell me about it.' Stanley looked out the window at a small monastery deep in a valley on the edge of the sea. 'Look at that man down there. Looks like a Greek Orthodox monk. Sometimes I think I should just join him and his friends and lock myself away. You know, the local priest here is ever such a naughty boy. Been after all the women, they say. Still, I told you before, it's no more playing around for me. I'll wait until a decent relationship comes along. Did I tell you Cal's been coming round to visit me back home a lot these days? We've been getting on famously. She's thinking of moving in, for the nights she's not in Latchmere House. I'd be a lot less lonely that way.'

'You and Cal living together? How would that work out? I mean . . .'

'It would work out fine, Nina. People can live together without sleeping together.'

'Then it sounds a perfect idea ' Nina turned her head and smiled at Stanley. His skin had turned by now an even shade of honey-brown. The hours of swimming had trimmed the fat off his body. 'You look great, Stanley. You really do. You look as if you've lost ten years.'

He stared ahead. He too had heard rumours that

Michael was visiting two lesbian prostitutes in town who put on private floor shows for him. Stanley was uncomfortable in withholding such knowledge from Nina, but what could he tell her? What he heard was only rumour. She'll have to learn for herself, was his conclusion.

They pulled up back at the villa. The evening sun hung low in the sky. The yacht, due to sail back to France soon, was moored in the bay. It's all so perfect, Nina thought. There was a message from Michael waiting for her when she got inside. The maid handed Nina the note: *See you at the taverna*. She couldn't wait.

She sat at a taverna table with Stanley and Sonia. Pakis was leading the dancing. The taxi driver that so nearly ran her down was singing, his head thrown back. He sent a glorious melody of sound into the air. Michael, standing next to Pakis, danced expertly. The taverna was swamped with tourists. Several silly, giggling German women tried to join the line of dancing men, but Pakis grunted, 'This dance not for women.'

The Germans fled. 'Ach, pig!' one spat at him.

'Oinky, oinky,' was his retort.

Nina had to laugh. 'Well, I suppose he is a bit of a chauvinist, isn't he?'

'More than you'd believe,' Sonia said dreamily. 'But he's *my* pig.'

'Really Sonia. I've never seen you this smitten. You've certainly never been this soppy about Myles.'

'That's because Myles is boring and unromantic. It's more like a business relationship between us. He gets my body, but I don't want his mother-fucked-up little heart. Pakis is different. Would you believe me if I told you he asked me to marry him?'

'Seriously? And what did you say?'

'I said let's wait and see,' she laughed. 'I really don't know if it's me he wants or all those Greek babies he has his heart set on.'

Nina felt suddenly envious. 'But just think, Sonia. You could live here for the rest of your life with a man who really loves you.'

'Yeah. And picture it: "Dear Agony-readers. your Agony Aunt has given up on Agony and is trying her hand at Happiness. She's taken herself off to Greece with a wonderful man to make lots of little Greek babies." Can you imagine it?'

'Yes, Sonia. I think I can.'

'Well, I'm not sure if *I* can.'

The men moved in a long sensuous wind, the sobbing wail of the song catching the hoot of the night owls as they floated by on silent wings. High over the tall night-smelling pine trees the moon looked down while the men broke ranks and joined their women.

Pakis went to the kitchen and brought out a tray. On it was a fat fish baked to perfection. Beside it lay a pile of fresh cut green parsley. A bottle of retsina stood on the tray. 'For my bride!' Pakis roared.

All the tourists clapped with enthusiasm.

Pakis put on a tape of music and Sonia, blushing, was dragged off to dance. Nina smiled.

Michael took her hand. 'Come on,' he said. 'Let's dance.' He held Nina securely in his arms, but somehow she was aware that he would have been more comfortable dancing by himself. When she had watched him dance alone he was elastic and graceful;

holding her, she did not seem to fit into his body. It was as if a carapace came between them. The real Michael was not there in the Greek moonlight. Still, she thought as she watched Stanley join a vigorous group of arguing men, we are all happy tonight. May tonight never end.

A telephone call came a few days later and Michael was gone.

Nina was too worried to be cross. 'Shit!' she heard him swear into the telephone. 'Don't they ever learn?'

Whoever *they* were, *they* were in trouble.

'Sorry,' he said. 'Something's come up.' He kissed her lightly on the forehead. 'I've got to go.'

'When will I see you again?' Nina could no help it if she sounded desperate.

'Can't say for certain. I'll give you a call in London when I get back.' Michael, at the thought of leaving, seemed enlivened by a greater energy than any he had shown when he had time at his disposal. She could see how much he wanted to be gone.

'Get back from where?'

'Business, Nina.' The carapace excluded her. 'You know that means it's private.'

Her mind was not satisfied. Uncontrollably it asked questions which she knew would never be answered. What went wrong? Was Titania calling him?

She sat on the villa's terrace all morning feeling more and more resentful. Sonia was at the taverna learning how to make moussaka.

Nina played with the moussaka on her plate at lunchtime.

'Come on, Nina,' Sonia scolded. 'Don't sulk. The moussaka's great. Made it myself.'

523

Nina looked down at the golden, bubbling concoction. The meat was freshly ground and the light, sweet raisins glinted in the deep brown gravy. 'It's delicious, Sonia. But that's not the problem.'

'You knew what Michael was like when you took him on. How can you be surprised now? In fact, you probably see more of him than most of his women do?'

'Most of his women?'

'Past relationships, I mean,' Sonia covered quickly.

'Hm. But I thought I could change him.'

'Nina, my love, people don't change that much. You get what you see most of the time, and that's the way things stay.'

Nina stuck her chin in the air. 'He *will* change,' she said firmly. 'We Tolmadges are a stubborn lot.'

Sonia said nothing in the face of Nina's uncomprehending determination. There was nothing she could say.

Chapter 69

Nina was again amazed at the amount of noise at Latchmere House. 'I've forgotten how to put up with the racket,' she commented to Monica.

'You get used to it. Little Richard took out the office window with a football, so Perry and Whiplash are installing a new one. All the kids are playing around with the putty. It's everywhere. Wow, you look good, though.'

Nina smiled. Monica and Cal were sitting in the office. Lilly was taking her turn at making lunch. 'I had a good time, but I'm glad to be back. Sonia fell in love with a Greek man called Pakis.'

'And you?' Cal asked.

'Me? What can I say? It was wonderful. Absolutely wonderful. Who's little Richard, by the way?'

'Oh, he's a Jamaican kid. About ten years old. He's on the run from his children's home. Lilly's taken him under her wing. They get on very well. He was sleeping rough on the streets until he found his way to us, but he's much better now.' Cal walked over to the door of the office. 'Is Richard down there?' she bellowed.

Nina heard the sound of scampering feet. A beaming black face appeared at the office door. 'Hello, Richard.' Nina extended her hand. 'I'm Nina.' He took her hand. 'How did you find out about us?'

'My sister was here with her husband, and they moved on to one of your squats. I don't want to live with her, though. She's too strict. I like it here, and I want to live with Lilly. I don't want to go back to the children's home ever.'

'His social worker's been on the blower from Leeds. Says they've been on to his sister.' Monica looked worried.

Nina thought a moment. 'I tell you what, Richard. I'll take you home with me until everything's safe. How about that?'

'Have you got a telly?'

'Hm.'

Richard smiled. 'I'll ask Lilly what she thinks.'

'Okay.' Nina sat down at the familiar desk. The sound of Perry's hammer was only a few feet away. The men flitted in and out of the office, carrying framing for the window and panes of glass.

'You look fantastic,' Perry whistled.

'Thank you, Perry.' She stretched out her brown legs and laughed. 'Stanley had a whale of a time, Cal. He says you might go and live with him?'

'Yeah, I've been giving it a lot of thought. We couldn't get along with each other any better. He has a terrific sense of humour. Strange, isn't it? An old dyke like me and a not-so-young-any-more gay guy?'

'You're not a dyke, Cal. Don't say things like that.'

Cal roared with laughter. 'I love it when you get proper, Nina. You look just like a schoolteacher.'

'And you wind me up just to tease me, don't you, Cal? But really I can't find it funny. Too many people killed themselves because they had been given labels and then became hated by everyone else.'

'True. Undoubtedly true. But a little humour was never lethal. And it's been lonesome with you gone.'

Lilly arrived with coffee. 'You want to take my little Richard, Nina? But he likes me. I like him.'

'I'd only take him home for a little while. The authorities will no doubt check the house here, so he'll be safe with me. Then I can bring him back, and you can join a squat.'

'Then me and Richard can live together?'

'He's a sweet kid,' Cal put in. 'A bit rough round the edges, but he'll have Lilly to look after him.'

Nina smiled. 'When do I go to your place?' Richard asked.

'This evening soon enough?' said Nina.

Nina was tired after the first day back. Latchmere House was a long way from a blue Greek headland. She very much ached for Michael . . . I must return Marietta's earring, she thought. I'll telephone her tonight.

In the car beside her, Richard was chattering like a

starling. 'You'll have fun with Hamish and Ryan,' she said to him. 'We're nearly home. You'll meet them in a minute.'

Janice looked surprised, but smiled happily.

'He can share my bedroom,' Hamish offered. 'Come on, Richard, I'll show you my trains.'

Richard took off his jacket and dropped it on the floor.

'Aye, Richard!' Janice pulled him back. 'We pick up our own jackets around here. We're not your servants.'

'Sorry.' Richard flashed a radiant grin and picked up the jacket. He went off with Hamish.

'Nice kid.' Janice went back into the kitchen and Nina followed.

'He's run away from a children's home in the North.'

Janice grunted. 'Don't blame him. Social workers drag the kids away from parents who abuse them, then they hand them over to child molesters who get jobs in the children's homes. I've no time or sympathy for them at all.'

'Well, we'll do what we can to keep him safe.' Nina poured herself a glass of wine. 'Sun's over the yardarm,' she said. 'Good health, Janice.' When she had swallowed her first sip she spoke. 'What I can't bear is to look into the eyes of a child and see he's been sexually abused for many years. You can see the total loss of innocence.' She shook her head. 'Instead of a child of seven, you see a child old long before his time.' She found herself thinking that some time in Michael's childhood someone must have done him a lot of harm. If only he had had somebody else to take him in and look after him and love him. A strange picture formed in Nina's head: the adult Nina caring for Michael as a little boy. Yes, she would have helped him.

She wandered into the drawing room and flipped on the evening news. For a moment all she could see was a heaving sea. Then she heard the voice of the announcer. 'A large shipment of cannabis has been found washed up along the Welsh coast, evidently set adrift when the ship smuggling the drugs foundered and sank. The cargo floated ashore in black plastic bags.'

'Good heavens!' Nina watched the police scrambling about the beach.

'Police are making enquiries,' said the news reporter.

'Somebody's going to be very unhappy,' she remarked as Janice came in to sit beside her. 'A whole pile of dope is washed up on a beach in Wales.'

'And that means they'll probably never catch the bugger who's shipping it in,' Janice grumbled. 'The bastards always seem to get away with everything.'

After dinner was cleared and the children were in their beds, Nina went upstairs and sat on the end of Richard's bed. 'What happened to your mum and dad, Richard? I remember your sister well, but I don't recall her saying very much about your family background.'

'Nah, Shelly wouldn't do. She's ashamed. My dad's in jail for raping a bird. And my mum ran off and left us. Shelly did the best she could, but they took us away all the same. I don't know where my other brothers and sisters are. They split us all up. Can I really live with Lilly, Miss?'

'Don't call me Miss, Richard. My name's Nina.'

'Okay, Nina.' Richard settled comfortably into his pillow. 'You've got a smashing house here.'

'Thank you.' She put her arm around him and kissed his forehead. She saw tears in his eyes.

'No one's ever done that since me mum left.' His voice was choking.

'Looks like we'll have to make Lilly an honorary grandmother.'

'You promise I don't have to go back to that awful place?'

'I promise, Richard. You don't have to go anywhere you don't want to go.'

Shit, she thought after she had given Hamish an extra-warm hug. State child care hasn't really changed much since Dickens's day.

A little later she fell into bed, too tired to telephone anyone. I'll ring Marietta tomorrow, she promised herself.

Chapter 70

At precisely eleven o'clock the next morning, Nina heard Lilly screaming at the front door of Latchmere House. 'Fuck off, you fucking bastards!'

Nina knew the police must be outside. Lilly hated all policemen. She noted down the time in the daily office diary. Policemen, with a few exceptions, were a valuable asset to Latchmere House. They knew how hard everybody worked, and they were also grateful to have a place that would take in the problems most agencies refused to touch. She could hear Lilly giving the officers an earful downstairs. 'Go down and see what they want, will you, Cal? If it's the bloody social worker after Richard, bring her or him up here and we'll sort them out.'

Monica stopped typing and watched to see what would happen next.

There was a commotion coming up the hall. 'Where is he? I want the boy found. You go and search this place from top to bottom. I'm going to see that dreadful woman Mrs Stockton.' A small, determined figure stormed into the office. 'He's here. I *know* he's here somewhere. Where is he, Mrs Stockton? I have a warrant to take him back to Leeds. Immediately. I have a car waiting outside.'

Nina smiled 'How very nice for you,' she said soothingly. 'I always think driving through the countryside is so relaxing. Don't you?'

The woman glared at Nina. 'I *know* you have the boy.'

'I'm sure I don't know what you mean. But if whoever you are looking for is here, then no doubt our goodly constables will bring him upstairs forthwith.' Nina had no intention of offering the woman a cup of tea. She knew the type well. An embittered old-style social worker, just waiting out her time to retire. Long lines ran down the face, and the eyes flickered. Nina let the sun shine on her engagement ring. She played with the refracted rainbow spectrum along the office wall.

One of the police came ambling up the steps. 'Can't find a thing,' he said, winking at Nina. Nina, delighted, recognized him. He was Police Constable No. 333, a godsend of an officer who had proved himself friendly and cooperative on a number of occasions in the past. 'Showed a photo of the lad around, but no one's seen him.'

'Do you really think they'd tell if they had?' the social worker spat.

'Oh, I don't know,' said PC 333. 'Seem like honest sorts round here.' He smiled knowingly at Nina.

'Lying lot of thieves and bastards is what they are,' said the social worker.

'Oh dear,' cooed Nina. 'I'm so sorry you think so little of us all. We do try, really we do.'

'*You*,' the woman said with an anger-constricted throat, 'you've been known to break the law before.'

'Only when necessary, I promise you,' Nina demurred. 'And even then, break is such a harsh word. Bend, perhaps?'

'Then I shall go to a judge and have you arrested.'

'On what evidence?'

'Oh, I'll find some. Don't you worry.' The woman stomped out of the house.

As he left the office, Police Constable 333 chuckled and tipped his helmet.

It was a week before Nina remembered to call Marietta. She was prompted to telephone simply because she so missed Michael: she hoped Marietta might know where he was. There was no answer from his office. The staff there were as tense and close-mouthed as ever. Lady MacLaughlin was complaining at his absence: 'I really don't know, dear. He's never been out of touch this long before. Even Titania doesn't seem to know where he is.'

Nightly stories on the news showed the police rounding up suspects in their efforts to get to the bottom of the drugs washed up in Wales. Wild stories ran like ever-changing gossip through Latchmere

531

House and in the squats. The police regularly invaded the squatters' houses because a rumour circulating at large hinted that the drugs were in some remote way connected to the charity for the homeless. The squatters made the police welcome any time they cared to inspect the premises. Nothing incriminating was ever found.

It was one of the tenets of Latchmere House that drugs were not allowed in any of their properties or squats. The people who went through Latchmere House had lost so much already that an easy consensus formed to the effect that drugs would only make their lives worse.

Richard and Lilly were due to go on to the next squat. 'I'll still come in and do the floors at Latchmere House,' Lilly promised.

'You do that,' Nina said, hugging her. 'I'll bring Richard to you when you're settled. I don't trust that old bitch of a social worker not to pay a surprise visit.'

It was quite late when Nina picked up the telephone. 'Marietta?' she said. 'Did you get my postcard?'

'Yes, I did. Don't bother about the earring. It's nothing.' Her voice sounded distraught. 'And don't come round here.'

'Why ever not? Marietta, is something the matter?'

'I think I'm being watched.'

'Watched? But what for?'

There was a moment's pause. 'Nina!' Marietta's voice was panic-stricken. 'I've got to tell you. You know the suspicion that the drugs are connected to Latchmere House? Well, they are, though not directly.'

'What on earth do you mean? I don't know a thing about drugs or . . .'

'I mean, Nina, that Michael's a drug dealer. That's what he does. That's how he makes so much money. His charities are just fronts to get him publicly accepted footholds in countries all around the world. The dope in Wales belonged to him. But I've got to get away. The authorities are on to me. I'm involved. I never wanted to be. And Michael's people don't want me saying anything. But the truth is, Michael used me as . . .' The line went dead.

Nina redialled. Silence.

She called the operator. 'Hello, operator? I was just talking to this number, but we seem to have been disconnected. And I can't get through again. Can you please check the line for me?'

'Checking. One moment please.'

Nina could not bring herself to believe what Marietta had told her. She's flipped the poor woman, thought Nina. She's tired and overwrought. Michael, a drug dealer? Impossible. But something inside Nina clicked together. No, I don't want to believe it . . .

'Yes, I've checked that number. There seems to be a fault on the line. I can report it to our repairs department if you wish.'

'Thank you,' said Nina, as she put down the telephone. I have to go to Marietta. She's in trouble.

'Janice?' she called as she grabbed her coat. 'I'm going out for a while. I'll be back soon.'

As she got into the car, she wondered if she should have told Janice to ring the police if she were not back home by midnight. Don't be so bloody dramatic, she told herself. It's probably just a technical hitch on the telephone line. But I'll check on Marietta anyway.

She started the car. Her hands were shaking. Calm down, you idiot! Marietta is just upset about something.

Deep, deep inside, a small voice said steadily, *You knew something was wrong all along, but you refused to think about it. You always were a stubborn Tolmadge.*

Nina clung to the wheel. 'Oh, the pain!' she whispered, dry-lipped as she drove into the night.

Chapter 71

Nina drove along what felt like an endless road, her eyes blind with anger. At moments pity managed to bludgeon its way through to her conscious thoughts. But mostly all she felt was raw, red anger. She did not know which hurt the worst. Pity produced a pain akin to a drill hitting a helpless nerve, while rage produced a bowel-intruding knife cut. The road, harsh in the night light, grew in the phosphorescence of the tall goose-necked streetlamps. High on the motorway approaching Chiswick roundabout, she saw other houses, their lights blinking contentedly. Families, she imagined fondly, sitting in front of television sets. A mother and father sitting closely together holding hands. One-point-seven children doing their homework at the back of the room. Why not me? she heard the question asked. The voice, she realized, was her own.

She had regressed to the happy teenager who met Simon all those years ago. She heard the cheerful, carefree voice of a young girl in love with her man.

But you chose to get out. There was an evil sneer in this voice. Who was speaking? Angela? Or was it Enid? *You disobeyed the rules, dear. You didn't realize*

534

that marriage is like a ship. A woman is the captain, and she can never abandon the vessel, though her pirate husband lays chase to every pretty boat passing by. You, the voice continued, *broke all the rules.*

Swirling around Hammersmith Broadway, she saw the buildings all begin to sway and shake. I'm going mad, she thought. The houses along the road looked as if they were going to melt like chocolate. The sticky runny stuff filling the road choked the wheels of the car. As fast as she tried to drive, she felt as if she were in a time warp. She was moving fast, the speedometer agreed that the car was moving, but outside the city looked as if it had been destroyed by some great catastrophe. *Serves you right*, the voice said again.

Finally she parked the car outside the block of flats which Marietta had moved to since breaking up with Gemma. Nina ran through the grim courtyard to the grimy stairs. The smell of stale urine and garbage was almost comforting. At least it was real.

The slimy concrete steps lay ahead of her. Courage, she heard Aunt Persephone's voice in her head. Grace under pressure.

She took a deep breath and walked up the stairs. She stopped in front of the door of the flat. She put out her hand and knocked. The sound was hollow. The flat felt empty. She tried again. The block of flats was silent. Did those people behind their front doors know something she did not? The silence was ominous. In areas such as this the dysfunctional members of society had secrets. They communicated like animals in the wild. They could smell fear and trouble. They lay silent in their lairs. She felt them crouched and waiting. She sensed a huge immutable mass of suffering, waiting. Waiting for what?

She pushed open the wide letterbox and peered in. Her knees bent at an awkward angle. Then she screamed. She heard her own voice ring hysterically in the night air. 'She's dead! Oh my God! Marietta's dead! Somebody do something!' She saw herself pushing at the door, kicking the peeled woodwork with her feet. Behind the door in the wide hall, Marietta lay sprawled. Her head was surrounded by a thick pool of red blood. 'Michael! Michael!' Nina screamed.

Her voice seemed to go on forever. She felt herself seismically shaking, her teeth chattering. The world had become an ice age. She felt a numbness creep over her body, and then oblivion. Before she finally felt herself cast into an abyss, she was dimly aware of blue flashing lights and hands lifting her up. That was all.

When she awoke, she was in a strange bed in a strange room. A kindly policewoman stood at the end of her bed. 'What happened?' Nina asked. She felt drowsy, her head full of bumblebees.

'You had an upset, dear.' The policewoman smiled down at her.

'Where am I?'

'In hospital, Mrs Stockton. We contacted your house, and your son is fine. Your housekeeper says . . .'

'Janice is not a housekeeper,' Nina contradicted wearily. 'She's my friend.'

'Your *friend* said not to worry. She'd take care of everything.'

'When can I go home?'

'Not just yet. You've had rather a shock.'

And then the awful scene came flooding back. Nina

felt her face crumble like a fearful child's. 'Is Marietta dead?'

'I'm afraid so. Look, love, don't take on so.' She pulled a chair up to the bed. In her hand she held a notebook. 'There's a very serious police investigation going on. When we came in, you were screaming a name.'

'I was?' A panic seized her. 'What did I say?'

The policewoman flipped back through her notebook for what felt to Nina like an eternity. 'You said, "Michael did it. Michael killed her." Michael who, dear?'

Nina shook her head. 'I have no idea. I don't want to answer that. Please, may I make a phone call?'

The policewoman picked up the phone by the bed and spoke down it. 'You have permission to make a call. But we will have to listen in.'

Gemma, Nina thought. Gemma will be devastated, Gemma who loved Marietta more than she loved her own life. I must get to her first. She uttered Gemma's telephone number to the invisible operator. 'Gemma? Marietta's dead. Killed. I'm in hospital under police guard. Can you go to my house and take care of Hamish? I'm afraid for him. Gemma?' There was a deadly silence on the telephone. 'Gemma, please. I know it's an awful shock.'

'How do you know she's dead?'

'I went over to the flat because she told me something, and her phone was cut off right in the middle of the conversation, so I had to go round to see if she was all right. But I looked through the letterbox and I saw her lying there . . . Oh, Gemma! I'm so sorry. Really I am.' Nina was weeping.

The policewoman put a tissue into her hand.

'Fine.' Gemma's tone was flat. 'I'll be down and I'll come and see you. Who's handling the investigation?'

Nina looked at the policewoman, who said, 'Tell her to contact Scotland Yard, Inspector Wiggins.'

Nina passed the name on.

'Don't worry, Nina. I'll take care of everything.' Gemma's voice reminded Nina of the slamming of a cell door.

She lay back on her pillow.

'This Michael . . .' Inspector Wiggins turned out to be tall and balding. He had very shrewd eyes and bushy eyebrows. Nina lay defensively in her bed. 'Is he a boyfriend, then?'

'No, not exactly.'

'Mrs Stockton, we have a murder on our hands, and you are refusing to cooperate.'

Nina shivered. 'I'm not refusing to cooperate. I'm just afraid of implicating anybody without having any real evidence, Inspector.'

'I understand,' he grinned. 'By the way. We told your father that we have you, and your parents are on their way up to collect your son.'

'Yes. Thank you.' Nina gave a sigh of relief.

The Inspector's inquisitorial eyebrows rose by themselves. 'Are you afraid someone might harm your son?'

'I don't know what to think or what to be afraid of. I'm confused. That's all. Whom should I trust?'

'Well, my dear, we have a visitor for you. I think you can trust him.' The Inspector went to the door and opened it. 'Come right in, sir. I'll leave you both to talk.' He crooked a finger at the policewoman who left with him.

'Justin!' Nina said. 'Justin, what on earth are you doing here?'

'I was about to ask you the same question.' Justin Agate took the chair by the bed. 'I've been called in to cover this case for *Time*. I'm working with Scotland Yard. Actually, I've been in England for the last two weeks. I've been undercover, so I couldn't call you. Nina, do you know where Michael is?'

Nina shook her head.

'Why did you scream, "Michael did it"?'

She shook her head again.

'Nina, you've got to tell me. How many other people are going to die while you put your loyalty to Michael first?'

The words punctured Nina's heart. The bullets that killed Marietta felt as if they lay in her own hand. 'It was because . . . because . . .' Her voice sounded as if it arose from a long way down, deep within her, from the part that loved and treasured Michael. 'Because the last words she said to me were that Michael was a drug dealer. I can't believe that, Justin. I refuse to.'

Justin sat quietly. Then he said, 'You'd better believe it.'

Nina moaned and the sound filled the room.

Justin pushed a button and a doctor came in with a hypodermic needle.

'I thought this might be necessary,' said the doctor, and he pushed the needle into Nina's arm. 'At least she'll get a good night's sleep.'

'Hm. Tonight. But what about tomorrow night?' Justin went into the corridor where Inspector Wiggins stood gazing at the glowing city lights through a dark window.

'We'll have to keep her here until we pick him up.

She might well be in danger.' The Inspector took out his handkerchief and blew his nose loudly. 'Poor woman. And what a bastard he is!'

'A charming bastard,' Justin said. ' I was stupid enough to believe he was a friend. But he uses people and then throws them away. I'll say goodbye now, Inspector. And thank you.'

Chapter 72

Time lost its measurement. Was it hours or days that Nina lay with her body too drugged to move but her troubled mind still restless? The moments of merciful oblivion felt brief indeed when, rising from total unconsciousness to a state of wretched mental activity, Nina participated involuntarily in scenes of her mind's making and tried with futility to push herself away from thought back into the sweet blackness. Among the tableaux passing before her inner eye came memories that she wished she could lose forever: Simon's confession to her, Susan's anger against her. One moment she found herself holding a teacup in Enid's sitting room, stuck in some ghastly, eternal Sunday afternoon ritual. The next instant she witnessed the most horrid yet most indelible image of all, that of Marietta's beautiful head inert in the crimson puddle of blood. Nina felt herself sob, yet, more aware than she wanted to be that such visions were produced by her own brain, she could not tell for certain whether she cried out in reality or merely in the same dark swirling sea of unstoppable sound and sight that swept her about in its relentless waves and whirlpools.

Sensations still tingled in her limbs. Michael's handed were on her, caressing her skin, thrilling her senses. But the shadowy pleasures she had received from Michael now appeared evil in themselves; all that she had shared with him had proved itself to be a prelude to horror. Her obsession must be no longer indulged. Never again could she allow herself the forbidden luxury of Michael's intimate company. She would have to tell him herself.

Nina stood before Michael. He sat on the bed at the Savoy Hotel, still in his formal clothes. His dinner jacket lay discarded on the chaise longue. He had taken off his shoes. He leaned back against the tall stack of pure white pillows, his golden skin made to look darker by its contrast to the linen. His shirt was open at the throat. His bow-tie, undone, hung from his neck. With one hand he turned his large diamond ring around a finger of the other. 'Don't sulk, Nina. You're ruining a perfectly lovely evening.' The raised corners of his mouth pushed the skin up over his cheekbones, crinkling his eyes.

Nina was shocked by his lack of feeling. She wore an evening gown that in past, happier days she had bought to make her look good, to make her feel good, for his sake. Now the dress hung upon her like a cloak of shame. How *could* she have been so seduced by Michael, so taken in by the power and comfort and luxury and energy that hovered about him, that she let herself put aside her better judgement? Marietta's death felt like the mysteriously-linked consequence of Nina's own weakness. No, she tried to tell herself. It was Marietta who first invited *me* to come to the meeting on homelessness, not the other way round . . . But rational thought was useless. Deeper feelings such as guilt cannot be so easily dismissed. Angry with herself, angry with her own sense that she should have done more to protect Marietta, she turned her anger to Michael. And he deserved her anger. *He* used Marietta. He corrupted her. He killed her. No, Nina could never be lovers with him again. 'A perfectly lovely evening, Michael? It's a night of death. How can you call that lovely?'

'Death *is* lovely, Nina.' He smiled like a nocturnal predator come awake in the shadows of the night. 'It's what I always offered. It's what makes me irresistible. Isn't that what you saw in me which thrilled you beyond control? You know that's what you wanted.'

'No.' Nina stood rigid. She would not approach the bed. She would not come too near his attractive magnetic field. 'I wanted peace. I wanted safety. I wanted love.'

'You wanted excitement. You wanted danger. You wanted lust.'

Nina refused to believe him. 'You are not what I wanted.'

'I am precisely what you asked for. And before you go accusing me of being the evil seducer, Nina, I will remind you whose fantasy nurtured our love first. Wasn't I your fantasy that you made real yourself?'

'Don't you dare use the word *love*.' Nina stood like a granite statue. Her mouth did not tremble as she spoke to him. Her voice remained even. Only her eyes, fixed on his smirking face, leaked slow tears steadily down her cheeks. 'You never loved me. I see it now. I thought I loved you, but I was wrong. You were my drug. You are everyone's drug. You make their darkest dreams come true. That is your power.'

'I only give people what they want. Is that a crime? Marietta asked *me* for help. Don't ever forget that.'

'You did not help her. You are the devil.'

Michael's smile widened. His dark eyes sparked as if in moonlight, though the elegant room was mostly in shadow. 'I assure you, I'm as human as they come.'

'No. Humans have consciences. Humans feel love. Humans have hearts.'

'I have a body, as you know fully well.' He stopped turning his ring and held out his arms to her. 'Let's put our bodies together again. It served us all along. It stopped all questioning. It silenced all doubt.'

'No, the questions about you never stopped.'

'Well then, they were never loud enough to make any difference. Now come. And don't be such a fool. You know your desire for me hasn't gone away. Why fight yourself? Give in. Come and be with me. You will have all that you ask.'

'I'm leaving, Michael.' She took her eyes off him and wiped her wet cheek with her hand. She turned to the door, far across the carpeted floor. 'You are evil.'

'I am what I am. I have never pretended.'

'You are what you are,' she echoed. 'You have always pretended. Goodbye, Michael. I will never see you again.'

'Nina!' He sounded angry, the strength of his wrathful voice a magnetic force itself, pulling her against her will.

She made herself move. She turned to the door.

'You will not go!' His volcanic, murderous anger grew.

She stepped again. The door was nearly in reach. She looked at him once more.

'Nina.' His voice was soft. His eyes, now gentle, began to show tears. His face was young and needy. This was what held her hand from turning the knob. This was the strongest pull of all. The once innocent child beneath all the evil called to her. She pitied him and wanted to bathe him in her love. 'Please,' he said.

She shut her eyes and faced the door. 'No.'

Holding her breath, as if she might never breathe again, she opened the door and walked from the room of darkness. She stepped into a world of light and immediate peace. The door closed behind her. Nina was free.

Nina's eyes fluttered. She rolled over and the hospital sheets brushed against her cheek. For the briefest of moments she approached the surface of her sea of dreams, feeling herself rise from the depths of somnolent imaginings. A bright bubble of blissful clarity drifted lightly upwards: She knew what she would have to do. She would tell him face to face, though she had not been able to find him for days. She would keep looking and she would not stop until she had found him. She would bid Michael goodbye.

Her decision made, she allowed some instinctive, protective gravity to suck her back down, deep into the waters of death-like silence.

Chapter 73

At the front door of Nina's house on Angel Walk, Janice pushed a piece of paper into Gemma's hand. Gemma looked white and drawn. Janice had not slept last night at all. 'Major and Mrs Tolmadge took Hamish back to the country, Gemma. Cal's holding the fort at Latchmere House. I'm so sorry.' She pulled Gemma to her, but Gemma stood looking at the note.

'Where did you find this?'

'Slipped under the door this morning when I went to get the newspapers.'

Gemma made a face. The note read: *Nina, meet me at the Lyme House Street dock. Eleven o'clock tonight.*

Gemma checked her watch. Plenty of time.

Gemma stood in the hall. Waves of exhaustion rolled off her.

'Shouldn't we tell the police?'

'No.' Gemma sounded distracted. 'No need to tell them. At least, not yet.'

Janice said, 'Why don't you go upstairs to Nina's room and try to rest.'

'Yes,' said Gemma, thinking quickly. 'That's a good idea. I'll try.' Her voice was bleak and arid, like a desert where there was no water.

On Nina's bed, Gemma lay wide-eyed, staring at the ceiling. Marietta was dead. Nina was in danger. She had no choice. Her father's wartime gun was filled with bullets and lay heavy in her handbag. Now it was just a question of whether she could get close enough to Michael. She went to Nina's cupboard and chest of drawers and found what she was looking for. She put on a borrowed coat, a scarf and a pair of dark glasses. Quietly she slipped down the stairs to the door.

Gemma heard her own footsteps ring out on the cobbles of the wharf in Lyme House Street. Huge cavernous warehouses lined the road either side. Men loomed in and out of the dark landscape, but Gemma was not afraid. Their antennae picked up that this woman was dangerous.

She walked slowly and stealthily, her head wrapped in Nina's silk scarf, her eyes shaded by Nina's black glasses, her thin shoulders bearing the weight of Nina's well-worn coat. She approached the dock and she saw the starboard light on Michael's yacht, the same yacht she had seen so often filled with Michael's fellow jet-setters in the newspapers, the yacht which Nina had reminisced about after returning from Greece. Now its steep sides glinted in the moonlight.

The note of invitation, intended for Nina, promised no party, no glass of champagne. What was Michael's intention in arranging this meeting with Nina? Gemma did not know.

She walked up the gangplank and silently handed the note to a man dressed in black with a woollen cap on his head. He read the note, then said, 'Mrs Stockton, please follow me.' Gemma pulled the gun from her purse and held it within the loose folds of the overcoat. She walked behind the man in silence down a panelled hallway into the main cabin.

Michael was on the telephone, his back to her. She watched his sleek head. The other man left. Gemma stood looking at Michael's head. First she felt a wave of nausea overcome her will, but then she was grateful to experience a detached, omnipotent calm.

He finished his conversation. 'Nina,' he said, reaching to put down the telephone. 'I understand our dear Marietta was talking to you on the phone when tragedy befell her.' He still had not looked up at her. His hands were busy opening a drawer. Then he lifted his face. As he turned, Michael's face showed no emotion.

Gemma knew he had reached for a gun. She also knew that the crew were waiting for a shot. She pointed the gun at Michael and squeezed the trigger. The bullet hit him in the forehead, making a neat round hole. 'Nina?' he said, his voice full of surprise, his hand dropping the revolver it held.

'No,' she said to his fast-falling body. 'Guess again, you bastard.'

He lay on the floor, his life leaving him. Gemma took off the sunglasses and she could tell he recognized her. She spat on his face then left the room.

She would have a few minutes' grace before she was caught. She slipped silently up the corridor to the gangway. Aft she saw crew members pulling up ropes, obviously unmoved by the expected sound of a gunshot. She stepped into the dark night before she was seen.

She ran panting along the road until she came to a telephone box. Picking up the receiver, she was relieved that the telephone was working. She dialled the operator, saying over and over to herself, 'Thank you, God. Bless me father, for I have sinned.' She was jabbering. 'Send the police fast,' she said to the operator. She turned quickly and kept checking over her shoulder. 'I've just killed a man,' she said, when she got through to the police switchboard. Gemma was shaking. 'His name is Michael Morningstar. I'm in the phone box on Lyme House Street. He's dead in his yacht.'

'Stay where you are. We're sending someone over.'

Gemma put the telephone down. She crouched as low as she could, hoping to become invisible in the gloom.

The sight of the flashing police lights was a relief and a sadness. She was relieved the police had found her before Michael's crew did. She was sad because she knew that these were her last seconds of freedom. Three police cars drove straight past her, their sirens screaming. Two other cars stopped by the telephone box. 'Come out with your hands in the air.'

Gemma, blinded by the lights, pushed open the door of the phone box with one hand, the other in the air. She left the gun on the floor. 'Don't shoot!' she said desperately. 'I'm unarmed.' She stood in the light, her arms raised. Tears ran down her cheeks. 'Oh. Marietta!' she wailed.

In her hospital bed, Nina, too, was crying. 'Michael,' she moaned in her sleep, mourning the relationship that she knew would never live. 'Michael.'

Chapter 74

Marietta dead, Michael killed, and Gemma in Holloway without bail. Nina lay in her own bed, at times too numb to feel anything. Other times she was wracked with sobs. Only Cal and Stanley kept her sane. Sonia tried to help, but Nina found it hard to come face to face with Sonia's radiance, the soft glow that surrounded a woman truly in love.

Sonia came to say goodbye. 'I know it's not a good time to leave, Nina. I ought to stay for Marietta's funeral, but Pakis is impatient for me to join him. Myles is furious and jealous.' Sonia stood by the bedroom window. 'Funny,' she said. 'Myles bought me roses for my birthday. It's a first, you know. Now that he's lost me, he wants me back. I feel mean leaving you, but I've finally found a man I really love, and I'm afraid what will happen to this chance if I don't grab it with both hands.'

Nina was dressed, sitting on her bed. 'You go, Sonia. And good luck. I thought I'd found a man I could love, but I was mistaken. The strange part about it now is that I never got a chance to tell him what I thought of him. That's what happens with a premature death: there's no such thing as a final goodbye because you never know if you're seeing the other person for the last time.' She smiled. 'But I said goodbye in my own way, in my own mind, even before I knew he was dead. And that does matter. It gives me some peace.' She rose and walked across the room. 'I wish you every happiness.'

How thin Nina was! thought Sonia. Her cheekbones pushed against her skin. Sonia hugged her friend. 'Thank you, Nina.'

'Well, at least some good did come out of my being with Michael. You got to meet Pakis and fall in love. I'll come to your wedding.'

'You'll *all* come to my wedding.'

Nina sighed. 'Tomorrow Hamish comes back from my mother's, and the next day Michael is buried. The police have released his body. Lady MacLaughlin has organized a huge funeral in St John's Wood. All the Great and the Good will be there. They'll close ranks, of course. Funny thing is, they can murder, rape, loot, and steal, but when a whiff of scandal comes their way, they form a united front. Though, of course, the press hasn't yet caught on to the fact that his death had anything to do with drugs. I'll go because I have to, but part of me will be hurling insults at them all, the bastards. Titania will make a beautiful widow. She's got Michael all to herself now.

'Do you know what amazes me, Sonia? The fact that he wasn't all bad. I mean, first I wouldn't hear a word against him. And after he had Marietta killed I knew deep inside myself that he *was* all evil. And then I hear . . . My God, can you believe it? He planned to kill me himself! If Gemma hadn't gone in my place and shot him first he would have gone through . . . I don't know. I can *almost* understand that. Whoever he sent to kill Marietta must have heard that she was in the middle of telling me what Michael really was. And it seems as if there was some sort of primitive animal instinct for self-preservation

550

organ solo began the heavy, solemn funeral in
Michael's honour. Nina wore a small hat with a heavy
black veil. No one would see her cry. The congre-
gation of elegant men and women did not shed tears,
neither did Titania who looked exceptionally radiant
in a black Balenciaga. Well, at least Nina's exposure
to this in-bred crowd of people had taught her to have
an expert eye for fashion. Lady Bobo Radnor, her
grizzled curly hair crowned with a black silk teapot,
looked ridiculous. For once her breathless baby voice
was stifled.

Cal stood beside Nina. She looked out of place
in her black jeans and a blue anorak. Stanley, on
the other side, looked elegant, but Nina was aware
that the three of them were nonetheless incongruous. Jimmy Donleavy, standing in the next pew,
also looked out of place. His haircut, though expensive, could not hide his early years of childhood
poverty.

Michael's body lay in front of the altar in a shining
mahogany casket. How he would have loved the
well-appointed ceremony of this event! thought
Nina, aware of the irony contained in the moment.
Michael was always the centre of attention, now for
the last time on earth. All she could do was pray
that Michael was at peace with God. In one lingering
affectionate thought, she imagined the good side of
Michael to be already fascinating the angels ri[...]
now, or at least what she had believed to h[...]
his good side. God, she told herself, pl[...]
nal and potentially divine soul [...]
could not but hope that t[...]
Michael had made of his [...]
around him, his spirit migh[...]
somehow purified. She wo[...]

in Michael to get me out of the way, even if that
meant killing me. I can understand it, but it scares
me. Could he really feel absolutely nothing for me?

'And just when I think I have it all figured out, I
find out something else. Did I tell you? His solicitor
wrote to me. Turns out Michael left me this house.
He also left me a lot of money, so I can continue to
work at Latchmere House. What am I supposed to
make of a man who at least at one time was capable
of a gesture that generous? God knows! I can only
assume that his intention, before he decided I was
some kind of mortal threat to him, was to look after
me, if anything happened to him first. I think he
found his pleasure in owning people, in buying my
house so that he'd own me, but then he planned to
provide for me anyway, as if he really came to care
. . . Maybe he did have some real feelings for me
after all.' She felt tears rise. 'That's the most painful
thought of all, that maybe I did mean something to
him. No, he couldn't have been entirely bad. That's
why I could never hate him, even though in the end
he wanted me dead. But I also can never love him.'
She sniffed. 'When were human emotions ever easy?'
She shook her head and wiped her eyes. 'So as of
tomorrow, I go back into the world. Janice has been
wonderful. Everybody's been wonderful. It's reassuring to know I have such amazingly good friends.'

Sonia kissed Nina's cheek. 'You can always count
me as a friend. I've got to finish packing. By the way,
Pakis and I want you to be a *kumbara* to our wedding.'

'*Kumbara*?'

'Yes, apparently in Greece they have five guardians
to a marriage, kind of like godparents to the couple.
Sounds like built-in marriage guidance to me, to help
see the couple through the rough spots. I thought of

asking you and Jimmy Donleavy to be two of the *kumbaras*. I don't know Jimmy very well, but what I've seen of him I like.'

'That would be great, Sonia. I'm honoured.' Nina smiled. 'I had a sweet note from Jimmy the other day. And I'll be seeing him at the funeral.' A black wave broke over her. 'Gemma is so resigned. It's terrible. I have permission for a visit the day after Marietta's funeral. Cal's arranging that. Marietta had no money at all. Cal tried to get the Latchmere House committee to donate the funeral expenses in memory of all the work Marietta did, but the committee refused. Said they wouldn't touch the idea with a bargepole. Lady MacLaughlin said, for all she cared, Marietta could be buried in a polystyrene coffin like all people on welfare. Cal got really angry at that. She offered to make arrangements for Lady MacLaughlin to be buried in a polystyrene coffin herself, and she slammed the phone down. What a bitch!'

'Yeah, but a miserable bitch. I wouldn't want her money or her way of life.'

The telephone rang shortly after Sonia left. Nina made a face upon hearing who it was.

'I do hope you're better now,' said the voice down the telephone. It was Simon. 'Thank goodness you haven't been roped into a scandal. Anyway I'm ringing to say that we will be happy to take you to Michael's funeral.'

'How kind of you, Simon.' So like him, she thought. A chance to wear his navy blue coat and sit in the same pews as the moneyed famous, and of course get in a quick dance on Michael's grave. 'But I already have friends to take me.'

'I trust you don't mean those circus freaks you spend your time with.'

'They are *not* circus freaks, and I won[...] speaking of my friends that way.' She felt [...] bling in her throat.

'Well, it all came to a bad end, Nina. You[...] turned out to be nothing but a comm[...] peddler.'

'At least he could fuck, which is more [...] could ever do.'

'There's no need to get personal.'

'There's no need to criticize, Simon. I'll arr[...] collect Susan at the weekend. Hamish will [...] tomorrow.'

'I should hope so, too. He's missed enough [...] already.'

Nina put the telephone down.

She ran downstairs. 'Simon is *such* a prick,[...] said.

Janice laughed. 'At least you can depend on [...] being a prick. Let's order Chinese for dinner[...] right?'

Later, sitting on the sofa, Nina found herself won[...] ing where the time went between the moment w[...] she was pushing cashew chicken into her mouth [...] the moment when she first saw on television the [...] ing black sea and the beached bags of drugs. No[...] newscaster was recounting disaster figures in a[...] way accident. All those people watching wh[...] loved ones in the disaster will drop through the[...] in the floor like I did, she thought. They'll lose al[...] [...]ol as the events take over your life and you are[...] [...] . . . But now I'm back in control, she told h[...] [...] as if I just rejoined the real world,' she sai[...] [...]e smiled. 'Welcome back.'

*

timeless torment. That much compassion she still felt and always would.

The vicar gave a sign for everyone to sit. The squelch of moneyed buttocks hitting the pews returned Nina from her reverie. She caught Jimmy's eyes. He winked at her. He understands, she thought.

When they walked out of the church, Nina caught up with Jimmy. 'Sonia says she'd like to invite the two of us to be *kumbaras* at her wedding in Greece. It means you and I will have to keep her marriage to Pakis on the straight and narrow.'

Jimmy laughed. 'Sounds good to me. I've never been to Greece, but I'd jump at the excuse to go.'

The September sun lay quietly on the grass. Most of the guests were going on to the cemetery for the interment of the casket. Nina said, 'I'm wondering if I can give the cemetery a miss. I really don't think I could handle going.'

'Then don't. Funerals are for the living, not the dead. Don't put yourself through any more than you feel you can manage. What time do we get together for Marietta's funeral?'

'Three o'clock at the Acton crematorium.'

'Then I'll see you there.' Her kissed her gently on the cheek. 'You will survive Michael's death, darling. I promise you will.'

'Yes, I have to believe I will, but the feelings are really quite overwhelming. I wonder if I'm to feel this torn in two for the rest of my life.'

'You'll feel better slowly, Nina. It takes time.'

'It's not just Michael I'm upset about. It's also Marietta and Gemma. I'm stunned by the possibility of Gemma getting a life sentence. She's being charged with murder in the first degree, after all. Her relationship with Marietta will be smeared all over the newspapers. It's like Simon's worst publicity nightmare coming true.'

'Oh, sod Simon,' Jimmy said with an irrepressible laugh. 'I'm sorry, Nina. But I've been meaning to say it for ages. Sod the bastard! He seems a right nasty little shit.'

Nina laughed, despite herself. 'Couldn't have put it better myself.'

'I'll see you at Acton then.' Jimmy moved off.

Cal and Stanley joined Nina. 'That cow of a wife of that ex-husband of yours,' said Stanley, 'is having a field day. Look at her over there! That Angela's giving interviews as if she actually knew the people involved.'

Reporters thronged the verges of the lawn around the church.

As Nina walked to her car with Cal and Stanley, a sudden golden leaf floated lazily to the ground in front of her. She stopped and picked it up. In the palm of her hand lay the perfectly shaped leaf. A gentle tracery of veins sprang from the centre and reached outwards. Somehow it seemed to have fallen from a clear sky. There was no tree nearby. For a moment Nina was transported by the leaf into another world where all was unity and harmony. She smiled at Stanley. 'I'll put this leaf in my Bible and keep it. It's a promise that peace is possible.' The pain in her heart became less intense. 'It is well with my soul, Lord,' she said, remembering the old church hymn written by Philip Bliss on the spot where a ship had gone down with his wife and daughters. 'It is well with my soul,' she whispered, as she climbed into her car.

*

The atmosphere at Marietta's funeral was very different. Lilly and Monica from Latchmere House were there. They sat alone in the rows of empty pews. Marietta had asked to be cremated.

Nina had never been to a crematorium before. The place frightened her. Lilly, Monica, Cal, Stanley, Nina and Jimmy were Marietta's only mourners. No doubt Gemma in prison was mourning, too.

When the coffin rolled under the curtain, Nina imagined the roar of flames that would engulf the body. Healing, cleansing flames, Nina hoped.

The small group of people left the chapel and stood for a moment in the silence of the garden. The flowers they brought with them lay on the ground. No one had much to say. Nina stored as much memory as she could. Tomorrow she would visit Gemma.

Chapter 75

'It was a quiet funeral, Gemma.'

Gemma sat on a chair, alone except for a warder. Nina had been warned on her arrival at Holloway that she could not touch Gemma. Gemma lowered her head.

'What are your plans?' Nina regretted the question as soon as it left her lips. Naturally Gemma could make no plans; her future was entirely out of her hands. She had decided to murder, and that was likely to prove her last free decision about her own life she would ever make. She had not meant the innocently-intended question to sound so ironic.

Gemma forgave Nina the question. It was clear to both that the warder's presence very much inhibited any easy, real conversation.

'I've had a very long talk with the governor. She says I can study for a graduate degree.' She smiled warmly. 'Whatever happens, Nina, I want you to know that in a funny way I'm quite happy. I've always been comfortable in my own company, so being in here's not too bad. And my conscience is clear. I couldn't let him get away with killing Marietta. And I knew that you were in danger yourself because you had found out the truth about him. I did what's right. That's all.' She glanced at the warder, and decided to say nothing more too pertinent to her case. 'Anyway, the governor's a good woman. All I've really done is exchange my ivory tower for a classroom with steel bars on the windows. And the sense of humour of the inmates is better here than at college, even if the food's a little worse.'

Even the warder laughed. For a moment, all three of them shared the warmth of women together. Nina was astounded by the equanimity that Gemma seemed to have achieved.

At the end of the visit Nina watched Gemma being taken away through the door on the far side of the room. She walked to her car thinking, well, there's still the trial to go.

The trial was a nightmare. Day in and day out Nina sat with Stanley and Cal. If Cal had to stay at Latchmere House, Jimmy kept Nina company. She came very much to rely on Jimmy's strong, quiet presence. For a man who made his living with his gift of speech, he also knew how and when to be quiet, which was a relief for Nina. She spent most of the time locked into a stunned daze. Barristers ran about in their white wigs. The judge, an ancient gargoyle of a man, sat stuffed on his chair, gavel in hand. His wig was woolly enough, and old and battered. He was peevish most of the time, especially on Friday when he wanted to get away to play golf.

Outside the court, cameras clicked. As Nina expected, the press took a prurient delight in the details of the case as they were revealed day by day. VENGEFUL LESBIAN SHOOTS MICHAEL MORNINGSTAR! screamed the headlines of the *Daily Globe*. DYKE PUTS FINGER ON DRUG BOSS TYCOON raged *The Voice of the World* as Michael's drug dealings came to light.

Inevitably, as if in accordance with some inviolable law that every small truth which one might wish to keep private, must eventually be uncovered and then distorted by the press, Nina saw her own face endlessly in the newspapers. Her affair with Michael became public property. She marvelled at the relish with which the press portrayed Nina Stockton, the angel of the homeless, as the scandalous 'other woman'. Indeed the media seemed to find greater pleasure in kicking her down than they had previously in building her up. Nina came to see that both images, the saint or the seductress, were untrue caricatures. But that was what the press dealt in, flat images of real people, reshaping them into forms unrecognizable even to themselves.

There was no point in trying to pinpoint who had leaked her secret. It could have been anyone; Nina suspected that Angela pieced together bits of Susan's recounted information. In the end she decided not to torture herself with unanswerable questions. She had been revealed and that was that. The best she could do was to carry on and soon life would return to something like normality.

The charity board, however, were not so quick to let the matter drop. Lady MacLaughlin was apoplectic. 'You've hurt us all by association, smearing your name all over the newspapers,' she accused. 'And you've made a thorough fool of yourself in the process. How dare you let the immoral details of your sordid carrying on become –'

'Immoral, Lady MacLaughlin? What about your relationship with Hugo?'

'What about Hugo?'

'I was merely wondering,' said Nina matter-of-factly, 'if your fornication is any purer than mine.'

There was an appalled silence for a moment on the telephone, followed by, 'How on earth do you know about my Hugo? It's none of your business anyway. And that's very different. I haven't caused a public scandal.'

'Oh, so the crime is in the detection, not in the action, is that right? No, you haven't caused a scandal. Not yet, Lady MacLaughlin, but it could be easily arranged. I'm sure certain members of the press would be most interested to learn that a respected English Lady is keeping a young Central American revolutionary as a love slave in an Eaton Square flat. I'll bet they could come up with some really catchy headlines . . .' Game, set and match, you bitch, Nina thought.

'I don't wish to discuss the matter any further,' Alison MacLaughlin said with audible anger. 'I'll say only this: things will have to change, now that Michael's dead.'

Nina could hear the door shut on her present path. Without Michael's protection and his promise to see that the committee did not interfere directly with the running of the programme, Nina dreaded that Lady MacLaughlin and the rest of the committee – with the probable exception of Antonia Hurst – would turn Latchmere House into just another institution. No more squatting. No more bending the law to protect individual cases. No more real help offered. And without fail they would insist on one further change – no more Nina.

Nina knew it was only a matter of time now.

Shortly before Nina was due to fly to Greece for Sonia's wedding, a meeting of the board was called in a conference room at the Savoy Hotel. Immediately after the start of the meeting, Lady MacLaughlin asked for Nina's resignation. Lord Ben and Lady Bobo Radnor did not appear surprised by Alison MacLaughlin's request, nor, for that matter, did Lady Germaine Phillips. Antonia Hurst looked put out at the possibility of Nina's leaving. Jimmy was at the meeting too. He had only one thing to say: If Nina left, so would he. Then he sat back and watched with his intelligent eyes wide open.

Nina sat in her chair and studied them all. Antonia Hurst, she could see, was grieving, not just for Nina, but also for Latchmere House, a project that had flourished under the love and effort of so many people and now would flourish no more.

Lady MacLaughlin's eyes were full of venom. 'We've no confidence left in you, Nina. You let us down.'

Nina drew a deep breath. 'Then to hell with you, Lady MacLaughlin,' she said. She saw Jimmy grin. 'Not with Latchmere House; just to hell with you. If you had anything good to say about me,' Nina continued, 'I would be afraid for my soul. The trouble is, *Alison*, you have never known poverty, never experienced the fear of homelessness. You also happen to be shockingly mindless and phony, locked away in your life of privilege. You live to party, and party you will. For the last couple of years, your party has taken place on the bodies of the homeless because that's all this charity means to you: a good excuse for a social life. You can throw fundraisers and hold committee meetings and congregate with your fellows endlessly over other people's misfortune, all because you have no other reason to have genuine friendships in your life. Next year, no doubt, the fashionable cause will be giant pandas, or saving the endangered sea urchin. Doesn't matter to you what the cause is, as long as you get your parties.

'The thing is, I always knew you were never there for Latchmere House, You were there for Michael. He was the maypole everybody loved to dance around. His money inspired lust in you.

'And now we're stuck with the problem that, without Michael, there's really no reason for you to stay. But so that you can have your little victory, you want me to leave. Then you can hang on for however long it takes to run the charity into the ground, turn it into a safe, mediocre institution like any other, take all the heart out of it, until it has no life left, and finally you can say, "Well, it's no use us wasting our time with this project any longer. So sorry." And off you'd go, having destroyed something exceptional. I'm not prepared to let that happen.'

'It's out of your control, Nina,' said Lady MacLaughlin, visibly enjoying her own strength. 'You have no say in the matter. You've made it quite plain that you and the board cannot work within the same organization, but I'm afraid there's no question who will be the one to leave. Again, Nina, I must ask: please hand in your resignation, and, with all due thanks for your past efforts, the board will be quick to accept it. And if our Mr Donleavy feels moved to go with you, then a hearty farewell to him, too, but we will not be swayed. You see you're really quite outnum –'

Antonia Hurst cleared her throat. 'No,' she said quietly, suddenly calling attention away from the struggle between Lady MacLaughlin and Nina. 'I don't think it's that simple, Alison.'

'What do you mean?' snapped Lady MacLaughlin, displeased to have her momentum broken.

'I mean,' Antonia Hurst continued in a strengthening voice, 'that I was hoping it wouldn't come to this. I was hoping you'd be more open-minded, Alison, and not put us all in this position.'

'Come to what?' Lady MacLaughlin was mystified. 'What on earth are you talking about?'

Antonia Hurst spoke clearly. 'I had an inkling, when you called for today's meeting, that things might not go too smoothly. So to find out exactly where affairs stand, I made a telephone call this morning. I spoke to Michael's personal solicitor, a delightful man named Mr Hicks.'

'George Hicks,' Nina said. 'Yes, I've spoken with him in the past. Very helpful person.'

'Indeed,' continued Antonia with a nod. 'And he told me something quite extraordinary. He said he's been sorting through Michael's legal business, tying up this and that, and evidently in a codicil to Michael's will, Latchmere House is left entirely to Nina Stockton.'

'Impossible!' spat Lady MacLaughlin.

'Very possible,' Antonia said calmly. 'What's more, it's true. Having a tidy, legal mind, Mr Hicks naturally wrote a letter to notify the board of this fact in writing. He said that you, as secretary, ought to receive the letter in a day or two.'

'But it can't be! The board runs Latchmere House, and certainly . . .'

'No.' Antonia's tone was patient. 'The building was Michael's private property. He was free to sign it over to whoever he pleased. And this charitable board which he assembled, well, we've only been here to help things run along. The building was his, and the people in it have always been there of their own free will, and now the building belongs to Nina.'

Nina turned to Jimmy and gave him a smile of immeasurable gladness. She said, 'It would appear he might indeed have had a drop of goodness in him after all. People are such complex creatures, don't you think, Alison?' She did not wait for an answer from the incredulous Lady MacLaughlin. She stood up at her place at the table. 'Yes. This is rather a different picture. I think the question now is whether or not the charitable board has any place at Latchmere House.'

'No!' Lady MacLaughlin slapped the table with an open palm. 'I refuse to accept this. I cannot believe that Nina has it within her authority to disband a board of such persons as ourselves. Why, she's a nobody!'

It was Antonia Hurst who spoke. 'You're right about one thing. She cannot disband us as a board. We have every right to elect a new chairman to take Michael's place, and we can carry on having our meetings and recording minutes and keeping accounts . . . But we will be a board without anything

564

to administer. Without a building to work in, and without the people whom our charitable work is supposed to be in aid of, what would we be but, as Nina says, a strange excuse for a social club? We seem to forget that the board must serve the charity. Not the other way around.'

'I shan't stand for this.' Lady MacLaughlin was livid.

'Quite right,' said Nina. 'Nor can you. You said it yourself, Alison. Clearly the board and I cannot work together in the same project. However, as a first gesture in my role as owner of Latchmere House, I would invite all sympathetically minded members of the board to stay on, if they wish. And anyone who can't work with me, obviously, will have to go. Antonia?'

'Staying, with pleasure,' the woman smiled. 'Thank you, Nina.'

'Thank *you*. Germaine?'

'Please,' said Lady Phillips.

'Very good. Lord and Lady Radnor?'

'But this is outrageous!' Lady MacLaughlin butted in.

Ben and Bobo Radnor looked at each other. Lady Bobo spoke up in her breathy, little-girl voice. 'You stopped being interesting years ago, Alison. Your parties never were any good anyway. Yes, Nina. Count us in.'

'Then that only leaves you, Lady MacLaughlin. As your opposition is quite open, I think you have no choice but to offer your resignation. I'm sure I speak for all at Latchmere House when I say we would be only too happy to accept it.'

Speechless for once, Alison MacLaughlin stared hard at Nina with eyes that seemed poised to explode. She rose suddenly from her chair and made her way to the door. Then, managing to find a word or two, she said, 'I won't give you the satisfaction of saying goodbye.' And she was gone.

'Good riddance to bad rubbish,' said Antonia Hurst.

Lord Ben Radnor settled himself into his chair. 'Perhaps we might get down to it and actually *do* something for a change.'

'As a start,' said Nina, fully in control, 'I suggest that we open the board to new seats. Our directorship should be expanded to include people who really care and people who know the issues first hand. My first nomination as director would be Jimmy Donleavy, the man who got me involved with this at the beginning. He really ought to be more to us than simply a public spokesman. Anybody second the motion?'

'Second!' said Lady Phillips.

'I'd be honoured,' said Jimmy, with a chivalrous bow of his head. 'And, once elected, I would be quick to nominate Monica Ficus, who has proved herself invaluable as an office administrator. She may have come to Latchmere House with problems of her own, but that's made her all the better in helping others.'

'Seconded,' Nina smiled. 'And we'll have to include Janice as well. And Stanley. And who knows? Maybe Lilly might find herself sitting on our board of directors.'

'Well done, Nina,' Jimmy called out. 'Truly. Well done.' His cry was met by an echo of 'Hear, Hears' around the table.

Chapter 76

Nina looked out over the horsehoe-shaped bay. The vision of Michael's yacht anchored in the harbour was only a ghostly memory. Far below the Greek headland where she stood with Jimmy at her side, Nina could see Sonia running across the sand. Her white dress billowed about her long brown legs. Her headdress, tossed by the warm, sweet-scented wind, flew behind her. Sonia was running barefoot to meet her future – Pakis, the man she loved. This was her long-awaited wedding day. Behind Sonia lay broken relationships washed up on the shore.

Nina watched and she remembered Michael. Somewhere out in space, she hoped, God had forgiven him in the same way as God answered Nina's own prayers for forgiveness. Nina was content to leave his troubled spirit in God's hands. She must let him go and turn to the man beside her, now her lover. Between Nina and Jimmy there lay no strange shadows. In the meeting of their souls was a quiet communication, a sense of eternal unity, sharing one path of wisdom and experience through the hazardous struggle of whatever might wait ahead.

The wedding ceremony proceeded. When her turn came to commit herself as *kumbara*, guardian to the wedding, Nina crossed and uncrossed her hands, holding the marriage garlands of flowers over the couple and then gently placing the garlands on the head of the bride and the groom. The wind whistled and danced as she watched Jimmy follow her lead.

At the end of the ceremony, she walked down the hill from the headland to the beach, with Jimmy's hand in her own. A goat went trotting past, its yellow eyes glinting in the sun.

She took endless pictures for Gemma of the island. Before leaving England, Nina had gone to visit her. The verdict had been as expected. The establishment of the mighty-moneyed would not tolerate the murder of one of its most powerful members, no matter how corrupt that member might have been. Gemma had taken it upon herself to deliver justice to the establishment, therefore the establishment hit back hard. Gemma was sentenced to prison for the rest of her life. But somehow she seemed to accept the sentence with a calmness that Nina found remarkable.

As Nina strolled back to the taverna, she was very aware of Jimmy's arm around her waist. They had been through so much together. Jimmy smiled. 'I can wait, Nina,' he said. 'If necessary, I'll keep on waiting forever.'

Nina kissed him. 'It isn't necessary to wait that long.'

As the bouzoukis and the mandolins sang in praise of the wedding, Nina moved in Jimmy's arms. She fitted comfortably against his body. 'It's been a long time, Jimmy,' she said into his ear. She knew he had understood her hesitation, just as he understood why and how she had risked herself with Michael. Then, when her eyes finally opened, she stepped back from the brink. And now she was home where she had always belonged. Nina was homeless no more.

The Cloning of Joanna May

Fay Weldon

Joanna May thought herself unique, indivisible – until one day, to her hideous shock, she discovered herself to be five: that though childless she was a mother: that though an only child she was surrounded by sisters young enough to be her daughters – Jane, Julie, Gina and Alice, the clones of Joanna May.

What will it be like for Joanna when she meets the clones? And what about the clones themselves? How are they different and how the same? Will they withstand the shock of first meeting? And what of the avenging Carl, Joanna's former husband and the clones' creator; will he take revenge for his wife's infidelity and destroy her sisters one by one?

In this astonishing novel, Fay Weldon weaves a web of paradox quite awesome in its cunning. Probing into the strange world of genetic engineering, *The Cloning of Joanna May* raises frightening questions about our very identity as individuals – and provides some startling answers. Funny, serious, revolutionary, this is the work of a master storyteller at the height of her powers.

Fontana

Shining Through
Susan Isaacs

'In 1940 when I was thirty-one and an old maid, while the whole world waited for war, I fell in love with John Berringer.'

Linda was a legal secretary; John Berringer was her indecently handsome, brilliant, unattainable boss, the man of her dreams. Four years later, Linda Voss Berringer emerged from the ruins of Berlin a self-determined woman of shining courage and a war hero.

Shining Through is the compulsive, engaging, heart-stopping saga of an American working girl and her transformation. Her story involves passion – a blazing affair with John Berringer; betrayal – when John's faithlessness rips their marriage apart; and intrigue – ultimately of a lethal kind when Linda joins the war as an OSS spy. Her story soars to its breathtaking conclusion in a blazing explosion of danger, death and unexpected love.

'Three cheers for Susan Isaacs, *Shining Through* keeps you turning the pages because you care what happens to the characters . . . her most ambitious novel to date'
Daily Express

'Give me the unashamed blockbuster any day, especially of the Susan Isaacs' tear-jerking, breath-catching variety . . . marvellously engaging'
Financial Times

'Truly compulsive . . . has all the hallmarks of a runaway bestseller'
Publishers Weekly

Fontana

King's Acre
Christine Marion Fraser

Author of the bestselling *Rhanna* series

Evelyn Grant started to come to terms with the loss of her
first love, Johnny, but the Grant family were overshadowed
by the unwelcome reappearance of a figure from Jamie's
past and by the terrible stories of the war told by soldiers
returning from the trenches. Among those fighting for King
and Country was Gillan Forbes, the son of the big house, on
whose friendship Evelyn increasingly relied and who still
hoped to win her love. But it was a handsome Gordon
Highlander, David Grainger, who captured Evelyn's heart,
sweeping her up in a whirlwind of passion that took her to
the heights of happiness and to the depths of despair . . .
Davie was a dangerous man to love . . .

King's Acre continues the entrancing story of the Grants of
Rothiedrum, Aberdeenshire, that began with *King's Croft*.

Fontana

King's Croft
Christine Marion Fraser

Author of the bestselling *Rhanna* series

ROTHIEDRUM, ABERDEENSHIRE

When Jamie King Grant, the travelling man, gave up his wandering life to wed Maggie McKenzie, their small farm had laughingly been re-named King's Croft. There they raised their family – straitlaced Nellie, lovesick Murn, lively Mary – and Evelyn, their youngest daughter.

Gifted and loving, Evelyn found herself torn between two different worlds and two very different young men. Johnny Burns, a child of the farmtouns like herself, had been her first love. Gillan Forbes was the son of the big house, and heir to the Lands of Rothiedrum. Neither man made any secret of his love for her – and the time was coming when Evelyn would have to make a choice.

King's Croft is the first novel in the enchanting new series from the bestselling author of *Rhanna*.

Fontana

The Hawthorne Heritage
Teresa Crane

'A finely crafted romantic novel'
Yorkshire Evening Post

Jessica Hawthorne grows up a strange, isolated child in the sumptuous beauty of her family's home, Melbury New Hall, in 19th-century Suffolk.

Robert Fitzbolton, a young aristocrat, is the companion of her lonely childhood, her comfort through family tragedy and the heartache of young love.

But is the support of Robert's friendship enough? Locked together in a disastrous marriage, they flee to Florence searching for freedom and fulfilment.

Robert finds what he is seeking, but Jessica is a true Hawthorne and is drawn – inevitably – back to Melbury, to her destiny . . .

Fontana

Rage of Angels
Sidney Sheldon

At the heart of the story stands the woman who is Sheldon's most unforgettable creation . . .

Jennifer Parker is brilliant, beautiful and indomitable – the most glamorous lawyer in America and one of the most successful.

Her life is shadowed by two men. Both of them powerful and both drawn irresistibly to her.

One is the politician, destined for greatness who fathers her son. The other is the Mafia boss, her only ally when crisis strikes and the man who brings her world crashing . . .

RAGE OF ANGELS

'The fast moving plot . . . with new surprises on every page . . . will keep his fans enthralled'   *Publishers Weekly*

Fontana

Fontana Fiction

Fontana is a leading paperback publisher of fiction. Below are some recent titles.

- [ ] GREEN AND PLEASANT LAND Teresa Crane £4.99
- [ ] KING'S OAK Ann Rivers Siddons £4.99
- [ ] THE EGYPTIAN YEARS Elizabeth Harris £4.50
- [ ] MAGIC HOUR Susan Isaacs £4.99
- [ ] THE RELUCTANT QUEEN Jean Plaidy £3.99
- [ ] TOMORROW'S MEMORIES Connie Monk £3.99
- [ ] WHEN SHE WAS BAD ... Kate O'Mara £4.99
- [ ] THE CLONING OF JOANNA MAY Fay Weldon £3.99
- [ ] FORBIDDEN GARDEN Diane Guest £3.99
- [ ] KING'S CLOSE Christine Marion Fraser £4.95
- [ ] MEMORY AND DESIRE Lisa Appignanesi £4.99
- [ ] THE ROAD TO ROWANBRAE Doris Davidson £4.50
- [ ] SACRIFICE Harold Carlton £4.99

You can buy Fontana Paperbacks at your local bookshops or newsagents. Or you can order them from Fontana, Cash Sales Department, Box 29, Douglas, Isle of Man. Please send a cheque, postal or money order (not currency) worth the price plus 24p per book for postage (maximum postage required is £3.00 for orders within the UK).

NAME (Block letters)_____

ADDRESS_____

_____

While every effort is made to keep prices low, it is sometimes necessary to increase them at short notice. Fontana Paperbacks reserve the right to show new retail prices on covers which may differ from those previously advertised in the text or elsewhere.